Praise for Tim Waggoner's Blade of the Flame...

"Diran is a kind of gentler, more thoughtful, but nonetheless formidable version of Conan and I look forward to his next adventure."
—Don D'Ammassa, dondammassa.com, *Forge of the Mindslayers*

"Fans of adventure fantasy series like Salvatore's Drizzt Do'Urden saga, Michael Moorcock's Elric of Melniboné and Raymond E. Feist's Midkemia sequence should definitely check out Waggoner's *Thieves of Blood*: a pedal-to-the-metal thrill ride of a novel featuring some of the coolest fantasy characters to come along in years. Highly recommended."
— *The Barnes & Noble Review*

"Waggoner is in possession of a talent that should be taken seriously, and I can't wait for his next book."
—Johnny Butane, The Horror Channel, on *Pandora Drive*.

"Waggoner is an excellent evoker of nightmarish terror, and his style is eminently readable."
—Horror Reader on *Nightmare on Elm Street: Protegé*

THE BLADE OF THE FLAME

BY ACCLAIMED AUTHOR
TIM WAGGONER

Thieves of Blood

Forge of the Mindslayers

Sea of Death

TIM WAGGONER

Sea
OF
Death

BLADE OF THE FLAME

BOOK
3

SEA OF DEATH
The Blade of the Flame · Book 3

©2008 Wizards of the Coast, Inc.

All characters in this book are fictitious. Any resemblance to actual persons, living or dead, is purely coincidental.

This book is protected under the copyright laws of the United States of America. Any reproduction or unauthorized use of the material or artwork contained herein is prohibited without the express written permission of Wizards of the Coast, Inc.

Published by Wizards of the Coast, Inc. EBERRON, WIZARDS OF THE COAST, and their respective logos are trademarks of Wizards of the Coast, Inc., in the U.S.A. and other countries.

Printed in the U.S.A.

The sale of this book without its cover has not been authorized by the publisher. If you purchased this book without a cover, you should be aware that neither the author nor the publisher has received payment for this "stripped book."

Cover art by Raymond Swanland
Map by Robert Lazzaretti
First Printing: February 2008

9 8 7 6 5 4 3 2 1

ISBN: 978-0-7869-4791-1
620- 21634740-001-EN

U.S., CANADA,
ASIA, PACIFIC, & LATIN AMERICA
Wizards of the Coast, Inc.
P.O. Box 707
Renton, WA 98057-0707
+1-800-324-6496

EUROPEAN HEADQUARTERS
Hasbro UK Ltd
Caswell Way
Newport, Gwent NP9 0YH
GREAT BRITAIN
Save this address for your records.

Visit our web site at www.wizards.com

DEDICATION

To Mark Sehestedt,
now a wizard of another coast. Thanks for sailing
the Lhazaar with me!

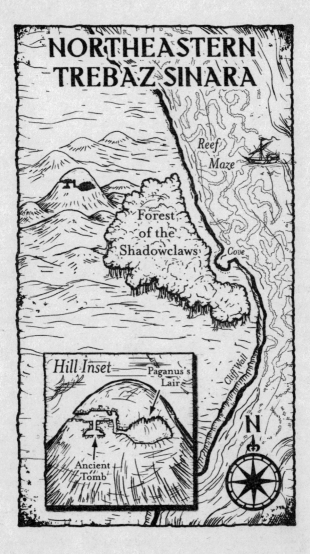

NORTHEASTERN TREBAZ SINARA

Reef Maze

Forest of the Shadowclaws

Cove

Cliff Wall

Hill Inset

Paganus's Lair

Ancient Tomb

N

CHAPTER

ONE

Dark clouds covered the heavens, smothering both stars and moons, leaving the sea blacker than night, blacker than sin. The wind howled like the wailing of a thousand lost souls crying out their misery to a cold, uncaring world. A sleek sailing vessel—a one-masted sloop mounted on runners—moved swiftly across the dark water, cutting through the turbulent waves with ease and grace, as if she traveled over solid ice, her runners fitted with razor-sharp blades. Though the sloop traveled against the wind, her sail nevertheless billowed full, thanks to a torrent of air issuing from a metal containment ring mounted behind the sail. The ring glowed with an aura of sizzling blue-white energy, and the scent of hot metal lay acrid on the salty sea air.

At the prow of the vessel stood a figure draped in darkness, bone-white hands gripping the railing, ebon fingernails long and sharp as bird talons. She faced the wind, and though the frigid sea-spray struck her like pellets of ice, she didn't wince, didn't so much as blink, for her dead flesh felt nothing. She appeared to be cloaked in living shadow, tendrils of liquid darkness trailing behind her, undulating in the wind like the fronds of a strange undersea plant dancing at the mercy of a strong current.

Nathifa gazed into the night, and though her eyes were dead,

1

still they saw—saw much farther than they ever had in life. She knew they were drawing near their destination, and her desiccated lips, which hadn't so much as twitched in all the hours she had stood motionless at the prow, now stretched into a slow smile, the movement cracking the layer of ice that had formed over her mouth during that time. Tiny shards of ice fell to the deck, taking bits of lip-flesh with them. Nathifa wasn't aware of the loss, and even if she had been, she wouldn't have cared. All she cared about—all she'd ever cared about, even back when she was alive—was satisfying her desires. And after over a century of patient, meticulous planning, she was now closer to her revenge than ever before. She had already gained possession of the golden dragonhead known as the Amahau, and on Demothi Island she would acquire the next item she needed. And after that . . .

"It shouldn't be much longer now."

A woman's voice, cold with a mocking edge. A new voice in Nathifa's undead existence, but one she had already grown to dislike. Nathifa responded without turning around.

"Indeed. It is as if you read my thoughts, Makala." Nathifa's voice was cold and hollow, like the inner chambers of an arctic tomb.

"Perhaps I did, lich."

Nathifa didn't move her body, but her head swiveled around to face Makala, rotating one hundred and eighty degrees like that of an owl. Nathifa no longer smiled. The woman who'd addressed her was medium height, with short blonde hair and fine, delicate features. Her pale skin was smooth, almost glossy like glazed pottery, and pinpoints of red light blazed within the depths of her eyes like crimson flame. She wore a red leather vest, brown leggings, boots, and a black cloak that fluttered behind her in the wind like the wings of a giant night raven. Makala carried a short sword belted around her waist, but steel was the least of her weapons. Ice crystals clung to her hair, skin, and clothing, but like Nathifa, she displayed no indication that she was aware of the cold, let alone bothered by it.

"Do not make sport of me, vampire." Nathifa's voice held a note of warning. "I can destroy you with a single whisper."

Makala smiled, revealing a pair of sharp incisors, and then

bowed. "My apologies, Mistress. I meant no disrespect."

Makala raised her head and met Nathifa's gaze. Crimson light similar to that which smoldered in Makala's eyes burned bright within the hollow sockets of Nathifa's. Normally, a vampire would have been unable to withstand the intensity of a lich's gaze. But Makala didn't turn aside, didn't so much as blink . . . and she continued to smile with infuriating smugness. Nathifa wanted to spin around, lash out with a clawed hand, and rip the lower half of the woman's face to shreds. And she might have, except that she knew that Makala wasn't *just* a vampire. She carried another spirit within her, a dark entity of a kind Nathifa was unfamiliar with. It was this spirit that allowed Makala to endure the power of the lich's burning gaze without shrinking. And until Nathifa knew the full measure of Makala's strength, she would stay her hand.

Besides, she needed Makala's help in order to bring her vengeance to its final fruition. So let the vampire mock her for now. In the end, Nathifa would stand laughing over the woman's cold ashes as her spirit—as *both* of them—was swallowed by everlasting darkness.

Nathifa turned her head back around and looked out across the sea once more. "We shall reach Demothi Island well before dawn, if that's what you're worried about."

"I'm not worried. Didn't I tell you the *Zephyr* was a fast ship?"

"That you did," Nathifa said grudgingly. Once again, her dark mistress had provided, just as she had always done.

Makala went on. "I'm rather enjoying our journey. It's been some time since I found sea travel tolerable, let alone pleasant."

Vampires, while useful servants, possessed a number of weaknesses—aversion to sunlight and holy objects chief among them. They also had difficulty traveling across running water: even the smallest stream could give them trouble, causing discomfort and even pain. Passage across a river was worse, and sea travel was nearly impossible. Makala possessed a mystic obsidian sarcophagus that allowed vampires to endure sea travel as long as they remained sealed within. But Makala hadn't made use of the sarcophagus once during this entire voyage. She strode the deck with ease, displaying no signs of discomfort. No doubt another strength granted by the dark spirit housed within Makala's undead body. How many more might there be, Nathifa wondered, and the thought troubled her.

"It's a good thing that we're almost there," Makala said. "Your barghest could use a rest."

Nathifa turned away from the prow and glanced back toward the containment ring. A short orange-skinned creature with a bat-like face and large pointed ears sat upon a wooden chair behind the glowing metal ring. Skarm's left hand lay flat on a depression carved into one of the chair arms. The depression was formed in the shape of a slender, long-fingered hand larger than the goblin's. An elvish hand. The flesh-to-wood contact allowed whoever sat in the chair to control the wind elemental that had been bound to the containment ring. At Nathifa's order, Skarm had been keeping the elemental producing wind at full strength ever since they had departed the secluded cove near the city of Perhata. And while it took little mystic skill to control the elemental, it did require a certain amount of mental strength and life energy. It had been a while since Skarm had fed, and he'd never been especially gifted mentally. His eyes were weary, his cheeks hollow, and—though Nathifa couldn't make out any color in the darkness—she knew his normally orange complexion would be pale peach.

Skarm would need to rest soon. Otherwise, if he expended all the life energy he'd absorbed from his last prey, he would die and be useless. Well . . . even more useless than he already was, Nathifa thought.

She glanced at Makala. Vampires were undead, but they *did* feed upon the living.

Might the stolen blood that flowed through her veins be suitable to sustain Skarm, at least for a short time? Nathifa knew that the vampiric taint carried by Makala's blood would have no effect on Skarm since he was a barghest. And as he was already bound to Nathifa, drinking Makala's blood wouldn't grant her mystic control of him.

The lich smiled, impressed anew by her dark mistress's wisdom at sending the vampire to her.

"Makala, I want you to give Skarm a measure of your blood,

enough to restore his strength until we reach Demothi Island."

The vampire looked at Nathifa for a long moment, face as expressionless as a marble statue. Nathifa thought that the woman might defy her, but in the end Makala simply inclined her head, turned, and began making her way sternward.

Satisfied that the pecking order had been re-established—for the time being, at least—Nathifa faced into the wind once more and gazed out into the darkness with eyes of flickering crimson flame.

◦ ◦ ◦ ◉ ◦ ◦ ◦

The dark shape of Demothi Island hove into view. Cold, desolate, barren, and rocky, it was a place of death and evil, though not entirely uninhabited. The island claimed one resident, and it was he whom they had come to collect.

They sailed toward the island's western side, and Nathifa noted the wreckage of a ship just off shore. The vessel had been reduced little more than splintered planks now, thanks to the constant pounding of the waves, and within a few more days, perhaps a week at most, there would be no sign left that the craft had ever existed.

"Have you been here before?"

Nathifa hadn't been aware of Makala's approach. She turned to face the vampire, ancient neck bones grinding and cracking.

"I have never set foot on the island, but I did see it once before, many years ago. When I was mortal." Though she had been undead far longer than she had drawn breath, Nathifa's memories of her previous life were as clear and sharp as ever.

"My brothers and I sailed past Demothi when we first discovered the gulf. I wanted to investigate, but both Kolbyr and Perhata convinced me that we should avoid it. Even from a distance, we could sense the evil emanating from the place." She smiled. "Of course, that was part of what intrigued me, but I deferred to my brothers."

Perhata and Kolbyr . . . the mortal bodies of her brothers were long dead, but their memories lived within her still. Memories of love, adventure, and conquest, but most of all of betrayal. *Kolbyr's* betrayal. After all these years, after everything Nathifa had sacrificed, she was close to finally achieving her revenge against her hated brother.

You killed my husband, Kolbyr, killed my son . . . all because you were too selfish to allow *my* child—your nephew—to become the heir you couldn't produce. Everything we built . . . everything you took from me . . . soon it will lie in ruins, and your name will become a curse upon the lips of all who inhabit the Principalities, until at last your name fades from all memory . . . even one as long as mine.

With a start, Nathifa became aware of Makala looking at her with a bemused expression. She feared Makala might take her momentary lapse as a sign of weakness, so to cover she said, "Tell Skarm to take us in."

Makala nodded, glanced down at the soarwood railing, and smirked before she turned and walked back to the barghest. Nathifa looked down to see what had amused the vampire so and saw that, in her anger, she'd gripped the railing so hard that her talon-fingers had dug deep furrows into the wood.

A loss of control. Another sign of weakness. One that she could ill afford with Makala and her evil spirit about.

Lady, guide me, she prayed.

Hollow laughter came in reply, but Nathifa told herself it was simply an auditory illusion caused by the howling wind and the pounding surf, nothing more.

❃ ❃ ❃ ❃ ❃ ❃ ❃

At the stern of the *Zephyr*, Skarm grunted as he lifted the vessel's anchor. In his present form he possessed no more strength than an ordinary goblin, but this was the best shape for him to use when he needed to perform manual labor—which, as Nathifa's servant, he had to do more often than he liked. In wolf shape, he had no hands, and while as a true barghest, he did have opposable thumbs, his spine wasn't designed for standing upright. The anchor felt as if it weighed a ton or more, and sharp pain shot through his lower back as he tossed it over the aft railing, rope playing out behind. His muscles quivered, weak as jelly, and despite the thick fur cloak that he wore—made of wolfskin, of course—he couldn't stop shivering. Commanding the *Zephyr*'s wind elemental had taken a great deal out of him, and though the vampire's blood, as bitter and foul-tasting as it was, had restored a certain measure of his strength, it hadn't been nearly enough. He would've liked nothing better than to crawl into the sloop's small cabin, curl up on a pallet and sleep for a decade or two. But not only wouldn't Nathifa permit him a moment's rest, she'd punish him severely for so much as asking. He had no choice but to keep going and hope he didn't drop from exhaustion, for if he did, Nathifa would most likely slay him and simply transfer his duties to her new servant.

Not for the first time, Skarm thought back to his life before he'd become the lich's slave—roaming free among the Hoarfrost Mountains, preying on unwary hunters and travelers, devouring sweet flesh and guzzling hot blood. But then one day he'd felt drawn to a series of caves located in the foothills just beyond the mountains. He'd tried to resist the pull, but he could not. He had no choice but to enter, and once he'd made his way through the tunnels to the cave system's main chamber, he discovered Nathifa waiting for him. Ever since that moment, Skarm had been the lich's slave, and he knew he would remain so until the day he died. He supposed there were worse lives for a barghest to lead, but offhand he couldn't think of any.

He tied the anchor rope to a metal cleat bolted to the railing, then turned to inform his mistress that she could disembark. But before he could speak Nathifa, who stood at the *Zephyr*'s stern as she had since they'd sailed from Perhata, bowed her head. Her cloak of living darkness seemed to swallow her, and an instant later her form broke apart into dozens of smaller shadow-fragments that resembled rats. The night-black vermin surged toward the railing and scuttled over the side.

Makala, who'd been standing next to Nathifa, glanced back over her shoulder and gave Skarm a grin. Then her form darkened, blurred, and reshaped itself into a large bat. Wind filled the vampire's leathery wings and bore her skyward.

Those two aren't the only ones who can play at shape-shifting, Skarm thought.

He ran to the stern, leather boots thumping on the wooden deck.

Just as he reached the railing, his boots became padded lupine feet as his goblin body reworked itself into the form of a wolf. He leaped into the air with bestial grace and soared up and over the railing.

Beware, Demothi Island! Skarm thought as he descended. The mighty barghest has come!

Then he landed in the frigid roiling surf just offshore and howled in shock at the sensation of a thousand ice needles piercing his hide. He scrambled out of the water and onto the rocky shore, whining like a wounded pup, and lost no time in vigorously shaking his coat dry. Or at least as dry as it could get, considering that half-frozen rain pelted the island.

I hate winter in the Principalites, Skarm thought. And the worst of it was, this was only autumn.

Nathifa and Makala stood on the shore, both having resumed their humanlike shapes. The lich shot Skarm a crimson-flecked gaze of irritation before turning and proceeding inland. She moved with an eerie gliding motion, as if she were floating above the ground instead of walking on its surface. Maybe she *was* floating, Skarm thought. After all, he'd never actually seen her legs and wasn't entirely certain she had any. Makala followed behind Nathifa, walking mortal-fashion, but moving with the serpent-like ease common to vampire-kind.

Skarm intended to shift into his barghest form then, for it was hardier than both his goblin and wolf shapes and thus better able to withstand the cold. But then his lupine nose detected a scent—a wonderfully rank odor of putrefaction that set his mouth to watering. Cold forgotten, Skarm padded toward the source of the tantalizing smell, a viscous mound of slime heaped onto the dark shore nearby. He lowered his snout to the ooze and drank in its deliciously foul stench. He judged the slime to be liquefied dead flesh—long dead, at that—and though barghests weren't by nature carrion eaters, Makala's blood had only done so much to restore his strength, and Skarm was still hungry . . . hungry enough to make even this muck seem like a fine banquet to him.

Skarm opened his mouth and extended his tongue, prepared to lap up the foul stuff when another scent drifted into his nostrils—the scent of living meat. *Human* meat. Skarm was always Skarm no matter his shape, but his thoughts were affected by the form he wore at any given time. As a barghest, he was cunning and cruel, as a goblin timid and scheming, and as a wolf a creature of appetite and instinct. Both of these latter qualities now combined into a single overpowering urge that told Skarm he must feed—*now*.

Skarm bounded off, nose to the ground, tracking this new scent. Others had been here not long ago, he knew—human, half-orc, elf, halfling—for their scents still clung to the rocks, but one scent, a human male's, was strong and fresh. Whoever the man was, he was still on the island and soon he'd be filling Skarm's belly. Skarm ran a zig-zag trail across the small island, heart pounding in excitement, air chuffing in and out of his nostrils as he searched for his prey. He heard voices yelling his name—both female—but he ignored them. Nothing mattered except filling the vast empty pit that lay at the core of his being.

Skarm found the man huddled behind a large outcropping of gray rock. He was blonde, bearded, broad-shouldered, and though half-frozen and trembling like a leaf caught in gale-force wind, the fact that he had survived exposure to the harsh elements on the island was testament to his great strength. This one would make a fine meal, indeed!

The man staggered to a standing position and brandished a knife as Skarm approached. He wore leather armor beneath a thick, red waterproof cloak, hood up as protection against the rain. Skarm's lupine vision was able to make out a tattoo of a stylized blue skull on the man's forehead. The image was meaningless to Skarm's wolf-mind, and he forgot it as soon as he saw it. The man's knife was a small, pitiful weapon, and his hand trembled so badly that Skarm doubted he would be able to do any serious damage with the blade. Not that it mattered if he did, for Skarm could heal with supernatural swiftness. But even if he had no special healing abilities, his hunger would still have driven him to attack, regardless of the risk of injury to himself.

Skarm ran at the man and leaped for his throat, already tasting the blood that would soon gush hot and sweet on his tongue.

But a strong hand grabbed hold of him by the scruff of the neck, stopping his attack in mid-leap. Skarm whipped his head around, growling and snapping at whoever dared to come between him and his prey.

"Easy, boy," Makala said, grinning, incisors longer and sharper than usual. "Nathifa would like a word with this gentleman before you tear out his throat."

Skarm writhed in Makala's grip, trying to twist free, but the vampire held him above the ground in a grip like iron, and there was nothing he could do.

Then Nathifa came gliding forward, the tendrils of her dark cloak probing the ground as she advanced like the feelers of a gigantic black insect. Her crimson-flame eyes burned with excitement as she regarded the bearded man, and her smile was a terrible thing to behold.

"Well, now. Who we do have here?"

❂ ❂ ❂ ❂ ❂ ❂ ❂

Haaken tried to put up a brave front, but he'd been marooned on Demothi Island for several days now—ever since the *Maelstrom*, the vessel he'd commanded, had run aground on this cursed shore—and he was half-dead from exposure. But even if he were at full fighting strength, still he would've quailed before the creature that glided toward him now. The wolf didn't frighten him overmuch, nor did the vampire. The wolf was a simple beast, and while the vampire was a formidable enough foe, they'd met in battle before and he'd managed to get the best of her then. But this . . . this *thing* coming toward him—bone-white flesh, fire-pit eyes, shadowy cloak that seemed somehow alive—exuded an aura of such malevolence that, if Haaken had had any fresh water to drink over the last few days, he would've lost control of his bladder.

"His name is Haaken Sprull," the vampire said. She continued to hold onto the snarling wolf, the animal showing no signs of calming down. "He is—or rather, *was*—the commander of the Coldhearts, the supposedly elite warriors who served Baroness Calida of Kolbyr. He made the mistake of kidnapping some former friends of mine, and he lost both his crew and his ship as a result. Quite frankly, I'm surprised the fool is still alive."

The white-faced *thing* glided closer to Haaken and scowled as she examined him. He wanted more than anything to run, to put as much distance as possible between himself and this horrible apparition, but he was too transfixed with terror to move. Besides, Demothi Island was so small, there wasn't anywhere *to* run.

"Kolbyr, eh?" The words were carried on breath redolent of dust and ancient bone. She regarded him a moment longer before letting out a brittle laugh and clapping her skeletal hands together in glee. "My mistress displays an unexpected sense of whimsy this night! How delightfully appropriate that she would send a servant of Kolbyr to now serve *me!*"

Haaken had no idea what the witch was talking about, and he didn't want to know. Better to die like a man than serve a creature like her! Though it took every bit of inner strength remaining to him, Haaken tore his gaze away from the witch's burning red eyes, turned, and ran. He staggered toward the sea, boots slipping on ice-coated rocks, so weak that he was barely able to keep his footing, but he continued on, knowing that if he fell it would be all over, and he would belong body and soul to the shadow-draped witch with the red-coal eyes. As he ran, he heard the vampire speak.

"Should I let Skarm go after him?"

The wolf yipped with excitement, as if it understood what she'd said.

"No need," the witch said. "He can't escape."

The witch spoke these words with such calm assurance that Haaken almost gave up in despair and stopped running. But then he heard the sound of waves breaking against the rocky shore, smelled the tang of saltwater, felt sea-spray wet his face, and his heart soared. Haaken was a Lhazaarite born and bred, and he'd spent more hours plying the sea than he had treading upon land. As a son of the Lhazaar, he couldn't imagine dying anywhere else but in its cold embrace. The sea had sustained him in life; now it would be his deliverance in death.

His boots splashed in the foamy surf, and he laughed with relief.

11

He'd made it! All he had to do now was dive into the water and let the Lhazaar have him. As cold as the sea was this time of year, and as weak as Haaken was, it wouldn't take long for him to die. A matter of minutes at most. It would be just like going to sleep, Haaken told himself. Peaceful, soothing . . .

Gathering what little strength he had left, Haaken crouched and prepared to dive into the welcoming waters of the Lhazaar and claim his deliverance.

But before he could enter the water, a large dark shape surged forth from the waves and slammed into him. The breath was forced from Haaken's lungs as he was driven backward toward shore. He reflexively grabbed hold of the creature that had attacked him. His hands clasped rough hide covered with barnacles, and he stared into a gaping maw ringed by triangular teeth—several rows of them—sharp and serrated. Shreds of ragged flesh were stuck between the beast's teeth, and its breath stank of rotting meat. Haaken saw an eye on the side of the creature's head, large as a dinner plate and black and cold as the bottom of the sea itself. Though the eye was inhuman, Haaken nevertheless had the impression that it glared at him with baleful intelligence.

At that moment the thought of death lost all appeal for Haaken.

In his terror to flee the white-faced witch, Haaken had unthinkingly held on to his knife. Suddenly realizing he still gripped the blade, the former commander of the Coldhearts decided to make good use of it. He rammed the knife into the beast's tough hide once, twice, three times.

But though foul black blood spurted with each strike, the wounds closed almost immediately, giving Haaken further confirmation—as if he needed it—that he was dealing with an unnatural creature.

The monster—a shark, but one far larger than any he'd ever seen—bore him up onto the shore, scraping Haaken's back bloody on the rough rocks. Haaken started to cry out in pain, but then he realized that he was holding onto the shark's snout with his arms; his legs were inside the beast's mouth. Haaken screamed in terror, but then the shark bit down, and Haaken's scream became one of agony.

SEA OF DEATH

* * * * * * *

The smell of fresh blood came close to driving Skarm insane. He howled and thrashed in Makala's grip, desperate to free himself so that he might steal a portion of the great shark's feast. At last, his wolf-mind understood that there was no way he could get away from the vampire in his present shape, and so he handed over the reins to the barghest persona. It was stronger than the wolf, and it would find a way to—

Nathifa stepped in front of Skarm just as his form started to shift. "Enough," she said calmly and backhanded him. Despite her withered, skeletal frame, the lich possessed incredible strength, and the blow was swift and strong enough to take the head off a mortal being. As Skarm was now nearly in barghest form, the strike merely cracked his skull in several places. It did, however, settle him right down.

Nathifa leaned close to Skarm's face so that her crimson eyes nearly touched his. "The human is mine, not yours. You cannot have him."

Skarm could feel Nathifa's power boring into his mind, and he knew that no matter how great his hunger became after this moment, he would have no choice but to obey her command. Slowly, he nodded.

Nathifa stepped back. "Release him, Makala."

The vampire let go of the barghest and Skarm dropped to the ground. He wanted to look in Haaken's direction to see if the shark had left anything for him, but he didn't want to risk Nathifa's anger again, so he kept his gaze trained on her.

"Makala, Skarm, I want both of you to go to the center of the island. There you will find a stone statue of a man rising forth from the rock, as if it had grown out of the earth itself. You are to *carefully* break the statue free from the surrounding ground without damaging it in any way, then carry it back to the *Zephyr* and stow it aboard. Do you understand?"

"Of course," Makala said. "I was present when Diran and Ghaji nullified the statue's power. They left a silver dagger embedded in its

13

chest. Should we attempt to remove it?" From the tone of Makala's voice, she didn't relish the idea.

Skarm didn't blame the woman. While silver had no particular ill effects on barghests, it was poison to a vampire. And this was no ordinary silver dagger; it had been wielded by a priest of the Silver Flame, one that Skarm had encountered before. Perhaps the priest had put some sort of blessing on the blade that would cause it to be harmful to any creature, undead or not.

Nathifa considered Makala's question for a moment. "Don't bother with the dagger. We can always remove it later, and if it currently is keeping the statue's power in check, it'll make it that much easier for us to transport." She smiled. "Like a cork contains the contents of a bottle and prevents them from spilling. Just be careful not to touch the damned thing."

Makala nodded. "One more thing. I know you told Skarm that Haaken is yours, but if you're just going to let the man bleed to death anyway . . ." She trailed off, her point made. She was a vampire, and she wanted Haaken's blood as badly as Skarm wanted his flesh and soul.

Skarm couldn't help it; he turned to look toward Haaken's body. The great shark was gone, the creature having presumably returned to the dark sea depths that had spawned it. Haaken lay motionless at the edge of the shore, both of his legs gone beneath from mid-thigh down. Even in his barghest form, Skarm could smell the blood flowing from the ragged stumps where the man's legs had been attached only moments before. His stomach gurgled, and he prayed that Nathifa wouldn't punish him for it.

"You can both forget about making a meal of Haaken," Nathifa said. "Though our toothsome friend has finished his work, the man's not going to die." The lich's dry lips drew away from her yellow teeth in a hideous mockery of a smile. "I have plans for him."

CHAPTER

TWO

The sun hung just above the eastern horizon as the small fishing boat sailed along the coast toward Kolbyr. The water was calm, the sky cloudless, and wind filled the sails. All in all, a good day to be out on the Lhazaar, even with the chill of approaching winter in the air.

A tall man with long raven-black hair, lean wolfish features, and intense blue eyes stood at the ship's stern, holding onto a rigging line with one hand to steady himself. He was garbed entirely in black, and though at first glance he appeared to be unarmed, the fur cloak he wore did not stir in the breeze kicked up by the ship's passage. An experienced observer would've guessed the cloak was weighted down, most likely by some manner of concealed weapon or weapons—and they'd have been right.

Diran Bastiaan inhaled the brisk salt air and exhaled with a sigh of contentment. Though born in the Principalities, he'd been sold into slavery as a child and had grown into adulthood in Karrnath, far from the sea. Still, Lhazaarite blood flowed through his veins, and he only truly felt at home when standing upon the deck of a ship, even one as small and humble as *Welby's Pride*. The *Pride* was a shallop, a single-masted fore and aft rig propelled by both oars and sails, designed for inshore fishing and limited coastal traveling. Hardly stylish transportation, but serviceable.

Diran turned and made his way back to the center of the deck where the rest of his companions stood huddled together in a circle. A red gem covered with a lattice of copper wire hovered in the air between them, and though it gave no sign of emitting energy—no glow of light, no shimmer in the air surrounding it—the gem exuded the warmth of a small campfire.

The others shifted to make room for Diran as he rejoined them, and he held his chilled hands out toward the gem. Diran rarely wore gloves, no matter how cold it was, for they interfered with his knife-throwing grip.

The crew of the fishing vessel—who'd been well paid to ferry Diran and the others to Kolbyr—ignored their passengers as they went about their work. Just because the crew had paying guests didn't mean they would pass up the opportunity to fill their fishing nets with additional profit as they sailed. The Lhazaar Principalities were a harsh, unforgiving realm, and its inhabitants had long ago learned to be both practical and frugal if they wished to survive. The animals in the Principalities were no exception: a mass of gulls hovered on the air currents around the vessel, hoping to snatch a free meal from the crew's nets. Whenever a fish fell out flopping onto the deck, the more aggressive of the birds swooped in, only to be shooed away with waving arms and shouted curses.

Ghaji, Diran's long-time companion in arms, stood to the right of the priest.

"Being a fisherman really stinks." The half-orc wrinkled his nose. "On multiple levels."

Ghaji's green-tinged features were a fairly even blend of orc and human, but he chose to accentuate the more bestial aspect of his heritage because of the edge it gave him. Ghaji was a seasoned warrior, a veteran of the Last War, and he knew that a soldier had to make full use of whatever advantages he possessed if he hoped to survive to see another sunrise. Thus Ghaji kept his black hair in a shaggy tangle and had a vertical strip of beard that drew attention to his large sharp teeth. He kept his prominent brow in an almost permanent scowl—though in truth this had more to do with his natural temperament than any conscious strategy on his part. The numerous scars that he'd acquired on the battlefields of the Last War served to make him look even more imposing than he already was.

Ghaji wore a battered breastplate—another souvenir of his soldier days—as his only armor, and he carried two axes tucked into his belt. One was a simple hand-axe he used as his back-up weapon, but the other served as his primary—an axe imbued with an elemental that, when Ghaji wished, became wreathed in mystical flame. It was on unofficial and—if Ghaji had anything to say about it—permanent loan from the prison island of Dreadhold.

Diran, his hands nicely warmed now, smiled at his friend. "You get used to the smell after a time."

Ghaji snorted as if to clear the stink out of his nostrils. "Easy for you to say. Your parents owned a fishing boat."

An elf-woman stood on the other side of Diran. Her brown hair was woven into an intricate pattern of braids, and she possessed the fine aristocratic features and pointed ears common to her people. Like the others, she wore a thick fur cloak, though she gave no sign that the cold bothered her.

"You grew up in marshlands, Ghaji," Yvka said. "Swamps have their own share of unpleasant odors."

"Sure," Ghaji said, "but they're *normal* unpleasant odors— brackish water, decaying plants. Not this stench! It reminds me of . . . well, let's just say I find it less than pleasant and leave it at that."

An elderly human male stood next to Yvka, and he frowned at Ghaji. "Just be grateful that you're a *half*-orc. Your sense of smell would be even stronger if you were full-blooded." A lean man in his sixties, Tresslar sported a scraggly white beard and mustache, but his eyes—though receded into the sockets somewhat and set above drooping bags—were intense, vital, and alive. The eyes of a much younger man, or a man who'd never forgotten what being young felt like.

"I can help alleviate your discomfort if you wish, Ghaji." Solus stood next in the circle, though he had no need of Tresslar's magic gem to warm himself. The voice that issued from the construct's throat was hollow-sounding and devoid of emotion, though not altogether inhuman. "I can temporarily reconfigure the sensory pathways in your mind so that you cannot detect the smell of fish. Or, if you'd prefer, I can cause you to experience any scent you desire, such as roses or perhaps a freshly cooked steak."

Solus wore a hooded gray robe with oversized sleeves to hide his three-fingered hands. He also wore a fur cloak, though it wasn't necessary since temperature extremes proved no discomfort for him. He had decided to wear the cloak for the same reason as he'd donned the robe: in order to disguise his true nature. Warforged were more common in the Five Nations than the Principalities, but they weren't unknown here. But Solus wasn't simply any warforged; he was special. Physically, he resembled a typical specimen of his kind. Roughly humanoid, body a composite of iron, stone, silver, obsidian, and darkwood. Glowing green eyes—though his were slightly dimmer than usual for a warforged—three-fingered hands, two-toed feet, and a hinged jaw.

But what made Solus stand apart from others of his kind were the crystals of various sizes, shapes, and colors embedded in the surface of his body. The crystals weren't simply decoration. They possessed the ability to absorb, channel, and intensify psionic energy. Solus was a psiforged, capable of astounding feats of psychic prowess—telekinesis, telepathy, illusion-casting and more. But he was untrained in the use of his abilities and thus potentially a great danger to those around him. Keeping his true nature concealed was necessary to prevent others from focusing their attention—and more importantly, their thoughts—on him. Until he learned a greater measure of control over his powers, the fewer minds he came in close contact with, the better.

"I'll stick with the stench," Ghaji said. "Nothing personal, but I'd rather not have my head explode if something goes wrong."

Hinto came next in the circle after Solus.

"That's not fair! Solus has gotten a lot better as using his powers!" Hinto smiled mischievously. "Though as homely as you are, Greenie, I doubt anyone would notice if your head *did* explode!"

Though in his early adulthood, Hinto stood no taller than a child, but he was of average height for a halfling. His skin was nut-brown, the result of a lifetime spent sailing the Lhaazar, and he wore a long-knife tucked under his belt, a weapon he wielded as if it were a sword built specially for someone his size. He wore a red bandana on his head, along with a long-sleeved shirt and pants, both woven from thick brown material. Sturdy boots, a scarf, and glove with the tips of the fingers cut off completed his outfit. A hardy Lhaazarite, he didn't bother wearing a fur cloak. As he'd said before they left Perhata, "I don't need one. It's not full winter yet."

Ghaji glared at the halfling sailor. "You're not exactly what I'd call handsome. And neither is your jewel-encrusted friend."

Hinto patted Solus's hand. "Don't mind him. He's always in a sour mood."

Hinto never strayed far from Solus's side. Ever since the construct had joined the companions, the instant bond the two had formed had only grown stronger. And, as Solus's eyesight had been damaged beyond Tresslar's ability to repair, the halfling served as the psiforged's eyes. His physical eyes, at any rate, as Solus had senses other than sight with which to navigate his environment.

The last member of the circle—standing between Hinto and Ghaji, which at the moment wasn't the safest place aboard *Welby's Pride*—was Asenka.

"I, for one, think a man covered by jewels is *quite* attractive," she said. "Even if he isn't human." She gave Diran a quick wink to show she was joking. She and Diran weren't lovers, not yet, but they were more than friends. Diran wondered if their relationship would continue to grow and deepen, and he surprised himself when he realized that he hoped it would.

Asenka had close-cropped strawberry-blond hair and a tattoo of a scorpion on the back of her right hand. Instead of the red cloak she normally wore with her uniform of black tabard over mail armor, she had on a fur cloak as protection against the cold. She was armed with a long sword, and though at first glance she didn't appear muscular enough to wield it effectively, Diran had seen her use the weapon to good effect on more than one occasion. Asenka served as commander of the Sea Scorpions, Baron Mahir's elite cadre of warriors, and it was she who had delivered Diran's proposition to the baron: the priest and his companions would travel to Kolbyr and see if they might be able to lift the curse that had hung over the ruling house for a hundred years. Mahir had been skeptical at first. After all, the Barons of Kolbyr had doubtless attempted to have the curse removed numerous times over the years, and without success. Not only would another attempt most likely prove futile, the fact that it originated from Perhata might well lead to an escalation of hostilities between the two cities. Especially since Diran and Ghaji had been responsible for the destruction of the *Maelstrom* and the Coldhearts. That action hadn't been authorized by Mahir—not that he wasn't pleased by it—but Baroness Calida might not see it that way.

In the end Asenka had managed to convince Mahir to sponsor the journey to Kolbyr. It helped that it wouldn't be too expensive, of course, and that they planned to conduct their mission as unobtrusively as possible. But Mahir's main reason for agreeing was a practical one. The longstanding enmity between the two cities had prevented both from progressing the way they might have otherwise. Mahir didn't exactly want to become friends with Calida, but the periodic clashes between their two cities were costly. If those Lhazaarites who made their homes in the Gulf of Ingjald ever hoped to compete economically with the rest of the Principalities, the feud between Perhata and Kolbyr had to end.

So with Mahir's approval—and more importantly, his money—Asenka was able to hire a cargo vessel to bear Diran and his companions to a small fishing village not far from Kolbyr. They couldn't use the *Water Dragon*—the Sea Scorpions' ship—lest she draw too much attention and be seen as an attack on Kolbyr, especially now that the Coldhearts were no longer there to protect the city.

After arriving at the village, they disembarked and hired *Welby's Pride* to take them the rest of the way. It was common for independent fishing boats to bring their catch in to either Kolbyr or Perhata, depending on which was closer and which happened to be paying more for fish at any given time. It was true that Diran, Ghaji, and the others didn't much resemble local fisherfolk, but then even in this less-than-cosmopolitan backwater of the Principalities, it wasn't unknown to see groups of odd strangers, and while some eyebrows might get raised, few questions would be asked.

"It seems like we've been sailing for days," Ghaji complained. "At this pace, we may not reach Kolbyr until summer."

"We wouldn't have to use this leaky wreck at all if we still had the *Zephyr,*" Yvka said. "In the time it's taken us to get this far, we could've already reached Kolbyr, lifted the curse, and be halfway back to Perhata."

Tresslar frowned. "You're not the only one who's lost something, you know."

The artificer had been in a foul mood for the last several days, ever since his dragonwand had been stolen at Mount Luster by the barghest. The elderly artificer had searched for the device night and day, forgoing both sleep and meals in his obsessive quest to regain the dragonwand. Diran couldn't blame the old man. The golden dragonhead affixed to the tip of the wand was a magical artifact of great power, enabling its user to drain mystical energy from enchanted objects and rechannel it to create whatever effects the user desired. Tresslar had possessed the dragonwand for forty years, ever since he'd sailed with the legendary explorer Erdis Cai in his youth. Tresslar was determined not to give up the dragonwand easily, but so far all his attempts to locate the artifact had met with failure.

Yvka's face reddened with anger at Tresslar's comment, and Ghaji—as he so often did—stepped in to lighten the mood. "I think you've been spoiled by your elemental sloop, Yvka. Now you're frustrated because you have to travel as slowly as the rest of us ordinary mortals."

But Ghaji's words had the opposite effect. Yvka's face turned a deeper red, and her delicate elvish brow furrowed into a scowl. "It's not a joking matter."

Her voice had a sternness to it that Diran had seldom heard before, like she was an adult lecturing a small child, and an annoying one at that. Yvka was an elf, and therefore older than Ghaji, perhaps quite a bit older. Diran forgot that sometimes.

Ghaji's jaws muscles tensed, and Diran knew his friend was fighting to keep from becoming defensive.

"I'm sure Ghaji didn't mean to make light of your loss," Diran said.

Yvka smiled and reached out to pat Ghaji's hand. "I know. It's just that the *Zephyr* doesn't belong to me. It's a loan from my associates."

The elf-woman had never directly admitted to any of them—not even Ghaji—that she worked for the Shadow Network, had in fact never acknowledged that the secret organization of spies and assassins even existed. But it was an open secret among the companions, though they avoided speaking of it out of respect for their friend.

The crew hauled another net full of fish out of the water and dumped the catch onto the deck. The fish, still alive and flopping, were mostly cod, Diran noted, and good-sized ones at that, each nearly the length of a man's arm. The fish would bring in good money once the crew put in to Kolbyr, Diran thought, and he found himself thinking of the path his life might have taken if his parents hadn't been killed, if he'd grown to adulthood fishing the waters of the Lhazaar. Certainly it would have been a simpler path than the one he now trod—he glanced at his companions and smiled—but a far less rewarding one.

Several of the crystals on Solus's forehead began to glow, and though the psiforged didn't possess the physiognomy to frown, the tone of his voice conveyed his concern.

"Something is wrong."

Before Diran could ask Solus to clarify, a chorus of shrill cries cut through the air, and a white mass descended upon *Welby's Pride*. The gulls, excited by the cod flopping on the deck, had abandoned making individual sorties to snatch fish in favor of a group assault. The crew yelled and cursed, flailed their arms, punched, kicked, even drew knives and struck out at the birds. But instead of frightening off the gulls, the crew's actions only served to further embolden the raucous scavengers. At first it proved to be an almost comical sight: grown men and women, toughened sea-hands all, battling birds that were little more than flying feathered rats for possession of a pile of flopping codfish. But then the gulls became more aggressive, forgetting the cod and turning their attention toward the crew. The birds pecked at every hand that came near them, flew past heads and dug their beaks into scalps. At first the crew merely yelped and swore, the injuries inflicted by the gulls little more than annoyances. But then the birds began to strike harder, sharp beaks drawing blood, and the crew's shouts of anger became cries of pain.

At first the gulls ignored Diran and his companions, presumably because none of them were standing near the fish, but that didn't last long. A single gull broke away from the flock and came flapping toward them, beady black eyes glittering with almost human hatred. The bird made straight for Asenka, clearly aiming for the woman's eyes, but before it could reach her, the commander of the Sea Scorpions drew her long sword, swung, and the gull's body fell to one portion of the deck while its head landed on another.

More gulls broke off their assault on the crew and came flying at the companions, harsh cries full of rage, as if they intended to avenge their flock-mate's death. Without a word, Diran and the others turned around, remaining in a circle but facing outward to meet the gulls' attack. Ghaji activated his elemental axe, and mystic fire burst forth from the metal. The half-orc warrior swung the enchanted weapon in wide, sweeping arcs, flames trailing from the axe head as he cut down one bird after another. Asenka continued striking out with her long sword, while Hinto did the same with his long knife. Yvka reached into the leather pouch that hung from her belt and withdrew a slender steel spike upon which three white acorns had been skewered. With a graceful flick of her wrist, she flipped the object—a product of the ever-inventive and always-devious artificers of the Shadow Network—toward the attacking gulls. The steel spike disintegrated in mid-air, and the acorns became ivory streaks as they shot off in three separate directions to bore large, bloody holes in the chests of three different gulls.

Tresslar appeared to do nothing but stand and watch the others fight, his brow slightly furrowed. But a moment later the warming gem he'd created floated out of the circle and toward a concentrated mass of gulls, the mystical object glowing more brightly with each passing second. When the light given off by the gem became too intense to look at directly—and when it was far enough away from any of the companions, the crew, and the ship's rigging—it exploded, killing at least a dozen birds. Like Tresslar, Solus seemed to be doing nothing more than observing the battle taking place around him, but the crystals covering his face and hands were flashing rapidly on and off in an intricate pattern, and Diran felt the psiforged was doing *something*, though the priest had no idea what.

Diran had drawn a pair of razor-edged steel daggers from the sheaths sewn into the inner lining of his cloak. His hands were blurs as he swept the blades through the air, slicing the wings of gulls as they swooped in to attack, cutting through feather and flesh, the birds falling to the deck, unable to remain aloft. Diran had no compunction about killing the gulls if it became necessary. He had served as an assassin during the Last War before forsaking that path to become one of the Purified. But as a worshipper of the Silver Flame, he held all life sacred and would only kill to defend the lives of the innocent, and even then only when he could find no other way to protect them.

Diran had no doubt that this attack was the trouble Solus had attempted to warn them of. Such aggressive behavior was unnatural for gulls, but during the Last War, Diran had seen animals ensorcelled and used as weapons to assault an enemy in a fashion similar to this. As one of the Purified, Diran could sense the presence of evil in the flock of mad gulls, but it was a diffuse evil, its nature difficult to grasp. Whatever the source of the malignant power that drove the gulls to attack, it didn't seem to be something Diran could exorcise using his priestly abilities. A notion struck him then: perhaps it wasn't magic at work here, but rather psionics. Diran turned to Solus, but before he could give voice to his question, the psiforged answered it.

"I do not know what is causing the birds to attack, but your technique for dealing with them appears to be sound. If you will allow me to borrow your daggers . . ."

Before Diran could reply, his blades were yanked from his grasp by an unseen force. They soared through the air, flying through the mass of gulls with blinding speed, cutting through wing after wing and sending birds tumbling to the deck one after another. Within moments, the air was empty of gulls, and Diran's daggers—steel blades smeared with avian blood—floated back into his hands. An instant later, the blood rose from the daggers in crimson beads, joined together to form a round mass of red liquid, then flew over the side of the boat and into the sea. His daggers now clean, Diran returned the knives to their sheaths within his cloak.

"Nicely done, Solus," Diran said.

"It was your idea," the psiforged replied. "I simply expanded on it."

Though Solus had been brought to life during the Last War, he'd remained in seclusion inside Mount Luster ever since the traumatic event of his creation. Only recently had he ended his isolation to emerge into the outer world, but while the psiforged lacked practical experience of life beyond the walls of Mount Luster, Diran thought the construct was proving to be a fast learner.

"Too bad you couldn't have used your mind tricks to make the gulls docile," Tresslar said. The artificer nodded at the wounded birds surrounding them. The gulls might not have been able to fly, but the creatures continued to cry shrilly and peck at anything near them that moved, including each other.

"I tried," Solus said. "But their minds were too simple, the rage that engulfed them too strong."

"That's all right," Hinto said. "I heard you tell Diran you didn't know what caused the gulls to go crazy. You can't counter magic if you don't know anything about it, right?"

"I said didn't know *what* power affected the birds, but I do know *something* about it. I know where it originated from."

Solus pointed sternward and everyone turned to look in the direction the psiforged indicated.

There, off in distance, lay the harbor of Kolbyr.

CHAPTER

THREE

As *Welby's Pride* headed into port, Diran healed the wounded crew members while Solus used his telekinetic abilities to remove the gulls from the deck. The psiforged placed the birds into the water, where the dead would become food for other scavengers and the wounded would have a chance for survival, slim though it might be.

Once the shallop was settled into a berth and tied down, Asenka paid the captain the rest of his fee, and the companions disembarked. Ghaji found the docks of Kolbyr to be quite a change from those in Perhata. Instead of using wood for pillars and planking, the Kolbyrites had fashioned their docks entirely from gray stone. The surfaces were worn smooth by decades of exposure to the elements as well as by the thousands of feet that had trod upon the docks over the years. Patches of moss clung to the stone everywhere, making the docks look more green than gray, as if they had grown from the sea floor rather than having been constructed with hammer and chisel.

The stink of fish hung heavy on the air here—no doubt due to all the fishing boats berthed at the docks—and Ghaji was grateful that a strong breeze was blowing to cut the stench, though gale-force winds would've been even better. He hadn't said anything to the others, but the smell of fish reminded him far too much of the stink of Karrnathi undead, which in turn reminded him of the months he'd spent serving as a mercenary on the Talenta Plains during the Last War. When he thought of those days, he thought of Kirai, and since *those* thoughts were too painful to recall, he did his best to cast them out of his mind. Doing so would've been easier if the damned air didn't stink like a horde of Karrnathi zombies, though.

Asenka led the way. Not only was she more familiar with Kolbyr as a citizen of the Gulf of Ingjald, she was also the representative of Baron Mahir, which meant she carried all the bribe money. Diran and Ghaji followed closely behind Asenka, while the others brought up the rear. Ostensibly their mission was a secret one, but Kolbyr had many spies in Perhata, just as Perhata had its own spies here. Often, these spies were one and the same, men and women who worked "both sides of the gulf," as the saying went. Thus the chances were excellent that word of their mission had preceded them to Kolbyr, and Asenka was authorized to play the role of official ambassador from Perhata—and spread Mahir's money around as liberally as necessary—should the need arise.

"Do you sense it, Ghaji?" Diran asked, his voice barely above a whisper.

Ghaji glanced sideways at his friend. "I assume you're not talking about the fish smell."

"Hardly. I sense the same sort of evil I did aboard the fishing vessel when the gulls attacked. Only it's stronger here, more focused."

Ghaji had traveled with Diran ever since the two had met when the half-orc had been working as a brothel bouncer in Kartan. Though not a worshipper of the Silver Flame himself, Ghaji had joined Diran's crusade against evil, and he had fought alongside the priest against threats so dire that just to stand in their presence was to risk one's sanity. They owed each other their lives a dozen times over, and there was no person in the world that Ghaji trusted more. If Diran said he sensed evil, Ghaji believed him, without question.

"My teeth have been on edge since we first approached the dock," Ghaji admitted, "and the hair on the back of my neck is standing at attention. What do you think is causing it?"

27

"The same force that drove the gulls to attack us," the priest said. "But other than that, I cannot say."

"Do you think it also has something to do with the way everyone's been looking at us?" Ghaji nodded toward a berthed sail boat as they passed. There were three men aboard—two humans and a half-elf—and whatever they had been doing a moment ago, they now stood upon the deck of their vessel, glaring at the companions as they walked by, faces contorted into expressions of pure hatred so intense they were almost comical.

Almost.

"We do seem to be attracting a great deal of negative attention," Diran said. "Far more than mere travelers should get for simply walking along the dock. It's almost as if our arrival was expected, though obviously not welcomed."

The trio in the sailboat wasn't the only ones staring at them with hate-filled eyes. Sailors, fishermen, dockhands . . . all fixed the companions with baleful glares that seemed to carry an almost physical force. If eyes were swords, then those gazes could've pierced flesh.

Ghaji's fingers toyed with the haft of his axe, but though the half-orc made no move to draw his weapon, Diran—with the awareness that only long-time companions possess—said, "Easy, my friend. They appear content to stare. For now, at least."

Ghaji nodded, though his perpetual scowl deepened in displeasure.

Diran glanced back over his shoulder toward Solus. "Do you sense anything more than you did aboard the shallop?"

The psiforged's crystals flashed briefly, then went dim. "No more than you do. The atmosphere of anger is stronger here, but I cannot locate its center. It seems to come from both everywhere and nowhere at the same time."

Tresslar snorted. "That's helpful."

Ghaji glared at the elderly artificer. Ever since Solus had joined them, Tresslar had been envious of the psiforged's powers, and his envy had only grown after the loss of the dragonwand. With the wand in his possession, Tresslar had been the most powerful member of their group in many ways. Without it, though he still possessed his skills at artificing, that distinction fell to Solus—and Tresslar was far from happy about it.

Diran stepped forward to walk alongside Asenka. "Is Kolbyr always like this?"

"I've only been here a few times. Most of my encounters with Kolbyrites have been at sea."

Ghaji knew that by "encounters" Asenka was referring to the Sea Scorpions' periodic clashes with the Coldhearts.

Asenka went on. "You met Haaken and his crew. By and large, most Kolbyrites are like them: ill-tempered, belligerent, ready to fight at the least provocation. But *this* . . . this is different."

Ghaji stepped forward to flank Diran. "Do you think this has something to do with the curse on the house of Kolbyr?"

Diran thought for a moment before replying. "The tales we've heard make no mention of it affecting anyone but the firstborn heir of the house of Kolbyr, and even then, only the heir's appearance is supposed to be affected. But rumors and stories never tell the entire truth, do they? I suppose it's possible, though. We'll just have to see for ourselves, and in the meantime, remain vigilant."

"In other words, business as usual," Ghaji said.

Diran smiled. "Precisely."

◦ ◦ ◦ ◉ ◦ ◦ ◦

Kolbyr's harbormaster demanded what seemed to Ghaji an exorbitant fee for allowing them passage into the city, especially since they didn't have a ship of their own to dock. But the man—sour-faced, with a scowl even more pronounced than Ghaji's—fairly trembled with suppressed rage while they talked, and Ghaji had the feeling that only the harbormaster's greed prevented him from summoning the city watch to haul them away. But though it took a good portion of their remaining funds, in the end Baron Mahir's money did the trick, and the companions were granted permission to enter Kolbyr.

Like the docks, the buildings were hewn from gray stone. The squat, blocky structures were plain and austere, their surfaces smooth and bereft of ornamental touches. The streets were stone as well, though cracked in numerous places and in dire need of repair. The oppressive pall that they'd sensed at the docks was stronger here, and it felt as if the companions shouldered an unseen and increasingly heavy burden as they walked.

"And I thought Perhata was unpleasant." Ghaji remembered Asenka was with them and quickly said, "Sorry."

The woman smiled. "Don't worry about it. My city may not be the jewel of the Principalities, but it has Kolbyr beat."

Ghaji couldn't disagree with that.

The people they passed looked little different than their counterparts in Perhata. Both men and women wore their hair in braids with intricate beadwork woven in—though theirs was less showy than elsewhere in the Principalities—and all were dressed warmly. The big difference was in attitude. Though the Perhatans were by and large rogues, thieves, and swindlers, the Kolbyrites appeared to be barely restrained killers. They glared, sneered, spat, and some even growled like beasts as the companions passed. More than a few hands twitched toward weapons, but none had been drawn—so far. Ghaji thought of the gulls that attacked *Welby's Pride*, and he wondered if the only reason the Kolbyrites hadn't given in to their antagonistic impulses was because they weren't simple-minded animals. He also wondered that, if the curse of Kolbyr was truly at work here, how long the citizenry would be able to resist the urge to attack.

Tresslar stepped forward until he trailed directly behind Diran. "I was thinking . . ." The artificer began.

Diran stopped and turned to face Tresslar. The other companions halted as well and turned to listen.

"Yes?"

"Now that we're here, I'd like to poke around a bit and see if I can detect any sign of my wand. I know it's no longer in Perhata or the surrounding environs. Perhaps the barghest brought it to Kolbyr for some reason."

"What of the curse?" Ghaji asked. "We might need your help to lift it."

"I'm an artificer, not an exorcist," Tresslar replied. "But to be honest, without my wand, I would be of little use to you. I've constructed a few other devices, it's true, but none that will prove effective against a curse. But if my wand *is* here and I can find it . . ." The artificer trailed off.

"As you wish," Diran said. "Let us meet at the docks around sunset."

Tresslar nodded, clearly relieved.

"I would like to accompany the artificer," Solus said. "Despite my efforts, I can fathom little of the nature of the dark power that grips this city. This leads me to believe that it is primarily magical in origin. I suspect I will be of far greater assistance in helping Tresslar in his attempts to locate his lost wand."

Tresslar scowled at Solus, and for a moment Ghaji thought the artificer was going to decline the psiforged's offer, but pragmatism won out over jealously, and Tresslar responded with a curt, "Thanks."

"I'm coming along as well," Hinto said. "My friend can't do without his eyes, can he?"

The psiforged looked down at the halfling pirate, and though his face didn't possess the ability to smile, Ghaji sensed the fondness Solus felt for his "eyes."

"Very true," Solus said.

Ghaji looked at Diran, an unspoken message passing between them. The loss of their two most powerful allies, if only temporarily, would seriously deplete their fighting strength. Given the reception they'd received so far in Kolbyr, Ghaji wasn't certain that splitting up was a good idea. But Diran gave a little shrug, as if to say there was no help for it, and Ghaji supposed his friend was right. Tresslar was obsessed with retrieving his wand, and he wouldn't be able to focus on anything else until the mystic artifact was once again in his possession. And with Solus's help, he just might be able to find it—assuming the wand was in Kolbyr at all.

Tresslar looked at Diran. "The docks at sunset," he said then turned to the psiforged and the halfling. "Let's go," he muttered, and the three headed off down the street. Ghaji kept an eye on them as they departed. The Kolbyrites glared at the trio as they passed, but otherwise did nothing. Then the three turned a corner and were lost to sight.

Ghaji turned to Diran. "Looks like it's just the four of us then."

"Actually . . ." Yvka said.

"Don't tell me you're going to desert us too!" Ghaji protested.

The elf-woman reached out to take Ghaji's hand and gave it a gentle squeeze. "We need the *Zephyr* back. *I* need her back. I have no idea if she was brought to Kolbyr, but there are certain . . . acquaintances I can consult with here in the city that might be able to help."

"We can book passage on other vessels if we need to," Ghaji said. "Diran and I got along fine without the *Zephyr* before."

Yvka's delicate brow furrowed, and she released his hand. "Are you saying you got along fine without *me?*"

Ghaji realized he'd inadvertently stepped into a cockatrice's nest. "Of course not." He knew he should say more, but not only couldn't he think of anything else, he was afraid he'd just make things worse by continuing to talk. So he fell silent.

"Perhaps it *would* be best if Yvka made her inquiries while we go to the baron's palace," Diran said. "I can think of only one person who knew where the vessel was hidden, and if *she* has her . . ." The priest failed to finish his sentence.

But Ghaji understood what his friend meant. Makala had most likely stolen the *Zephyr*, not only because of the ship's speed, but because the obsidian sarcophagus that allowed vampires to endure sea travel had been aboard. After the final confrontation with Aldarik Cathmore at Mount Luster, Makala had changed. She'd been a vampire for months, ever since being bitten by the undead pirate Onkar at the fortress-city of Grimwall. But while she'd been infected with the taint of vampirism, she'd fought to keep from being consumed by the darkness that now dwelled within her. But she'd lost that struggle at Mount Luster and had become a true creature of evil. With the *Zephyr*, she could go anywhere she wished and spread her contagion throughout the Principalities. Diran had failed to prevent Makala's transformation into a vampire, and he'd failed to keep her from being claimed by evil. Now the priest was determined to slay Makala—even though she had once been the mortal woman he'd loved above all others. He would not fail her a third time, no matter what it took.

Ghaji gazed at his friend with understanding before turning to face Yvka. "Sunset at the docks?"

She smiled. "Sunset." She leaned forward to give Ghaji a quick but passionate kiss, then jogged off down the street in the opposite direction the others had taken, moving with the silent, liquid grace that only elves possessed. Soon, she too was lost to sight.

Ghaji sighed. "I've never really understood women, but of all the women I haven't understood, I understand that one the least."

Diran laughed and clapped the half-orc on the shoulder. "Let's continue on to the baron's palace, my friend. Helping me exorcise a curse will hopefully take your mind off Yvka for a time."

Ghaji nodded, but he wasn't thinking about Yvka, at least, not *only* about her. He was also thinking of another woman he'd known—or rather had *thought* he'd known.

The half-orc thrust thoughts of both women from his mind. "Well, if we're going to do it, then let's get moving," he growled. And without waiting for Diran and Asenka to resume walking, he stalked past them and continued down the street. He didn't look over his shoulder to see if they followed. He knew they would. Besides, he didn't want either of them to see how much the cold air was making his eyes water. And as he walked, the thought of Kirai.

CHAPTER

FOUR

Ghaji wrinkled his nose as a horrid stench curled its way up his nostrils. He tried to ignore the churning in his gut and the splash of hot bile at the back of his throat—tried hard.

"Karrnathi undead stink bad enough as it is, Kirai." His voice was strained, and he fought to keep his gorge from rising any further than it already had. "Why make their stench worse by spreading that foul-smelling glop all over them?"

Aligned in rows of six and positioned less than a hand's breadth apart, a squadron of zombies clad in half-plate armor, two dozen in all, stood motionless upon the arid grassland of the Talenta Plains. It was only mid-morning, but there were no clouds in the sky to filter the punishing rays of the sun here on the edge of the Blade Desert, and it felt as if they inhabited a vast, open-air blast furnace. Ghaji wore a white cloth over his head tied in place with a black headband to ward off sun-poisoning. The rest of his uniform—if you could call it that—consisted of a white loin-cloth, a vest of boiled leather, sandals, and a belt beneath which he'd tucked the handle of his war-axe. Though he was a mercenary and not an official soldier in Karrnath's army, he was currently employed by them and therefore required to wear the army's standard uniform. But it was simply too damned hot for the half-orc to bother with such a foolish technicality, and whenever anyone tried to remind him of it, he just bared his teeth and growled until they left him alone. It never took long.

Kirai knelt before the zombies, a clay jar sitting on the ground at her right. Periodically, she reached inside the jar and brought out handfuls of thick, greasy paste which she rubbed liberally onto the zombie's skin. At times, for reasons Ghaji wasn't clear on, Kirai would look at the paste on her hands, frown, then reach into a satchel sitting on the ground next to the jar. She'd pull out a few ingredients—a root, a vial of greenish-blue liquid, or perhaps a cylindrical object that resembled a spice dispenser—and add a touch of this, a sprinkle of that, presumably to adjust the formula's potency. Right now she tossed in what Ghaji would've sworn was a dried spider carcass before continuing to rub unguent on a zombie's left leg.

Kirai was dressed for the heat, but their commander allowed that as the woman was an alchemist and not a soldier. She wore a white robe made of light cloth that covered her arms and legs, and while the clothing helped keep her cool, it did little to accentuate her appearance—much to Ghaji's disappointment. Kirai kept her raven hair cut short because of the heat, but she didn't wear a hat to shield her head from the sun. Instead she used a salve of her own making as protection against the sun's rays, which she rubbed daily all over her body, including the top of her head. She'd gotten Ghaji to try it once, but he'd broken out in a painful rash that had lasted the better part of three days, and so he stuck to his trusty cloth head-covering and otherwise took his chances with the sun.

Kirai smeared unguent on an undead knee-cap. "We've been here for the better part of a month, and you've complained about the smell ever single day. You should've gotten used to it by now."

Ghaji tried breathing through his mouth. It helped . . . a little. But inhaling the hot dry air made his throat feel as if it were caked with burning sand. "Some things you never get used to," he said in a queasy voice.

Kirai laughed. "Have you been taking that potion I mixed for you? It's supposed to help keep your stomach settled."

Kirai wasn't what most humans would deem beautiful. She was

tall, lanky instead of thin, small-breasted, with bony elbows, knobby knees, and overlarge hands. Her face was plain, but when she smiled her green eyes shone, and she had full lips that Ghaji never got tired of looking at.

"I drink a dose every morning without fail," he said. "That's why I finally stopped throwing up every time I guard you."

"Are you saying that I induce vomiting?"

Ghaji felt suddenly flustered. "No! I meant—" He broke off when he saw Kirai grin. "Very funny."

Kirai continued smearing the greasy unguent on the zombie's leathery brown flesh. The undead creature remained completely motionless, displaying no sign that it was even aware of Kirai's ministrations, let alone that it felt them.

"You know I have to do this, Ghaji. Stink or no stink."

Ghaji understood quite well. He just enjoyed hearing Kirai talk – and not only because their conversations helped keep his mind off his roiling stomach. He enjoyed the sound of her voice and the way she laughed when she teased him.

Karrnathi zombies were more durable than ordinary undead because of the alchemical treatments they received. Those treatments not only prevented further decay, they kept the zombies functioning physically, though the undead warriors didn't move as swiftly as their living counterparts. But the zombies more than made up for their slowness in durability and savagery, as Ghaji had witnessed numerous times in battle since he'd signed on with the Karrnathi army.

But the harsh conditions on the Talenta Plains took a great toll on the zombies, further drying their already leathery skin and tightening their muscles and tendons. Because of this, they required almost daily alchemical treatments to continue functioning. That was one important advantage warforged had over zombies, Ghaji thought. The artificial constructs could operate in any environment—not to mention their scent was far more tolerable. They smelled of stone, metal, and wood . . . natural things. Zombies smelled like death. No, worse than that, for death was a natural part of the cycle of existence, but there was nothing natural about raised corpses. They stank of *un*death, and to an orc—even a half-orc like Ghaji—there could be nothing more unnatural.

Though no one had ever come out and said so to his face, Ghaji knew he'd been assigned to this unit not only because he was a mercenary, but because he was half-orc. Who better to work with zombies than a half-blood like him? That way true Karrnathi soldiers—*human* soldiers—would be freed up for more important and less odious duties. Ghaji told himself that he was a mercenary, and a job was a job, even if it did literally stink at times. But this assignment had its positive side: he'd gotten to know Kirai well during their time working together. She was quite talkative, and he'd learned a great deal about her—more than he'd ever learned about any human, as a matter of fact. At first he'd been annoyed by how chatty she was, but he'd soon come to appreciate their often one-sided conversations and, in a strange way, to even need them.

The other soldiers, about a dozen in all, remained inside the stone tower that lay several hundred yards to northwest—upwind of where Ghaji and Kirai worked. Because of their stench, the zombies were permitted no closer to the Karrnathi outpost, and while Ghaji couldn't blame the humans, tending to the maintenance of the undead would've been marginally less unpleasant if they could've done it in the shade provided by the tower's shadow. Instead Kirai and he had to stand out here in full sunlight, rivulets of sweat pouring off of them.

A faint scuttling sound came to Ghaji's ears from off in the distance, and he drew his war-axe.

"Halfling riders," he warned Kirai. Without waiting for the alchemist to respond, Ghaji whirled about to face the direction he judged the sound had come from. A group of halfling warriors wearing hunting masks and sitting astride clawfoots raced across the plains toward them, the man-sized two-legged lizards kicking up a cloud of dust as they bore their riders onward. The Talenta Plains were home to tribal halflings, fiercely proud hunters who'd domesticated the savage clawfoots, one of the breeds of giant lizards that roamed this land. For years, Karrnath had sought to extend its territory into the Plains—hence the outpost where Ghaji was stationed. But the halflings—understandably enough—were reluctant to allow their ancestral homeland to be conquered piece by piece by the Karrnathi. Ghaji didn't blame the halflings for their reluctance to roll over and submit to Karrnathi rule, but they didn't pay his salary; the Karrnathi did.

Ghaji did want to leave Kirai, but it was his duty to alert the human soldiers within the outpost. Besides, he knew from experience that the alchemist could take care of herself. Ghaji ran toward the outpost, shouting back over his shoulder, "Kirai, get the zombies ready!"

Karrnathi zombies possessed a rudimentary intelligence that allowed them to fight with little to no instruction, but they were most effective when given specific, direct orders.

"Arm yourselves and defend the outpost against the halflings!" Kirai commanded.

Ghaji didn't look back to see if the zombies obeyed her. He knew they would, for they had no choice: it was how they were made. The zombies normally carried wickedly curved scimitars and shields that they never put down, but because they'd been receiving alchemical treatment from Kirai, the undead warriors had been instructed to discard their weapons. Two dozen scimitars and an equal number of shields lay on the ground in two neat rows, precisely where the zombies had put them. Ghaji knew the animated corpses were even now moving stiffly but deliberately to reclaim their weapons to fulfill Kirai's order. As soon as the zombies were armed once more, they would move toward the outpost as fast as their desiccated limbs would allow and engage the attacking halflings in battle.

But Ghaji had no intention of waiting for the zombies to catch up. After all, the halflings weren't going to rein their clawfoots to a halt and politely give the zombies a chance to reach the outpost.

The half-orc warrior drew in a breath and bellowed in the loudest voice he was capable of. "To arms! To arms!" He hoped he'd shouted loudly enough to rouse the soldiers in the outpost. The fort grew so hot during the day that they usually left the main entrance open to permit air to flow through the tower. A necessary step to make the atmosphere within the stifling tower walls bearable, perhaps, but one that seemed awfully foolish now. If the halflings reached the outpost's wide-open entrance before the zombies got there, the warriors would dismount, run inside, and attack the Karrnathi soldiers with the spears they carried and which they could wield as well in close quarters as they did out in the open while seated on the backs of their clawfoot mounts. The Karrnathi were skilled fighters, but the punishing heat sapped their strength, while the halflings, being native to this region, weren't bothered by the temperature in the least. The Karrnathi would be lethargic and clumsy, and once inside the halflings would make short work of them. But if Ghaji could reach the entrance first and seal the iron door shut . . .

He ran faster.

As he ran, he gauged the halflings' strength. Ten riders armed with spears, each riding a clawfoot with mottled gray-green hide, a wide maw filled with sharp teeth, and a sickle-like talon on each foot that could disembowel prey as easily as a white-hot dagger could cut through lard. Clawfoots were savage beasts, but their riders controlled the animals with almost supernatural ease. Before signing on with the Karrnathi, Ghaji had heard rumors that the Talenta halflings had some sort of mystical bond with their monstrous mounts, and after serving on the Plains for the last month, he believed it.

The halflings resembled elves after a fashion, though they were of shorter stature and possessed deeply tanned skin. They wore ritual hunting masks fashioned from clawfoot jaws, tunics made from animal skin, and armored vests constructed from clawfoot hide. They were beardless, and their long hair trailed out behind them as they rode full out toward the Karrnathi outpost.

As Ghaji drew near the outpost, he noticed one thing more. He'd been mistaken in his first assessment of how the halflings were armed. Of the ten riders, only *nine* carried spears. One halfling rode in the middle of the group, and instead of a spear, he carried an ivory bone-staff with runes carved deep into its surface. This halfling appeared older than the others, his hair white, skin wrinkled and leathery.

He's a shaman, Ghaji realized, and he felt a sudden unease. He'd never heard of a halfling shaman riding into battle before. Maybe the halflings hadn't come to fight, but rather were here for a different reason.

Yeah, right.

Ghaji put on a last burst of speed and reached the tower's entrance. One of the Karrnathi soldiers—a woman who normally refused to look at Ghaji, let alone speak to him—was already standing inside the doorway.

"I'll bar the entrance, half-blood" she said. "You and the zombies can deal with the halflings." She gave Ghaji a smirk before slamming the iron door shut in his face. A second later he heard the sound of an iron bar being slid into place.

Fury surged through Ghaji, and he felt like pounding his fist on the door and calling the woman a few choice names. But he didn't have time to give in to his emotions. Not if he wanted to survive the next few moments. War-axe gripped tight, lower incisors bared in a snarl, the half-orc spun to face the oncoming riders—

—and saw that they had stopped.

Not a dozen yards from where Ghaji stood, the halflings had formed a semi-circle behind the shaman. The shaman wore the same animal-hide tunic as the other riders, but without the extra protection of a clawfoot-scale vest. Bone-staff held lightly in his left hand, the shaman sat relaxed but alert in the saddle of a clawfoot whose head was marked with a patch of deep red that might or might not have been natural. The shaman regarded Ghaji for several seconds with the confident, unconcerned air of a man who was completely in control of the situation.

The shaman spoke with the lilting accent of the Talenta halflings, his voice surprisingly deep for one of his diminutive stature.

"You are not Karrnathi. Why do you stand guard before their outpost?"

Ghaji glanced sideways and saw the zombies, scimitars and shields grasped in their undead hands, lumbering toward them. The halflings couldn't have been unaware of the approaching undead, but they appeared not to notice, let alone care. Ghaji wasn't sure why that was so, but if he could keep the riders distracted for a moment or two longer, the zombies would arrive and the half-orc just might be able to take to his sleeping pallet tonight with the same number of limbs and major organs he'd started the day with.

"Because the Karrnathi pay well and they pay on time."

The shaman's lip curled upward in distaste. "A mercenary. You fight for profit. We fight to repel invaders from our land."

Ghaji didn't know this man, didn't have any reason to care what he thought. Yet the shaman's blunt assessment of Ghaji's motives cut through him as sharply as any blade ever had, and he felt ashamed.

Ghaji intended to say something bold and equally cutting to show the shaman that his words hadn't bothered him—even if it was a lie. But before he could speak, the shaman raised his bone-staff high and spoke a series of rapid syllables in a strange language that hurt Ghaji's ears to hear.

Ghaji risked another glance to check on the zombies' progress, and he was gratified to see they had closed to within half a dozen yards. Another few seconds . . . then he realized the zombies had stopped. The undead warriors stood motionless, seeming to stare at the shaman's upraised staff, their heads cocked slightly to the side in the manner of confused hounds. Ghaji then noticed something almost as disturbing. Instead of hanging back and remaining out of harm's way, Kirai had followed in the zombies' wake. She stood not ten feet behind the last of the zombies, her satchel of alchemical supplies slung over her left shoulder. She probably thought she could help somehow, and Ghaji admired her courage, but this was a battle in the offing—a far cry from smearing goo on undead flesh as part of daily zombie maintenance.

The zombies straightened their heads, their momentary confusion gone. Their full attention was focused on the halfling shaman, and Ghaji thought they seemed almost eager to hear his next words.

"Slay the Karrnathi—every one of them." And then, almost as an afterthought, the shaman added, "And slay the half-orc as well."

Two dozen leather-fleshed heads swiveled to look at Ghaji, two dozen scimitars were raised high in the air, and two dozen pairs of dry dead lips stretched into wicked, blood-thirsty smiles.

Ghaji sighed. It looked like it was going to be a long morning.

He lifted his war-axe, bellowed a battle cry, and rushed forward to meet the first of the oncoming zombie horde.

❧ ❧ ❧ ❦ ❧ ❧ ❧

In the mouth of an alley across the street from Diran, Ghaji, and Asenka, a man sat with his back against the cold stone wall, knees drawn to his chest, hands wrapped around his legs, hugging himself for what meager warmth his body could provide. He was garbed in a tattered cloak that provided little defense against the late autumn winds, but though his clothing marked him as a man whose fortunes had taken an ill turn, the brown hair that hung past his shoulders had recently been washed, and his thick beard and mustache were neatly trimmed. Around his neck, concealed by his ragged clothing, a silver arrowhead hung from a chain. Lying on the ground next to him rested a longbow and a quiver full of arrows.

The man watched as the seven companions on the other side of the street spoke for several moments before going their separate ways. They were an interesting lot, but his gaze remained fixed on a single individual: the tall man garbed in black. Grim-faced, cold-eyed, he was the sort of man that exuded an almost palpable aura of danger, and yet there was gentleness about him as well. It was in the easy way he smiled at his friends, how he focused his full attention on them as they spoke, and the fondness in his tone of voice as he replied.

But despite his obvious kindness, at his core the man in black was a stone-cold killer. The man in the ragged cloak knew this. It was, in fact, why he had gone to such lengths to seek Diran Bastiaan out.

Images flashed through the cloaked man's mind: moons blazing bright and full, a shadowy form emerging from the darkness and bounding toward him, growling low in its throat, mouth opened wide to reveal sharp white teeth—

Shuddering, the man thrust the images from his mind. His breath now came in ragged gasps, and sweat rolled down his face despite the cold.

Diran moved off down the street, accompanied by the half-orc and the blond woman. The cloaked man waited several moments until he'd collected himself, then he gathered his bow and arrows, rose to his feet, and followed.

CHAPTER

FIVE

Tresslar, Hinto, and Solus walked side by side along the street, the human and the halfling flanking the psiforged. Though the Kolbyrites they passed continued to glare at them, their animosity seemed somewhat muted now. Tresslar guessed Solus was using his psionic abilities to blunt the citizens' anger, and before he could ask, the psiforged said, "Yes, I am. I have been doing so since we made port."

Tresslar was taken aback. If Solus had been protecting them since their arrival in Kolbyr, did that mean psiforged was the only thing that had been keeping the citizens from attacking them? And if so, what did that mean for Diran and the others now that they no longer had Solus to shield them?

"Fear not, my friend," Solus said. "The protective aura I extended around the others will linger for some time yet, and the citizens of Kolbyr have much experience at resisting the dark magic that hangs over their city, though I sense that it is stronger this day than usual. We should all be safe enough—for the time being."

Tresslar nodded, though he could've done without Solus's qualification of "safe."

"So where are we going?" Hinto asked.

Tresslar didn't want to answer the little pirate's question, but he knew if he didn't the halfling would only keep pestering him.

"Tinker's Room."

"Is that a tavern?" Hinto said. A chill breeze wafted down the street, and the halfling shivered. "It's a bit early in the day to start drinking, but I *could* use a little something to warm me up inside."

"No, it's not a tavern, and Tinker's Room isn't its real name. It's a customary nickname. There's a Tinker's Room in every city across Khorvaire, and while they're a bit rarer in the Principalities, Perhata has one, and so does Kolbyr."

Hinto frowned. "If they're that common, why haven't I heard of them before?"

Before Tresslar could reply, Solus said, "Because you aren't an artificer, my friend."

Tresslar scowled at the psiforged. "It's impolite to read people's minds without their permission, you know."

Solus bowed his head. "My apologies, master artificer. I'm finding it more difficult to block out the thoughts of my new friends than I anticipated. The more time I spend in your company, the more my mind becomes . . . accustomed to yours, causing me to sense your surface thoughts without intending to."

Tresslar, somewhat mollified by Solus's referring to him as *master* artificer, decided to accept the psiforged's apology. "Very well, but I'd appreciate it if you would allow me to keep my thoughts to myself in the future. Now, to return to Hinto's question, while the existence of Tinker's Rooms isn't precisely a secret, it's not something that artificers go out of their way to publicize. While both wizards and artificers work with magic, wizards deal with the more theoretical aspects of the craft, while artificers take a practical approach. Wizards research and study magic for the sake of acquiring knowledge and increasing their own personal power. Artificers, on the other hand, *use* magic, applying it for practical purposes. Wizards tend to work in isolation and guard their secrets jealously, but artificers—because of their more pragmatic approach to magic—are much more open about sharing their knowledge. Hence the existence of Tinker's Rooms, places where artificers gather to talk shop, admire one another's craftsmanship, and trade for materials and supplies as needed."

"And you hope to learn something of your missing wand at the Tinker's Room in Kolbyr?" Solus asked.

Tresslar shrugged. "No one at the Tinker's Room in Perhata had any news about my wand, but someone here in Kolbyr might. Whenever an artificer is unsure how to begin tackling a problem, we have a saying: 'Go to your room.' So that's what I'm doing."

"Are you sure the people there won't mind if we accompany you?" Hinto asked. "Neither Solus nor I are artificers."

"Don't worry," Tresslar said. "While outsiders aren't encouraged, they aren't forbidden." He then smiled at Solus. "In fact, I think you will be especially welcome, my bejeweled friend. Psiforged are extremely rare, and there's nothing artificers love better than seeing a magical device—or in your case, a construct—that they haven't encountered before."

They continued walking through Kolbyr, and though Tresslar had never been here before, he'd received directions from artificers in Perhata before setting sail for this side of the gulf, and after a short time the three companions stood before a domed building with a single wooden door hanging slightly askew on its hinges.

"This is it?" Hinto said, eyeing the building skeptically. "Kolbyr's artificers must not be very good if they can't fix a simple door."

"I told you, Tinker's Rooms aren't advertised," Tresslar said. "The door's state of disrepair is no doubt intended to help disguise the building's true nature." Which was possible, but it was equally possible—and Tresslar had to admit, more likely—that Kolbyr's artificers hadn't even noticed the door's condition. If there was nothing magical about the door, there wouldn't be anything about it to interest artificers. "But you don't have to take my word for it."

Tresslar removed his backpack, reached inside, and withdrew a small metal ring with a wooden handle attached. Tresslar held the device, which resembled a magnifying glass that had lost its lens, up to the stone wall to the right of the door. He moved the device slowly up and down until a golden light began to glow within the center of the ring. The glow grew brighter, and the illumination began to take on a distinct shape: a hand grasping a tool that looked like a small trident wrapped in a coil of wire.

"Behold the Tinker's Mark," Tresslar said. He held the revealer steady for a moment while he gazed upon the mark, his mind filling with fond memories of the many Tinker's Rooms he'd visited over the years—especially back when he'd been a young adventurer sailing on the *Sea Star* with Erdis Cai. Without a doubt, those had been the happiest days of his life, and he missed them.

Tresslar sensed he was being scrutinized, and he turned to see Solus looking at him, though it wasn't always easy to tell when warforged had their artificial eyes trained on you. He was certain Solus had been reading his thoughts, purposefully or not, and he turned away, embarrassed. He deactivated the revealer and the golden image of the Tinker's Mark winked out. Tresslar put the revealer away, slid his pack over his shoulders once again and, without looking at either of his companions, pushed open the door. The hinges creaked and the door wobbled, but it opened smoothly enough. Tresslar stepped inside without hesitation, and Solus and Hinto followed.

This was Tresslar's favorite part of entering a Tinker's Room: seeing what the outer chamber looked like. Tinker's Rooms always had a legitimate business as a front in order to conceal their true nature and to create a plausible reason why people—quite often strangers such as themselves—would be entering and leaving at all hours. In his time, Tresslar had seen Tinker's Rooms that had such wildly diverse disguises as a chandlers' shop, a garment merchant, and once even a taxidermist's. But this rivaled them all.

The outer chamber was set up as a shop, with a main counter and display shelves. But the wares for sale were like nothing Tresslar had ever seen before. At first he thought they were some sort of glass sculptures, but after a moment's inspection, he realized that the beautiful arrangements of translucent blue-green orbs were, in fact, structures created out of water bubbles. The bubbles were of various sizes, configurations, and hues, but the arrangements all had two things in common: the bubbles were frozen in space without any visible sign that anything was holding them up, and they were all set atop triangular jade bases. A number of the bubbles glowed with soft, gentle light, providing illumination for the room.

A beautiful woman in her late forties or early fifties emerged from a back room behind the counter. She had long flowing hair that was tinted blue and bereft of the usual beadwork favored by most Lhazaarites. Her dress—if that was the right word for her garment—was made from the same blue-green bubbles as the sculptures that filled the room, though hers were less translucent, providing only a suggestion of the body they concealed.

She took Tresslar's breath away. She was the single most beautiful woman he had ever seen, and considering how widely he'd traveled during his youth, that was saying something.

"It may be rude to read people's minds without permission," Solus said, "but if I'm not mistaken, it's equally rude to stare."

Tresslar felt his cheeks burn, and he knew he was blushing.

Hinto ignored the exchange between the artificer and the psi-forged. He walked over to one of the displays and rose on his tiptoes, stretching out his hand to touch the nearest sculpture.

"Please don't," the woman behind the counter said. "Those are actual water bubbles harvested from the sea. The spells that keep them intact and in place are quite fragile. A single touch could well disrupt them and destroy the sculpture."

With an almost childlike expression of disappointment, the halfling lowered his hand and came back down on the flats of his feet.

The woman came around from behind the counter, moving with such easy grace that it seemed that she didn't so much walk as glided toward them.

"My name is Illyia," she said. "Are you art lovers? It may be immodest of me, but I daresay my sculptures are among the most unique objects to be found in the Principalities." Her voice was like the breaking of gentle surf upon a sandy beach.

A moment of silence passed before Tresslar realized everyone was waiting for him to speak, and when he did, his voice was huskier than usual. "Indeed, though the word I would use is spectacular."

Illyia smiled, and a mischievous gleam came into her eyes. "Are you speaking of my bubbles?"

Tresslar had to force himself to keep from gazing at the way her garment clung to her chest—and wondering if those bubbles would be "disrupted" by a single touch like those that comprised her sculptures. *"Everything* I see here is spectacular."

Hinto rolled his eyes. "You've spent too many years on Dreadhold, Tresslar. That line is as stale as decade-old sea rations."

Tresslar glared at the halfling, but Illyia continued smiling. "Just because something is . . . seasoned doesn't mean it's no longer good. Often, quite the opposite is true, wouldn't you say . . . ?"

"Tresslar. And these are my companions, Hinto and Solus."

Illyia nodded briefly to the halfling, but she took her time regarding Solus. "We don't get many warforged here in Kolbyr, Solus, and I doubt we've ever had any quite like you."

Solus bowed his head. "I shall take that as a compliment."

Illyia's eyes twinkled. "Good, since that's how I meant it." She turned back to Tresslar. "So, you spent time on Dreadhold. You don't look like a hardened criminal, but then looks can be deceiving, can't they?"

Tresslar smiled. "I worked there as an artificer, helping to maintain the facility's magical wards and defenses."

Illyia hmphed. "You must've had your work cut out for you, then. The artificers of House Kundarak aren't exactly known for their attention to detail."

The dwarves of House Kundarak were responsible for running Dreadhold, but while most of the prison staff were members of the House, many—like Tresslar—were not.

"I must admit, I *did* have occasion to double-check their work from time to time," Tresslar said, trying to sound more modest than he felt. A sudden realization hit him then, and he forgot all about the artificers of Dreadhold. "You're being nice to us."

Illyia laughed. "Why do you find that so surprising?"

"Up until this point, we haven't had the warmest of welcomes here in Kolbyr," Tresslar said.

Illyia's merriment ebbed and she grew serious. "I'm afraid you've experienced the effects of the curse that plagues our city. We call it the Fury."

"It hasn't seemed to have affected you," Hinto said.

"It's her dress," Solus said. "It radiates a field of mystic energy that protects her from the curse's effect."

Illyia spread her arms and slowly spun around, as if modeling her dress for them. "Stylish *and* practical, that's me."

"Indeed," Tresslar said with appreciation. "It's a most impressive piece of work."

Hinto groaned, and it took all of Tresslar's self-discipline to keep the artificer from striking the halfling.

"The Fury is like the weather," Illyia said. "Some days it's worse than others. On mild days people are merely more rude and brusque, but on bad days people brawl in the streets. On extremely bad days, the streets run red with spilled blood. We don't leave our homes on bad days and try to avoid contact with anyone else, lest we find ourselves in the grip of a murderous fury."

"It sounds awful!" Hinto said. "How can you live with it?"

Illyia shrugged. "If you grow up in Kolbyr, as I have, you become accustomed to it. The effects of the curse are manageable, though it does take some effort to resist them. Newcomers to the city, such as yourselves, are the most vulnerable to the Fury. Since they aren't local, there's less reason for citizens to care about not harming them, which makes it more difficult to resist the Fury. Newcomers aren't affected by the curse right away, but the Fury is both powerful and insidious. Over the space of just a few hours, it will slowly worm its way into your heart without your realizing it, and it will fill you with anger . . . anger that you have no experience at managing. Newcomers often succumb to the Fury within their first day in Kolbyr. It's why we're so leery of strangers, as I'm sure you noticed as you made your way through the city."

Tresslar didn't feel any anger building within him. All he felt was the general irritation he often experienced at the annoyances presented by day-to-day living. Was Solus—?

The psiforged's voice whispered in Tresslar's mind.

I cannot counter magic, but as we first approached Kolbyr, I used my psionic abilities to strengthen everyone's emotional self-control to help slow the effects of the Fury. So far, my efforts seem to have been successful.

Tresslar's first impulse was to chide the psiforged for altering people's minds without permission, but he decided not to worry about it, especially since it *did* appear to be working. Still, before long someone would need to explain to Solus that it was a good idea to ask before using his psionic powers in such a fashion—especially on friends.

Illyia frowned slightly, and Tresslar wondered if she were somehow aware of the telepathic communication that had occurred between Solus and him. But when she spoke, she said, "So, have you come to acquire one of my sculptures, or are you perhaps here for a different purpose?"

"We're friends of Tinker," Tresslar said.

"Tinker?" Hinto said, scowling. "Who's . . . ?" He trailed off, a sly smile coming onto his face. "Oh . . . *right*." He winked knowingly at Tresslar.

Now it was the artificer's turn to roll his eyes.

Illyia laughed. "Come with me, and we'll see if Tinker is home."

She turned and, for the briefest of instants, Tresslar thought the bubbles of her gown turned transparent. But before he could get a good look at what lay beneath, the bubbles returned to their blue-green hue.

Illyia headed toward a door at the back of the shop, walking with perhaps a bit more sway in her hips than was strictly necessary, and Tresslar, Hinto, and Solus followed. Suddenly Kolbyr—curse or no curse—didn't seem like all that bad a place to the artificer.

Not bad at all.

❀ ❀ ❀ ❀ ❀ ❀ ❀

Yvka stood across the street from a two-story building decorated with elaborate stonework. Intricate designs of sea creatures had been carved into the building's face, a quartet of granite gargoyles perched upon the roof, and a pair of manticore statues flanked a huge oak door at the top of marble steps. Casual passersby would appreciate the building's beauty, but few would realize that, should the need arise, the gargoyles and the manticores would come to swift and deadly life.

There was no sign to indicate the name or even the nature of this establishment, but then none was necessary. Only those who already knew of the Culinarian sought it out, and few of those were permitted entrance. And of and those who got inside, even fewer knew the restaurant's true nature.

Though Yvka hadn't let on to her companions, this wasn't her first time in Kolbyr. She had no specific reason for not telling them the truth, and she wasn't sure why she'd kept that information from them, and especially from Ghaji. Habit, she supposed. By necessity, operatives of the Shadow Network lived by a strict code of secrecy, but living by that code came with a price. Operatives couldn't afford to get too close to anyone, even other members of the Network. *Stay silent, stay guarded, stay alone, stay safe.* That was an operative's motto, and while Yvka had never come out and directly admitted to belonging to the Network, her friends knew the truth. That was why she stood out here hesitating. It was possible—no, almost certain—that the man she had come here to see was aware she'd become too close to Ghaji, Diran, and the others. The question was what, if anything, he planned to do about it.

She took a deep breath, let it out slowly, and started across the street.

She walked casually, seeming relaxed and comfortable, but inside she was tense and alert. As she approached the stairs, she had to force herself not to look at the gargoyles and manticores. She could feel their cold stone eyes upon her, and though she knew it was probably her imagination, she sensed displeasure in their gazes, as if even the guardians knew of her failure to remain detached and professional.

She reached the steps, ascended them, and stopped before the oak door. There was no knob, no handle, no device for signaling those inside. Yvka simply stood there, and after several moments—a bit longer than strictly necessary, she thought—the door swung inward, and Yvka stepped inside. She found herself standing at the end of a narrow corridor lit by tiny everbright lanterns hovering close to the curved ceiling. The lanterns gave off a soft blue light that only dimly illuminated the way, but they provided more than enough light for elvish eyes to see by. Yvka started down the corridor, and she didn't look back as she heard the door close behind her with a gentle *snick* that sounded all too final to her ears. No one came forward to greet her, but that was normal here. If the door opened for you, you already knew you were welcome in the Culinarian.

The corridor ran straight for a few dozen yards before opening onto a vast dining hall. The hall was illuminated by cerulean everbright lanterns floating in the air to simulate an underwater environment, and saltwater aquariums filled with exotic sea creatures were placed in various locations around the hall to further enhance the illusion. A long table constructed from coral stretched the length of the hall, and spread out on its craggy surface was a buffet of seafood dishes: lobster, shrimp, squid, crab, clams, mussels, mullet, salmon, scampi, prawns, grouper, conch, blowfish, octopus, halibut, monkfish, and many more. Dishes were served raw, baked, broiled, and fried, along with a wide assortment of vegetables.

The diners sat at smaller tables in groups of two, three, or more. Like the main table, the diners' tables had been fashioned from coral, with animated centerpieces enchanted to resemble seaweed drifting in an underwater current. Servers moved constantly throughout the room, some bringing new dishes in from the kitchen, others carrying plates loaded with food to diners too lazy—or self-important—to serve themselves. The diners themselves came from all strata of society. Some were clad in expensive finery and adorned with jewelry of rare craftsmanship and incalculable value, while others were barefoot and wore torn, dirty rags that could only charitably be referred to as clothing at all. But despite the variance in dress, the rich and poor—or at least, those who appeared to be so—often sat at the same tables, talking, laughing, and behaving as equals.

Yvka stood in the great hall's entrance for a moment as she scanned the tables searching for the man she had come here to see. It didn't take her long to spot him sitting at a table alone, almost as if he had been expecting her. He probably was, Yvka thought.

Zivon was a handsome man who appeared to be in his mid-forties, though Yvka knew he was older, perhaps quite a bit so. Half-elves weren't as long-lived as full elves, but their lifespans were significantly longer than those of their human cousins. His brown hair was pulled back and bound with a leather thong, and he sported a neatly trimmed goatee with more than a bit of gray mixed in with the brown. Full elves didn't grow facial hair, but half-elves could, thanks to the human side of their ancestry. Zivon wore a fine silken robe of aquamarine with white trimming the color of sea foam, in keeping with the Culinarian's underwater theme.

Zivon smiled with what appeared to be genuine delight when he spotted Yvka and waved her over to his table. Yvka returned the smile, acknowledged the invitation with a nod, and began making her way across the room toward Zivon. As she drew near, she saw that the capillaries in the half-elf's eyes were tinted purple, and she knew that he'd been indulging in urchin-sting, a common narcotic enjoyed in the Principalities. She also knew that he was far from the only one in the great hall who had done so this day. Sitting on the table before him was a plate piled high with seafood delicacies, and before Yvka could sit across from him, a server brought her a plate similarly loaded. As soon as that servant departed, another appeared carrying a wine jug. She refilled Zivon's mug, then moved to fill the mug already sitting at Yvka's place, but the elf-woman waved the servant away and the woman moved off to tend to other diners.

As Yvka took her seat, Zivon said, "I'm surprised you declined the wine. You know I select only the finest vintages for my cellar." The half-elf's voice was steady, though his words were slightly slurred.

"I also know you lace your wine with urchin-sting to blunt the effects of the Fury," Yvka said. "I'd rather my perceptions remain undulled. Besides, if all goes well, soon no one in Kolbyr will need to worry about resisting the Fury any longer."

Zivon took a long sip of wine, and when he put his mug back down, the veins in his eyes looked thicker and more purple than they had a moment ago. "You speak of course of your friend the priest."

There was something in the way Zivon said *your friend* that made Yvka uncomfortable. Half-elves were known for their silver tongues, and Zivon was no exception. He used words with rapier-like precision. He was undoubtedly making a comment about Yvka getting too close to her companions.

Zivon lifted an oyster to his mouth and swallowed it in a single deft motion. He set the empty shell aside and took another sip of wine. Half-elves tended to be thin, though not as ethereally slender as full-blooded elves. With his hybrid metabolism Zivon could regularly eat twice as much as a human without putting on excess weight, which made the Culinarian a perfect place for a devotee of fine dining like him to serve the Shadow Network.

"We were aware of the priest's vow to lift the curse on the House of Kolbyr moments after he made it," Zivon said.

The half-elf was exaggerating, Yvka thought, though probably not by much. The Shadow Network knew virtually everything that happened in the Principalities—in some instances, before it occurred. "Then you also know that Diran stands a good chance of succeeding."

"You're not eating," Zivon said, the merest hint of disapproval in his voice. "Try the mussels. They're delectable."

Yvka wasn't especially hungry but tried a mussel for the sake of not offending her host.

"Well?"

Yvka chewed, swallowed. "It's good."

"Good? I have some of the finest cooks in the Principalities working in my kitchen, and all you have to say in response to experiencing their art is 'good'?"

Yvka shrugged. *"Very* good."

Zivon shook his head and laughed. "Fortune save me from uneducated palates!" He took yet another sip of wine, set his mug down, then pushed his plate aside—an indication that he was ready to get down to business. "You truly believe the priest is capable of dispelling the Fury?"

"His name is Diran, and I've seen him do remarkable things."

"Rumor has it that you've seen his partner do a few remarkable things as well."

Yvka felt her own rage take hold at Zivon's remark—a rage that had nothing to do with the House of Kolbyr. But before she could say anything, Zivon held up his hands in a placating gesture.

"You've managed to maintain our code admirably—*until* the night you met Diran Bastiaan and his companions in a seedy tavern in Port Verge. At first you joined them in order to discover the secret of the Black Fleet, for information is the Network's lifeblood, is it not? But it didn't take long for you to come to admire your new companions and, despite your many years of experience at maintaining professional distance from others, for the first time in a long time you found herself becoming close to others, didn't you? Especially the half-orc.

"Oh, you made excuses, told yourself that the best way to gain your new companions' trust was to appear to become friends with them, and your association proved even more beneficial than you'd hoped when, after you'd defeated Erdis Cai, you informed us about the vampire's hidden lair in Grimwall. We were quite pleased with the treasures we discovered in the ancient goblinoid city. And if you'd had a little fun with the half- . . . with *Ghaji* in the process of performing your duties, what was the harm? You received a new assignment not long after that, and when you were forced to say goodbye to Ghaji, you pretended that parting from him didn't hurt. And you almost managed to make yourself believe it.

"But a few months later you learned that Aldarik Cathmore, one of Bastiaan's former teachers in the art of assassination, had come to the Principalities, and you used that information as an excuse to rejoin your new friends once more . . . as an excuse to see Ghaji. Once again, your association with the others benefited you: you informed us of the existence of the creation forge within Mount Luster, and our artificers are even now investigating the facility to ferret out the delicious secrets it holds. You've done well, Yvka. Quite well, indeed." Zivon paused a moment before adding, "All things considered."

Zivon's tone remained pleasant enough, but his words sent a chill rippling down Yvka's spine. "You're speaking of the *Zephyr.*"

"A valuable asset. One that we are disappointed to have lost."

"Makala took it." It was as much a question as a statement.

"Yes. Though she wasn't alone."

Yvka frowned. "Who else was with her?"

"A lich and a barghest. The same barghest, we believe, who stole the wand of your artificer friend."

"A lich?" Could it be the same one that Diran, Ghaji, Tresslar, and Hinto had slain in the mountains outside Perhata? How could it be any other? The barghest had been her servant, after all. But how had the lich been resurrected, if that was the right term to apply to the reanimation of an already undead creature? Had the barghest somehow used Tresslar's dragonwand to perform the task? Yvka supposed it didn't matter how the dark deed was done. A more important question was why Makala had joined forces with the lich and her servant, and most important of all, where were they bound aboard the *Zephyr*? Aboard *her* ship?

Anticipating her question, Zivon said, "The three set sail from Perhata in the dead of night, appropriately enough, bound for the open sea. They did not make port here in Kolbyr, but otherwise I cannot say where they went. Given their last heading, my guess is that they intended to leave the gulf entirely, but it is only a hunch, based on no solid information."

Yvka smiled. "Your hunches are better than most people's facts."

Zivon acknowledged the compliment with a slight nod.

Yvka decided she'd gotten all she was going to from Zivon, and she'd better not push her luck any further.

"My thanks. Knowing that the *Zephyr* and the dragonwand are together will make things simpler. If we find one, we'll find the other." She started to stand, but Zivon gestured for her to remain seated. Yvka gritted her teeth. She didn't like being told what to do, but the Culinarian was Zivon's domain, and so she had little choice but to do as he wanted.

"I wish you all success in regaining possession of the *Zephyr*. But before you leave, there is another matter we need to discuss."

Yvka didn't like the sound of this. "If it's about my companions, I assure you—"

"It isn't," Zivon said. "At least, not primarily. As I said earlier, we are greatly pleased with the treasures that you've delivered unto us, thanks to your most profitable association with Diran Bastiaan and his friends. But you know our philosophy: too much is never enough, not when it comes to information and power. In the end, they're really both the same, are they not?"

Yvka was disturbed by the sudden turn this conversation had taken, and she dreaded Zivon's next words.

"If you wish to find yourself in our good graces once more, not only will you recover the *Zephyr*, you will bring us two things more: the artificer's wand and the psiforged called Solus."

CHAPTER

SIX

I didn't know what to expect, but this surely wasn't it," Ghaji whispered.

Diran couldn't help but agree with his friend. The two companions, led by Asenka and flanked by a pair of guards, walked down a corridor in the palace of Baroness Calida. Up to this point, the architecture they'd seen in Kolbyr had been austere at best and forbidding at worst, and the outside of the palace had been no exception. The face it presented to the world was that of a severe-looking edifice of gray stone bereft of ornamentation or humanity. No windows or battlements, no towers or crenellations . . . nothing but featureless cold sterility. The air around the palace felt heavy and stale, making every breath an effort, and worst of all, the palace itself exuded an aura of sheer malevolence, as if waves of hate emanated from the stonework.

But inside was a very different story. The walls were painted soothing colors—soft yellows, placid greens, and gentle pinks. Potted ferns rested in corners, vases filled with aromatic blooms sat on tables, and hanging plants dangled from ceilings. Tiny bright-feathered songbirds flew through the air, free to sing wherever they pleased. Musicians performed at strategic locations throughout the palace—soloists, trios, and quartets—all playing their instruments with deft, light touches, producing tunes both soft and tranquil. The air smelled of sweet incense, and where breathing outside had been a chore, inside breathing was a pleasure and every inhalation filled one's body with a sensation of peace and contentment.

"Obviously, the palace's interior has been designed to soften the effects of the Fury," Diran whispered. "An absolute necessity, as this is where the curse is centered."

Neither of the two guards—tall, broad-shouldered men wearing chainmail vests and longswords belted at their waists—reacted to the two friends' exchange. But Diran could feel the tension radiating from both men. Their muscles were tight, jaws tense, lips pursed, brows furrowed, and their breathing was labored, as if some great struggle was taking place within them.

Ghaji must've sensed the guards' anger as well, for he drew his lower lip back to better display his bottom incisors. Diran had seen his friend perform this action on numerous occasions, and he'd also seen the aftermath. It usually involved a great deal of blood being spilled.

The priest laid a hand on his friend's shoulder. "Peace, Ghaji. Don't let the curse of Kolbyr take hold in you." Diran concentrated on projecting a sense of calm, not only in his manner, but also spiritually. As one of the Purified, Diran could mystically soothe a turbulent soul in much the same way that he could heal an injured body.

Ghaji sighed then nodded to show he was all right, and Diran was relieved. He doubted Baroness Calida would grant them an audience if they began brawling with her guards in the palace corridors.

Diran looked to Asenka, and though she appeared tense, she seemed to be handling the urgings of the Fury well enough. She was made of stern stuff, that woman: strong steel with a sharp edge. And yet she was also one of the most genuinely warm people Diran had ever met, with a gentle loving gaze and a delightfully earthy laugh. He was older than she by a few years, but the difference in their ages wasn't that great. But the gulf between them was much wider in terms of experience. Asenka had spent her life in Perhata, training to be a warrior, joining Baron Mahir's Sea Scorpions, and eventually becoming their leader. She had seen her fair share of battle, no doubt, but Diran had lived the first part of his life as an assassin. He had killed heartlessly, efficiently, and without remorse. So many men and women had felt the deadly kiss of his daggers that he'd lost count of the number he had slain. As one of the Purified, he knew death was not to be feared, for the passing away of the mortal shell allowed one's spirit to join with the Silver Flame in the afterlife. But as wondrous as that joining was, as much as it was to be desired, never should it be hastened. It should take place in its own time, and not be dictated by the desires of the rich and powerful, those with money enough to pay to have their enemies slain.

But after becoming a priest of the Silver Flame and dedicating his life to using his assassin's skills to combat evil in all its myriad forms, Diran had seen sights far worse than anything he'd ever experienced during the war. Purified he might be, but that didn't mean he was unaffected by the evil he battled, and he wondered if the shadows that had touched his soul over the years had changed him *too* much, set him apart from ordinary men to the point where he couldn't love and be loved the way he wanted to. The way Asenka deserved.

As they continued toward the Baroness's court, Diran found himself thinking back to a time when he'd learned what it truly meant to be touched by shadow, when he began to realize that he'd only *thought* he'd understood what evil was . . .

When his education as a priest of the Silver Flame began in earnest.

❂ ❂ ❂ ❂ ❂ ❂ ❂

Nighttime along the banks of the Thrane River, southwest of Sigilstar, a week shy of Victory Day in the month of Barrakas. A priest and two acolytes sat cross-legged around a campfire, cloaks draped around their shoulders against the night's chill, heavy travel packs lying on the ground at their sides, bedrolls spread out behind them. The flames of their campfire burned with a silver tint, but the fire produced little smoke. A cloud of insects, mostly moths, hovered over the flames, drawn by the light, encouraged to come closer by the absence of smoke. The three men had finished a tasteless meal of travel rations and were now watching the silvery flames dance, thinking whatever thoughts happened to drift through their minds.

"Pass the wineskin, Diran, if you would be so kind."

Diran did as his teacher asked. Tusya shook the wineskin once, then frowned.

"That's all we have left? There can't be more than a couple swallows in there."

Diran smiled. "I have even worse news: that's the last of the wine."

Tusya slapped a hand to his chest. "Say it isn't so! Your words strike me to the very quick!"

Diran chuckled, but Leontis only continued staring at their campfire, scowling as he stirred the silvery-white coals with a stick. Tusya had added silverburn to the fire, a common—if somewhat expensive—practice among the Purified. It symbolized the Silver Flame offering light to its followers and warding off the darkness. Diran had been surprised by their teacher's largesse. Normally, he was by necessity a thrifty man, for wandering priests possessed little but what they could carry with them on their travels. Indeed, this was the first time Diran had known Tusya to use silverburn, and he wondered what the occasion might be. For certainly there was some reason; despite Tusya's seemingly haphazard way of approaching life, he always had a reason for the things he did, even if that reason wasn't readily apparent to those around him.

Like Diran, Leontis Dellacron was in his mid-twenties. His brown hair hung almost to his shoulders and was in need of a good trimming, and he'd recently begun growing a beard that looked as if it might never fill in properly. Both Diran and Leontis had served as acolytes under the tutelage of Tusya Vanarden for the last six months. Before petitioning for admission to a seminary, acolytes of the Silver Flame were required to serve under a priest for an undetermined period of time, learning the basics of the faith. When the sponsoring priest thought they were ready—and only then—could acolytes be accepted as seminarians. During their time as Tusya's students, Diran and Leontis had become companions, if not the closest of friends. Leontis tended to be moody and withdrawn, while Diran, due to his training in the Brotherhood of the Blade, was stoic and guarded.

Leontis's longbow sat within easy reach, but though it was the signature weapon of the order of the Silver Flame, neither Tusya nor Diran carried one. Diran had practiced with bow and arrow on occasion, but he had yet to develop any skill with them. Instead he carried a dozen daggers—the tools he'd employed in his previous life—secreted about his person. Tusya, however, carried no weapons at all. Diran had once asked his teacher why he chose to go about unarmed. Tusya had simply given Diran a mischievous smile and replied, "What makes you think I'm unarmed?"

The best word to describe Tusya, Diran thought, was *nondescript*. There was nothing physically about the man to make him stand out in any way—a quality that would serve an assassin well, Diran mused, but could at times be something of hindrance to a priest engaged in the holy task of ridding the world of evil. Tusya was hardly a commanding or intimidating presence, and thus it struck Diran as no surprise that he had chosen to serve in the Order of Friars as opposed to becoming a templar. Tusya was in his late sixties, of medium height, and carried a rather sizeable paunch, especially considering how much he walked. Only a few wisps of snow-white hair clung to his bald pate, but he'd grown a full beard as if to make up for it. He smiled easily and often, and he spoke with a soft, gentle voice though his laugh was loud enough to scare the birds out of the trees. His eyes were kind, but if you looked beneath the surface, you could see a sharp, calculating intelligence that belied the priest's easygoing veneer.

"Is something brothering you, lad?" Tusya asked Leontis. His tone remained good-humored enough, but his voice now held an edge of seriousness.

Leontis continued stirring the coals for a moment longer before responding. "Forgive me for saying so, Father, but your . . . fondness for wine confuses me."

Diran wasn't surprised to see Tusya grin at Leontis's words. Where others might take offense at being challenged—even in such a mild way—Tusya always seemed delighted, as if he thrived on conflict. No, that wasn't right, Diran amended. In his former life as an assassin for hire, Diran had seen many men and women who lived for conflict . . . and died because of it. What energized Tusya was the chance to engage in a lively dialogue.

"How so?"

Leontis glanced up from the fire to look at Tusya for a moment, before turning his gaze back to the flames. Diran liked Leontis, even considered him a friend, the first real one he'd made—not counting Tusya himself, of course—since the priest had cast out the dark spirit that Diran had shared his soul with for so many years. But though Leontis and Diran were close in age, they were very different in terms of experience. Diran had begun training as an assassin during childhood, and he'd been a full-fledged member in the Brotherhood of the Blade for over a decade before turning away from the dark path of the killer and embarking on his studies to become one of the Purified. Leontis, on the other hand, had grown up as a cobbler's son in Danthaven and had become interested in the priesthood because his maternal aunt served as a priest in a temple of healing there.

Leontis continued looking at the fire as he spoke. Diran had long ago noted his friend often had trouble meeting others' eyes when he was discussing what he thought were sensitive matters. "You are Purified, are you not? Strong drink can impair one's judgment, causing one to lose control of one's emotions. As you've taught us, becoming Purified—and staying so—requires the constant vigilance of both a strong mind and a strong heart."

Tusya finished off the last of the wine before answering his young charge. "I'm not sure I'd call this vintage particularly strong, either in alcohol content *or* taste." He smiled as he laid the empty skin on the ground next to him. "There are many lessons to be learned from the symbol of our faith, many truths and insights to be gained. For example, Leontis, what shape is our campfire?"

Leontis turned to Tusya and frowned. "What?"

"The shape, son. It's a simple enough question. Square, round, triangular . . . which is it?"

Leontis scowled. "Forgive me for saying so, Teacher, but sometimes I wish you would just come out and say what you mean." But the acolyte looked back to the fire and answered. "It has a general shape, one that's not like anything else except other fires. Our campfire is smaller than some, larger than others. Its specific size and dimensions vary with the amount of wood used to fuel it, and the flames themselves dance and move about."

"So would you say that while the essential nature of the fire remains the same, its particular shape varies from one moment to the next?"

"Yes," Leontis answered.

"And thus it is with Purification. The shape it takes varies from person to person, depending on their personalities"—Tusya glanced sideways at Diran—"and what demons drive them. Some men drink alcohol as if it were water, without experiencing any significant lasting effects. Others merely take a few sips of strong drink and become its lifelong slave. For these latter souls, resisting their need for alcohol is a struggle far greater than battling couatls or lycanthropes. You have little taste for wine, Leontis, so abstaining from it would be no hardship for you. I enjoy wine, so abstaining would be more difficult for me, but I could do so with minimal effort. So it would be no great feat for either of us to forgo strong drink. And the lesson in this, Diran, is . . . ?"

Now it was Diran's turn to smile. "Without struggle, there is no Purification, and what defines the struggle is different for each person."

Tusya nodded, pleased. "And it also varies for individuals in different circumstances and at different times in their lives."

Leontis frowned, as he so often did after one of Tusya's lessons, but it was an expression of contemplation rather than consternation.

Diran noticed a moth dip precariously close to the fire. "What insight might that insect have to offer us, Teacher?"

Before Tusya could answer, the moth dove too close and ignited in a bright silvery flash. Its charred remains fell into the fire and were quickly consumed.

Tusya's smile was grim this time. "I think that speaks for itself, don't you, boy?"

"I suppose it does," Diran said softly. He thought of the upcoming Victory Day, and the lycanthropic purge it commemorated, when the followers of the Silver Flame had at last rid Khorvaire of the scourge of the evil shapeshifters. Some of the templars, believing that the ends justified the means, had used rather questionable methods to reach this holy goal. In the end, a few priests had become just as evil as any lycanthrope they had ever fought. They had flown too close the flame, and instead of being Purified, they'd been consumed by its heat.

"But as I said earlier, the symbol of our faith can reveal many truths," Tusya said. "Forget the moth for a moment and consider instead the wood that feeds our campfire. Fire consumes wood for its fuel, and in so doing, the wood is transformed. It becomes one with the fire, fulfilling its true purpose. To serve the Flame well, we must willingly give ourselves over to its heat and light."

For a time after that the three men sat quietly, listening to the crackle of the fire, the leaves of nearby trees rustling in the night breeze, and the gentle rushing waters of the Thrane River. It was peaceful and soothing, and soon Diran found himself becoming drowsy. He was about to say goodnight to his companions and crawl into his bedroll when a strange sensation began to come over him. The training he'd received at Emon Gorsedd's academy of assassins had honed his senses to a razor-fine edge, and on more than one occasion those senses had saved his life on a mission. The feeling he had now was something like that, an awareness of danger, but there was more to it. He also felt a sense of *wrongness*.

Diran was instantly alert. "Teacher, I feel something . . ."

Tusya raised an eyebrow. "Is that so?"

Diran turned in the direction of the river. "That way . . . on the bank of the Thrane. But upstream a ways, I think."

"What are you going on about, Diran?" Leontis asked. "I sense nothing."

Tusya kept his gaze focused on Diran as he spoke to Leontis. "Our friend lived with a demonic spirit inside him for many years, lad. Thus he is more sensitive to evil's presence than most people, even though he has yet to have any tutelage in the ways of dealing with such dark powers."

Diran turned to look at Tusya. "Surely you were aware of this evil long before I was."

Tusya shrugged. "Perhaps."

"You have many fine qualities, Teacher," Diran said. "But acting talent isn't chief among them."

Tusya grinned but said nothing.

Leontis sighed as he reached for his bow and quiver of arrows. He withdrew half a dozen shafts and began rolling their tips in the silvery ashes scattered around the burning wood.

"What are you doing?" Diran asked.

"Getting ready. Obviously Tusya wants us to investigate the source of this evil. Why else would he have insisted we camp here for the night? And why else would he have added silverburn to the fire unless he wished for us to make use of it?" Leontis finished coating the last of his arrowheads with ash and then returned the shafts to their quiver. He strung his bow, stood, and slung the quiver over his shoulder.

"Shall we?" Leontis asked.

Diran looked at his friend and fellow acolyte with newfound respect. Leontis might not have Diran's life experience, but that didn't make him stupid by any means.

Diran nodded to Leontis and stood. He turned to Tusya and asked, "Will you be joining us?"

During their travels through Thrane with Tusya, they'd had occasion to encounter evils both mundane and supernatural. But while the young acolytes had assisted their teacher in whatever capacity he required, Tusya had always been the one to take the lead when dealing with anything otherworldly.

The priest appeared to consider for a moment. "I'm a bit tired. I believe I'll just stay here and warm my old bones by the fire."

Diran and Leontis exchanged glances. Their teacher's message was clear: he wished them to go alone this time.

"We'll be back as soon as we can," Diran said. He nodded to Leontis, and the two acolytes began walking away from the silvery flames of the campfire and into the dark of the night. When they were almost out of earshot, Diran heard Tusya speak in a voice close to a whisper.

"Go with the Flame, lads. But be careful not to fly too close."

● ● ● ◉ ● ● ●

Baroness Calida took her time examining the letter of introduction from Baron Mahir. Not, Ghaji thought, because she had trouble understanding the missive's meaning or doubted its authenticity. Rather, because she was uncertain how to respond to the words before her.

Ghaji, Diran, and Asenka stood quietly in front of Calida while she thought. Calida's chamber was nothing like what Ghaji had expected. There was no throne on a raised dais to put the Baroness above her audience, no large open area for courtiers to gather, gossip, backstab, and generally attempt to curry favor with their ruler. The chamber resembled nothing so much as a private sitting room, with chairs and couches that looked almost *too* comfortable. Paintings of placid landscapes hung on the walls, and a woven rug of gentle sea-green covered the floor. As elsewhere in the palace, flowers and hanging plants were located throughout the chamber, their aromas mingling with the smells of the scented candles that lit the room, the combined odors keeping the air pleasantly perfumed.

Calida herself didn't look particularly regal. In fact, if Ghaji had to pick a single word to describe her, it would have been *tired*. At first glance, he guessed Calida to be somewhere in her forties, but on closer inspection he realized she was likely ten years younger. The Baroness's weariness added years to her appearance. Her eyes were red and sore, the flesh beneath them puffy and discolored. Her long flowing brunette hair was shot through with strands of gray, and she was so thin she looked as if she might be suffering from malnutrition. Calida's simple yellow dress hung on her emaciated frame like a blanket someone had tossed carelessly over her to keep her warm.

She looked up from the letter and attempted to focus her gaze on them, though she seemed to have trouble doing so. She kept blinking as if to clear her eyes, and her head swayed from side to side slightly, as if she were having difficulty staying awake Ghaji wondered if Calida's condition was entirely due to weariness, or if perhaps, living so close to the center of the Fury, she was forced to take narcotics simply to function. Perhaps both were true, he decided.

"Others have tried to remove the curse on the House of Kolbyr. What makes you think you can succeed where so many have failed before?" Calida's voice was surprisingly strong, and Ghaji's estimation of her went up a notch. It was the voice of a woman who was used to ruling, a woman whose inner reserves of strength, while depleted, were not yet exhausted.

Ghaji looked to Diran, expecting his friend to make their case to the Baroness. But to the half-orc's surprise, it was Asenka who spoke first.

"I'm Perhaten, Baroness, and a faithful servant of Baron Mahir. As a Sea Scorpion, I have fought against your Coldhearts on numerous occasions, and I've slain more than my fair share. I think it safe to say that I hold little love in my heart for Kolbyr or its citizens."

Ghaji grimaced. "I'm just an ignorant half-orc, Asenka, so feel free to correct me if I'm wrong, but isn't it generally a good idea for diplomats to speak *diplomatically?*"

Calida held up her hand to silence Ghaji then nodded to Asenka. "Go on."

Asenka bowed her head to the Baroness. "Forget for the moment that Mahir thought enough of these two men to write them a letter of introduction and send me, the captain of his Sea Scorpions, to accompany them. Forget for the moment that the citizens of Kolbyr have lived with the curse upon their city for the last hundred years. Forget that, should the curse be lifted, it may well lead to improved relations between our two cities, and perhaps a better life for all who inhabit the Gulf of Ingjald. All that matters is that within this generation, the curse has manifested itself in *your* firstborn child, Calida. Do you really want to hear assurances that Diran and Ghaji can help you? You already know you're going to allow them to try. As a mother, you won't pass up any chance, no matter how slim, to save your child?"

The Baroness regarded Asenka for a long moment, the expression on her weary face unreadable. Finally, she rose out of her overstuffed chair, picked up a scented candle mounted in a pewter holder off of the end table, and began shuffling toward the door.

"Come with me," she said.

As the three companions followed the Baroness, Asenka gave Ghaji a grin as if to say, *Was that diplomatic enough for you?*

Ghaji grinned. He was beginning to understand what Diran saw in this woman.

❋ ❋ ❋ ◉ ❋ ❋ ❋

Ghaji expected Calida to lead them down into the bowels of the palace, where they'd find the cursed child sealed away in a subterranean cell, dwelling in darkness, forever denied the light of day. But instead the Baroness—along with the two guards—led them up a flight of stairs to the uppermost floor of the palace. At the end of a long featureless corridor lay a single door made entirely of metal, an iron crossbar set firmly in place to seal the room shut from the outside.

It must be a very lonely way to grow up, Ghaji thought. Curse or no curse, he felt sorry for the child forced to live behind the metal door. Strange and unfamiliar sigils and runes had been scratched into the surface of the door, dozens of them over the long years since the curse first took hold. Ghaji was by no means an expert, but he felt certain the markings were all protective charms of one kind or another. A glance at Diran, a nod from his friend, and Ghaji's suspicion was confirmed.

As they drew near the iron door, Ghaji could feel waves of anger radiating from the chamber within, so strong that it was nearly a physical force. It took an effort to move forward, almost as if they were walking into a strong wind. He clenched his jaw tight and concentrated on ignoring the Fury that buffeted him, but he could feel it sinking into his mind, making itself at home, and beginning to grow.

They hate you, you know. Half-orc. Half-human. Half a man . . . Show them how strong you are. Take hold of your axe. Will its flames to life. Strike swiftly and without mercy . . .

Ghaji's hand reached for his elemental axe. But before he could draw the weapon, Diran laid his hand on the half-orc's shoulder, and Ghaji felt soothing calm spread through him. The Fury was still there at the core of his being, but its urgings were quieter now, more easily ignored.

Ghaji gave his friend a nod of thanks then looked to Asenka. From the strained expression on her face, it was clear the woman was fighting her own battle to resist the Fury, but he saw that Diran held her hand tight, and Ghaji knew that his friend was also helping Asenka hold the Fury at bay.

When they reached the door, Calida stopped and turned to regard the three of them.

"I'm impressed. Most outsiders can't make it this far without trying to kill each other . . . or themselves."

"What of you?" Diran asked. "You seem unaffected."

The Baroness gave the priest a lopsided smile. "Unfortunately, I am used to resisting the Fury . . . as are all who serve me." She nodded to the two guards that had accompanied them. "Do not underestimate my son's power. After Taran was born, he . . . his father was gripped by the Fury. My husband was driven to slay me, but enough presence of mind remained to him that he took his own life rather than harm me." She then looked away from them, as if suddenly embarrassed, and gestured at the door. "I do not have the strength to unbar it. If you wouldn't mind . . ."

Ghaji stepped forward. As soon as he slipped away from Diran, he felt the Fury whelm into him anew, but because he knew what to expect—and because of the lingering influence of Diran's calming touch—he was better able to withstand it this time. With a grunt of effort he raised the heavy iron crossbar then took hold of the door handle. He didn't open it yet, though. He looked to Diran to see if his friend was prepared to enter the chamber.

The priest looked at Asenka. "I think it best if Ghaji and I go in alone," he said. Asenka started to protest, but Diran cut her off. "I mean no insult, but we have much more experience dealing with this sort of thing. If we fail to withstand the Fury, we might well end up attacking one another . . . or you."

"I'm not afraid," Asenka said.

"It's not your fear that's at issue," Diran said. "It's mine. I will not be able to fully devote myself mind and soul to the task ahead if

71

I'm distracted by concern for your safety. Remain in the corridor and guard the door. If we need you, we'll call out." When Asenka didn't answer right away, Diran added, "Please?"

For a moment, Asenka looked as if she might protest further, but she assented with a single curt nod. "Very well, I'll remain. But don't even think of asking me to lower the crossbar while you're inside. I won't do it."

Now it was Diran who looked as if he might protest, but like Asenka, he merely nodded.

"I shall return to the chamber where we first spoke," Calida said. Her tone was flat, her gaze dull. "Let me know how you fared . . . assuming any of you survive ." Without further comment, she turned and began shuffling back down the corridor.

The guards said nothing as they took up positions on either side of the door. Ghaji had thought at first that the guards' impassive silence was just an intimidation act. Now he understood that they were concentrating on resisting the Fury.

"Call if you need me," Asenka said. She then leaned forward and gave Diran a quick kiss on the lips. "For luck," she explained.

Ghaji expected his friend to say something suitably pious and heroic, such as *Thank you, but I have no need of luck as long as I have my faith to sustain me.* Instead, Diran simply smiled at Asenka before turning to Ghaji and giving him a nod.

Time to go to work.

Ghaji opened the door and stepped inside. Diran followed and moved past the half-orc, slipping into the room as silent as a shadow, and Ghaji closed the door behind them.

The room was dark, so much so that even Ghaji's orcish night vision couldn't make out any details. There were no windows, no candles or lamps. Knowing an attack might come at them any instant, Ghaji drew his elemental axe and willed it to activate. Mystic flames burst into life around the blade, revealing a stone room devoid of furnishings, the only exceptions being a rumpled bedroll in the middle of the floor and a chamber pot that smelled as if it hadn't been emptied in a while located in one corner. Sitting on the floor next to the bedroll, cross-legged and looking at them with an almost serene expression on his face, was a boy who couldn't have been more than ten. He was completely naked, the flesh of his body criss-crossed with scratches—some scabbed over, some fresh and bleeding—as if the boy had been clawing at his own flesh. The child's resemblance to Calida was obvious both in his face and brunette hair. But as disturbing as the boy's appearance was, the aspect that bothered Ghaji the most was his eyes: they were completely black, moist and glossy, like the eyes of a beast.

"Are you Taran, son of Baroness Calida?" Diran asked. The priest's voice was firm, but kind.

The boy's beatific smile grew wider and became sinister, almost mocking. "She thinks so. The stupid cow."

Ghaji remembered an important element of the curse of Kolbyr. "Diran, wasn't the firstborn child supposed to be an indestructible monster? This boy may be in dire need of a lesson in manners, but he looks human enough . . . except for those eyes."

Diran smiled grimly, but he kept his gaze fixed on the child. "It appears the details of the curse have become distorted over the last century, starting with its very name. You see, my friend, the Curse of Kolbyr isn't a curse at all. This boy is possessed by a demon—one that has cast a foul enchantment over the city, causing the Fury."

Ghaji could feel waves of hatred and fury rolling off the naked boy, and he had no trouble believing Diran's words. Then a thought occurred to him, and he frowned. "But what of all the other firstborns that preceded Taran? Were they possessed by demons as well?"

"My guess is they were," Diran said. "But not by other demons: by the *same* demon. That's why each cursed firstborn is reputed to be indestructible. They're individual bodies may perish, but the demon that possesses them simply waits to return in the next generation."

The boy's grin grew even wider, his mouth stretching farther than was humanly possible. The corners of his mouth tore and thin lines of blood ran down past his chin. "Well done, priest. I knew when I first sensed you and your friends approaching the city—and by the way, I *did* send those gulls to attack you as a greeting—I knew you would prove to be a worthy adversary. Perhaps the most worthy I've faced since first being summoned."

Ghaji snorted. "Spare us. Your kind always thinks you can put opponents off balance by alternately complimenting then castigating them. We've heard it all before."

The boy turned to regard Ghaji with his glossy black eyes, and despite his earlier courage, the half-orc warrior felt a chill shiver down his spine.

"Is that so? Then perhaps you'd like to hear something new. My body may be locked away in this chamber, but my mind roams free. I know many things . . . things you and your companions would dearly love to know."

Ghaji rolled his eyes. "And now you're trying to make deals with us. Is there some kind of infernal school where they teach you this sort of thing, or are demons bereft not only of souls but of imagination as well?"

The demon grinned even wider, and this time Ghaji thought he could hear the boy's mouth tear. The blood flow increased, and now drops fell from Taran's chin to patter onto his claw-marked chest. "Let me give you a sample of my wares. I know where your elven lady-love is right now, half-orc. I know who she's talking to and what they're talking about. I could relate their conversation to you word for word, if you wish. It would be as if you were standing there beside her, listening unseen."

Ghaji clenched his teeth in anger. "Shut up."

The demon continued speaking, its voice a hideous parody of sympathy and concern. "She's such a mystery to you . . . you have so many doubts. You keep them to yourself, struggle to tell yourself that you understand and that not knowing doesn't matter. But it does matter to you, doesn't it, half-orc? It matters very much indeed."

Ghaji's gripped the haft of his axe tighter, and without realizing it he took a step toward the possessed child. Diran took hold of his arm and stopped him.

"He's just trying to goad you," the priest said. "If you slay the demon's host body, the Fury will be dispelled, but Calida will lose her son. The demon will be banished, but only until such time as the next Baron or Baroness produces an heir."

"As long as that ruler is a descendent of the House of Kolbyr," the demon said. "When the line of Kolbyr ends, so too ends the curse, and I shall return to your world no more. Needless to say, I hope that doesn't occur for many, many years. I'm having too much fun playing with the city and all the foolish mortal toys that inhabit it. I love to make them angry, make them fight each other, *kill* each other . . . I'm a naughty child, I suppose, always breaking my toys." The boy shrugged. "But no matter. There are more where those came from, are there not?"

"The one who summoned you was Kolbyr's sister," Diran said. "Nathifa was her name."

"I should make you barter for confirming that information, but I'm in an especially good mood today. Yes, that's true."

"She must've have been an especially powerful sorceress to call forth a demon of your strength," Diran said.

The demon's laugh was so much like that of a normal little boy that it startled Ghaji.

"So now it is *your* turn to attempt to appeal to *my* vanity, eh? What fun! You amuse me, so here's another free tidbit: the sorceress is powerful, yes, but the one she serves—and from whom her power flows—is far stronger."

Diran frowned. "You speak of the sorceress in present tense, but she summoned you a century ago. Are you telling us that she still lives after all this time?"

A sly look came over the boy's face, as if he were hiding a secret. "She is not alive, and that's the last thing I shall tell you without receiving payment first."

Ghaji glanced at Diran. "Not alive isn't the same thing as being dead."

"Indeed," Diran agreed.

"Are you now convinced that the information I have to offer is worth the cost?" the demon said. "Are you ready to bargain with me?" The demon sounded almost as if it were pleading, like a child begging an adult to play.

Diran appeared to consider the demon's offer. "I don't know . . . you haven't really told us anything *new*. And quite frankly, you could be making up what you *have* told us. Demons aren't known for their scrupulous adherence to the facts."

"My friend means you're a bunch of damned liars," Ghaji translated. "Literally."

The demon scowled, and the waves of anger pouring off of him became more intense. "Do not push me, half-orc. Cease to amuse me, and it will go all the worse for you." The demon considered for a moment. "Very well. Another sample for you, but I warn you, this is the last. I know where your vampire lover is, priest. I know who she travels with and where they are bound. Not only do they sail the vessel the half-orc's love lost, they also carry with them an object that your artificer friend is most anxious to regain possession of." The fiend's smile returned. "Now are you interested in bargaining with me?"

Ghaji was stunned by the demon's words. He'd learned a great deal about infernal creatures since beginning his travels with Diran, and he knew that demons did far worse than simply lie. They seasoned their falsehoods with truth, mixing the two together until you couldn't tell where one began and the other ended. It was this diabolical tactic that ensnared more fools than any other, and even though Ghaji knew better, he found himself tempted by the demon's offer.

If I could return the *Zephyr* to Yvka . . .

Ghaji turned to Diran, looking to his friend for support. Diran wouldn't be tempted by the demon's sly words. He'd take hold of his silver arrowhead, the sacred symbol of the Silver Flame, and he'd thrust it toward the demon's face, and in a commanding voice reject the fiend's offer.

But Diran said nothing. The priest only stared at the demon wearing the face of a young boy, his gaze dark, jaw clenched as if he were struggling to hold back his voice. He made no move to reach into his vest pocket and remove his silver arrowhead. His arms remained slack at his sides, hands empty.

Ghaji couldn't believe it. Was Diran actually *considering* the demon's offer?

The demon, like a hunter sensing weakness in its prey, pressed on. "I can tell you much more if you wish, priest. I can reveal to you secrets about Emon Gorsedd, about your teacher Tusya . . . secrets that would completely shatter your views of them and forever change the way you see yourself. It will be my great privilege to share my knowledge with you . . . for a price."

Ghaji knew that all it took to seal a bargain with a demon was a single word of assent. Sometimes, with the most powerful demons, even speaking aloud wasn't necessary; simply the *desire* to make the bargain was enough.

Ghaji didn't want to harm the child whose body the demon possessed, but he couldn't allow his friend to damn his soul in a moment of weakness. He owed Diran his life a dozen times over, and he'd do anything to protect the priest—even if it meant taking the life of an innocent.

Ghaji raised his flaming ax high and stepped forward to strike. But just as he was about to swing, he saw a flash of motion out of the corner of his eye. A dagger slammed hilt-first into his axehead with a metallic clang, throwing off the weapon's trajectory and sparing the child's life.

Ghaji looked back at Diran and saw the priest held a second dagger in his left hand. In his right he held a silver arrowhead. The flames from Ghaji's axe should've coated the arrowhead's metal surface with orange-red light, but the holy symbol shone with a bright silvery illumination of its own.

"Your honeyed words are laced with poison, demon," Diran said, "and they fall on deaf ears."

Ghaji grinned. Now *that* was more like it!

The demon squinted against the light from the arrowhead, but it didn't look away. The creature then let out a long, theatrical sigh. "Oh, well. You can't blame a fiend for trying. To be honest, I was getting rather tired of that game anyway. I'd much rather play another, one that I've always wanted to try but somehow have never gotten around to."

Ghaji knew the demon wanted them to ask *What game?* But the half-orc warrior was done playing. "The fun's over. It's time for you to return to whatever hellhole you crawled out of, and this time you're going to stay there."

The demon did not appear overly impressed with Ghaji's taunt.

"I don't think so. You see, the game I've always wanted to play is called the Destruction of Kolbyr. And I'm going to start playing it with you two."

Before either Ghaji or Diran could do anything, the demon's black eyes turned a baleful crimson, and rage unlike anything the half-orc had ever experienced surged into his heart. All positive emotions were driven out of him, along with the memory that he had ever experienced such feelings. All that remained was hate and fury and the lust to kill.

Ghaji turned to see the man garbed in black glaring at him with a hatred bordering on madness. Ghaji knew just how the bastard felt.

The man in black dropped the sliver arrowhead to the floor and grabbed a dagger. He now held a blade in each hand.

For a moment, the two partners stood glaring at each other, and then the demon said, "Let the games begin."

Ghaji and Diran shouted their Fury and rushed toward one another to the accompaniment of the demon's dark, delighted laughter.

CHAPTER

SEVEN

So this is a Tinker's Room," Hinto said. "Looks like a trash heap tossed about by a hurricane."

The halfling's comment might have irritated Tresslar if it hadn't been so apt.

The cellar of Illyia's gallery was crammed full with wooden tables, so many that there was barely room to walk between them. There were no chairs or other furnishings of any kind, simply for the fact that there wasn't any remaining space. Row upon row of shelves lined the walls, and the room was lit by a dozen or so of Illyia's bubbles that floated near the ceiling, glowing with greenish-yellow phosphorescence like some kind of spherical deep-sea creatures. Mounds of junk covered every flat surface in the cellar—tables and shelves alike. Fragments of metal, chunks of minerals, pieces of wood, jewels and gems in a variety of colors and sizes—including a few small dragonshards here and there—along with bits of string, twisted lengths of wire, nubs of wax, an assortment of nails, screws, bolts, and nuts . . . There were tools as well, everything from mundane hammers, wrenches, and chisels to exotic objects designed to help balance magic matrices, bind minor elementals, and merge incompatible energy sources.

A dozen men and women of various races were present, either working alone at tables or standing in groups of two and three, chatting and, in more than a few cases, arguing good-naturedly.

"—impure dragonshards *do* have their uses, I agree on that point, but you have to concede the danger in—"

"—crazy? If you try to bind an elemental *that* way, the containment ring will blow up in your—"

"—and then she said to me, 'I didn't realize artificers could build things like *that!*' "

Laughter followed that last comment, and Tresslar couldn't help smiling himself. He'd spent so many years working on Dreadhold, hiding from the monster Erdis Cai had become, that he'd forgotten how much he missed the simple camaraderie of other artificers. Oh, he hadn't been the only artificer working at Dreadhold. Far from it. But the dwarf artificers of House Kundarak had never really accepted him as one of their own. Or perhaps, Tresslar mused, *he* had never accepted *them*. Perhaps things would be different now, if he were to return to the prison island.

Most of the artificers in the room were too involved in their work or conversations to notice the newcomers, but a few glanced their way and immediately fixed their gazes on Solus. They stared at the psiforged with undisguised interest. Tresslar was certain they were eager to come over and inspect the construct, but the protocols of Tinker's Rooms everywhere discouraged approaching new arrivals unless they made it clear they were open to socializing.

Illyia led them down the stairs into the cellar and stood next to Tresslar, a little closer than was strictly proper—not that he was complaining.

"Are you here for anything in particular," she asked, "or is this just a recreational visit?"

One of the duties of a Tinker's Room host was to help artificers find the tools and materials they might need if they'd come to tend to a specific task, such as repairing a magical device or even building one from scratch.

"Please tell me you're not going to feed her another of your moldy old lines, Tresslar," Hinto said. "They stink worse than goat cheese that's been left out in the sun too long."

Tresslar glared at the halfling before turning to Solus. "I don't suppose you would consider psionically suppressing his so-called sense of humor."

The psiforged cocked his head to the side. "I find his wit amusing."

Tresslar couldn't tell if Solus was being serious or not. He'd never heard a warforged laugh or tell a joke, but that didn't mean the constructs didn't appreciate humor in others.

Tresslar decided to ignore the halfling and the psiforged and answer Illyia's question. "Actually, we've come in search of information. One of my devices—a very special one—was recently stolen. I'm hoping to find some leads as to where it might be so I can get it back."

Illyia frowned. "This is a Tinker's Room, not a place where stolen good are fenced."

Tresslar held up his hands. "Please, I mean no offense. But if your Tinker's Room is anything like the others I've visited over the years, more than information is exchanged here. *Tinker's gossip* is what they used to call it."

Illyia's frowned faded and she smiled. "And they still do, at least here in Kolbyr. But you have to know just how reliable that gossip often is."

"Not very," Tresslar admitted. "But I have to start somewhere."

Illyia considered for a moment. "Perhaps it would be best if you allowed me to make inquiries on your behalf. I'm someone they know and trust. They'll be more forthcoming with me."

"I'd appreciate that," Tresslar said. "The object I'm looking for is a wand with a golden dragon's head affixed—"

"Tresslar," Solus interrupted. "Something is happening."

Tresslar looked to the psiforged, but before the construct could explain further, the conversations in the room rose in volume. The voices not only got louder, they took on a harsh, angry edge. Soon the gathered artificers were shouting at one another, gripping tools in clenched fists and waving them about as they yelled, almost as if they intended to wield the objects as weapons.

Tresslar felt a wave of anger wash over him. He was about to rebuke the impertinent psiforged for interrupting his conversation with Illyia, but before the artificer could speak, the emotion faded, though it didn't completely vanish. Tresslar still felt irritated, but his level of anger had diminished to the point where he could handle it.

"The Fury is growing stronger," Illyia said. The enchanted spheres that formed her dress began to glow, and Tresslar knew their magic was protecting her against the curse of Kolbyr.

"Why would it suddenly get worse?" Hinto asked. "You likened the Fury to weather, Illyia, but it can't be like a storm that blows weak one moment then strong the next . . . can it?"

"Not in this case, my friend," Solus said. His artificial eyes shimmered with green light, and the multicolored crystals embedded on the surface of his body pulsed with psionic energy. "Diran and Ghaji are confronting the creature responsible for the Fury, and it's fighting back—not only by striking out at our friends, but by attacking the entire city. Illyia has her magic to protect her, and I can continue to shield the three of us from the worst of the Fury, but that's all I can do."

"If Diran and Ghaji are in trouble, then we should go to the palace and help them!" Hinto said.

Tresslar regretted splitting off from the others to go in search of his dragonwand. The mystic object was undeniably powerful, but in the end it was just a thing. Diran and Ghaji were good men, good companions, good *friends*, and they mattered far more than any number of magical artifacts ever could.

"You're right," Tresslar said. "We might not be able to reach the palace in time to be of any assistance to them, but we have to try." He turned to Illyia to make his farewell to her, but his words died in his throat before he could speak them.

The room had gone completely silent.

They looked to the artificers who had only moments before been arguing amongst themselves. Every man and woman now glared at them, eyes wild with hate, teeth bared in animalistic snarls. They clutched a variety of objects in their hands—mystic tools, magical devices, even metal rods that they gripped like clubs.

Then, as if obeying some unspoken signal, the artificers bellowed like mindless beasts and came running toward them.

SEA OF DEATH

❀ ❀ ❀ ❀ ❀ ❀ ❀

Yvka didn't know how to respond to Zivon's pronouncement—more like a warning, really—that she was expected to deliver both Solus and Tresslar's dragonwand to the Shadow Network. She desperately tried to think of a way to stall Zivon until she could come up with an appropriate answer, but she was so stunned by this development that nothing came to mind.

Zivon popped a well-seasoned mussel into his mouth and chewed while he waited for Yvka to speak. She knew he would gauge her level of compliance and, more importantly, its sincerity by the amount of time she took to think before responding. She had only seconds to speak, and whatever she said, it had to be good.

"You ask a great deal," she said. "I'm not sure that simply remaining in the Network's good graces is payment enough."

Zivon looked at her while he swallowed the last of the mussel. Then, though it appeared he was trying hard not to, he smiled.

"Spoken like a true operative. Of course, whether you mean what you say or are merely putting on a front to protect your *friends*"—he sneered as he said this word—"is debatable. But then, a little mystery is the spice of life, is it not?"

Yvka gave Zivon a sly smile before reaching across the table to take his wine cup. She raised the cup in a toast, then lifted it to her lips and drank. But as she started to put the wine back down in front of Zivon, she felt a cold, prickling sensation on the back of her neck. She'd worked many years as an operative for the Shadow Network, longer than a human lifetime, and that experience had sharpened her survival instincts to a keen edge. Now those instincts were screaming at her that there was danger nearby. She glanced quickly around the room but saw nothing that could account for her feeling. The sensation of danger didn't dissipate, though. Instead, it continued to grow worse, until it felt as if the threat were all around her, as if the Culinarian *itself* were the danger.

She looked to Zivon to see if he felt it too, but before she could broach the subject, the man bared his teeth at her, snarled like a wild animal, and lunged across the table, hands twisted into claws as he

83

attempted to grab hold of her. Yvka leaned back in her chair, pressed the soles of her boots against the edge of the table, and pushed with all her strength. Though she was petite and slender, she was an elf and far stronger than she appeared. The table slammed into Zivon's stomach, knocking the breath out of him. Yvka's chair fell backward, and just before it struck the floor she performed a graceful reverse somersault and finished standing on her feet.

She reached into the pouch that dangled from her belt and withdrew what seemed to be a simple goose feather with tiny arcane symbols etched into the quill. Zivon still sat, face red, gasping for breath, but despite his discomfort, he continued to glare at her with undiminished hatred. She knew that he intended to kill her and that nothing would stop him—nothing except the mystical weapon she held in her hand.

Anger took hold of her. How *dare* Zivon attack her like that? He might rank higher on the Network hierarchy than she, but that didn't give him the right to treat her with such disrespect! She was Yvka w'Ydellan, member of House Phiarlan by birth, now member of House Thuranni by choice. She allowed no one to lay hands upon her person—no one!

She began whispering the charm that would activate the poison-tipped quill-dart and send it flying straight into Zivon's heart with all the swiftness and force of a crossbow bolt. But before she had gotten halfway through the spell, her voice died away. She saw that the room had descended into total pandemonium. Diners and servers alike were attacking one another, using utensils, bare hands, even morsels of food as weapons. They fought with wild-eyed ferocity, yelling with incoherent fury as they struck blows frenzied and savage.

Where had this sudden rage come from? It wasn't like her to become so emotional, especially in the midst of a hazardous situation. It was her ability to think calmly and rationally during moments like these that had kept her alive for so many years. How . . .

Then it hit her. Sudden rage.

The Fury.

Something had happened to make the Fury intensify, and she had a good idea what: Diran and Ghaji had reached the palace of Baroness

Calida and had begun their attempt to remove the curse on the House of Kolbyr. If that were the case, and the Fury was this intense here, how much worse would it be in the palace, the center of the curse? She feared for Diran, but most of all, she feared for Ghaji.

Gods be with you, love.

Perhaps it was the knowledge that her anger was false, forced upon her by foul magic. Perhaps it was the cool rationality that she had cultivated and relied on for her entire life. And perhaps it was simply concern for the safety of the man she loved. Whichever did the trick, the Fury lost its hold on her, and she no longer felt a burning desire to send a mystic missile shooting into Zivon's heart.

Unfortunately, that didn't mean that Zivon had abandoned his desire to slay *her.*

The man had caught his breath at last. He grabbed hold of one of his utensils—a fork—and with a growl, he overturned the table, leaped to his feet, and charged.

Armed only with a magical quill she no longer wished to use, Yvka steeled herself to meet his assault and wondered how—or even *if*—she could stop Zivon without killing him.

❂ ❂ ❂ ◉ ❂ ❂ ❂

The man in the ragged cloak stood in the street outside the palace home of Baroness Calida. He had tracked Diran, Ghaji, and Asenka here, but—as he had no excuse to allow him entrance—he had been forced to remain outside. He'd overheard enough of the three companions' conversation as he'd followed to know what Diran intended to do, and he also knew that Diran, strong as he was, would have difficulty dealing with the evil that dwelled within the halls of the palace. And so he waited outside, bow in hand and strung, quiver slung over his shoulder, waiting for the moment his aid would be needed.

It didn't take long.

He could sense the evil the palace radiated, could almost see it as a foul black cloud spreading outward in all directions from the building. More, he could *smell* it: like the carcass of an animal that had been gutted and cast into a sewage pit to rot. The stink offended him on a primal level, and—though it shamed him to acknowledge this—it excited a part of him, too. His mouth began to water and without his realizing it, a soft growl of desire began rumbling deep in his throat.

Then, like a sudden violent cloudburst, the dark energy emanating from the palace doubled, tripled, quadrupled in intensity. The cloaked man felt the evil power slam into him with almost physical force and then move past as it rolled like an ebon wave to inundate the streets of Kolbyr. For an instant, the cloaked man's spirit was almost swept away by the dark tide, but he resisted the call of the Fury. He'd had much experience resisting such urgings over the last few months, and though it had been an ordeal, that experience saved him now.

Unfortunately, the citizens of Kolbyr, though used to withstanding the day-to-day effects of the Fury, had no preparation for dealing with it at full intensity. The Fury grabbed hold of their minds, instantly transforming them into murderous fiends intent only one thing: shedding as much blood as they could as swiftly as possible. The air filled with shrieks of fury, maniacal laughter, and cries of agony as the ensorcelled Kolbyrites began a sickening orgy of pain and death. The cloaked man hesitated, torn as to where his duty lay. He didn't wish to abandon the people in the street to their fate, but if Diran and Ghaji failed to lift the curse, every man, woman, and child within the city would perish, and there would be nothing he, one lone bowman, could do to save them.

His duty was clear.

Leontis ran toward the palace's main entrance.

❂ ❂ ❂ ◉ ❂ ❂ ❂

The throat and the heart, Diran decided. Slash one, pierce the other . . . do it at the same time, and even a creature as strong as a half-orc would perish within moments. He'd have to make sure to stay clear of the beast's flaming axe, but even if he did take an injury, as long as it wasn't a mortal blow he would be able to heal himself after his opponent had been reduced to a cooling corpse. Then . . .

The half-orc swung his elemental axe in a wide arc designed to separate Diran's head from his body. It was a clumsy attack, fueled by emotion rather than directed by skill, and Diran knew he could easily evade it and get in his planned strikes. But instead of lashing out at the half-orc with his daggers, Diran threw himself to the side, tucked in his right shoulder, rolled, and came to his feet. He spun around to guard against another attack by the half-orc, and—though his hands itched to hurl his daggers at the green-skinned half-blood—Diran stood and regarded his foe.

Something about what was happening bothered Diran. The situation seemed wrong somehow, but he couldn't quite put his finger on why. On the surface, it all appeared simple enough: he hated the half-orc, the half-orc hated him, and each wanted the other dead. But . . .

You thought of healing yourself a moment ago. Your power to heal flows from the Silver Flame. You are a priest of the Silver Flame, one of the Purified. You do not kill without reason, and you certainly do not want to kill your friend.

Friend. It was a simple word, but a profound one, and as if it were a charm to counter to effects of the Fury, once he'd thought it, Diran found himself released from the demon's influence.

Ghaji moved in for another strike, features contorted into a mask of pure hatred. Diran wanted to speak to his friend, to try to reach the real Ghaji, but there was no time. The demon had unleashed the full force of the Fury upon Kolbyr, and Diran knew that at this moment men, women, and children throughout the city were in the grip of the Fury's killing madness. Innocents were dying, and Diran couldn't afford to waste any more time.

With a bestial roar, Ghaji swung his axe in an upward arc designed to gut Diran from stomach to throat. Diran sidestepped the blow— the heat from the elemental axe's flame stinging the skin of his face—then he moved in close and, wielding his daggers with surgical precision, he sliced through Ghaji's right bicep with one blade while at the same time that he rammed the second into the half-orc's right quadriceps, sinking the dagger into the leg muscle all the way to the hilt.

Ghaji bellowed in pain and released his grip on the axe. The weapon's flames extinguished the instant physical contact with its wielder was broken, and the axe fell to the floor. Without the illumination provided by the elemental weapon, the windowless chamber plunged into darkness. Before Diran could move out of the way, Ghaji—maddened with pain—head-butted him, and bright light flashed behind the priest's eyes. Diran staggered backward, struggling to hold onto consciousness, knowing that if he passed out, the demon would be victorious and dozens, perhaps hundreds, of Kolbyrites would die. He reached into a pocket and withdrew a small light gem. It wasn't very powerful, but when Diran activated it, the gem shone brightly enough for him to see.

Blood gushed from Ghaji's wounds, but the half-orc limped toward Diran, teeth bared, eyes burning with a hatred born of madness and evil. Diran still held the dagger he'd used to slice Ghaji's arm—the other was still embedded in Ghaji's leg—and he flipped the dagger into the air, caught it by the blade-tip, and hurled it directly at the point between Ghaji's eyes. The dagger hilt struck the half-orc a solid blow before bouncing off and falling to the floor. Ghaji stood, fighting to remain upright, but then his eyes rolled white and he collapsed.

"That's a surprise. I would've put my money on the half-orc."

Diran turned around to regard the demon. If Ghaji hadn't been under the fiend's spell and had been able to fight with a clear mind, Diran might well have died at the hands of his friend. It had been a near enough thing as it was.

Diran's vision was blurred and his head swam, but he managed to keep on his feet. He walked over to where his silver arrowhead had fallen. He bent down to retrieve the holy symbol. Once his fingers closed about its cool metal surface, he felt renewed strength, and when he stood again his vision had cleared and his dizziness was gone.

"It's over, Demon. Vacate the boy's body now or I'll eject you by force. This is your last warning."

The demon chuckled, but the sound lacked confidence. "I have plagued the House of Kolbyr for a hundred years, and I'll continue to plague it long after you've rejoined your precious Silver Flame, priest."

Diran hadn't expected a demon this powerful to give up easily. He glanced at Ghaji's unconscious form to make certain that his friend wouldn't rise and attempt to kill him while he worked to exorcise the demon, and then he started walking toward the naked scarred body of Calida's son.

The demon made no move to defend itself—no physical move, that is. The body it inhabited was no stronger than that of an ordinary boy. But the fiend redoubled its efforts to ensnare Diran's spirit with the force of its Fury. Diran felt as if he walked against gale-force winds, but he concentrated on the image of a silvery flame burning at the core of his being, and he continued moving step by tortuous step toward the demon. When he reached the boy, Diran knelt before him and pressed the silver arrowhead to his forehead. Silver light flashed bright as a lightning strike, and the demon let out an agonized shriek so loud Diran could feel the floor vibrate beneath his feet.

The priest began speaking the Rite of Exorcism in a strong, clear voice, and the demon's howling increased in volume, as if it thought it could negate the rite by drowning out Diran's words. But Diran continued praying aloud, silver light blazing forth from the arrowhead and filling the chamber with its pristine energy.

The demon's screams reached a crescendo, and Diran knew from long experience that the rite had almost done its work. Just a little longer . . .

"Fine!" shrieked the demon. "If I can't stay here, then I'll just have to find myself a new home, won't I?"

Diran felt a cold, foul wave of infernal power wash over him, and he knew that the demon had been forced out of the boy and was seeking to enter the next closest body available: his.

Such a nice strong, body . . . and there's already a place for me here! Once you've played host to darkness, it leaves a hollowed-out space inside your soul, Diran Bastiaan. All sorts of nasty things can find their way inside you and make themselves right at home.

Diran felt the demon's spirit attempting to wriggle its way inside him, like a worm invading the flesh of a potential host. But Diran wasn't without his defenses, and he fought back with all the spiritual strength at his command.

It goes both ways, demon, Diran thought. *I once shared my soul with one of your kind, and that does make me more susceptible to possession. But I also know what it's like to resist evil and cast it out of my heart.*

Diran closed his eyes. In his mind he saw the fiend as a cross between a spider and a squid, with a touch of boar tossed in for variety. He didn't recognize the demon's species, but that wasn't important. What *was* important was the thin dark thread that emerged from the demon's back and trailed off into the distance. It was this astral thread that connected the demon to the physical world, and more particularly, to the House of Kolbyr. The mystic connection had been created by the sorceress who had originally summoned the demon a century ago, and it was what allowed the fiend to continue returning generation after generation to possess one innocent child after another.

Diran visualized a dagger forged from purest silver, a stylized flame etched into the blade. He imagined the dagger positioning itself over the ebon astral thread, imagined the blade rising to strike . . .

Wait! I wasn't lying when I said I can show you things! I can reveal to you important information about the present, even draw aside the veil that conceals the future . . .

New images flashed through Diran's mind, obscuring the demon, the astral thread, and the silver dagger. He saw the *Zephyr*, sailing across the choppy waters of the Lhazaar, an obsidian sarcophagus resting on the deck, its lid sealed shut. Sitting behind the elemental containment ring and guiding the vessel was an orange-skinned goblin wearing a gray cloak. No, not a goblin. A barghest. The one who served the lich Diran and the others had destroyed in the foothills outside of Perhata . . . the one who'd stolen Tresslar's dragonwand in the psi-forge facility housed within Mount Luster. Diran tried to look up at the sky so that he might note the position of the sun and perhaps get an idea of which direction the craft was headed, but the image faded too soon. It was replaced by a vision of a dank cave where the skeleton of a dragon lay in final repose, and as swiftly as that image appeared, it was supplanted by another. A city at night: cobblestone streets, fine architecture, everbright lanterns illuminating the way for crowds of well-dressed pedestrians . . . Diran recognized the city as Regalport, the gem of the Principalities. And though he wasn't certain how, he knew he was looking at a scene not far off in the future.

Sudden alarm crossed the faces of the men and women in the vision, and though there was no sound to accompany the images, Diran could tell from the pedestrians' terrified expressions that they were screaming. He soon saw why: creatures emerged from the alleys and poured into the street, half-human monstrosities with smooth gray skin, mouths filled with rows of triangular teeth, and eyes black and cold as death. The monsters attacked anything that moved, rending flesh with sharp claws, tearing away bloody hunks of meat with their teeth . . . and though the vision showed one street only, Diran knew that the scene was being repeated throughout Regalport. Hundreds, perhaps thousands of the half-human creatures swarmed throughout the city, killing wherever they went.

One last image superimposed itself on the horrible scene: the face of a brown-furred wolf, teeth bared in a snarl, human intelligence shining in its eyes . . .

The vision faded and once more Diran saw only the demon, the thread, and the blade.

Let me in, and I'll serve you well! All these visions will I reveal to you in full, and far more besides! Think of all the good you could do, priest, with the knowledge I can provide!

Diran's only reply was to imagine the blade slicing downward. The astral thread was severed, and the demon's form faded with a last echoing cry of despair.

Diran opened his eyes.

Sitting cross-legged on the floor in front of him was Calida's son. The boy's skin was smooth and unmarked, his eyes clear but confused. Diran could feel the lingering taint of the Fury hanging in the air about them, but he could sense no evil from the child. The demon was gone; the curse of Kolbyr lifted.

Diran took his hand away from the boy's forehead and tucked the silver arrowhead back into his pocket. He then reached out and smoothed a lock of hair from the child's forehead. "Everything's going to be all right now, Taran."

The boy's eyes went wide as he stared at a point beyond Diran. The priest heard the faint scrape of boot leather on stone and turned to see Ghaji staggering toward him. The half-orc's right arm dangled useless at his side, and he dragged his left leg behind him, the dagger still embedded in muscle. He held his elemental axe in his left hand, though he had not activated its flame, perhaps because he lacked the presence of mind to do so. His face was contorted with furious hate, and Diran knew that even though the demon had been banished, the Fury had not released its hold on his friend.

"It's over, Ghaji. You don't have to do this." Diran didn't want to harm Ghaji any further, but if the Fury continued roiling within his soul unabated, he might well prove a danger to the child, and Diran couldn't allow that. More to the point, Ghaji—the *true* Ghaji—would want Diran to stop him.

Diran reached back into his cloak's inner lining and withdrew a dagger.

"Please . . ." Diran pleaded. "Don't make me do this."

Ghaji frowned in confusion and looked at Diran as if truly seeing him for the first time since being gripped by the Fury. But then the hate returned to Ghaji's face and he lifted the axe over his head.

Diran, his heart breaking, was just about to hurl the dagger toward the point just below Ghaji's throat apple when he heard the unmistakable *twang* of a bowstring. Ghaji stiffened, took a stagger-step forward, then dropped his axe. The half-orc turned around to face the chamber's entrance, and as he did, Diran saw the end of a feathered shaft protruding from between the half-orc's shoulder blades.

Standing in the open doorway was a bearded man in a ragged cloak. He held a bow at the ready, another arrow already nocked and trained on Ghaji. The half-orc took three hesitant steps toward the door before his knees buckled and he collapsed.

Leontis gazed at Diran, his expression unreadable.

"Greetings, my brother. Looks like I arrived just in time—as usual."

❀ ❀ ❀ ❀ ❀ ❀ ❀

As the artificers attacked, Tresslar wished he'd foregone the Tinker's Room tradition of not entering with a weapon in hand. The Fury-crazed men and women would be on them in seconds—not nearly enough time for Tresslar to rummage around in his pack for a device to defend himself and his friends.

"Solus?" Tresslar shouted.

"The Fury has too strong a hold on them," the psiforged said, sounding eerily calm in the face of the artificers' murderous fury. "I cannot reach their minds."

Tresslar was about to suggest Solus try telekinesis, but before he could say anything, Illyia spread her arms and the mystic bubbles that comprised her outfit burst outward in a shower of translucent spheres. Separate bubbles flew toward each of the attacking artificers, growing larger as they went. The spheres molded around the artificers' heads without popping and sealed themselves tight.

The men and women stopped their attack, frowning and blinking in confusion, as if they had just woken from some manner of strange group dream.

Solus nodded in appreciation. "Very impressive."

Tresslar looked to Illyia, who now stood completely and unashamedly naked. He opened his mouth to echo the psiforged's comment—though with an entirely different meaning—but then Hinto, as if his short time as Solus's companion had granted him telepathic powers of his own cut off the artificer.

"Don't you dare say it!"

Tresslar scowled at the halfling while Illyia laughed.

❀ ❀ ❀ ❀ ❀ ❀ ❀

Yvka prepared to send the mystic quill streaking into Zivon's heart, and damn the consequences. Either the Grand Hierarchs of House Thuranni would understand or they wouldn't, but whatever final judgment they might render upon her, she wasn't going to die at the end of a glutton's fork.

She danced aside as Zivon swiped his improvised weapon at her, but in so doing she lost her grip on the quill, and the enchanted feather fell to the floor. Zivon tried one more strike, this one coming closer to landing, and the elf-woman barely avoided being skewered.

"Bilge-rot!" Yvka swore, and reached into her pouch to find another weapon. But as her fingers rifled through the remaining objects within, Zivon lunged at her a third time, the tines of his fork aimed for her jugular.

Yvka prepared to throw herself to the side to avoid Zivon's strike, but she felt a sudden burning sensation on the inner flesh of her left forearm, and she winced, momentarily distracted by the pain—but a moment was all Zivon needed.

But before Zivon could plunge the fork into Yvka's neck, a patch of darkness appeared in front of the man's face and sealed itself tight to his features, as if it were an ebon mask. Zivon broke off his attack, dropped his fork, and clawed at the darkness clinging to his face. He staggered backward. His foot landed on some kind of bright-red glop that Yvka thought might have once been sorbet, and his legs flew out from under him. He fell backwards and landed on his rump with a tailbone-jarring thud.

Yvka realized then that the sounds of fighting—angry shouts, cries of pain, blows landed by fists, feet, and utensils—had ceased. The Fury was over.

The dark mask covering Zivon's face was gone, and he sat looking up at Yvka as if he didn't quite recognize her, his expression no longer contorted by madness, his features calm, if confused.

The burning sensation on Yvka's forearm had subsided somewhat, but it still hurt. She rolled back her sleeve to examine her forearm, and for a moment she stared in stunned disbelief at the stylized blue mark on her flesh.

Sovereigns! She'd manifested a dragonmark! She recognized it as the Mark of Shadow, one of the dragonmarks carried by both House Phiarlan and House Thuranni.

Zivon recognized the mark, too, and smiled. "Well, well, well ... the Hierarchs will most definitely be interested in *this* development!"

SEA OF DEATH

Zivon held out his hand and, after a moment's hesitation, Yvka reached out to help him up.

CHAPTER

EIGHT

Two dagger wounds and an arrow in the back . . . and not one of the blows came from an enemy." Ghaji shook his head in disgust. "If someone is ever foolish enough to write our adventures, Diran, I hope they leave this chapter out."

"I'm sorry, my friend, but I had no choice."

Ghaji brushed Diran's apology aside with a gesture. "Of course you didn't. I would've been upset if you'd done anything else. I am, however, grateful that you took the time to heal me before I bled to death."

While divine magic could raise the dead, priests of the Silver Flame refused to perform that particular feat and nothing could get them to consider otherwise. The Purified believed that once a spirit departed the world of the living, it joined with the Silver Flame. That joining was, in the view of their religion, the Ultimate Good and much to be desired—though of course one's death should never be intentionally hastened to fulfill this destiny, wondrous and beautiful though it might be. Ghaji knew that as much as Diran cared for him, the priest would never raise him from the dead, and while Ghaji didn't share Diran's religion, he respected the priest's views and accepted them.

Diran, Ghaji, and the rest of their companions stood outside in the inner courtyard of Calida's palace. Though the air was chilly, the sky was clear and the sun bright. Statues of rabbits being chased by a fox encircled a fountain. Clear water burbled from the top of the fountain to splash into the basin below. Despite the temperature, the water remained warm so that it wouldn't freeze. According to Tresslar, this was due to the presence of a minor fire elemental that was contained within the fountain. The animal statues were tall as halflings, and they stood on their hind legs, as if they weren't true representations of a fox and hares, but rather people wearing costumes. Ghaji hadn't seen any books during his time growing up in the Eldeen Reaches—who would waste time trying to teach a dumb half-orc to read? But the statues made him think of the illustrations one might find in tales written to delight children.

The animals certainly seemed to amuse Taran. The boy—dressed in a fur-lined doublet, trousers, boots, and a warm cloak—ran laughing from one statue to the next, climbing this one, pretending that another spoke to him in words only he could hear, running to the edge of the fountain's basin and scooping a handful of water to splash on another. The boy played as if he'd never played before in his life, and Ghaji supposed that he hadn't.

Calida stood watching her son, smiling, her eyes moist with tears. The woman had begun crying when Diran first brought Taran to her, and she hadn't stopped since. Ghaji was surprised that she still had any tears left to shed. But then, Calida had been storing her tears for a long time.

"Words cannot express the depth of my gratitude, Father."

Ghaji was taken aback to hear Calida refer to Diran that way, though as a member of the Order of Friars, the appropriate honorific for Diran was *Brother*. Sometimes Ghaji forgot that his friend was a priest, and that his position inspired a certain amount of deference from others, even from the non-Purified.

"Words aren't necessary," Diran said gently. "Your tears of joy and your son's laughter speak more eloquently than words ever could."

Calida still appeared tired and weak, but her color had improved, and she was no longer listless. She wore a long fur-trimmed robe, with a hood and large sleeves that, when put together, functioned as a muff. There were no guards within the inner courtyard to keep watch on the Baroness and her son. The courtyard was completely enclosed, and Calida—though she hadn't said so directly—obviously trusted her visitors to ensure the safety of herself and Taran.

Ghaji glanced at the others. They stood a dozen yards from where the half-orc and the priest spoke with the Baroness, watching Taran play and speaking in low tones. Ghaji had been relieved when their companions reached the palace unharmed. According to reports from the city watch, many people hadn't been so fortunate when the full, unfettered force of the Fury had been unleashed on Kolbyr. The watch was still tallying the number of dead. Ghaji had been especially glad to see that Yvka had suffered no injuries, though he'd tried his best not to appear unduly concerned about her when she'd arrived at the palace. Yvka could take care of herself just fine, and she expected Ghaji to respect that—and he did, but he'd still felt like giving her a fierce bear hug when she'd entered the courtyard unharmed.

Tresslar, Hinto, and Solus were also none the worse for wear, though for some reason the artificer seemed distracted, as if his thoughts were elsewhere. Probably worrying about his lost wand, Ghaji decided. Ironically, of all the companions, only Ghaji and Asenka had sustained any serious injuries during the Fury. Ghaji had taken dagger blows from Diran, and then an arrow in the back from the priest who'd arrived to help at the last moment. The man sat by himself on the edge of the fountain's basin, looking down into the pool of water within, lost in thoughtful solitude. Ghaji wondered if the priest, who evidently was an old acquaintance of Diran's, was praying. The man, named Leontis, seemed too grim, and somehow too sad to be praying, though.

Asenka had also suffered a number of wounds: the first batch from the palace guards she'd attacked when the Fury had taken hold of her, but the last and most serious injury was delivered by an arrow strike compliments of Leontis. The priest had been forced to disable Asenka to gain entrance into Taran's chamber. Ghaji had expected Leontis to make amends by healing Asenka, but he'd left that task to Diran, who'd also healed the guards that Asenka had come near to slaying. Ghaji had only ever met a few Silver Flame priests besides Diran, but he'd never known any of them to not give aid to others when it was needed. He was puzzled by Leontis's reluctance to heal Asenka, and he intended to ask Diran about it when the two of them were alone.

"If there's anything you need," Calida said, "anything at all . . ."

"There *is* something you could do," Diran said. "Not for us, but for your people—and the people of Perhata. The enmity between your two cities originated from the curse, but now that the Fury has been dispelled, there is nothing to prevent you and Baron Mahir from making peace. Together, your two cities could take full advantage of all the Gulf of Ingjald has to offer, and the Gulf could become an economic power to rival any in the Principalities."

"Not to mention the fact that your people wouldn't have to kill each other anymore," Ghaji added. "Unless they felt like it, that is."

Calida smiled at the half-orc's joke. "A hundred years *is* a long time to hold a grudge. I'll send an envoy to begin talks with Mahir, and we'll see how things go from there." Before she could add anything more, Taran came running up to her and began tugging on her sleeve.

"Mommy, come splash in the fountain with me!" He lowered his voice and cast a sideways glance at Leontis. "The man in the robe scares me a little."

"Of course, sweetheart." She looked back to Diran and Ghaji. "If you'll excuse me?"

Diran and Ghaji nodded and the Baroness allowed her son to lead her to the fountain—on the other side from where Leontis still sat brooding. As mother and son began playing in the mystically heated water, Ghaji turned to Diran.

"What's wrong with your friend? I'm not always the most sociable man myself, but even I find it odd that he's keeping apart from the rest of us like that—especially after making such an effort to help us fight the demon."

"I'm not certain," Diran said. "Leontis and I trained with Tusya, and afterward attended seminary together. Although we were once close as brothers, we drifted apart over the years. I haven't seen him since the day I took my vows. It's obvious that something is troubling him, and I suspect it's no coincidence that he is here in Kolbyr the same time we are. I shall speak with him alone later."

Leontis wasn't the first person from Diran's past to turn up since Ghaji had begun traveling with the priest—there was Makala—but the fact that Diran said the two men had once been like brothers made Ghaji feel a twinge of jealousy. He knew it was ridiculous of him to feel like that, and more than a little embarrassing, but Diran was the only true friend the half-orc had ever had in his life. The priest was the closest thing Ghaji had to family, and childish though it might be, Ghaji didn't like the idea of sharing his friend with someone else. Plus, there was something about Leontis that bothered Ghaji on an instinctive level. Something that told the half-orc that the grim priest was more dangerous than he appeared.

Ghaji wanted to dismiss the idea, to put it down to another manifestation of the jealousy he felt, but he couldn't shake the sense that something was profoundly *wrong* with Leontis. And from the tone in Diran's voice and the concerned way he looked at Leontis, the priest sensed it too.

"Let's go talk to the others and see how they fared in their separate missions," Diran said.

Ghaji nodded, gave Leontis a final glance, and then the two men walked over to where their companions stood talking. The others turned as Diran and Ghaji approached and made room for the two men to join them.

"So what news do you have for us?" Diran asked.

"Good, I hope," Ghaji added. He smiled at Yvka, but though she returned his smile, there was something hesitant in her gaze, as if she were having a hard time meeting his eyes. She rubbed her left forearm as if she'd sustained an injury there, but when Ghaji raised a questioning eyebrow, she dropped her hand from her arm and looked away, as if he'd caught her doing something she'd preferred he hadn't seen . . . something almost shameful. Yvka's reaction bothered Ghaji, but now wasn't the time to make an issue of it.

Tresslar shrugged. "I suppose it depends on what you mean by *good*. We've compared notes, and we've managed to learn a few things, though I'm not certain they'll ultimately be of much help to us. We've confirmed that Makala took the *Zephyr*, and that my dragonwand is aboard, along with the infernal barghest who stole it."

"We also know that they sailed the *Zephyr* out of the Gulf," Yvka said. "But beyond that, we have no clue as to their destination—or even why they would want the *Zephyr* and Tresslar's wand in the first place."

Hinto frowned. "What I can't understand is why Makala would be working with the barghest. I mean, I know she's a vampire and all, but she's still *Makala*, isn't she? Why would she do these things?"

Diran let out a weary sigh. "When Makala bit Aldarik Cathmore within Mount Luster, the dark spirit that shared his soul entered her, and she became its new host. The spirit tainted her even further, and I fear she had become a true creature of evil, with little or nothing of the Makala we know remaining."

An uneasy silence fell over the companions after that. It was Asenka who finally broke the silence. "This makes things simpler, doesn't it? The wand and the *Zephyr* are together: reclaim one, you reclaim the other."

"Simpler, perhaps," Diran allowed, "but not easier. We don't know where the *Zephyr* is bound, and we have no way of tracking her across the Lhazaar. Unless Tresslar has managed to discover a way . . ."

The artificer reached around into his backpack and withdrew a small device that resembled a miniature sundial. "I began work on this in Perhata, and I was able to find the parts I needed here in Kolbyr to finish it. It should allow me to detect the dragonwand's thaumaturgical energy signature—but only within a radius of a mile or so."

"Which puts us right back where we started from," Ghaji said. "Without a way to locate the *Zephyr*."

"I don't believe that's entirely accurate," Solus said softly.

All eyes turned to focus on the psiforged.

"Tresslar has informed me that it isn't good manners to read the thoughts of my friends without their permission."

Yvka's eyes widened for an instant as if she were startled, but her expression quickly returned to one of calm neutrality. The elf-woman's reaction had occurred and passed so swiftly that Ghaji doubted anyone else had noticed it. But then, no one in their group knew Yvka the way he did. *What is she worried about?* he wondered. Did she fear Solus might ferret out all the Shadow Network secrets she kept locked up in her head? That would make sense, but Ghaji couldn't help thinking that it was something more than that.

"I have taken my new friend's advice," Solus said, "so I do not know for certain, Diran, but I believe the answer to where the *Zephyr* is headed lies within your mind."

Now it was Diran's turn to look startled. "What makes you think this?"

"The palace was the center of the Fury, and extremely strong psychic turbulence occurred here. Traces of this turbulence yet remain, and I have examined them, primarily out of curiosity."

Ghaji wanted to ask *examined how?* He hadn't seen the psiforged actually *do* anything. But then he realized Solus didn't have to take physical action to use his psionic powers. The construct had probably examined the traces—whatever they were—while the others had been talking.

Solus continued. "The strongest psychic residue was left behind by your struggle with the demon, allowing me to piece together what I believe is a fair representation of what occurred during the exorcism. The demon attempted to take possession of your corporeal form, did it not?"

"Yes, but the demon failed," Diran answered.

"No matter. For during the few moments you were joined, the demon tried to coerce you into letting it inhabit your body by showing you visions of past and future events—including the location of the *Zephyr*."

This revelation was news to Ghaji, but then he and Diran hadn't had much time to discuss how the exorcism went—and the Fury-possessed half-orc had been too busy trying to kill his friend at the time to pay much attention to the actual rite itself.

"It's true," Diran said, "but though I tried to get a sense of what direction the *Zephyr* was traveling, I failed."

"It doesn't matter, Diran," Tresslar said. "The demon was probably just trying to trick you."

"No," Solus said. "The demon told the truth—at least, it *believed* it told the truth. If you will grant me permission, Diran, I can attempt to read your mind and see if the answer we seek is buried within."

"I don't know about this," Ghaji said. "Nothing personal, Solus, but you're still learning to use your abilities. If you make a mistake while attempting to read Diran's mind . . ."

"He won't!" Hinto said. The halfling smiled up at his psiforged friend and patted the construct's stone hand. "Will you?"

"I shall do my very best to ensure your safety, Diran," Solus said.

"It's the *very best* part that worries me," Ghaji muttered.

Diran considered for a moment. "Even if there is a risk, I believe it is one worth taking. The demon showed me images other than the *Zephyr*. They made no sense in and of themselves, but I fear they might portend ill for the future. Any information we can learn about the demon's visions might help us prevent them from coming to pass. Go ahead, Solus."

The psiforged nodded once, then lowered his hood and stepped toward Diran. He reached up and gently touched his blunt stone fingers to Diran's temples, and his eyes glowed a brighter green. Diran gritted his teeth and winced a couple times, but otherwise he appeared to be in no discomfort. Within a few moments, it was done, and Solus lowered his hands.

The psiforged then spoke two words. "Trebaz Sinara."

❃ ❃ ❃ ❃ ❃ ❃ ❃

Haaken Sprull drifted in feverish delirium, his dreams filled with sharp teeth and the stink of fetid breath seasoned with rotted flesh. Over and over in his mind he saw cold-black shark eyes roll white, saw a tooth-filled maw clamp down on his legs, felt white-hot pain burn through his nerves as those teeth shredded meat, snapped bone, and spilled his life's blood into the freezing surf . . .

He screamed and his eyes snapped open.

The Coldheart commander lay on a pallet in a darkened cabin, the sheet beneath him soaked with sour sweat. Haaken sensed motion and thought he might be at sea, but if so, the water must have been especially calm today, because the ship's passage was smoother than any he'd ever experienced before. At first he thought he was aboard the *Maelstrom*, the Coldhearts' vessel, but this cabin was more cramped than his: the walls closer together, the ceiling lower, and the pallet softer than he preferred. Then he remembered—the *Maelstrom* had run aground on Demothi Island when he'd attempted to strand the priest and his half-orc friend there. Not one of his more brilliant schemes, he had to admit, considering how it had turned out. His crew dead, his ship destroyed, his legs . . .

He sat up in sudden panic. He remembered everything: hiding out on the island when the undead rose from the waters surrounding Demothi, seeing Diran Bastiaan and the half-orc defeat the zombies, witnessing the arrival of the elemental sloop and the dark creatures that sailed upon it . . .

He remembered the lich summoning a huge shark from the sea, remembered the foul beast biting off his legs. But he felt no pain . . . true, his legs felt odd in a way that was hard to define, but they didn't hurt. The light in the cabin was too dim to see by, so—hands trembling—Haaken reached down slowly to feel his legs.

They were still there, but that came as little relief to him. For what he felt protruding from below his knees were small, stumpy limbs, hardly longer than a child's legs. What's more, the skin felt smooth when he ran fingers down it, but rough when he slid his fingers back upward. Each foot had only three stubby toes, all with sharp claws. There was something familiar about this strange new flesh he possessed, but his mind refused to supply the answer to the mystery, almost as if Haaken was too terrified by the truth to allow himself to recognize it.

"You're awake. Good."

The voice sounded cold and hollow, like winter wind blowing between ice-coated gravestones. Haaken remembered that voice. It belonged to the lich.

He turned toward the direction the voice came from, and in the darkness he saw two small pinpoints of crimson light. The lich's burning eyes.

A cold chill gripped his heart, and it was all he could do to force words out. "What . . . happened to me?"

The lich made no noise as she moved, but her crimson-fire eyes grew larger as she came closer. Haaken wanted to flee, but he was too paralyzed with fear to do more than sit and watch as the undead sorceress approached his pallet.

"You've been granted a great honor, Haaken Sprull," the lich said in her whispery graveyard voice. "My mistress has chosen to include you as part of her glorious plan."

"Uh, and that mistress would be . . ."

"Vol," the lich said. "I am her most devoted servant. You also serve her . . . *now*."

Haaken couldn't see in the dark, but he could hear the lich's smile in her voice. He tried to put up a brave front as he responded. "I serve no one but Baroness Calida!" But despite his intention, his words came out sounding timorous and weak.

The lich released a hissing laugh that sounded like a nest of venomous snakes had taken up lodging within her throat. "You have no choice but to serve Vol, Haaken. She's in your blood."

The Coldheart commander thought of the loss of his legs and the strange limbs that had replaced them. "That shark you summoned . . ."

"You are doubtless aware of what those who worship the Silver Flame call the Purge, when the so-called Purified caused the near extinction of Khorvaire's lycanthropes. But even warrior-priests as mighty as those of the Silver Flame have their limits, and while the Purified carried out their Purge on land, they were unable to do anything about the lycanthropes that inhabit the seas. The creature that attacked you was a wereshark, Haaken. A very old and powerful one. It passed its curse on to you through its bite. Your new lycanthropic healing abilities are already in the process of regenerating your lost legs, and you should be completely healed well before midnight. At that time you will be able to begin your new life as a servant of our most dread mistress."

If Haaken hadn't seen the ancient wereshark with his own eyes, he would've thought the lich was insane. But more than the evidence of his eyes, he could sense that the lich's words were true. He could feel it in his blood.

A wereshark . . . Haaken had heard of them, of course. Every sailor had. He'd never seen one before, but then again, maybe he had and just hadn't realized it. He'd seen hundreds of sharks over the years, and any one of them might have been a lycanthrope. The thought that he was now such a creature should've filled him with loathing, but it didn't. Instead, he felt curiously good, even excited. Like all Lhazaarites, Haaken was more at home on the water than off. Now he would know what it was like to be able to breathe underwater, to swim free and strong, to hunt prey, capture it, and devour it whole.

Without realizing it, he smiled, revealing two rows of sharp white teeth.

"What must I do?"

And there in the dark, while Haaken's new legs continued to grow, Nathifa told him.

CHAPTER

NINE

"Diran, are you sure you don't want to come with us?" Ghaji asked. "You know a lot more about hiring ships than I do."

Dusk was approaching, and the inner courtyard of the palace was cloaked in shadow. Baroness Calida and Taran had gone inside a while ago. The boy had been eager to have his mother show him his bedroom; tonight would be the first night he'd ever slept in it. Their other companions had already left the courtyard for Kolbyr's docks. Only Ghaji and Diran remained behind—and Leontis. The cloaked priest still sat on the edge of the fountain and stared into the water, as unmoving as any of the animal statues that ringed the fountain.

"Asenka and Hinto know just as much as I, if not more," Diran said. "And thanks to Calida's generosity, we'll be able to hire the fastest ship in port, no matter how much the captain charges. You'll have no difficulty finding a suitable vessel with or without me."

After Solus had identified a destination for them, Diran had told the Baroness that he'd changed his mind about accepting a reward from her. Calida had been only too happy to fund their expedition to Trebaz Sinara.

Diran glanced at Leontis then lowered his voice. "There's a reason my old friend has sought me out, and if I'm to discover what it is, I'll need to speak with him alone."

Ghaji scowled—which didn't surprise Diran since the half-orc scowled all the time, even when he was happy—then nodded once. "Very well. I'll be down at the docks with the others . . . if you need me."

Diran smiled and clasped his friend's shoulder. "When have I ever not needed you?"

Ghaji grinned. "Truer words were never spoken." Then with a last suspicious look at Leontis, the half-orc turned and left the courtyard.

After Ghaji had departed, Diran stood for a moment regarding Leontis, whose attention was still fixed on the water within the fountain's basin. It hadn't been that many years since Diran had last seen Leontis, and the man looked almost untouched by the passage of time. Oh, there was some gray in his beard, but not much . . . a few more lines around the eyes, perhaps. But the greatest change in Leontis wasn't physical. He seemed weary, as if he were weighed down by a heavy burden. Depression and spiritual malaise were hardly uncommon among the Purified, especially in those who took the most active role in combating the evils that plagued the world. There was a saying in the Church: "Gaze into the Darkness long enough, and you'll see that the shadows you find there are your own."

And never had that bit of wisdom been driven home for Diran like that night many years ago by the banks of the Thrane River. . . .

* * * * * * *

"Do you see it?" Diran whispered. "There, up ahead."

There were enough moons in the sky to provide sufficient illumination to allow even someone without an assassin's training for night-work to see. At least, there should have been.

"Where?" Leontis whispered back, sounding vexed.

Diran tried not to sigh. He was fond of Leontis, and they got along well, but he sometimes found it difficult to have patience with his fellow acolyte's lack of experience. "Ahead of us on the riverbank, about a hundred yards away. A mill, I think. That's where the evil is located."

Leontis's teeth flashed white in the moonlight as he smiled. "How much are you willing to wager that Tusya knew about the mill long before we came to the area, and that's why he chose to make camp here?"

Diran smiled in response, but he didn't draw his lips away from his teeth. Emon Gorsedd had taught him to be more cautious than that. A bit of moonlight reflected off one's teeth at the wrong time could well mean the difference between success and failure for an assassin. And failure too often meant death, and not for one's intended target.

"Not a single coin," he said.

The river burbled on their left, its gentle sound accompanied by the soft whisper of the wind. Despite the lateness of the hour, birds sang to one another, perhaps stirred by the blue-white light of the moons, and their trills added notes of beauty to the night's symphony. During his years as an assassin, Diran had learned not to be taken in by false appearances, and this lesson had only been reinforced during his time with Tusya. Just because all seemed peaceful here didn't mean they weren't in danger. Evil all too often disguised itself as innocence and beauty, a sweet-smelling poison waiting for someone foolish enough to drink it, as Aldarik Cathmore might have said.

The two young acolytes approached the mill warily, walking side by side, their footfalls making no sound on the grass as they drew closer to the shadowy structure. Diran hadn't had any formal training in sensing evil. Those sorts of priestly skills—assuming one had an aptitude for them—were taught in seminary. But he had a natural ability, Tusya said, honed by his previous life as a hired killer, and that sense was screaming now. He felt a tingle on the back of his neck, as if burrowing insects had dug their way beneath the skin and were crawling around. Diran had never sensed evil this strong before, and he paused, his gorge rising, and feared he was about to vomit.

Leontis stopped and look at him with concern, but Diran focused his mind just as Emon Gorsedd had taught.

Forget everything, boy. Forget where you are and what you're doing.

Forget even who you are, and just breathe. In and out, in and out . . . until your mind becomes clear.

Diran did as his old teacher had instructed, and after several moments he felt better. He gave Leontis a reassuring nod, and the two of them continued approaching the mill.

When Diran had first begun studying the ways of the Silver Flame with Tusya, he had been reluctant to make use of his assassin's training in any way.

I used those skills in the service of evil, Teacher, Diran had once asked. *Doesn't that make the skills themselves evil?*

Tusya, as always, had possessed a ready answer for Diran's question.

Skills are simply tools, the priest had said. *It's what we do with them that results in good or evil. It would be wasteful for you to abandon skills you already possessed just because you once misused them. Far better to redeem those skills by employing them for good.*

"Should we go in together or separately?" Leontis asked. He was well aware of Diran's practical experience as an assassin and, just like Tusya, he didn't hold it against Diran.

Diran considered for a moment. His experience didn't extend to entering lairs of evil without Tusya's guidance.

"Together, I think. If we were facing a mortal foe, it might make sense to approach from different directions. But as our foe is a spiritual creature of some sort, we will be stronger if we remain together and combine our faith against it." Diran frowned. "Besides, I have a feeling that whatever evil lairs within the mill is already well aware of our presence."

"So much the better," Leontis said. "Evil should be confronted head on."

Diran knew that life was never that simple. Sometimes the direct approach got you killed. But he saw no benefit to sharing this information with Leontis right now, and the two acolytes continued making their way steadily and cautiously toward the mill's entrance. It wasn't difficult to find.

Now that they were up close, they could make out the mill's features. There was nothing remarkable about it, nothing to differentiate it from dozens of others Diran had seen before. The mill had been constructed from wood and stone on the eastern bank of the river, and a waterwheel provided the motive force for grinding grain. Effective enough, Diran supposed, though a contained water elemental would've performed more efficiently. Not that it mattered anymore. The wheel hung slightly askew and was frozen in place, resisting the river's current. The mill's stonework remained in good repair, but its wood was weathered, a number of the planks cracked, broken, or missing altogether. The mill had been abandoned for some time, Diran judged. Decades, at least.

Of *course* it's abandoned, Diran thought. What self-respecting evil spirit would want to haunt a newly constructed mill?

"Do you feel it?" Leontis asked. "The temperature is several degrees colder this close."

Diran nodded. He'd noticed. He'd also noticed that now that they stood at the mill's threshold, Leontis seemed hesitant. Diran wondered if he were talking in order to postpone entering.

Leontis went on. "Should we take a light with us?"

If he were going in alone, especially to confront a mortal enemy, Diran would've wanted to use the darkness to his advantage. The shadows are an assassin's greatest ally, Emon had always said. But Tusya had taught him that light could be a powerful weapon against spiritual evil. Besides, if Leontis were to make the most effective use of his bow, it would help if he could see what he was aiming his arrows at.

Diran reached into a pocket and withdrew a light gem—a favorite tool of the Brotherhood of the Blade. Each gem contained a tiny fire elemental that began to glow in response to the touch of a human hand. The gems provided light: not too strong or harsh, just enough to see by without giving away one's presence unnecessarily. In addition, they were small and easily portable, and their light could be shut off simply by closing one's hand or tucking the gem into a pocket. Of course, the gems had their drawbacks, chief among them being how easy it was to lose hold of the damned things. If Diran had a gold piece for every light gem he'd lost over the years . . .

"I'll go first," Diran suggested, but Leontis shook his head.

"You open the door for me, then I'll go first. If you weren't so tall, maybe I could shoot over you. As it is, you'll be in the way of my arrows."

Diran nodded and Leontis—who already had an arrow nocked and ready—stepped back and raised his bow. Diran held the light gem steady as he took hold of the mill's door handle, depressed the catch, and gently pushed.

The handle tore free from Diran's hand as the door fell inward with a thunderous crash. A cloud of dust billowed forth from the now open entrance, and Diran turned to regard his fellow acolyte.

"If whatever is inside didn't know we were coming before, it surely does now."

Leontis grinned wryly. "I suppose that means the time for stealth has passed."

Diran grinned back. "I'd say that was an accurate supposition."

He stepped aside so Leontis could enter the mill. As his companion stepped past, Diran slipped a silver dagger out of a hidden sheath in his cloak. He'd owned the dagger for years, having acquired it on a job when he was seventeen, when he'd been hired to assassinate a baron in Adunair who'd turned out to be a vampire. It had been Diran's first and only encounter with one of the undead fiends, but he'd kept the dagger, just in case. It had come in handy on several occasions since he'd begun studying with Tusya, and he had the feeling he'd have further need of it this night.

As soon as Leontis had passed across the mill's threshold, Diran slipped inside after his friend with silent grace. The air inside the mill was even colder than outside, and the dust from the collapsing door had yet to settle, making visibility poor, even with the aid of the light gem. Leontis continued holding his bow at the ready, but he didn't loose the arrow. Leontis wasn't one to act on impulse.

Inside, they saw only what they expected: a large room with floorboards warped and broken, sacks filled with old grain piled against the walls, millstone set in the middle of the floor, wooden rods and gears for turning the stone, ceiling beams overhead, missing roof tiles allowing shafts of moonlight to fall upon the dust-covered floor. But Diran noticed something else. The grain sacks had no holes from where hungry mice had nibbled their way inside, no bats hung from the ceiling beams, and there were no spiderwebs anywhere, only strands of cobwebs. There was no life of any kind within the abandoned mill.

"Now what?" Leontis spoke in a low voice even though there was no longer any need to maintain secrecy, but Diran knew the man couldn't help it. The mill's atmosphere of dread inspired one to speak in soft tones.

Now what, indeed? Up to now, Tusya had always taken the lead whenever they'd "bearded evil in its lair," as the old priest half-jokingly referred to it. And whenever they'd done so, the evil had obligingly made its presence known—usually by leaping out and trying to slay them. But it appeared that the evil that infested this place had no intention of being so cooperative.

"I suppose we could always try summoning the evil forth," Diran suggested.

Leontis kept his silverburn-coated arrow ready and swept his gaze slowly back and forth, continuous alert for danger. Diran noted with approval that Leontis's hands were steady, and the tip of his arrow didn't waver.

"And how, pray tell, are we supposed to do that?"

Good question. Diran knew such rites existed in Church lore. Tusya had spoken of them a time or two, and Diran had read about similar rituals during his years at Emon Gorsedd's academy, when—at Emon's encouragement—he'd read widely about all manner of subjects, including the supernatural. But to how those rites were carried out specifically, Diran had no idea. But that didn't stop him from giving it a try.

He knelt down and wedged the light gem into a small crack in the floorboard near his foot. He then straightened and, still gripping the silver dagger in one hand, he reached into his tunic pocket and withdrew an arrowhead. Leontis had once asked Diran why he chose to keep the symbol of his new faith hidden when it was the custom among the Purified to carry their arrowheads in plain sight. Diran had responded that it was a practical decision. Just as with smiling in the moonlight, displaying a piece of silver where light might glint off of it wasn't conducive to approaching an enemy without being noticed. Leontis had seemed less than satisfied with this explanation, but he'd never challenged Diran on it again.

Diran planted his feet apart, raised his hands into the air, and spoke in what he hoped was a commanding voice.

"Spirits that inhabit this place, in the holy name of the Silver Flame, we beseech you to reveal yourselves!"

Diran thought he could almost feel the mill tremble in response to his voice, but no unearthly voices answered, and no undead creatures came charging toward them out the shadows. After several moments passed without anything happening, Diran lowered his arms and looked to Leontis.

"Beseech?" Leontis asked with a raised eyebrow.

Diran shrugged.

Despite the failure of Diran's exhortation, Leontis continued to hold his bow steady. Just because nothing had responding to Diran's summons didn't mean nothing was present. After all, they could both still sense the evil permeating the mill.

"So what do we do next?" Leontis asked. "Tear the place apart looking for hidden chambers? Rip up the floorboards to see if any bodies are hidden beneath?"

Diran thought for a moment. "I say we burn the mill down."

Leontis looked at Diran as if he'd taken leave of his senses. "Are you possessed?"

Diran smiled. "I hope not. If the evil will not come forward to confront us, then it must be because for whatever reason it's hiding from us. So the best way to flush it out is to take away its hiding place."

Leontis mulled over his fellow acolyte's suggestion. "It's worth a try. Given how old this place is, we shouldn't have any trouble getting a good fire going in short order. And who knows? Perhaps by destroying the mill we'll also destroy the evil presence that inhabits it. I'll keep watch while you start the fire."

Diran nodded. He slipped his dagger back into its sheath, then reached into his tunic for his flint and striker. He knew a way to release the fire elemental from the light gem if necessary, but he didn't want to waste the little flame spirit if he didn't have to. But as he brought out the flint, he felt a sudden chill gust of wind waft through the mill and enfold him in its icy grasp.

No . . .

It sounded like the mournful wail of a distant wind, but Diran knew he was hearing a voice. The coldness surrounding him intensified, and he thought he could feel delicate fingers gripping the wrist of the hand that held the flint. But when he looked down, he saw nothing but his own flesh.

"Diran, what is it?"

Diran tried to answer his friend, but his lips felt sluggish and numb, as if he'd been outside in winter cold for too long, and his voice refused to come. He felt his strength begin to ebb, and he knew that the unseen creature holding onto him was stealing his life essence.

"Use your arrowhead, Diran! Thrust it toward the creature!"

Excellent advice. Unfortunately, Diran couldn't move. Whatever foul power the invisible creature possessed, it had rendered him immobile. But then again, perhaps not entirely. He tried to wiggle the fingers of his right hand—the hand holding the flint—and though his fingers were too numb for him to tell whether or not he succeeded, Diran was rewarded with the sound of the flint hitting the floor. Marshalling all the strength remaining to him, Diran concentrated on speaking a single word.

"F . . . fffff . . . *Fire* . . ."

Leontis understood. He dropped his bow and ran forward to snatch up Diran's flint. He moved quickly away from Diran lest he be caught by whatever force had taken hold of his companion and then drew a fresh arrow from the quiver slung over his shoulder. Holding the arrow near the metal tip, Leontis knelt down close the floor and began using his makeshift striker on Diran's flint. Sparks leapt forth from the flint, arcing into the air and landing on the mill's wooden floor, only to fizzle out in the layer of dust covering the planks.

Diran felt vertigo wash over him, and his vision was starting to go gray. As consciousness began to desert him, he prayed that Leontis would be able to get a fire started before their unseen attacker finished draining the rest of his lifeforce. If not . . . well, then Diran would just have to experience his reunion with the Silver Flame a bit earlier than he'd expected, wouldn't he?

Diran heard the spectral voice whisper mournfully once more.

No . . . fire . . .

And then the voice spoke a word that startled the young acolyte.

Please . . .

A spark hit the floor and ignited into flame, causing Leontis to let out a shout of triumph. The flame grew quickly, and Diran knew that within moments the mill would be beyond saving.

Though he had virtually no strength remaining, Diran somehow managed to speak three more words. "Put . . . it . . . out . . ."

They were little more than whispered exhalations, and Diran wasn't sure that Leontis had even heard them, let alone that he would understand and heed them. But the other acolyte looked at Diran for a long moment before finally rising to his feet and stomping out the fire he'd just made. It took several tries, but Leontis managed to extinguish the flames.

"I sure hope you know what you're doing, Diran Bastiaan."

Diran wanted to say, *So do I,* but he couldn't force out any more words. If he'd guessed wrong, he was dead, and perhaps Leontis was too. But if he'd guessed right . . .

Diran felt the icy fingers let go of his wrist, and the cold that gripped his body began to recede. He was weak as a newborn, but he no longer felt dizzy and in danger of passing out. He looked to Leontis and gave his friend a reassuring, if somewhat shaky, smile.

Before either acolyte could speak again, the air between them began to shimmer as strands of white mist appeared. The strands grew thicker, joined together, and coalesced into the ghostly apparition of a young woman in her late teens. She appeared solid enough, but her flesh and clothing—a simple dress with an apron tied over it, a cloth wrapped around her head to keep her hair in place—were both marble-white.

She looked at the two acolytes and gave them what was unmistakably a grateful smile.

"I take it we're looking at a ghost," Leontis said. He sounded oddly calm, given that a specter had just manifested before them, but then the priesthood did run in his family, and he'd been training with Tusya for a while now—long enough for strange sights not to seem so strange anymore.

"That would be my guess," Diran said. "I've seen a few in my time." Caused more than a few as well, he thought wryly.

"And she evidently would prefer that we don't burn down the mill," Leontis added.

My mill . . . the ghost's voice sounded clearer and more distinct now, though still very ethereal. But when she spoke, the movements of her lips lagged behind the sound of the words themselves, adding to the unearthly effect.

Keeping his gaze firmly on the ghost-girl, Leontis tucked Diran's flint into one of his pockets then retrieved his bow and silverburn-coated arrow. The spectral girl watched him, but made no move to stop him. Why would she? Diran thought. Silver had no effect on ghosts.

"Why do you think she's haunting this place?" Leontis asked, his arrow trained on the ghost-girl's heart—or rather, where her heart used to be. Diran was certain Leontis knew the arrow would prove little more than an annoyance to the girl, but he supposed his friend felt a need to do something other than just stand there while they talked.

The girl shook her head emphatically, the motion making her ghostly features blur a bit. *Home* . . . she said.

Diran thought he was beginning to understand. "From the way she's dressed, I'd say she used to work here. Perhaps she died here as well."

The girl nodded, the action again making her features blur.

"All right, so this is her *home*," Leontis said. "But what does that matter? She's a creature of evil! You can feel it all around us! We shouldn't be standing around here having a conversation with her. We should be destroying her!"

"You said it yourself: evil is all *around* us. But do you sense any evil emanating from her?" Diran gestured at the ghostly mill girl.

Leontis looked at her and frowned. "Actually . . . no, I don't."

"She didn't manifest when we first entered," Diran pointed out. "And she didn't appear when I attempted to summon her. She had ample opportunity to attack us if she wished to harm us, but she only acted when we attempted to burn down the mill . . . her home."

"That may be," Leontis said, "but then where is the evil coming from? Is there another creature of some sort lurking here?"

Though he'd had no formal training in how to do so, Diran attempted to stretch his senses outward, to feel what could not be seen. "I don't think so. I think the mill itself is the source of the evil. Something wrong happened here . . . something that bound this girl's spirit to this place and infused the structure itself with the echoes of the evil that was done here."

Leontis looked at the girl once more. "You mean she was . . . killed here?"

"I believe so," Diran said. "Remember what you said earlier, about tearing up the floorboards to see if any bodies were hidden under them?"

The two acolytes lowered their gazes to the floor beneath their feet.

● ● ● ◉ ● ● ●

Diran and Leontis sat atop the unmoving waterwheel, legs dangling over the side. The ghost-girl hovered in the air beside them, her malleable features contorted in an exaggerated mask of fear, her terrified eyes larger than a human's could ever be, her mouth a grotesque slash of a grimace. Diran wondered how many ghosts assumed a hideous appearance not to frighten others, but simply because they were themselves afraid. The Thrane River rushed by less than thirty feet below them, moonlight sliding across the surface of the water like a liquid silver sheen. The river smelled clean and pure, but another scent hung in the air, growing stronger by the moment: the scent of smoke.

"How did I let you talk me into this?" Leontis grumbled.

"I believe all I had to do was ask," Diran replied.

It hadn't taken the two acolytes long to find the girl's skeleton hidden beneath the floorboards, along with the remains of a half dozen other unfortunates. Why hers should be the only spirit bound to the mill, Diran couldn't say. Perhaps of all those who had died here—or at least been buried here—she was the one whose death had been traumatic. Dying in great grief, fear, or rage was often the cause of spirits becoming earthbound. At least the number of skeletons explained why the mill itself reeked of evil. Deeds of great wickedness had been performed here, and their spiritual taint had seeped into the wood and stonework of the mill, turning it into a Bad Place.

Diran and Leontis had spent a couple hours digging graves well away from the mill and then transporting the skeletons as carefully and respectfully as they could to their new resting places. They'd attempted to lay the girl-ghost to rest first, but after they'd finished burying her and returned to the mill, they found her ivory-white form waiting for them. So they finished with the others and, after Diran had convinced the girl there was no other way, they'd set a fire inside the mill. But in order to get the girl to agree to let them start the fire, they had to acquiesce to one request: she didn't want to be left alone while her home burned.

The girl couldn't leave the mill, and Diran and Leontis could hardly remain inside. But they *could* sit atop the waterwheel for as long as it was safe, and the girl *could* manifest outside the mill, as long as she remained close enough to reach out and touch it.

Diran looked at the girl's almost comically distorted features and reminded himself that he was looking not at a monster, but rather at the soul of a person who was afraid to die for a second time.

"Don't be afraid," Diran said. "The destruction of the mill will not mean the destruction of your spirit. Instead, you will be released from your earthly prison. You will be free at last."

The smell of smoke was much stronger now, the wood beneath them began to feel hot, and a new sound joined that of rushing river water: the crackle of hungry flames.

Phantom tears streamed down the girl's face, wearing channels in her insubstantial flesh, as if her fear would literally be her undoing.

Diran reached out to take the ghost-girl's hand, and though he shouldn't have been able to touch her, though it was more than likely only his imagination, he intertwined his fingers in hers and found them not cold and dead but very much warm and alive.

The girl's features returned to normal, and she gave Diran a grateful smile.

"Uh, Diran . . ." The usually unflappable Leontis sounded as if he'd edged a step closer to panic. "It's getting rather toasty up here."

Diran could feel sweat beading on his skin despite the coolness of the night air.

"And in case you hadn't noticed, breathing is becoming something of a chore . . ."

Smoke billowed up around them now, obscuring his vision and making his eyes sting, and he could no longer see the ghost-girl. But he could still feel her hand entwined in his.

Diran had to fight to keep from coughing as he answered. "I promised her we wouldn't leave her until it was over."

Then the smoke parted and the girl's ivory face came toward his. He felt soft lips brush his gently, and then she withdrew back into the smoke and was gone.

Thank you . . .

Diran tried to tell her she was welcome, but he burst out with a fit of coughing. He felt Leontis grab him by the shoulders and shove him off the waterwheel, and he tumbled down into the waiting waters of the Thrane, Leontis following right after.

They climbed onto the bank many yards downriver, wet, shivering, and chilled to the bone. They flopped exhausted onto the grass and turned to view the bright orange glow of the burning mill set against the black of the night sky.

"You lads might consider getting a bit closer to the mill so you can dry off. It'd be a shame to let a fire like that go to waste."

❁ ❁ ❁ ❁ ❁ ❁ ❁

Only a smoldering pile of ashes and blackened stone remained by the time dawn pinked the eastern sky. When they'd first arrived, Tusya had added the last of his silverburn to the mill fire and spoke a series of prayers, asking the Silver Flame to forgive any impurities in the girl's soul and accept her as part of the divine Flame. Diran and Leontis had prayed along with their teacher, and when the rite was concluded the three men sat in silence and watched the mill burn.

It was Leontis who first broke the silence. "It's too bad we finished the last of the wine, Teacher. I could use a drink right now."

Tusya smiled. "I'm proud of you boys. You served the Flame well tonight. So, though we're all tired and could use some rest, I would be remiss in my duties as your teacher if I didn't ask what you've learned here this night."

Both Diran and Leontis thought for a time before answering.

"There are many kinds of evil in this world," Diran began. "I've known this since I was a child. I once served one of those evils . . . carried it within me like the blood that flows within my veins. The evil we discovered in the mill tonight wasn't of a supernatural nature. It was the result of someone who long ago could not restrain his own selfish need to wield the ultimate power over others—the power of life and death. I understand now that all evil—natural or not—comes from the same impulse to put one's desires above all else, no matter the cost to others. Evil is the ultimate form of selfishness, and it must be opposed in all its manifestations, whether small or great, mundane or mystical. That is what the Silver Flame asks of us."

Tusya nodded approvingly. "And you, Leontis? What did you learn tonight?"

"That things are not always as they appear on the surface, and in order to combat evil, one must see a situation not as one thinks it is or should be, but rather as it truly is." Leontis looked at Diran then. "You taught that to me tonight, my friend, and I am grateful."

Diran smiled and nodded his acceptance of Leontis's thanks.

Tusya stood, groaning at the stiffness in his joints. "I think it's time we returned to our camp and got some rest don't you? There's a village not far from here, and once our strength is restored, perhaps we'll pay the good folk who live there a visit and see if there's anything three faithful servants of the Silver Flame might be able to do for them."

Diran and Leontis rose to their feet.

"And perhaps we'll see if they have some inexpensive wine for sale?" Diran teased.

Tusya grinned.

● ● ● ◉ ● ● ●

Diran walked over to the fountain and sat beside Leontis.

"I thank you for your earlier assistance, my friend. If you hadn't arrived when you did, I'd most likely be one with the Flame right now, and Ghaji would have the burden of my death on his hands. Even though he wasn't in control of his actions at the time, he would still feel responsible."

Leontis didn't look at Diran as he replied. "I was glad to help, but I really didn't do much. You had the situation well in hand before I arrived."

"Remember what Tusya always told us: 'Humble or grand—' "

" '—all good actions brighten the Flame's light in the world.' " A ghost of a smile crossed Leontis's face. "I haven't forgotten."

The entire time he'd been in the courtyard, Diran had felt uneasy, as if evil were present nearby, though for some reason it seemed muted and restrained. He'd put the feeling down to the lingering aftereffects of the Fury, but now that he sat close to Leontis, he could tell the evil he felt was centered on his fellow priest. Something was seriously wrong, and Diran felt confident that was the reason Leontis had kept himself apart from the others while they talked in the courtyard.

"It is good to see you, my brother," Diran said. "It's been too many years since last we saw one another. I would like to think you sought me out for old times' sake, but I suspect otherwise. Something is clearly troubling you. Tell me what it is."

Diran reached out to put his hand on Leontis's shoulder, but the other priest jerked away, as if he feared Diran's touch.

"I . . . I would prefer that you do not lay hands on me," Leontis said.

Diran frowned, but he withdrew his hand. "Of course." He waited several moments for Leontis to continue speaking, but his fellow priest remained silent, and Diran knew that whatever matter was plaguing his friend was so serious that Leontis couldn't bring himself to discuss it, even though that was surely why he had come to Diran.

"May I see your arrowhead?"

Diran was puzzled by Leontis's request, but he removed the holy symbol from the pocket where he kept it and held it out for his fellow priest to take. But instead of reaching out for the arrowhead, Leontis turned his palm up and waited. Even before he dropped the silver symbol into his friend's hand, Diran had a bad feeling, and once the metal touched Leontis's flesh that feeling was confirmed by the sound and smell of sizzling meat. Diran quickly snatched back the arrowhead, but the damage was done: a blackened scorch mark in the shape of the holy symbol had been seared onto Leontis's palm.

As Diran stared at the mark in horror, Leontis gave him a sad, grim smile.

"I've come to ask you to kill me, my friend . . . for old times' sake."

CHAPTER

TEN

The setting sun cast an orange sheen on the gray water of Kolbyr's port, creating an illusion of warmth. A poor illusion, Ghaji thought, considering the wind felt as if it were blowing down from the top of a glacier. The half-orc, Yvka, Tresslar, Hinto, Solus, and Asenka were walking down Kolbyr's dock back toward the wharf, their destination a tavern called the Ill Wind.

Asenka had already spoken with the harbormaster about hiring a ship, and since they had a letter of credit from Baroness Calida, the man was only too happy to make recommendations—especially since the letter promised him a substantial finder's fee if he could find them transport as quickly as possible. He'd given Asenka several names, but he'd told her that if it what she was looking for was a swift vessel, the *Turnabout* was their best bet.

"She's a galleon," Asenka explained to the others when she rejoined them. "A fast one, too. Faster than she should be given her size, according to the harbormaster. He suspects magical enhancement of some sort, though there's nothing obvious about the ship to indicate what kind. She's anchored not far offshore. The harbormaster is going to send the captain a message to let him know we'd like to hire his vessel and how much we're willing to pay. The harbormaster seems to think the captain will at least want to talk with us, and he suggested we wait for him at a nearby tavern."

After that, they walked to the end of the dock to take a look at the *Turnabout*. She lay at anchor a quarter mile from the port—a bit farther than convenient, Ghaji thought. Almost as if the captain wanted to keep people from getting a close look at his vessel. Or perhaps so the ship was far enough out to sea in case there was a sudden need for hasty departure. A pirate ship, he decided, though in the Principalities any vessel might suddenly fly raider's colors if the need—or for that matter, the whim—arose. Lhazaarites were nothing if not pragmatic, and given the harsh environment in which they lived, Ghaji supposed he couldn't blame them.

Despite the harbormaster's words, the *Turnabout* didn't look like anything special, just a typical three-masted galleon. She didn't leave the shipyard yesterday, but she wasn't ready to be scuttled and sent to her final rest at the bottom of Lhazaar, either. Ghaji figured it likely that the harbormaster had made up the ship's mysterious reputation for speed in the hope that they'd book passage and he'd get his finder's fee before they discovered the vessel was slower than a leaky tugboat with a broken rudder and a hold full of lead ingots.

None of the others were impressed by the galleon's appearance, either, but they agreed that they might as well head for the Ill Wind and hear what the *Turnabout*'s captain had to say. They found the tavern easily enough, and though it was crowded, once Ghaji stalked in glaring, a table near the back suddenly became free. The companions sat, ordered drinks that only a man with his tongue cut out would've believed was ale, and settled in to wait for the *Turnabout*'s captain to show—assuming he was interested in doing business with them at all.

The atmosphere in the tavern was subdued due to the aftereffects of the Fury. Patrons talked quietly among themselves or sat silent and alone, struggling to come to terms with the violence that had occurred—and which they'd all participated in one way or another. Tresslar, Hinto, Yvka, and Solus talked for a while, sharing stories of the difficulties they'd experienced during the Fury, but instead of contributing to the conversation, Ghaji only listened in moody silence.

After a while, Yvka had had enough of his being withdrawn, and she elbowed him in the side none too gently to get his attention. She then learned close to his ear and whispered, "What's bothering you?"

Ghaji remembered how uncomfortable Yvka had seemed around him in the palace courtyard after the Fury had ended. "I know that your . . . profession prevents you from telling me certain things, and I accept that. But if there was anything that I really needed to know—about us, I mean . . ."

Yvka smiled and touched his cheek with her long, delicate fingers. "Come now, Ghaji. You know how I feel about you."

Yvka gave him a quick kiss, a smile, and a wink. Ghaji returned the smile, but inside he was thinking: Does anyone ever *truly* know how another feels about them?

❧ ❧ ❧ ❧ ❧ ❧ ❧

The harsh, unforgiving light of the desert sun blazed down upon the Talenta Plains, causing sweat to pour off Ghaji's body as the half-orc hacked away at one zombie after another. One good thing about fighting the undead creatures—the *only* good thing, as far as Ghaji was concerned—was that they were slower than living foes. Unfortunately, no matter how much damage you inflicted on the undead warriors, they couldn't be killed, only disabled. Decapitation was the most efficient way of putting a zombie out of action, even though losing something as minor as a head didn't destroy it. The body would continue to fight on, but since the zombie could no longer see to direct its attack, it could only flail about, hoping to score a blow by accident. It was then a relatively simple operation to remove the zombie's arms and, if necessary its legs. The detached body parts would continue to move, but they could do little damage in and of themselves.

The Karrnathi zombie masters weren't fools, though. Each of their zombies wore metal collars around their necks and flexible but tough leather bands around their shoulders, elbows, and wrists. One of Ghaji's duties was to inspect this protective armor on a regular basis, which he'd just done this morning, and he knew the zombies' gear was in good order.

Fire was an effective weapon against zombies, though the undead warriors would continue fighting until enough of their muscles and tendons had been destroyed to render them immobile. But the Karrns had thought of this as well, which was why all their zombies were alchemically treated to be resistant to flame. Not that Ghaji could afford to take the time to get a flint and striker and start a fire at the moment. He was too busy hacking away at zombies with his axe and trying to stay alive for a few moments longer.

Ghaji wasn't concerned with the finer points of combat, nor did he employ a carefully thought-out battle strategy. Given the sheer number of zombies that were trying to kill him—two dozen in all—Ghaji knew the only hope he had of survival was savage brute strength. Luckily for him, that was his specialty. He stood in the midst of the attacking horde of zombies, his war-axe gripped in both hands, swinging it from side to side as if he were a woodcutter trying to fell two dozen murderous, animated trees. Zombies came at him, wielding scimitars as if the curved blades were extensions of their arms. Ghaji bled from numerous cuts and slashes, but he'd been wounded in combat before and he ignored the pain. Every warrior knew that the only wound that mattered was the one that killed you.

Ghaji wasn't sure how many zombies he'd taken out so far. Not enough, he figured as he continued hacking with his axe.

He was distantly aware of the halfling riders sitting on their clawfoot mounts, watching with grim interest as he fought for his life. When the halfling shaman had first cast his spell to make the zombies attack, Ghaji had been surprised. The Talenta halflings were consummate hunter-warriors, and he hadn't expected them to employ such a cowardly—though admittedly effective—tactic as getting the zombies to fight their battle for them. But then he'd realized that he wasn't thinking like a hunter. The halflings were using the zombies the same way that a houndmaster might use a dog: to flush prey out of its lair. The halflings knew they couldn't breach the Karrnathi tower, so instead they planned to make the zombies do it for them.

The undead warriors would go inside, kill everyone they could, and if any Karrns were left alive when it was over, the halflings would finish them off. It was, Ghaji was forced to admit, a brilliant tactic. And one that looked as if it might have a chance of succeeding. There was no way that he could stop two dozen zombies on his own, and if the Karrns stationed inside the tower didn't emerge to aid him—and it looked like they wouldn't—then he'd be cut down soon. After that, the zombies would batter open the tower entrance, rush inside, and in close quarters the Karrns would have a difficult time trying to stop the zombies. They'd have a much better chance fighting them out here, in the open, where there was more room to maneuver. And if the door held and the zombies couldn't get inside, the halflings would order the zombies to surround the tower while they made camp, and the sly hunters would simply wait for hunger and thirst to drive the Karrns out.

At least Ghaji had managed to keep the zombies' attention on him so far. He hoped that Kirai would do the smart thing and try to escape while the battle raged on, but that hope—faint as it was—was dashed a moment later when he heard Kirai call out.

"Ghaji, close your eyes!"

Ghaji wanted to shout back, *Are you insane?* Closing his eyes in a fight like this was an excellent way to commit suicide. But he trusted Kirai, and so, after only a half-second's hesitation, he did as the alchemist instructed. Spinning around in a circle, axe held out before him to keep the zombies at bay, Ghaji closed his eyes.

He heard the sound of a clay pot breaking nearby, and then an acrid smell filled the air. The stench burned his nose and throat, and even though Kirai hadn't warned him to hold his breath, Ghaji did so anyway. The half-orc continued spinning around, and his lungs soon began to ache and he felt dizzy. He knew he had to take a breath soon or his body would give out on him. He'd fall unconscious, and the zombies would make quick work of him.

"The gas has dispersed enough!" Kirai shouted. "You can open your eyes!"

Ghaji did so, taking in a deep breath of air at the same time. The wisps of yellowish gas that filled the air stung his eyes and made them water. He stopped spinning and focused his attention on the nearest zombie. The creature stood near the broken shards of the clay pot Kirai had thrown, its normally brown-leather skin now the color of sun-blasted stone, and its movements significantly slower. The zombie still moved, but with obvious effort, as if trying to fight while deep underwater.

Ghaji grinned. Kirai had done something to reverse the effects of the unguent she used to prevent the zombies' flesh from drying out in the heat of the Talenta Plains. The zombies' skin and muscles had hardened, rendering them nearly immobile. As slowly as they now moved, Ghaji would have no trouble destroying the lot of them. But even if the zombies were no longer a threat, the clawfoot riders—and especially their shaman—still would be.

Ghaji stepped out of the way of a torturously slow scimitar strike and sought out the halfling shaman among the gathered riders. Ghaji picked out the shaman right away, sitting on his red-marked clawfoot mount at the forefront of the hunting party, rune-carved bone staff held high, still chanting in a lilting foreign tongue. The half-orc warrior took careful aim and, though his arm and shoulder muscles ached from fighting the zombies, he put every bit of his remaining strength into hurling his axe at the shaman.

The weapon spun through the air, hit the bone staff, and broke it in two. The top half tumbled to the ground and the bottom joined it an instant later, as the impact of the striking axe knocked it out of the shaman's grip.

The shaman stopped chanting and cradled his injured hand to his chest. The zombies, whether because Kirai's potion had dried their muscles completely or because the shaman's spell was broken, froze where they stood, now little more than undead statues. Ghaji bent down to pick up a scimitar dropped by one of the zombies he'd managed to dismember. If the halflings planned to attack, he would be ready for them.

The shaman glared at Ghaji with a mixture of fury and respect, then with his good hand he took hold of his clawfoot's reins, urged the giant lizard to turn, and the beast bore him away from the tower at a quick trot. The rest of the hunting party followed, and soon the halflings and their clawfoot steeds were nothing more than a distant cloud of dust moving toward the horizon.

Ghaji dropped the scimitar with a weary sigh before turning to check on Kirai. The alchemist rushed to him, threw her arms around him, and hugged him with a fierce strength that he wouldn't have thought her slender body capable of.

"We did it!" she cried. "We stopped them! Just the two of us!"

Tentatively, Ghaji raised his arms and hugged Kirai back.

"I guess we did."

❦ ❦ ❦ ❦ ❦ ❦ ❦

The sun had almost set for the night, and the temperature on the Talenta Plains had become nearly bearable, though evening did bring out clouds of gnat-like pests that seemed to find Ghaji's skin particularly tasty. Kirai knelt next a small fire across which she'd erected an iron spit. A trio of metal pots hung from the cross-rod, their foul-smelling contents bubbling as the chemicals they held simmered.

Ghaji—his wounds smeared with healing ointment and bandaged by Kirai—approached the fire, carrying a clay bowl filled with stew. He crouched next to the alchemist and held out the bowl to her.

"I figured you weren't cooking dinner for yourself out here, so I brought you something to eat. I have to warn you, though: don't ask where the meat in the stew came from."

Kirai laughed. "I don't have to ask. It's plains rat. What else would it be?" Still, she took the bowl and the wooden spoon Ghaji had brought and gave the half-orc a grateful smile.

Ghaji was silent while she ate, and he gazed up at the twilight sky. A palette of colors spread above them—pink, red, orange, blue, purple, and more—all swirled together as if the gods were in an artistic mood and had decided to use the sky as their canvas this evening. He looked at Kirai's face, and though she might be plain by human standards, he found her every bit as beautiful as the gods' sky-painting. He'd been trying all day to think of a way to tell her how he felt about her, but he still had no idea how to express his feelings without sounding like an idiot. Maybe if they started talking about something else first, the words he truly wanted to speak would come to him.

"Any luck with the zombies?" he asked.

Kirai swallowed a mouthful of plains-rat stew before answering. "Not yet. It's possible that their musculature has desiccated to the point that they cannot be made to function again. It's too early to tell for sure, though. I still have a few more tricks that I can try. That's why I'm brewing more of my 'foul-smelling glop.' " She gave him a wink, and Ghaji felt his heart lurch in his chest.

Tell her now . . .

He cleared his throat, not that he had any real need to. "Kirai . . . there's something I want to tell you. Or maybe ask you." He scowled, irritated at himself. "Something like that."

Kirai paused, another spoonful of stew halfway to her mouth. She raised a curious eyebrow. "From the tone of your voice, whatever it is must be serious. Is the commander angry about the zombies? Did you explain that we didn't have any choice but to immobilize them?"

In truth, the Karrnathi commander *was* less than thrilled, but that wasn't what Ghaji wanted to talk about right now. "It's not that, it's . . . about earlier. After we stopped the zombies."

Kirai frowned and laid her stew bowl on the ground. "I don't understand."

"The way you hugged me, it . . ." Ghaji gazed upon the fire, unable to look Kirai in the eyes. "No one ever hugged me like that before."

"I was just so relieved that we'd won. I couldn't believe it!" A teasing tone crept into her voice. "Don't tell me that I hugged you too tight! Did I bruise the big strong warrior?"

He smiled but still didn't look at her. "I think I'll survive. I liked how hard you hugged me. It was . . . nice."

Kirai didn't respond right away, and for several moments the only sound was the bubbling of her chemicals in their pots. And then Kirai began to laugh.

"I'm sorry, Ghaji, really! I know I shouldn't laugh, but it's just *too* funny! I mean, you know . . . I'm human and you're an *orc!*"

Ghaji stiffened and his heart turned to a cold lump in his chest.

Though it was the hardest thing he had ever done in his life—harder by far than fighting a horde of blood-thirsty zombies—he forced out a hollow laugh.

"I was just joking. Enjoy the rest of your stew." Before Kirai could say anything else, Ghaji rose to his feet and walked away from the fire, heading north as night continued its descent upon the Talenta Plains.

Come sunrise, he was still walking.

*   *   *   *   *   *   *

Ghaji was just about to suggest that they give up on the *Turnabout*'s captain and seek passage elsewhere when the tavern door burst open and a tall, broad-shouldered man walked in, followed by a dwarf wearing a heavy cloak.

All eyes turned toward the newcomers. The dwarf stood with a taciturn expression on his face, while the tall man met the patron's curious gazes with a broad grin. "Good evening to you all! Word has reached me that there are good people present in this establishment who seek to hire a vessel swift and true!" His voice was a warm, honeyed baritone, and he sounded as if he had come for a reunion with old friends rather than a meeting with potential passengers.

The man was in mid-fifties, with sea-weathered skin, a hook nose, and a bushy black beard. A gold earring hung from his left ear, and he wore his hair in a small pony-tail tied with a tiny red ribbon. He wore an overlarge black tricorner hat with gold trim and a large red feather sticking up from the back. His red long coat was unbuttoned over a green tunic with a white ruffled collar and a purple sash around his waist. The coat had large black gauntlet-like cuffs, past which his ruffled white shirt sleeve collars were visible. He had thick-fingered, calloused hands, and wore gaudy jeweled rings on all ten of his fingers. Black trousers, brown boots, and a cutlass sheathed at his waist completed his outfit.

Ghaji took one look at the man and burst out laughing.

"You have *got* to be joking!"

● ● ● ◉ ● ● ●

Diran stared at the blackened arrowhead shape seared onto the flesh of Leontis's palm.

"I assume you have a good reason for asking me to kill you."

"Isn't it obvious?" Leontis closed his fingers and made a fist to hide the scorch mark, as if he were ashamed of it. "I've been cursed."

Diran didn't reply. He knew his old friend would speak when he was ready. After several moments, Leontis took a deep breath and began.

"Six months ago I was traveling in the Principalities near Tantamar, at the behest of a village priest who'd contacted the cathedral. Livestock in the area were being slaughtered by some kind of animal, and there were rumors of a strange beast prowling the hills at night. The priest feared that a lycanthrope might be active in the area, and he asked that a priest with battle experience be sent to investigate. The Order of Templars chose me, and I was dispatched immediately. The Templars didn't expect me to discover anything more than some rogue beast or another—quite possibly nothing more sinister than a normal wolf—that had found an easy source of food to fill its belly. You know as well as I that lycanthropes of all kinds have been extinct in Khorvaire since the days of the Purge . . . or nearly so."

"But it's that *nearly so* that caused the Templars to send you," Diran said.

Leontis nodded. "In the years since you last saw me, I've made something of a specialty of investigating reports of lycanthropy. I'd always been fascinated by tales of the Purge—the heroics and the atrocities the Purified committed in the name of the Silver Flame. It sounds foolish now, but I thought that I could help balance the scales for the Flame, help redeem the Purified that were involved in the Purge by investigating lycanthropy now with a clear head and a pure heart . . . fighting evil with strength, determination, but also with compassion." Leontis smiled at Diran. "Just as you taught me by the banks of the Thrane River so many years ago."

"It doesn't sound foolish to me at all," Diran said. "And I know Tusya would agree."

Leontis shrugged. "Perhaps. At any rate, during my investigations over the years I'd discovered and fought any number of creatures, both mystic and mundane, but not once had I encountered a true lycanthrope."

"Until you went to the village near Tantamar."

Leontis nodded. "Despite the rarity of true lycanthropic outbreaks, the Templars take no chances when a report comes in. They dispatched me to the region by airship, and within a few days of the village priest making his report, I was scouring the woods near his village for signs of lycanthrope activity. For two weeks, I roamed those woods, hiking by day, camping at night, my senses ever alert for even the merest hint of supernatural evil. I didn't find any, nor did I find any physical signs. I found no tracks, and no animals were killed during my time there. Then one night—my last night in the area, I'd already decided—as I was about to drift off to sleep in my bedroll I finally felt it: the presence of true evil. I grabbed my bow and strung it, then slipped the quiver of silver-tipped arrows I'd brought over my shoulder. Then I walked off in into the night to begin the hunt."

"But you weren't the only hunter stalking the darkness," Diran said.

Leontis let out a bitter laugh. "Hardly! There's always *something* hungry roaming the night, isn't there? But you're right. As I was hunting the lycanthrope, so too was it hunting me. I suppose it was my arrogance that proved my undoing. After all, I was one of the Purified, a warrior of the Silver Flame . . . I'd battled evil on so many occasions, faced creatures so powerful that ordinary men and women would've been driven to the brink of madness merely to gaze upon their dire countenances. How could a single lycanthrope compare to that?" Leontis shook his head. "Pretty damned well, as it turned out.

"Lycanthropes are different than other evil beings, Diran. They combine the best and worst aspects of both man and beast. Intelligence and cunning, savagery and cruelty, instinct and forethought . . . that's what makes them so deadly, and that's why the Purified fought so hard to eradicate them during the Purge. If their contagion were allowed to spread, Khorvaire—perhaps all of Eberron—might be lost."

Diran waited for Leontis to continue, but when the man had remained silent for a time while he stared into the fountain's basin, Diran said, "So you encountered the lycanthrope."

"Yes. It came at me out of the darkness, moving far more swiftly than I would've thought possible. I had an arrow nocked and managed to release it before the beast was upon me, but I had no idea whether I had struck the monster. It knocked me to the ground, clawing, biting . . ." Leontis shuddered at the memory, grimacing as if he felt the pain of the attack anew. "I couldn't even tell what kind of lycanthrope it was. All I knew was that it had fur, claws, and teeth, and that it was doing its best to tear me into ribbons. The agony was incredible, but I fought to ignore it and reached for the silver knife sheathed at my belt. And that's the last thing I remember before awakening to see a canopy of trees above me and beyond their leaves the blue sky of morning.

"My clothes were shredded and caked with dried blood, but I had no wounds. Lying next to me on the grass was a young man who most likely hadn't seen his twentieth year. He was naked, his skin covered with blood—some of it his, but much of it mine, I warrant. The shaft of my arrow protruded from his shoulder, and my blade was lodged in his heart. He had a number of stab wounds on his chest and abdomen, and I was amazed that I had been able to strike so many times as I was losing consciousness."

Diran smiled sadly. "You've never understood just how much inner strength you possess, my friend."

Leontis ignored Diran's comment and went on. "I disposed of the boy's body, first performing the Rite of the Death of the Foe, then burning the corpse. Afterward, I buried the bones in an unmarked grave and prayed over them. Then I returned to the village priest to tell him what had happened. The priest was relieved, thanked me for my service, and told me he was glad I had received no injury during my battle with the werewolf. I didn't . . . couldn't tell him the truth. And so I left the village and began the journey home."

Diran wanted to ask Leontis why he hadn't tried to prevent the lycanthropic infection from taking hold in his body. There were rites that could be performed using silverburn, flame, and priestly magic . . . but then Diran realized what had happened. Leontis had fallen unconscious before he'd had the opportunity to attempt such rites. Even when conducted immediately after infection, the rites didn't always prove effective, but after several hours, they would've been useless. The curse of lycanthropy had transformed Leontis, and there was no going back.

"I wanted time to think, so I decided to walk back to Flamekeep instead of returning by airship. Several days into my journey, I . . . changed for the first time. I don't recall exactly what I did while in beast form, but I know that I roamed the countryside without encountering anything more than rabbits and deer which I killed and . . . devoured. When I awoke the next morning, I was human once more. I considered attempting to take my own life, but I knew that, once unconscious, I could not perform the rites to make certain I did not rise again. And so I've been wandering ever since, avoiding cities and villages, anywhere that people might congregate, lest I harm anyone or worse, pass my curse on to some other unfortunate, and allow the evil of lycanthropy to begin spreading throughout the land once more."

"What kind of beast do you become?" Diran asked.

"A werewolf. Or so I believe, based on tracks I've made while in my lycanthropic state. I have memories of what I do when I change, but they're different than human thoughts . . . not words or ideas, but rather images and sensations."

"I assume you've continued to change," Diran said.

Leontis nodded. "I always try to fight it, though, and sometimes I'm successful." His voice grew softer. "But only sometimes."

Diran was filled with sorrow and sympathy for his friend. "It sounds horrible."

Leontis gave a hollow chuckle. "If only it were that good."

The two men were silent for a time, but then Diran asked the question he feared to speak, but which he knew he had to.

"Have you killed anyone?"

Leontis's answer was swift and sure. "No. I have hunted and slain only animals and other night creatures. Never have I taken an intelligent life."

Diran wondered how, if Leontis's memories of being in his wolf-state were unclear, how the priest could know for certain that he had never killed a person. But he decided to let the matter go for now.

"I've spent the last several months trying to find a Knight of the Flame, one with the strength to slay me and make certain I don't rise again. And, as fate would have it, you're the first priest I've encountered." Leontis gave Diran a sad smile. "In truth, I'm glad it's you, for if I must die, I prefer it be at the hands of a friend. I first saw you in Perhata. I almost caught up with you there, but you left the city before I could make contact. I learned you and your companions had left for Kolbyr, so I booked passage on a swift sailboat. Evidently you traveled by slower means, for I arrived in the city a full day before you did and have been searching for you ever since." The templar rose to his feet. "So, now that we're finally reunited, let us tarry no longer, Diran. Strike and be swift about it."

Diran stood and drew a silver dagger from its cloak-sheath. Leontis's jaw was set in a firm line, and his gaze was strong and clear. Diran gripped the handle of the dagger tight. He had no need to think about where to strike. He knew from long experience exactly which ribs to slide the blade between to pierce the heart in an instant. Leontis would be dead before he even knew the dagger had entered his body. Diran's muscles tensed, and he was about to lunge forward, but he hesitated. He remembered the last vision the demon had shown to him—the face of a wolf with a man's eyes. He then thought of the ghost of the mill girl that Leontis and he had encountered so many years ago. There were many ways to purge evil, and not all of them required a dagger-thrust to the heart. At least, not immediately.

Diran sheathed his blade with a fluid, graceful motion and smiled.

"Before I kill you, what do you say to going on a little trip with me and my friends?"

CHAPTER

ELEVEN

Makala stood on the deck of a sloop, gazing upward at a black sky—no clouds, moons, or stars, just featureless, unbroken darkness. But though the sky appeared empty, she had the sensation that a malevolent presence resided within the unrelieved blackness, a baleful force that was watching her with cruel amusement. She couldn't bear the oppressive weight of the dark watcher's gaze, so she lowered her head and looked past the ship's starboard railing. Startled by what she saw, she quickly looked port, aft, and stern, but each glance only confirmed what her eyes had first revealed to her: the elemental sloop was surrounded on all sides by the turbulent waves of a blood-red sea.

This didn't make sense. A few moments ago she had been lying on a blanket in a moonlit glade with Diran holding her close. They had just made love for the first time, and it was more tender, sweet, and exciting than she could ever have imagined. But how did she come to be here, and where was Diran?

She shook her head, as if such a simple action of denial could make this distorted reality disappear. But the sky remained black, the sea remained red, and she could still feel the pressure of the watcher's dark gaze bearing down upon her like a giant invisible hand slowly but inexorably crushing her.

"This isn't real," she whispered.

"Of course not. You're dreaming."

Makala turned toward the owner of the voice. An instant ago she had been alone on the *Zephyr*, but now an elderly man wrapped in a fur cloak stood less than half a dozen yards from her, grinning to display enlarged canines, dark shadows writhing within empty eye sockets.

"Cathmore." But it wasn't him, not exactly. The being resembled the master assassin in general—emaciated frame, wrinkled skin, hook nose, claw-like hands. But those fangs . . . those *eyes* . . .

Makala was terrified, but she'd been trained to be a cold, calculating killer, and she knew how to keep a tight rein on her emotions.

"What are you?" she demanded, her voice steady and strong. "What is this place?"

The man . . . no, the *creature* resembling Aldarik Cathmore spread its hands, as if to indicate that it intended no deceit. "I told you: you're dreaming. Not a very pleasant dream, I'll grant you, but then you're in so much torment these days, aren't you, my sweet? No wonder that even your dreams are filled with darkness and fear."

The creature stepped forward as it spoke. Makala reached for her short sword, intending to defend herself, but when she drew the weapon, she saw that the blade was covered with reddish-brown rust. It was the only weapon she had, though, so she brandished it before her as if it were newly forged and held a razor's edge.

"Stay back!" she commanded.

The creature grinned wider. "Or what? You'll shake flakes of rust on me?" The creature pursed its lips and blew a stream of air toward Makala. A strong breeze kicked up out of nowhere, and her sword trembled in the sudden wind. Bits of reddish-brown sheared away from the blade, only a few at first, but then dozens more joined them. Within seconds, the corroded sword had completely disintegrated, and Makala was left holding the hilt.

The creature with Cathmore's face continued its approach. "I told you that you're dreaming, but I neglected to say that even though it's your dream, you're not the one in control here: *I* am."

Makala hurled the useless sword hilt at the creature's smiling face. Not because she thought it would do any real damage, but because it was the only thing she *could* do. The Cathmore-thing batted the improvised projectile aside with a casual flick of its hand, and the hilt flew over the railing, hit the surface of the blood-sea, and sank beneath its thick crimson waters.

The creature pursed its lips in annoyance. "Every dusk it's the same thing: you draw your rusty sword, I blow it away, then you throw the hilt at me. It's all getting rather tiresome, my sweet."

The air grew colder the closer the creature came, and Makala began to shiver as much from the temperature as from fright. But she continued to put up a brave front. She recalled something Emon Gorsedd had once taught her. *The moment you surrender to fear is the moment you're lost.*

"It's not dusk. It's . . ." She glanced up at the featureless black sky once more. "I don't know what it is. But it surely isn't dusk."

The Cathmore-thing had closed to within ten feet of her now. "Not here it isn't, but it's dusk in the waking world."

Makala had no idea what the creature was talking about, but the cold continued to intensify, and that's when she realized the frigid sensation emanated from *within* her body, not without. The creature was only five feet away now, and despite her intention to keep up a brave front, Makala couldn't help stepping backward.

"If this place isn't real, then neither are you," she said. She'd meant for the statement to come out as a bold accusation, but her words were little more than terrified gasps of air.

"Untrue," the creature said. "You and I are the only real things here." He glanced upward. "Not counting our Dark Queen, of course. From far away among the ice-covered peaks of the Fingerbone Mountains, seated upon her throne of bone and sinew in Illmarrow Castle, she watches."

The Cathmore-thing continued its slow approach, and though Makala wanted to hold her ground, she couldn't stop backing away from the creature.

"What do you want?" This time her words came out as little more than a whispered plea, like a scared child hoping to find some way, any way, of placating an angry, dangerous adult.

"Nothing dire, I assure you. I simply want to help you wake up. Think of me as your own personal alarm. You're sleeping right now, Makala. In that." The creature nodded toward something behind Makala. She turned just in time to keep from bumping into an obsidian sarcophagus with strange runes carved into the sides. Makala frowned. The sarcophagus looked familiar, but she couldn't remember where she'd seen it before.

The creature laughed at the expression of puzzlement on her face. "The undead slumber during the day and wake come nightfall. But though they appear to lay in a mindless stupor during the daylight hours, the truth is that vampires are very much active during the day—within their own minds. It's an aspect of the curse, you see, and a most delightfully cruel one at that. During the day, what remains of your mortal soul is allowed to dream . . . to recall what it was like to be human. This day—as on numerous others—you relived your first time Diran and you made love. Then at dusk, the hunger that has claimed your soul takes over and the vampire Makala awakens."

"If that's true, then what are you?" Makala asked.

"I'm the dark spirit you received from Aldarik Cathmore when you attempted to drain his blood. A parting gift from one of your former teachers." The creature glanced skyward, and though there had been no obvious change in the darkness above, the Cathmore-thing said, "The sun has fallen, and it's time for you to rise."

The creature dashed forward and before Makala could react, it grabbed her by the arms and lifted her into the air. She looked over her shoulder and saw the lid of the sarcophagus had opened of its own accord and hovered in the air next to the obsidian coffin. Inside was nothing but darkness, just like that which filled the sky above. The Cathmore-thing shoved Makala into the sarcophagus, and she found herself falling downward into endless darkness. As she fell, she wailed in despair, knowing once again what she had become and what she had lost.

And from the sky above came the sound of cold, dark laughter.

❀ ❀ ❀ ❀ ❀ ❀ ❀

Makala opened her eyes to darkness. She started to take a breath—a habit from her days as a living woman—but then stopped. Since her rebirth, she only needed air to speak.

Deep within what remained of her mortal soul, Makala screamed in frustration and sorrow as the woman she had been was once more consumed by darkness, leaving only a vampire's animalistic desire to rise from its resting place and feed. She reached up and rapped knuckles cold as ice on the inside lid of the obsidian sarcophagus. A moment later the lid was removed and laid aside, and she found herself looking up at the face of a goblin framed by a starlit night sky.

"Good evening, Makala," Skarm said. "Sleep well?"

Makala hissed like a cat and lunged for the barghest, intending to slake her thirst. She grabbed hold of the barghest's tunic and pulled him toward her, the scent of his blood pumping just beneath his orange skin sending her into a near-frenzy.

"Hold!"

Makala froze, her teeth mere inches from Skarm's jugular.

Nathifa glided out of the *Zephyr*'s cabin and across the deck toward the sarcophagus. The lich was living darkness, her undead eyes burning with crimson anger. "I'll admit Skarm's not much use, but until I have no further need of him, you will not drain him dry."

"I'll just take a little," Makala said, chafing from the way the sorceress had asserted control over her with a single word. As much as she wanted to sink her teeth into the barghest's throat, she was unable to do so. She could not move her mouth a single fraction of an inch closer to Skarm's neck. "His blood tastes like sour milk, but it will do until we reach our destination, and I can hunt for a finer vintage."

"You've fed recently enough that you will lose little strength by fasting this night," Nathifa said. "And Skarm would be weakened by the loss of blood. You will have to suffer your hunger."

Makala glared at Nathifa for a long moment, fighting to break free from the lich's mystical control. At first nothing happened, but then she began to feel Nathifa's hold slipping. But the sorceress's red eyes blazed like twin flames as she redoubled her efforts, and Makala knew that this was a battle she could not win . . . yet.

"Fine," Makala growled, and tossed Skarm aside. The barghest landed rear-first onto the deck and yelped in pain. Makala ignored both Skarm and Nathifa as she climbed out of her resting place, picked up the heavy stone lid as if it weighed no more than a thin sheet of vellum, and replaced it atop the sarcophagus.

Skarm rose to his feet and rubbed his sore rump. He gave Makala an angry glare, feeling bold because his mistress was near. Makala considered tearing the barghest's head off his shoulders and heaving it out to sea, regardless of what punishment Nathifa might dish out, but she decided the satisfaction of killing Skarm wasn't worth the trouble. Besides, she could always slay the barghest later.

Then she realized something: Skarm wasn't piloting the ship. She looked back to the elemental containment ring and saw that it had been deactivated. The *Zephyr* traveled now by natural wind power alone.

Makala looked at Nathifa. "What's going on?"

As if in response to Makala's question, a figure came shuffling out from the sloop's cabin. Haaken appeared much stronger than the last time Makala had seen him, and she could tell by the scent of his blood that not only had he recovered from his injuries, but he was fairly bursting with health and vitality. She took a step toward Haaken but stopped when she remembered Nathifa was present. No doubt the undead bitch wouldn't let her take any of the man's blood either.

Haaken's legs had regrown, but they weren't human limbs, and he was having trouble walking. He moved like a baby that had only recently taken his first steps and still doesn't trust his legs to keep him upright for more than a few seconds at a time.

"I told Skarm to deactivate the elemental come nightfall," Nathifa said. "We don't want to be moving too fast when Haaken takes his first swimming lesson."

The man gave Nathifa a horrified look. "What do you mean?"

"You now possess abilities I wish to make use of," the lich said.

"But in order for me to do so, you must learn to master them. It is time for you to start." She turned to Makala. "Throw him overboard."

Before Haaken could protest, Makala stepped forward, took hold of the man's left arm, and flung him over the railing. Haaken yelled as he soared through the air, but his voice was soon cut off as he hit the water and sank.

Makala grinned. Serving Nathifa had its good points from time to time.

❂ ❂ ❂ ❂ ❂ ❂ ❂

The Lhazaar Sea is always cold, but it becomes far more so in winter. A sailor who falls overboard without a protective charm of some sort will be dead soon after plunging into the deadly winter waters. It was only late autumn, but the open sea was still cold enough to kill, and Haaken—who'd sailed aboard one vessel or another all his life—knew this with the same certainty that he knew which way was up and which way was down. He was dead as soon as Makala hurled him into the air—it would just take his body a few minutes more to realize it.

When Haaken struck the frigid waters of the Lhazaar, he wished he *had* died the moment Makala grabbed hold of him. The shock made his heart seize up in his chest, and his teeth clamped down so hard he thought they might shatter. If his tongue had been between them, he would've bitten it in two. Every nerve in his body went numb, and his thoughts became unfocused, gray, and sluggish. He could feel the cold of the sea penetrate his bones and begin to freeze the marrow within.

Not much longer now, he thought. A few more moments, and it'll all be over.

In a way, it was a relief. Life in the Principalities was harsh and unforgiving, and from the day Haaken Sprull was born, he'd lived a life of constant struggle and battle. At least now he'd finally have a chance to rest.

Cold numbness was replaced by comforting warmth as oblivion slowly began to claim him.

But then he felt a spark deep within the core of his being, as if something new was being born inside him. Energy surged through his body, giving him a strength that he had never known before, had never even conceived was possible. He felt his body begin to grow long and sleek, his legs merge into a single limb, his arms retract, fingers joining together, hands flattening, eyes sliding to the sides of his head, nose and mouth lengthening, jaws growing wider, teeth becoming sharp and pointed. The transformation was agonizing beyond belief, and he tried to scream, but all that escaped his mouth was a fount of bubbles. His clothes tore, fell away, and were lost to the depths. He was free to move, to swim, to glide through the water like an arrow through air. The sea no longer seemed cold, no longer felt like a hostile force intent on claiming his life . . . it felt like home.

Haaken no longer relied on sight as his primary sense. Smell was far more useful here in the sea, and he had new senses upon which to draw as well. He could detect the slightest change in the currents around him, could feel the vibrations of other bodies moving through the water, creatures of various kinds and sizes, and his instincts automatically sorted them into two categories: prey and not-prey. A large not-prey moved ahead and above him, and from its vibrations, he understood that whatever this Not-Prey was, it wasn't alive, which meant it was not food, and thus of absolutely no interest. And yet, he felt compelled to swim toward it, and so he did, not questioning his instincts, not even possessing the ability to question them. He surged through the water, moving swift and sure, angling upward, toward the place where the surface of the sea touched the Great Nothing beyond. He felt a twinge of reluctance and almost veered off. The Great Nothing was not a place for his kind, but his instincts continued to insist he head for the Not-Prey, and so he did, tail fins thrashing wildly, impelling him higher, higher . . .

His dorsal fin cut the surface, and then with a final effort he leaped forth from the water and into the air. For an instant his body—all seventeen feet of it—hung suspended above the waves. He saw the Not-Prey in front of him, tantalizingly close, but just out reach of his massive jaws. But Haaken was determined to reach the Not-Prey, and he felt the power within him respond to his desire.

His body reshaped itself once more, lateral fins becoming arms and hands, tail fin shortening as legs and feet sprouted from his trunk. As Haaken reached the apex of his leap and began to arc downward, he lunged forward with clawed hands, grabbed hold of the *Zephyr's* aft railing, and heaved his bulk onto the deck.

He stood near the empty pilot's seat and the deactivated containment ring, his cold black eyes focused on three beings staring at him from the center of the deck. Haaken regarded the trio warily, his gills opening and closing as his newly grown lungs drew in oxygen, trying to decide if the strangers were prey or not-prey. An aching pit of hunger lay at the core of his being, and he decided he might as well take a bite out of one of the strangers to see what they tasted like. He took a step forward, thick strands of saliva dripping from his tooth-filled maw and spattering onto the soarwood deck.

The white-faced stranger cloaked in living shadow spoke then. "That's enough, Haaken."

Haaken . . .

The noise was familiar to him for some reason, and hearing it made his head hurt. Then he remembered: that sound was his name.

The man-shark's form blurred and shifted, and Haaken Sprull—naked and dripping with freezing cold seawater—stood upon the deck of the *Zephyr*. The frigid late autumn wind began to turn the water coating his body to a shell of ice, but Haaken barely noticed. He no longer felt the cold. He was powerful and strong . . . stronger than he'd ever been before, than he'd ever imagined was possible.

"Not that I'm complaining," Makala said, "but do we really want him going about naked?"

Nathifa looked at the vampire as if she had no idea what the woman was talking about, but then she took hold one of her robe's dark tendrils and tore it free. She flung it toward Haaken, and the tendril flew toward him like an ebon leaf tumbling in the wind. The patch of darkness grew as it came toward him, then it wrapped around his groin and rear, sealing itself to his body to form a pair of black trunks.

"Not the most stylish solution, perhaps," Makala said, "but I suppose it'll do."

Haaken ignored the vampire's words, and he was only distantly aware of the clothing provided by the lich sorceress. His thoughts were filled with the memory of water, strength, and hunger so intense it was almost agonizing.

He smiled, displaying teeth that still very much resembled those of a shark. He was looking forward to his next lesson.

＊ ＊ ＊ ＠ ＊ ＊ ＊

Later that night in Kolbyr's palace, Diran, Ghaji, and the others slept in comfortable—if not quite luxurious—rooms provided for them by a grateful Baroness Calida. The captain of the *Turnabout* had been only too happy to accept Calida's money, and they would be embarking for Trebaz Sinara at dawn's first light. Everyone had turned in early, agreeing they should all get a good night's rest before they set out on the morrow. Each companion had his or her individual room, save for Solus who had no need of sleep. The psiforged stood outside in the inner courtyard, watching heated water bubble forth from the enchanted fountain as he used his psychic abilities to cleanse the last traces of Fury from the palace.

Sometime near midnight there was furtive movement in the palace corridors, followed by two knocks—one on Diran's door, and one on Ghaji's. Both doors were opened, guests were welcomed, and four people got little sleep that night.

＊ ＊ ＊ ＠ ＊ ＊ ＊

And hundreds of miles to the north in a frozen palace made of ice and bone, a claw-like hand stroked the pate of a glossy black skull, and a pair of bloodless lips stretched into a satisfied smile.

Everything was proceeding exactly as planned.

CHAPTER

TWELVE

So when am I going to meet Captain Onu?" Diran asked.

"I'm not sure you want to," Ghaji replied. "He . . . takes some getting used to."

Diran gave his friend a quizzical look, but Ghaji just shook his head. "It's difficult to explain. You'll have to experience the good captain for yourself. As for his first mate Thokk . . . well, he's as night to the captain's day. Where Onu is honey-tongued and effusive, Thokk is plain-spoken and all business." In fact, it was the dwarf who'd negotiated the terms of their passage while Onu drank ale and regaled the tavern-goers with sea stories, each more outrageous than the last.

It was an hour after sunrise, and the *Turnabout* sailed eastward into the Gulf of Ingjald, Kolbyr little more than a speck in the distance off their aft bow. The slate-gray surface of the Lhazaar was choppy today, but not so bad that the galleon rode rough across the water. A strong wind blew from the northwest, filling the three-master's sails with bitterly cold air that seemed to waft straight down from the Fingerbone Mountains. Gray clouds blocked the sun, casting an oppressive pall over the *Turnabout*. The crew worked in silence for the most part, men and women making a point of staying out of each other's way as they tied lines, worked sails, scraped ice from deck planking, any of the thousand and one never-ending tasks that defined a life a sea as much as the motion of the waves and the tang of saltwater in the air. The crew were of various races, which was unusual for the Principalities, where ships were manned primarily by humans. There were a scattering of half-elves and gnomes and—despite his people's dislike for water in general—a lone dwarf who served as first mate. The crew dressed for practicality in heavy wool clothing and fur-lined cloaks.

The *Turnabout* was a typical three-masted galleon with bowsprit, forecastle, main deck, quarterdeck, and poop. And two balconies at the rear, one above the other, with large stern windows. Longboats were stacked upside down on the main deck, tied down and covered with burlap to prevent them from sliding around and hurting anyone if the sea became too turbulent. The sails billowed. Ghaji hoped the wind would last for the eight days or so it would take the vessel to reach Trebaz Sinara. He wished they still had the *Zephyr*. The sloop was smaller than the galleon, but because her sails were perpetually full, thanks to the magic of the elemental bound within the containment ring bolted to the deck, and also because of the soarwood runners, the vessel could skate across the surface of the water with astounding speed. If Yvka still had possession of the *Zephyr*, they could reach Trebaz Sinara in—Ghaji did a quick mental calculation—two, maybe three days at the most. But if wishes were hippogriffs . . .

Diran and Ghaji stood on the port side of the main deck. The others remained below in their quarters, doing their best to stay warm. So far, they'd seen no sigh of Onu, and Ghaji was wondering if the captain simply had no interest in meeting Diran and *Sir* Leontis, or if the man was still sleeping, exhausted after staying late at the tavern last night after Ghaji and the others had departed. Onu had certainly seemed the type to spend the night carousing.

Ghaji looked at Diran and gave his friend a sly smile. "So, did you sleep well last night?"

Diran returned the smile. "As well as you, I expect."

"Asenka's a wonderful woman."

"That she is."

Ghaji was happy for his friend. While he doubted Diran would ever truly be over Makala, he was moving on with his life, and that was a positive sign. These last few months the priest had been carrying so much guilt over Makala's transformation into a vampire—a transformation he blamed himself for—that at times Ghaji thought the burden would prove too much for him. Ghaji knew Diran still felt responsible for Makala's current state, but perhaps he no longer *blamed* himself for it. It was a small change, perhaps, but Ghaji thought it an important one.

The two companions stood in silence for a while after that, watching as the crew worked around them. Ghaji wasn't sure what to make of the way the men and women of the *Turnabout* ignored them, almost as if they were invisible. Were they simply absorbed in their tasks, or did they transport cargo of a questionable nature often enough that they'd learned that the less they knew, the better? The latter, Ghaji suspected.

"So our merry little band has increased by one," Ghaji said. "I'm a bit surprised Leontis joined us. He doesn't seem the sociable type."

"Look who's talking." Diran's gentle smile alleviated whatever sting his words might otherwise had held.

"There's something about the man that I don't quite trust, Diran. You vouch for him, and that's good enough for me, but there's still something about him that sets my teeth on edge." Ghaji did trust Diran, more than he'd ever trusted anyone or anything in his life. Nevertheless, he hoped that the priest would take the opportunity to tell him why Leontis had decided to travel with them. If Ghaji were going to fight by someone's side, he wanted to know as much about the person as possible.

Diran seemed to consider for a moment before responding. "Leontis told me his motivations in confidence, and I cannot reveal them—not even to you, my friend. Suffice it to say that he's searching for something, and I hope to help him find it."

Diran's explanation didn't *suffice* at all, but Ghaji decided not to make an issue of it—at least, not right now. "As you well know, I'm no sailor, but something strikes me as odd about the crew, and I don't mean the way they're acting as if we don't exist."

"There aren't enough of them," Diran said.

Ghaji nodded. "Exactly."

"A ship this size should have a crew of sixty or so. But it appears that the *Turnabout* is manned by only twenty sailors. And there's something else . . ."

"The way the air ripples near each of the masts," Ghaji said.

It was Diran's turn to nod. It was subtle, and Ghaji doubted that anyone not on board would notice, but all three masts had some sort of distortion in the air behind them, resembling the effect created by heat rising off desert ground.

"Kolbyr's harbormaster said the *Turnabout* was rumored to travel more swiftly than a normal galleon should," Ghaji said. "He suspected the ship is magically enhanced, though he wasn't sure in what manner."

"Magic is definitely at work here," Diran said. "But what kind and for what purpose, I cannot say. Perhaps Tresslar can—"

"Can do what?" the artificer asked.

Diran and Ghaji turned to see their companions—Leontis included—coming toward them, led by the dwarf first mate. Bartalan Thokk was a typical member of his race: squat, broad-shouldered, powerfully muscled, with a dour countenance hidden behind a full reddish-brown beard that held more than a few flecks of gray. He dressed like the other crewmembers in thick tunic and trousers, boots, and fur-lined cloak with the hood pulled up to further conceal his face. Ghaji noted the absence of jewelry—no rings on the dwarf's fingers, no bracelets or pendants, no ear or nose rings. Dwarves respected hard work and wealth, and they appreciated the finer things life had to offer. They tended to display their wealth by carrying well-made weapons and wearing beautiful jewelry and fine clothes. To dwarves, making a show of one's wealth proved an individual's success and power, though they always kept their greatest treasures hidden from anyone outside their family. But Thokk presented no such display, and Ghaji wondered if that were due to practical reasons—such as the risk of ruining fine clothing while doing shipboard chores—or if there were perhaps another, more personal reason for the dwarf's modest presentation.

Ghaji was about to explain to Tresslar when Diran cut in. "Nothing at the moment, my friend. Something far more important must have prompted you to forsake the warmth of your cabins and join us above deck."

Ghaji saw Tresslar glance toward the *Turnabout's* masts—or more specially, the distortion in the air behind them—and narrow his eyes suspiciously. Ghaji should've known, as Diran obviously had, that the artificer wouldn't need them to alert him to the presence of magic.

Tresslar turned back to Diran. "We're not sure why we're here, but First Mate Thokk was most insistent we accompany him." The artificer sounded even more irritated than usual, and considering how cold it was, Ghaji didn't blame him. The *Turnabout's* cabins weren't the most comfortable of accommodations, but they beat standing on deck exposed to the frigid wind."

Ghaji looked to Solus. The psiforged wore a fur cloak like the others, though Ghaji doubted he even felt the cold, let alone was bothered by it. Solus could easily discover what Thokk intended simply by reading the dwarf's mind, but as Ghaji had learned after their meeting with Captain Onu last night, the construct had decided not to read anyone's mind without express permission to do so. Ghaji had tried to explain to Solus what an advantage it would be to divine the thoughts of potential adversaries, but the psiforged refused to be persuaded. He said Tresslar had told him it wasn't polite to read people's minds without permission, and that the memories he had inherited from his kalashtar makers concurred. Thus, Solus had decided to stop secretly reading minds, and that was that.

While on one level Ghaji understood and respected Solus's choice, he couldn't help also feeling frustrated. Warforged in general tended to think of right and wrong in a simplistic, cut-and-dried fashion, almost the way a small child might. And since Solus had little experience of the world beyond the interior of Mount Luster, the child analogy was more than apt. As he matured, Solus might eventually come to understand that there were times when good manners needed give way to sheer pragmatism, but that wasn't going to help the rest of the companions now.

It's a good thing Solus is abstaining from sneaking a peek into others' minds, Ghaji thought. The psiforged wouldn't like to know what Ghaji was thinking about him at the moment.

"We've just about put enough distance between ourselves and Kolbyr," the dwarf said in a voice that rumbled like distant earth tremors. "The captain will want to get underway in earnest."

Diran gave Ghaji a questioning look, but the half-orc warrior only shrugged.

Thokk cleared his throat and gestured toward the door of a cabin just off the main deck. He then began speaking in an awkward, stilted manner, as if reciting lines that he'd been forced against his will to memorize. "Ladies and gentlemen, it is both my pleasure and my very great honor to introduce you to your host for this voyage . . . a man known in ports throughout the Principalities as the Master of Maelstroms, the Sage of the Trade Winds, and"—he momentarily lowered his voice to a murmur—"he likes this one best of all: the Lion of the Lhazaar! I give you . . . Captain Onu!"

The cabin door burst open and Onu stepped out onto the deck, highly polished boots thumping on the planking as he walked toward them. No, *strutted* would be a better word. He moved with a swaggering confidence that was so exaggerated it was almost comical. He was dressed in the same uniform he'd been wearing last night, and despite the cold, he wore no cloak for additional protection against the temperature. His captain's uniform was spotless and appeared to have been recently pressed, which was some feat, given that the last time Ghaji had seen the man, he'd been so drunk that he'd spilled ale all over himself.

"Greetings, my friends! Allow me to officially welcome you aboard the *Turnabout*, the finest ship to ever ply the jeweled waters of the Lhazaar!"

Ghaji glanced off the port bow at the murky gray sea. He'd heard many words used to describe the Lhazaar—*harsh, unforgiving, treacherous*—but never *jeweled*.

Diran leaned close to Ghaji. "I see what you mean," he whispered.

"I was privileged to make most of your acquaintances last night at the Ill Wind, but I see there are two fine worthies with us this day that I have not yet had the pleasure of meeting face to face." Onu walked over to Leontis and clapped the grim priest on the shoulder. "Sir Leontis Dellacron, my humble vessel is graced by your presence!"

Leontis bowed his head to acknowledge the captain's welcome, but otherwise didn't respond. If Onu was disappointed by Leontis's lackluster reaction, he gave no sign of it. Grinning broadly, he grabbed the priest's right hand in both of his and shook it vigorously.

Ghaji leaned close to Diran this time. "*Humble* vessel? Didn't he just say she was the finest ship to ply the Lhazaar a moment ago?"

Onu released Leontis's hand and spun around so quickly that Ghaji thought the boisterous mariner might lose his balance and fall to the deck, but he remained upright. Ghaji wondered if Onu's problem was a fondness for strong drink. It would explain his over-enthusiastic manner and why he'd slept in this morning—not to mention his abrupt and at times almost spastic movements. But when the half-orc sniffed the air, he detected no trace of alcohol on Onu, and if the man had been drinking recently, Ghaji would've smelled it.

The captain, near-maniacal grin firmly in place, approached Diran and shook his hand with the same enthusiastic energy as he'd greeted Leontis.

"Diran Bastiaan! To imagine the much-lauded Blade of the Flame stands upon the deck of *my* ship . . . more, that I am at this very moment shaking his hand! It as if I stand in the presence of a legend made flesh!"

Ghaji scowled. "You weren't this excited when you met *me* last night. You know, the half-orc warrior who's Diran's partner? The man who's stood by his side against the forces of darkness and who's saved his life a dozen times over?"

Onu didn't take his gaze off Diran as he responded to Ghaji. "Yes, yes, yes . . . and to be sure, it was a great honor and transcendent joy to meet you as well, Ghaddi."

"That's Gha-*jee.*"

"Of *course* it is! My most sincere apologies!" Onu still didn't take his gaze off Diran, and he continued to shake the priest's hand vigorously, as if it were a small animal he was attempting to throttle.

"The stories I've heard about the two of you . . . To be honest, and I pray that you can both find it in your oh-so-generous hearts to forgive me. I didn't realize that it was *that* Diran who wished to hire the *Turnabout* until after I left the tavern last night. Tell me, is it true what they say? Did you single-handedly end the curse of Kolbyr when no one else had even come close in the last hundred years?"

An expression of embarrassed annoyance crossed Diran's face, and he gently but firmly pulled his hand away from Onu's grasp. "I was happy to play a role in the lifting of the curse, but it was far from an individual effort. Ghaji, Asenka, and Leontis all—"

"Yes, of course, I meant no slight!" Onu said. "But you simply *must* tell me all about it! What was it like? Was the Fury more intense in the presence of the Baroness's firstborn? Did the boy attempt to stop you? How did you manage—?"

Thokk cleared his throat loudly. "Captain, I believe you have something of importance you wish to do . . . something that will help us make better time on our journey?"

Onu looked at Thokk and frowned in momentary confusion, but then his face brightened. "Ah, yes! Of course! Master Thokk, if you would be so kind as to do the honors?"

The dwarf reached beneath his tunic collar and brought out a medallion on a metal chain. It was nothing special—just a misshapen lump of iron, really. But Thokk held it in the palm of his hand with a gentle reverence that suggested it was of great value, at least to him.

"Normally we don't carry passengers," Thokk said. "But the amount of money the Baroness offered was more than enough for us to make an exception in your case. What you're about to see is something . . . private, and all who sign on to the *Turnabout*'s crew swear a magically binding oath never to reveal any of the ship's secrets. This medallion ensures that they'll keep their word. We'll need you to take the same oath before we can proceed any further."

Diran and Ghaji exchanged doubtful looks. Neither was thrilled at the prospect of being bound to an oath of which they knew nothing and, from the expressions on their faces, neither were any of their companions.

"Come now, my friends," Onu said. "It's a mere technicality, but

I'm afraid we *must* insist. Trade secrets an all that, you understand." He gave them all a smile that was at once apologetic and reassuring.

"And what happens if we decline?" Diran asked.

"Nothing," Thokk said. "We will continue on our present heading to Trebaz Sinara." The dwarf paused meaningfully. "At our present speed."

"Which means we won't arrive for eight days," Ghaji said.

Neither Onu nor Thokk said anything more. The dwarf continued holding the iron medallion in the palm of his hand, waiting for them to make up their minds.

"I swear," Solus said.

Light glittered across the gray surface of the medallion as its magic bound the psiforged to his oath.

"Do you know something we don't?" Tresslar asked the psiforged.

Solus's artificial face was incapable of expression, but one of his green eyes momentarily went black before returning to its normal color.

Ghaji had to fight to keep from grinning. Had Solus just *winked?* Perhaps the psiforged had decided to make an exception to his no mind-reading rule.

Hinto was the next to swear. "If Solus thinks it's safe, then I do, too."

That was enough. The medallion glittered as the halfling's oath was accepted.

The rest of the companions swore in turn: Tresslar, Yvka, Asenka, Leontis, Diran and, with much reluctance, Ghaji.

Satisfied, Thokk tucked the medallion back into his tunic. He then spoke in a language Ghaji recognized as Dwarven, though he didn't understand the words. The distortion in the air behind the three masts grew more pronounced, and then three towers appeared, atop of each a large metal circle. Ghaji recognized them as containment rings, through much larger than the one aboard the *Zephyr*.

"This is an elemental galleon!" Tresslar said. "No wonder your ship has a reputation for being fast. I assume the runners are visible now as well?"

Thokk said nothing, but Onu answered with his usual enthusiasm. "Everything about the ship's true nature is now visible—to those of us who swore on the Oathbinder, that is. It wouldn't be very practical to have crew and passengers stumbling about on deck, bashing into elemental containment towers and such that they can't see, now would it? Would you like to take a look at the runners? All you have to do is peer over the side. I especially enjoy watching the spray they make when the ship's running at full speed. On a sunny day, you can see little rainbows in the mist. It's quite lovely!"

Thokk scowled and Onu looked suddenly embarrassed. "But I suppose it's too cloudy today, isn't it?"

"The illusion spells cloaking the containment towers aren't bad," Tresslar said, "but they won't stand up to scrutiny. I suppose that's why you make anchor so far from the docks: to keep anyone from getting a close look."

"That, and to keep our distance from the Fury," Onu said. "When the curse was still active, that is. It would've been most inconvenient to have our crew suddenly trying to kill one another."

"What I don't understand is why you bother to hide the true nature of your vessel," Asenka said. "You'd get far more business if people knew how fast the Turnabout can travel."

"Perhaps concealing their true speed is what allows them to attract the kind of business they want," Yvka said. She gave Onu and Thokk a meaningful look. "The kind that pays a hefty sum to have cargo transported swiftly and discreetly."

Onu began to open his mouth, but Thokk spoke first, cutting the captain off. "You've paid your fee—or at least Calida has paid for you—and you've sworn your oaths. Now I'll inform our pilots to rouse the elementals, and we'll get well and truly underway. We should reach Trebaz Sinara within two days—perhaps a touch less if the pilots can squeeze a bit more wind out of the elementals. Calida has certainly paid enough for them to try." The dwarf turned to Onu. "If you wouldn't mind coming with me, Captain, I'm sure the pilots will work harder if you offer them some personal encouragement."

"Of course, Bartalan! I'm always delighted to do whatever I can to help keep the crew's spirits high!" Onu turned to Diran. "I insist that all of you join me in my cabin for dinner this evening. It'll be somewhat cramped, but I think we'll be able to manage. And I fully expect you to regail with me with wondrous tales of adventure for as long as the wine holds!" He laughed, clapped Diran on the back so hard that the priest staggered forward from the impact, and then Onu followed Thokk and the two began to make their way over to the closest containment tower, the captain talking loudly the entire way, and the first mate pointedly ignoring him.

Diran watched them go. "They're an odd pair. And before you say anything, Ghaji, I know others have spoken the same about you and me. I suspect there's more to their relationship beyond captain and mate, though I have no notion what."

Ghaji looked at Solus. "Do you know?"

The psiforged shook his head. "I limited myself to probing the dwarf's surface thoughts, going deep enough to determine if taking the oath would prove to be a danger to us but no farther. Even so, I sensed some vague background thoughts and emotions . . . enough to make me believe that Diran is correct in his assumption. Just as the true nature of the *Turnabout* was hidden from us, so too is the true nature of Onu and Thokk's relationship."

"I wonder if we'll learn the truth about them," Asenka asked.

"If we do, we won't be able to speak of it to others," Tresslar said. "We are now physically incapable of speaking, writing, or in any way communicating information regarding the *Turnabout* to anyone who is not already bound by the magic of the Oathbinder. And remember what Thokk asked us? To swear that we wouldn't reveal any of the ship's secrets. He didn't limit us to just the one secret, either."

Anger clouded Yvka's delicate features. "You knew that and didn't tell us? Who knows what we might learn about the *Turnabout* and her crew? And we won't be able to *tell* anyone? *Ever?*"

"I'm sure you're employers would've preferred you didn't take the oath," Tresslar said. "But I saw no point in informing the rest of you about the scope of the promise we allowed ourselves to be mystically bound to. I want the Amahau back, and swearing that oath was the only way to ensure that we reach Trebaz Sinara as swiftly as possible. We all had to swear. If even one of us refused, Onu would never have given the command to use the ship's elementals."

Yvka looked as if she'd gladly cut Tresslar's throat right then, but she fell silent. Ghaji knew that as an operative of the Shadow Network, it galled her to be tricked into anything, let alone being tricked into taking a magically-binding oath as broad in scope as this one. Secrets were the Network's stock in trade, but what good were secrets to an operative if she couldn't use them?

Ghaji was about to say something to Yvka, but before he could, the three containment rings flared to life as the pilots seated within the towers activated the spells that woke the air elementals. Gusts of wind blasted forth from the rings to fill the *Turnabout*'s sails, and the galleon leaped forward, the sudden acceleration almost knocking the companions off their feet.

They were on their way to Trebaz Sinara at last.

CHAPTER

THIRTEEN

It shouldn't be long now."

Nathifa stood at the prow of the *Zephyr*, her bloodless white hands gripping the ice-covered railing. She looked eastward into the darkness, toward Trebaz Sinara. Skarm sat in the pilot's seat behind the glowing containment ring, keeping the air elemental active. The barghest, while possessing more stamina than a mortal creature, was on the brink of exhaustion. The magic that controlled the elemental was contained within the pilot's chair itself, but wielding that magic still required the contribution of the pilot's will. Someone trained in using the seat's magic could do so with minimum effort, but Skarm had no such training. Thus the energy drain on the barghest was significant. Not that Nathifa cared what happened to Skarm. All that concerned her was reaching Trebaz Sinara and obtaining the last object she needed to realize her dark dreams—and those of her mistress, of course.

The lich sorceress sensed more than heard Makala approach her from behind. A moment later, the vampire joined Nathifa at the railing.

"Haaken is still sleeping. And before you ask, I didn't take any of his blood . . . much as I might have wanted to."

"I would've known if you'd tried. And I would've punished you."

Makala smiled, as if to show that Nathifa's threat didn't impress her. The vampire was becoming far too bold, and the lich was beginning to regret accepting her as a servant. She reminded herself that Vol sent Makala to her, and that meant the vampire had an important role to play in fulfilling the queen's plan. But Nathifa vowed to continue keeping close watch on the woman, for she had no doubt that Makala was going to attempt some manner of treachery, and sooner rather than later.

"Why does the man sleep so much?" Makala asked. "He's no longer human, but he still seems to possess a human's weaknesses."

"He's no longer *only* human," Nathifa corrected. "He still requires rest, though less than a mortal needs. While you slumbered during the day, Haaken spent several hours practicing his new skills. He's unused to transforming back and forth between his various forms, and he's unaccustomed to the physical exertion of swimming so much."

Letting Haaken swim meant deactivating the air elemental so that he could keep up with the *Zephyr*. Nathifa didn't like slowing down and adding hours to their journey, but Haaken would be useless to her as a servant if he didn't possess at least a minimal mastery of his lycanthropic skills. Nathifa forced herself to view the delay as an investment, though it wasn't easy. She'd bided her time for a hundred years, but now that the culmination of everything she had worked for was finally at hand, she found herself becoming increasingly impatient, almost as if she were a mortal woman again.

She gazed up at the night sky. The cloud cover was light, and the Ring of Siberys was visible off to the south, a luminescent band of golden dragonshards that encircled the world high above the equator. A number of Eberron's twelve moons could be seen as well, four of them full and bright.

Nathifa frowned. Something tickled at the edges of her memory . . . something about full moons and sailing on the Lhazaar. It was a memory from her living days, when she and her two brothers had raided throughout the Principalities. But she couldn't quite—

The moons dimmed and winked out, followed closely by the Ring of Siberys. Nathifa was a lich, and thus couldn't know fear, but she felt something distantly akin to that emotion as she looked up at the black sky.

"The sky's gone dark," Makala said. "Is a storm coming?" The vampire didn't sound afraid, merely curious.

Nathifa struggled to call on more memories from her life as a mortal woman. "It doesn't *feel* like a storm. You can smell a storm coming, even when it's still miles away." Not that she could—her sense of smell had died with her mortal body a century ago. But the vampire's senses were sharp, and Makala should be able to detect a change in the wind's scent.

The wind began to kick up then, almost as if purposefully contradicting Nathifa's words. It gathered strength quickly, and was soon blowing with gale force, the air so cold that even Nathifa's undead flesh could feel it, and for the first time since she'd died, Nathifa shivered.

"It certainly feels like a storm to me!" Makala had to shout to be heard over the roaring of the wind.

"It's worse than that!" Haaken shouted. "It's a Ragestorm!"

The two undead creatures turned to see Haaken approaching. Though the newly reborn lycanthrope wore only the black trunks Nathifa had given him, he appeared unaffected by the wind's icy blast. Nevertheless, the fear he felt was evident in the panicked expression on his face as he gazed up at the blackened sky.

It had been many years since Nathifa had sailed the Lhazaar as a living woman, but she was confident she'd never heard of anything called a Ragestorm. She was about to demand Haaken tell them what he knew, but the lycanthrope spun and headed aft.

"We have to deactivate the elemental!" he shouted over his shoulder as he made his way across the ice-covered deck toward the pilot's seat. Skarm still sat, hand pressed palm down on the control arm of the chair, keeping the air elemental active.

Nathifa felt a surge of anger. Haaken was *her* servant, and she should be giving orders to him, not the other way around. But the man's sailing experience was far more recent than hers, and she decided to trust that he knew what he was doing. She once again looked skyward to see what she might be able to discern about this Ragestorm.

Despite the absence of moon and starlight, Nathifa's undead eyes could see well enough to make out an amorphous, shifting cloud hovering over the *Zephyr*. Some portions of swirling vapor seemed to form suggestions of eyes and mouths—dozens of them. The gale buffeting the sloop blasted down from the cloud, and Nathifa thought the creature—for she was certain the thing, whatever it was, was alive—resembled an air elemental. Or, more accurately, a number of air elementals that had joined together. She sensed malevolence in the cloud, a deep, fierce anger.

"Perhaps we should consider taking shelter in the cabin!" Makala shouted, her voice edged with terror. "Or better yet, the hold!" The vampire, despite her great strength, was having trouble withstanding the force of the Ragestorm. She held onto the handrail for support, gripping it so tight that her fingernails sank into the wood. No doubt she was terrified of being hurled overboard by the gale-force winds, since vampires were weakened by running water. A fast-flowing river was dangerous enough, but the Lhazaar Sea was another degree of peril entirely.

Still, Nathifa ignored Makala's suggestion. The lich hadn't been one to run away from a fight when she was alive, and death hadn't changed that aspect of her personality.

Haaken came stumbling back toward the *Zephyr*'s prow, a terrified Skarm in tow.

"We deactivated the elemental, but I fear we were too late!" Haakan shouted. "The Ragestorm has our scent now, and it won't let go of us until it gets what it wants!"

"And that is . . . ?" Nathifa asked.

Haaken kept his eyes on the roiling cloud above them as he answered. "A Ragestorm is a group of air elementals that were once bound in containment rings on sailing vessels or airships. During the Last War, when elemental vessels were damaged in battle and their air elementals were released, sometimes they merged into a single creature. I'm not sure why—something to do with the release of the magic within the containment rings themselves. Once a Ragestorm is created, its only purpose is to seek out other bound elementals of its kind, free them, and absorb them into its mass, growing larger and stronger. The Ragestorm sensed our air elemental and was drawn to our ship. But though we shut down our containment ring, the storm knows we have an air elemental onboard, and it won't leave until it's absorbed it!"

Nathifa looked back up at the Ragestorm with renewed interest and pondered what, if anything, her magic might be able to do to drive the creature off, if not destroy it altogether. Elementals of any stripe were notoriously hard to work with, and it required a high degree of mystic finesse and skill to deal with them. Nathifa had no training in the handling of elementals, and very little practical experience to drawn on. She wished she had Espial with her, but the obsidian skull that allowed her to hear her mistress's voice was inside the cabin, and she feared there wasn't time to retrieve it. She would've liked to consult her goddess on the best way to deal with the Ragestorm. But then, Vol preferred to help those who helped themselves.

The wind increased until it felt as if claws of ice raked their flesh. Nathifa could feel a column of air surround her, and a quick glance told her the others were experiencing the same thing. The Ragestorm was reaching out with invisible hands and grabbing hold of each of them. She felt air spinning rapidly around her, pressing inward with each revolution. The Ragestorm was attempting to crush them. Accompanying the sensation of increasing pressure was a feeling of movement, as if Nathifa were being lifted upward by the small whirl-wind that had taken hold of her. But her feet remained on the *Zephyr*'s deck, as did the others'. She was puzzled for a moment until she realized that they *were* being lifted upward because the *ship* itself was rising. The Ragestorm had grasped the sloop within its winds and was bearing the craft aloft, most likely intending to dash the *Zephyr* back into the sea, cracking the ship open like an egg, destroying the containment ring, and releasing its trapped brother. Voices shrieked in the wind, screaming rage in a language Nathifa didn't recognize, though she was able to divine the basic meaning from the tone.

You hunt us . . .

. . . capture us, enslave us . . .

Now it is we who hunt you . . .

You shall pay for what you've done to us, what you've done to our brother . . .

Nathifa knew that she had only seconds to act to prevent the Ragestorm from ruining everything she had worked so long and hard for, had sacrificed so much for . . .

She knew only a little about elementals, but from what Haaken had said, the release of mystic energy which occurred when the containment rings were destroyed acted as a binding agent of some sort, fusing the elementals and holding them together. But if a different sort of mystic energy were introduced into the mix, perhaps the binding agent could be disrupted.

You shall pay . . .

. . . pay, pay, pay!

The column of whirling air that pressed against her like the squeezing hand of an invisible giant prevented her from filling her lungs, and without enough air to speak, she couldn't use any spells that required a spoken component. And since her arms were pinned to her sides by the Ragestorm, the same went for spells that needed mystic gestures. That severely limited her options. If only she held the Amahau . . . but no, she'd left it back in the cabin. For safekeeping, of all things.

PAY, PAY, PAY!

She felt her ribs beginning to crack under the pressure the Ragestorm applied, and though she experienced no pain, she didn't relish the idea of being an undead ragdoll, her body crushed to the point of uselessness. With no time left, she chose to forego subtlety in favor of sheer power. She concentrated on gathering the necromantic energies at the core of her foul being—the dark power that dwelled where her mortal lifeforce once had—and using only the power of her will, she thrust the energy toward what she sensed was the heart of the elemental conglomerate that held them and their ship in its grasp.

A bolt of crackling ebon energy lanced forth from Nathifa's forehead and streaked into what she judged was the center of the creature—though in truth, she had no idea if this thing even *had* a center. The voices of the Ragestorm raised in pitched and took on an edge of desperation as the necromantic energy she'd released began to eat away at the ties binding the air elementals to one another.

No, you mustn't!

Stop . . . please!

We beg you!

"You want me to stop? Fine!" Nathifa shouted into the wind. "Release us and be on your way! Otherwise, I'll keep attacking, and you'll be *forced* to let us go!"

The shrieking stopped and the wind's anger abated somewhat, though it didn't entirely vanish. The *Zephyr* remained aloft, though Nathifa had no idea how high above the sea she hovered. Nathifa had the impression the Ragestorm had paused in its attack and was trying to decide its next move.

They didn't have long to wait.

The wind ceased, and the *Zephyr*—possessing all the aerodynamic properties of a large boulder—plunged to the waiting sea below. The sloop hit the water, sending up great plumes of seaspray. The whirling column of air that had held Nathifa withdrew, and when the *Zephyr* struck the surface, the lich was knocked off her feet. Before she could stand, a wave washed over the rail, engulfed her, and carried her away.

* * * * * * *

Nathifa had been bobbing on the surface of the Lhazaar for only a short time before she saw a dorsal fin slicing through the water toward her. As it drew close the shark slowed and turned its side to her. The lich took hold of the creature's dorsal fin, and the shark began swimming with powerful strokes of its tail. Within moments, they were in sight of the *Zephyr*—or at least what was left of her. The vessel was still afloat, but she listed to starboard and a set of runners was missing. The shark brought Nathifa up to the sloop's hull, and the lich let go of the creature's fin and, using her own magic, levitated up and over the ship's railing. Once her feet touched the deck, she took hold of the railing behind her to steady herself. She wasn't about to waste something as precious as magic energy to help her keep her footing on a canted deck.

A moment later, a humanoid shark climbed over the railing and joined Nathifa. The creature's facial features began to soften, and its eyes became less cold. Soon, a nearly naked Haaken stood next to the undead sorceress, also gripping the railing to keep from sliding on the slanted deck.

"I thank you for coming to my aid, Haaken." The words were as sawdust in her mouth. She wasn't used to needing help, and she was even less used to thanking anyone. She glanced around, searching for Makala and Skarm. She found the latter in his barghest form clinging to the mast, fur soaked and body trembling with fright. As for Makala . . .

A black-winged bat swooped down from above and circled the lich and the wereshark once before transforming into Makala. The vampire smiled weakly.

"All present and accounted for," she said, her voice tinged with weariness. It was clear to Nathifa that it had taken a great deal of strength for Makala to resist the energy-draining power of the Lhazaar. But resist she had, if only just.

Nathifa gazed skyward and was pleased to see the moons and stars once more. She didn't know whether she'd destroyed the Ragestorm or merely driven it off. Either way, she was glad the damned thing was gone.

She turned to Haaken. "How bad is the damage?"

"Bad enough. When I was underwater, I swam around the *Zephyr* to get a good look. We lost the starboard runner, which is why the ship is listing so badly. There are no leaks as yet, but the hull's been weakened in a number of places. Even if we shore up the weak spots by spreading pitch on them, it's only a matter of time before we start taking on water. The mast and sails look fine, and the containment ring seems undamaged. We'll have to check, but I don't think the Ragestorm was able to absorb the ship's elemental. Not that it matters. We can't travel at top speed without both runners, and even if we could somehow fashion a new starboard runner, the hull wouldn't be able to withstand the stress of traveling that fast. We can remove the port runner so that we can sail by natural wind power alone, but our speed will be greatly diminished."

"I don't want to spend any more time at sea than necessary," Makala growled. "My sarcophagus survived the *Zephyr*'s fall. It slid about and damaged the starboard rail, but at least it didn't break through and sink to the bottom of Lhazaar. I have a place to rest during the day, but I still don't have a source of nourishment." She shot Nathifa a quick glare. "None that I'm permitted to avail myself of, anyway. The sooner we make landfall, the better as far as my thirst is concerned. But my own selfish considerations aside, we aren't in any hurry, are we? Trebaz Sinara will still be waiting for us whether we arrive in one day or a half dozen."

"And when we reach the island, we should be able to find the materials needed to repair the *Zephyr*," Haaken said. "We can't make her as good as new without a supply of soarwood, but we can get her strong enough to withstand the force of the air elemental again."

Normally, her servants' logic would've swayed Nathifa. After all, what were a few more days after all the time she'd already waited to see her vengeance finally done? But there was something she hadn't shared with Makala and Haaken yet—something she had learned earlier when she'd been alone in the cabin listening to the whispers of Espial.

"We cannot afford any delay," the lich said. "The priest and his companions have learned of our destination, and they have acquired transport upon an elemental galleon. Even now they speed toward us, coming closer with each passing second."

Makala laughed. "I'm not surprised. Diran may have been foolish enough to ally himself with the so-called Purified, but he's as much as a hunter as any of us. He'll never stop, not so long as breath remains in his body."

Nathifa gave the vampire an appraising look. "You sound as if you still love him."

Makala opened her mouth and displayed her fangs. "I'd love to sink my teeth into his neck, if that's what you mean."

Nathifa wondered if the evil that infested Makala's soul didn't have quite the firm foothold that she'd originally thought. If so, it was a useful thing to know. Nathifa might be able to use that against Makala should the need arise.

When the need arose, the lich amended.

"Unless you know a spell that can repair a damaged sloop, I'm afraid we're not going anywhere fast anytime soon," Haaken said.

Nathifa looked up at the sky, noted the four full moons, and remembered at last what they signified.

"I just may," she said.

* * * ◉ * * *

Nathifa stood alone at the *Zephyr's* slanted prow, Espial tucked beneath one arm. Her servants had locked themselves in the cabin as she had ordered. Not only didn't she wish them to interfere in what was to take place, they would be safer there. She hoped.

She rubbed chalk-white fingers across the smooth surface of the skull's glossy obsidian pate, her gaze fixed on the eastern horizon. It was well past midnight, but dawn was still some hours away. Nathifa was a creature of darkness, but right now she would've preferred to see at least a hint of coming sunlight in the distance.

It's not too late to change your mind, she told herself. But of course it was. She'd sent the summons. The ship would come, and no power on Eberron could stop it now.

Was she really willing to make the terrible bargain she had in mind? Perhaps it would be better to remove the remaining runner and sail without the aid of the *Zephyr's* bound air elemental. What did it matter that the priest and his companions would catch up to them? Nathifa and her servants were powerful. Diran Bastiaan and the others wouldn't stand a chance against them. There was no need to make the deal she was contemplating.

But of course there was. She'd only faced Bastiaan once, in her lair located in the hills beyond Perhata, but that had been enough for her to take the man's measure. Power ran strong in him—far stronger than anyone Nathifa had ever encountered before. She sensed darkness in the man's soul as well, and she wondered if his knowledge of darkness, instead of weakening the good in him, actually strengthened it. It was a disturbing thought, for if a man like Diran Bastiaan could learn to let go of his past, what did that mean for a creature like her? Could she, like Bastiaan, step off her path and decide to walk another, even after all this time?

She shook her head and cursed herself for a fool. Her brother Kolbyr had wronged her grievously, had wronged her child by not giving him the chance to be Kolbyr's heir. And even though Kolbyr had long ago gone to his grave, she couldn't bear to allow his name to live on through his descendants . . . descendents who ruled a city bearing her brother's very name! She'd sacrificed so much in the name of vengeance: long years spent studying fell sorcery, pledging herself to the service of the Lich Queen, surrendering her mortal life so that she might become a lich and live long enough to see her vengeance fulfilled at last. If she turned aside from her path now, all her work, all her sacrifices would be wasted.

And her thrice-hated brother would win in the end. That, more than anything else, she simply could not bear. She would walk her chosen path to the bloody end, regardless of the cost. No price was too high to finally see her vengeance done.

And then, as if in response to her thoughts, a wall of greenish mist rolled in from the east, heralding the arrival of the *Ship of Bones*.

The dread vessel slid forth from the mist in complete silence—no splashing of water against its hull, no flapping of sails or creaking of rigging. In fact, the ship seemed to swallow all sound, for Nathifa could no longer hear the wind or the waves, or even the dry rasp of her hand as she rubbed Espial for whatever cold comfort the mystic object could give. The green mist reached the *Zephyr* and rolled across the sloop's deck, bringing with it a cold more intense than that of even the most frigid winter nights on the Lhazaar, for this was a cold that affected not the body, but the spirit.

Like all born and raised in the Principalities, Nathifa grew up hearing the legend of Prince Moren and his *Ship of Bones*. An evil man cursed for his misdeeds in life, Moren was doomed to sail the Lhazaar Sea with a crew of undead pirates in search of living sailors upon which to feed. As the tales would have it, on nights when two or more moons were full, the *Ship of Bones* silently sailed the dark waters of the night searching for any vessels unfortunate enough to cross its path. Although in this instance, Moren found the *Zephyr* because

Nathifa had summoned him.

Nathifa had always wondered what the *Ship of Bones* would look like. Was it just a name to inspire fear or was the vessel truly constructed from bone instead of iron and wood? She now knew it was the latter.

The hull was made from the curving rib bones of some enormous creature—a dragon, perhaps, though one larger than any Nathifa had ever heard of. The ship's three masts were formed from massive leg bones that appeared human, save for their great size. Giant bones, Nathifa guessed, but from giants larger than any she'd ever dreamed could exist. The sails were fashioned from sewn-together patches of leathery skin, torn from the bodies of Moren's victims, she wagered, most likely while they were still alive and screaming in agony. At least, that's how she would've done it. The bones were lashed together with strips of flesh, lengths of muscle, strands of sinew, and coils of intestines. It was, in its own dark way, magnificent.

Nathifa could see none of the crew as the *Ship of Bones* drew alongside the *Zephyr*, but she knew they were there. She could sense them watching her with curiosity, wondering who this madwoman was who was suicidal enough to summon the Prince of Bones and his deathly crew.

A gangplank made from interlocking arm and hand bones was lowered over the side, and a pair of skeletal hands on the end grabbed hold of the *Zephyr*'s railing. Nathifa waited to see if any of Moren's crew would disembark, but when none did, she knew they were waiting for her to board their ship. After all, hadn't *she* summoned *them?*

Rubbing the top of Espial's head once more for luck, Nathifa stepped up onto the skeletal ramp and began walking upward.

❧ ❧ ❧ ❧ ❧ ❧ ❧

"How long has she been over there?" Haaken asked.

Makala peered through the porthole of the *Zephyr*'s cabin. She could see no sign of activity aboard the *Ship of Bones*. It was as if the vessel was deserted, a thing possessed of its own unearthly life that plied the waters of the Lhazaar without need of a crew. But she knew Nathifa was aboard, had seen the lich embark.

"The better part of an hour, I'd say. Whatever they're talking about, they're evidently in no hurry."

"Time doesn't mean the same thing to the dead as it does to the living," Skarm said. Then, realizing who he was talking to, he added, "No offense."

Makala considered backhanding the barghest, but she restrained herself. Depending on how Nathifa's meeting with Prince Moren turned out, they might well end up having to fight for their lives. If so, she wanted Skarm uninjured and ready for battle.

Haaken sat cross-legged on the sleeping pallet, face pale, eyes haunted. "Do you think they're . . . going to *eat* us?"

Makala turned to the lycanthropic sea raider and sneered. "Depends on whether or not they like the taste of fish."

Any reply Haaken might have made was cut off by a knock on the cabin hatch. Both Haaken and Skarm jumped, but Makala just looked at the hatch for a moment with a narrow-eyed gaze before starting toward it.

Haaken leaped off the pallet, rushed to Makala, and grabbed hold of her arm to stop her. "Are you mad? If you let them in they'll devour us!"

Makala bared her fangs, hissed, and slashed Haaken's face with claw-like fingernails. Haaken released her arm and staggered backward, blood pouring from wounds that were already beginning to heal. Makala inhaled, savoring the scent of fresh blood, and it took every bit of self-control she possessed not to fall upon the man, tear out his throat, and gorge herself on his life's fluid.

"Don't be an idiot," she snarled. "If Prince Moren and his crew had come for us, do you really think they would bother to knock?"

Makala continued to the hatch and opened it. She stepped back as Nathifa glided into the cabin. The lich's face—normally bleached of all color—looked even whiter than usual, and the crimson fire that burned in her eyes had dimmed to the point where it seemed as if it might go out altogether.

"It's done. We have what we need to repair the ship. Begin

working. I . . . need to rest for a bit."

Without another word, the lich crossed over to the sleeping pallet and lay down with her back to her three servants.

Makala looked at Skarm and Haaken with a raised eyebrow before walking out of the cabin and onto the deck of the *Zephyr*. The *Ship of Bones* was gone, and there was no sign of her in any direction, even though the ghostly craft couldn't have sailed very far away in the time since Nathifa had disembarked. It was as if the ship had simply vanished. A pile of lumber lay on the deck, along with a new runner . . . no, it was the *Zephyr*'s runner, recovered and returned to them. The planking was mismatched—the boards different types of wood, along with varying widths, and lengths—and the lumber was wet, covered with moss and barnacles.

"They salvaged the wood from shipwrecks," Haaken said softly.

Makala hadn't noticed the man's approach. Skarm stood next to him, and all three of them stared at the lumber left by Prince Moren.

"What price do you think Nathifa had to pay to get that wood?" Skarm asked.

"I don't know," Makala said. "But I can tell you one thing: when she went aboard the *Ship of Bones* she had Espial with her, but she returned empty-handed." She glanced up at the night sky to gauge the time, though she had no real need to do so since her vampiric instincts told her how long it would be until sunrise. "We still have a few hours of darkness left to us. Let's get to work."

As Haaken and Skarm started toward the lumber, Makala glanced back at the *Zephyr*'s cabin.

What price indeed? she thought, and wondered how she might be able to turn this most recent development to her advantage. Then she joined the others to begin the repairs to the *Zephyr*.

CHAPTER

FOURTEEN

Thokk was as good as his word, and the *Turnabout* reached the northeastern shore of Trebaz Sinara a bit less than two days after they'd set out. The sun had edged up over the horizon, and the sky was a bright, clear blue with barely a cloud in sight. Despite the beauty of the dawning day, the island was as forbidding as legend painted it, surrounded by treacherous reefs and enclosed by high, sheer cliff walls. Off in the distance, a flock of winged creatures circled lazily above the island. Birds, perhaps, or something else. They were too far away to tell for certain.

Captain Onu stood at the ship's rail, gazing out upon the island, eyes shining as if its cliffs were made of gold instead of stone.

"Trebaz Sinara," he breathed. "How I've longed to look upon its fabled shores!"

Thokk stood at the railing next to his captain. The dwarf had summoned Diran, Ghaji, and the others to the deck when Trebaz Sinara had first come into view, and the companions stood at the railing alongside the *Turnabout*'s master.

"If we don't drop anchor soon, we may well run aground on those shores," Thokk said.

"Hmm? Oh, yes, of course. Give the order if you would, Master Thokk."

The first mate signaled to a crewman and the ship's anchor was released.

"Those reefs are like a maze," Ghaji said. He turned to Tresslar. "Are you sure you remember the route through? It *has* been forty years since you were here last."

The artificer glared at the half-orc. "Assuming that the visions the demon revealed to Diran are true—and I haven't the faintest idea why the lich would want to go to the dragon's cave where I discovered the Amahau—I'll be able to get us there. My memory's as sharp as it ever was. I may be hazy on one or two minor details, I'll admit, but once we get started I'm sure it'll all come back to me."

Hinto groaned. "We'll be scuttled before we're halfway through!"

Tresslar started to protest, but Diran laid a gentle hand on the artificer's shoulder to silence him. "I've been giving the matter some thought, and we shouldn't have to rely solely on Tresslar's recall—as strong as it is, I'm sure. Assuming Nathifa and the others made it here before us—"

"Which they almost certainly did," Asenka put in.

"Then once we're on the island, Tresslar should be able to locate the dragonwand using another of his mystical devices. Isn't that right?"

The artificer nodded. "*If* the lich brought the Amahau onto the island with her."

"Would *you* leave such a valuable artifact behind on your ship?" Yvka asked.

"Good point," Tresslar said. "In that case, as long as we're within several miles of the Amahau, I'll be able to detect it." He reached around into his backpack and withdrew one of his homemade magical devices: a metal ring attached to a wooden handle. "I've modified my revealer to sense the unique energy signature of the Amahau." He gripped the tool by the handle and held it out in front of him. Several seconds passed, but nothing happened. Obviously disappointed, but trying to hide it, Tresslar returned the device to his backpack. "As I said, the range *is* somewhat limited. Nathifa and the others might be too far inland, and even if they aren't, those cliffs are likely interfering with any signals I might pick up. We'll need to get closer."

"But if we can't maneuver through those reefs . . ." Hinto said.

"That's where Solus comes in," Diran said, turning to the psi-forged. "Can you use your psionic abilities to strengthen Tresslar's memory of the proper route through the reefs?"

"Yes," Solus said. "But I can do better than merely strengthen Tresslar's recollection. Once I locate the memory, I can reproduce it and transfer it into each of your minds. That way, we shall all know the route in case something should happen." No one said anything for a moment, and the psiforged added, "Trebaz Sinara *is* reputed to be a dangerous place, is it not? I wish no harm to Tresslar, but we should prepare for all possibilities."

Yvka nodded appreciatively. "Quite sensible."

"An unnecessary precaution," Tresslar said, "as I am quite capable of taking care of myself, but I see no harm in it. What do I need to do?"

"Just come off to the side with me for a few moments," Solus said. "There will be little discomfort, and the procedure won't take long. After we're done, if each of you would come over to me one by one, I'll implant the route into your minds."

Tresslar and Solus walked off several yards, and the psiforged told the artificer to close his eyes. The construct then gently placed his three-fingered stone hands on the sides of Tresslar's head, and his artificial eyes glowed bright green as the memory transference began.

"I'll have a longboat prepared for you," Thokk said, "along with enough food and water for several days. If you're on the island longer than that . . ." The dwarf trailed off, leaving the rest of the thought unspoken, though it was clear enough. If Diran and the others remained on Trebaz Sinara that long, they were probably dead.

Onu frowned. "You speak as if our friends are going to be making landfall on their own, but surely we're going with them!"

Thokk stared at the *Turnabout*'s captain with shock, as if the man had suddenly sprouted a second head.

Onu made a grand gesture in the island's direction. "It's *Trebaz Sinara*, Thokk! According to legend, it holds the wealth of two thousand years of pirate raids! Gold! Dragonshards! Priceless relics!

Treasures beyond imagining and number! You can't expect me to stay onboard, lean on the rail, and be content to just *look* at the island!"

Thokk's face reddened with frustration. "It's too dangerous, *Captain!* I don't care how much treasure may be waiting for us there, it won't do us any good if we're dead!"

For the first time since Diran and the others had met Onu, the captain's good humor deserted him and his expression clouded over with anger. "Bartalan Thokk—ever the hard-headed businessman without even the most minimal sense of adventure. Well, I *am* the captain of this ship, and I *am* going to accompany these good worthies on their journey . . . unless, of course, you have anything more to say about the matter, *First Mate* Thokk?"

The dwarf's jaw muscles tightened, and his hands clenched into white-knuckled fists.

"No . . . *Captain!*" With that, Thokk spun around and stalked off to see to the preparation of the longboat.

Onu turned to Diran and the others and gave them an apologetic smile. "Forgive me. Thokk is a good man, and I couldn't do without him, but sometimes he oversteps his bounds and needs his leash yanked. You understand." The captain then turned back to the railing and gazed across the water at the fabled island of Trebaz Sinara.

Diran and Ghaji exchanged glances. They understood, all right. They understood that there was far more going on between Onu and Thokk than first met the eye. The question was whether or not their problems were going to interfere with the mission to retrieve Tresslar's dragonwand, and whether that interference would prove a distraction at the wrong time, resulting in disaster for the landing party—or even death.

❧ ❧ ❧ ❧ ❧ ❧ ❧

Ghaji was almost disappointed by how uneventful the passage through the twisting barrier maze of reef was. Thanks to Solus, they all knew the route, so there were no surprises there, and since the psiforged used his telekinetic abilities to move and steer the longboat, there was nothing for any of them to do but sit and enjoy the ride. Trebaz Sinara was reputed to be home to all manner of terrible monsters, and the companions kept close watch as they drew closer to the island, but no ravening creatures burst out of the sea to devour them. Ghaji wasn't foolish enough to believe that meant they were safe, though, and he continually scanned their surroundings for any sign of danger, elemental axe held at the ready.

Tresslar sat in the prow of the boat, revealer held out in front of him, slowly moving it back and forth through the air. Ghaji didn't know what the magical device would do once it detected the dragonwand—make some sort of sound, emit a burst of light—but it did nothing. Either it was failing to function properly, or the dragonwand was out of range, assuming it was even on the island at all.

Hinto sat next to Solus in the back of the longboat, the halfling occasionally reaching out to pat the psiforged's hand. The little pirate looked afraid, but he seemed to be handling it well enough. He'd come a long way since they'd found him shipwrecked in the Mire. No longer did he experience paralyzing bouts of panic. But then again, he'd never faced the sort of dangers that Trebaz Sinara held, and Ghaji wondered if the halfling would be able to manage his fear once they made landfall.

Asenka sat next to Diran in the middle of the longboat, close enough that their knees were touching. Despite the situation, she appeared happy and content, and though it might have seemed incongruous to some given what they would soon be facing, it didn't to Ghaji. He'd been a warrior all of his life, and he knew the importance of appreciating the good moments in life as they came, for those moments were often all too brief and the future uncertain. The orcs had a saying: *Live today and let tomorrow take care of itself.* It seemed Asenka had decided to do just that.

Ghaji and Yvka sat behind Diran and Asenka, the elf-woman's hand resting lightly on the half-orc's leg. Yvka leaned forward, eyes wide, taking everything in, working to memorize every detail so that she could make a full report to her "associates" in the Shadow Network. Ghaji knew she was also keeping a sharp eye out for anything—treasure, magical artifacts, rare plants or animals—that she might be able to claim and take back to her people. When he'd first met the elf-woman in Port Verge, when Diran and he had been working to unravel the mystery of the Black Fleet, he'd been instantly attracted to Yvka's free spirit and love of adventure. But in the months since then, he'd come to know another side of her. She could be calculating and opportunistic, qualities that admittedly served her well in her profession, but which made it difficult to remain emotionally close to her. At times like these, he couldn't help wondering if Yvka was with him because she truly cared about him or because she'd found their relationship advantageous to her career. Thanks to her association with Ghaji, she'd been able to turn over both Erdis Cai's stronghold of Grimwall and the psi-forge facility in Mount Luster to the Shadow Network. Though he knew he should work harder to trust her, he couldn't help wondering which Yvka loved more: him or the professional opportunities their relationship afforded her.

Leontis sat in the back of the boat in front of Solus and Hinto. Ghaji had never expected to encounter a Silver Flame priest as grim as Diran could sometimes be, but Leontis was that man. He held his longbow with an arrow nocked, prepared for whatever danger might threaten, but he stared straight ahead, eyes focused on a point far more distant than the island looming before them. Ghaji had seen similar looks in the eyes of warriors who had witnessed so much blood and cruelty on the battlefield that they no longer believed life was worth living and were merely marking time until Death finally came for them.

None of the companions, Ghaji included, felt comfortable around Leontis, but they accepted his presence because Diran vouched for him. They'd all tried speaking with the priest at one time or another during the voyage from Kolbyr, and though Leontis had responded to their overtures, he had always done so briefly and without enthusiasm, and before long even the ever-curious Hinto gave up.

Ghaji didn't like heading into an almost certainly dangerous situation with a man he didn't know well enough to trust. He hoped Diran knew what he was doing. So far, the priest had never steered

Ghaji wrong, but Diran was only human, and could make a mistake as easily as any other man.

Onu and Thokk sat behind Tresslar. The captain continued to wear his garish regalia, despite the fact that his red longcoat made for a very effective target. Thokk had attempted to explain this to Onu before they'd lowered the longboat and departed the *Turnabout*, but the captain had refused to listen. Onu grinned like an excited child as the longboat slowly wound its way through the reef maze, bringing them ever closer to Trebaz Sinara. When Ghaji had first met Onu, he'd thought the man eccentric. Now he was beginning to wonder if the sea captain was in truth insane. Thokk certainly seemed to think so. The dwarf sat with his arms crossed, brow furrowed in a scowl, occasionally shooting dirty looks at Onu and grinding his teeth in frustration. Ghaji had no idea why the dwarf continued to serve as Onu's first mate if the man upset him so much. Perhaps in his own way, Thokk was just as mad as Onu.

Diran's face was impassive, only the slightest crinkling of his brow giving any indication that he was anything but relaxed and calm. But Ghaji knew his friend well, and he was certain Diran was running one scenario after another through his mind: debating strategies, calculating odds, anticipating problems, and exploring alternatives. *Careful preparation is the assassin's greatest weapon,* Diran had once told him. But Ghaji knew Diran wasn't making his plans dispassionately. He understood the risks they were all taking to recover Tresslar's dragonwand and prevent the terrible visions revealed by the Fury-demon from becoming reality. The priest wanted to make certain he had done everything within his power to ensure the safety of his companions, and so he continued to think, plan, and plot, and he would keep doing so until the time came for action. And when that time arrived, Diran would act swiftly, confidently, and—if the situation called for it—utterly without mercy.

As for Ghaji . . . well, he wasn't anticipating their landfall with the insane glee that Onu was, but he had to admit that he *was* curious to see if Trebaz Sinara lived up to its fearsome reputation. So far, it had been something of a letdown. He'd expected—

The twang of a bowstring vibrated through the air, and out of the corner of his eyes, Ghaji saw the shaft of an arrow blur by as it flew skyward. A second later, came the sound of the arrow striking something meaty with a dull *thwok!* followed by an ear-splitting screech of pain. Ghaji looked up in time to see a monstrous winged lizard that looked something like a wyvern with the head of a jungle cat come spiraling downward, Leontis's arrow buried in its heart. The creature was easily the size of the longboat, and when the thing struck the reef on their port side, the rock cracked and partially crumbled. The beast ended up laying half in, half out of the water, eyes wide and staring, forked tongue lolling out of the corner of its mouth.

Everyone in the longboat, including Onu and Thokk, turned to look at Leontis. The dour priest already had a second arrow nocked, its point trained on the cat-headed lizard, just in case the thing turned out not to be quite as dead as it appeared.

"My apologies if I startled you," Leontis said, never taking his gaze off the cat-head. "But the beast was flying a little too close to our vessel for my liking."

Ghaji noticed Diran staring intensely at Leontis, and for a moment, the half-orc couldn't figure out why. Then he realized: Leontis' beard had grown fuller, his eyebrows bushier, the hair on the back of hands more pronounced. A feral gleam had come into his eyes, and—though Ghaji thought this last might just be his imagination—Leontis's teeth seemed sharper.

After that everyone kept a closer watch, especially on the sky, as Solus continued using his mental powers to pilot the longboat through the reef-maze toward whatever dangers awaited them on Trebaz Sinara. Everyone except Ghaji, that is.

He watched Leontis.

❂ ❂ ❂ ❂ ❂ ❂ ❂

Even with Solus's expert guidance, the longboat took several hours to maneuver through the reef-maze, and it was late afternoon by the time they reached a secluded, shadowy cove. Diran had hoped they might find the *Zephyr* anchored here waiting for them, but the cove was deserted. The lich had likely moored the elemental sloop elsewhere. They reached shore, disembarked, drew weapons, and scanned their surroundings, alert for the least sign of danger. While the others kept guard, Solus employed his telekinesis to pull the longboat onto the rocky beach, tie the craft down, and secure it with rope lashed to pitons.

"You keep that up, Solus, and we'll start getting fat from all the exercise we'll miss," Ghaji joked.

It was difficult to interpret warforged body language, but from the way Solus thrust his arms down stiffly at his sides—not to mention the way the psionic crystals embedded into his stonework began to flicker erratically—Diran guessed that the construct was upset.

"I did not mean to deprive you of the opportunity to maintain good health," Solus said. "As I am a construct, I have some difficult understanding the physiological needs of others."

Hinto glared at Ghaji. "Don't let the green-faced blowhard upset you, friend. He's just making a joke at your expense."

Solus looked at Ghaji for a moment, and Diran feared the psiforged might use his mental abilities to take some manner of revenge. But then a strange noise issued from the construct's throat, a combination coughing and choking sound.

"By the gods!" Onu said. "I do believe your stone and metal friend is attempting to laugh!"

Solus stopped. "That is the proper response to a joke, is it not?"

Diran smiled. "Yes, my friend. It is."

Solus nodded in satisfaction. "Good. But there is little ambient psionic energy in the area for me to strengthen my crystals. I will therefore need to be cautious in expending what energy remains to me." The psiforged looked at Ghaji. "I'm afraid you will get more opportunities for exercise, my friend."

The companions laughed, and Ghaji gave Solus a friendly slap on the back. Diran then turned to examine their surroundings. Craggy black stone covered the shoreline, giving way to dirty-white sand a dozen yards inland, and beyond that a thick forest. The trees were a strange mixture. Some, such as fir, ash, oak, evergreen, and elm, were common to the Principalities and their presence on the island came as no surprise. But other trees—palm trees, orange blossoms, and cyprus—rightfully belonged to far warmer climates. And even though winter was drawing closer by the day, the warmland trees looked as robust and healthy as their Lhazaar counterparts.

"Is this how you remember the area?" Diran asked Tresslar.

The artificer nodded. "It was a patchwork conglomeration of different landscapes and flora, just like this. While I don't recall this cove specifically, since Solus ransacked my memory for the directions to get here, I'm confident this is the location where we made landfall. I remember Erdis leading us into a forest." Tresslar pointed toward the treeline. "That one, I suppose."

"That is what your memories showed me," Solus said. "But time and emotion can color one's recollections, rearranging them, blocking unpleasant details, or re-interpreting them so they seem better or worse. I did my best to sort out truth from misremembered half-truths and outright distortions, but . . ." The psiforged trailed off with a very humanlike shrug.

"We understand," Diran said. "We shall go cautiously and assume nothing." The priest took a quick inventory of the group. All wore backpacks containing food and water, among other supplies, and all were armed with their chosen weapons. Diran held a pair of daggers—one steel, one silver—and Ghaji gripped his elemental axe. Asenka had drawn her longsword, and Hinto his long knife. Yvka held no obvious weapons, but Diran knew the pouch hanging from her belt contained various magical items constructed by the devious artificers of the Shadow Network. He'd seen the elf-woman use her devices to devastating effect in the past, and he had no doubt their magic would serve her well again this day, if required. Solus needed no physical weapon, just the power of his mind. Thokk held a mace whose handle was pitted with small concave spaces, as if it had once been encrusted with jewels, The weapon might not be a thing of beauty, but it would still perform its function well enough when wielded with dwarven muscle. Onu's weapon was a light rapier that he kept swishing back and forth through the air as if it were a toy. The captain of the *Turnabout* hadn't removed the tiny metal ball on the rapier's tip used to prevent accidental injury when simply sparring with an opponent. Diran was certain everyone else had noticed as well, but no one had said anything, perhaps having come to the same conclusion as Diran: given Onu's overly enthusiastic personality, everyone might be safer if he left the little metal ball where it was.

Leontis held his longbow with an arrow nocked and ready. Diran's old friend appeared calm enough, but there was a gleam of excitement in his eyes as if he were eager to head off into the forest to begin exploring—or perhaps hunting. Diran hadn't failed to notice the minor transformation Leontis had gone through after slaying the aerial monster earlier—the increased length of his beard and hair, as well as the sharpening of his teeth. Diran had hoped that those feral touches might recede as time passed, but they had remained. It was as if Leontis had held the bestial side of himself in check as long as he could, but the wolf was beginning to fight its way out. Back in the inner courtyard of Kolbyr's palace, Diran had been fully prepared to honor Leontis's request and release him from his curse, much as it would have pained the priest to do so. But he'd remembered the visions the demon had shown to him, especially the image of a wolf's head, its eyes shining with human intelligence. Diran had stayed his hand then, because he realized that Leontis had a role to play in the events to come—though for good or ill, he couldn't say. Now, seeing the first signs of lycanthropic change in his old friend, Diran was beginning to question his decision. Had he once again allowed emotion to cloud his judgment, just as he had with Makala? Would more weight be added to the burden of guilt Diran carried on his shoulders. And if so, how would he ever be able to bear it?

Tresslar held his revealer out before him and slowly moved it from left to right then back again. When he was finished, he lowered the device to his side, a disappointed look on his face.

"No sign of the Amahau yet. Perhaps once we get moving . . ."

Diran nodded. "Then let's be on our way. We have precious little daylight remaining to us, and we shouldn't waste it."

The companions set off toward the forest in single file. Ghaji took the lead, with Diran right behind him. Asenka came next, with Tresslar after that, periodically holding up the revealer to check for the presence of the dragonwand. Thokk and Onu were next in line, the dwarf muttering to himself as walked, the garrulous captain commenting on anything and everything he saw that took his fancy. Leontis followed those two, and though Diran would've preferred to keep his fellow priest closer to him, and had suggested as much, Leontis insisted it made more sense for him to take a position in the middle of the line, where he would be free to loose his arrows in any direction an attack might come from. Though Diran agreed with Leontis's reasoning, he didn't like it. Yvka and Hinto came after Leontis, and Solus brought up the rear, using his psychic powers to scan the surrounding area for threats.

During the journey from Kolbyr, Tresslar had told them all about his previous voyage to Trebaz Sinara in the company of Erdis Cai. So Diran knew what to expect from this portion of the island, but experiencing it for himself was a different matter. As they entered the forest and began making their way northwest between mismatched varieties of trees, Diran was struck by how still and stale the air was, and after only a few minutes, it began to feel as if some unseen force was weighing them down, its pressure increasing with each step they took. Though it was yet daylight, the treecover blocked out the sun, and the forest gloom only added to the oppressive atmosphere. The forest should've been home to all manner of insects, birds, and animals, but the only sounds they heard were their own footfalls and breathing—well, that along with Onu's incessant chattering. Thokk had managed, with no little effort, to get the man to keep his voice to a near-whisper, but no amount of urging could get Onu to be silent. If Diran hadn't already known about the eerie silence of the forest from Tresslar's account, he would've thought Onu had scared off all the life in the area.

Solus's psionic powers confirmed the absence of anything living nearby except foliage.

"I cannot sense even a trace of thought beyond our own," the psiforged said. "It is as if the entire island is devoid of life."

Since they knew that was not the case, Solus's words were far from reassuring. Indeed, they made things worse, for *something* had to be blocking the construct's psychic abilities. But what?

The quiescence soon became maddening. At first, it seemed preferable to hearing the roaring of fierce beasts close by or the rustling of underbrush as something large and hungry stalked them. But the silence grated on the nerves and eroded the spirit, preying on the mind, if not the flesh. As Diran and the others continued trudging through the forest, the minutes stacking up and becoming hours, the companions became increasingly on edge, and even Onu finally fell quiet. The forest gloom deepened as night came to Trebaz Sinara, and though they seemed to be completely alone in the forest, Diran deemed it was too risky to use any illumination, and so the humans in the party had to rely on the night vision of the nonhuman members to guide them.

Since making landfall, they'd been traveling without rest to take advantage of the daylight left to them, but now that night had fallen, Diran thought it high time they took a break. But just as he was about to broach the subject, light flashed in the darkness behind him, and the priest whirled about, prepared to hurl his daggers.

Diran saw Tresslar's grinning face lit by a yellow glow emanating from his revealer.

"I've detected the Amahau!" Tresslar said, his voice rising in excitement. "That means we're close!"

Diran smiled, all thought of rest forgotten. "How close?"

"No more than a few miles."

"Let's keep moving," Diran said. "We—"

Diran's words were cut off as the darkness surrounding them came alive.

CHAPTER

FIFTEEN

Nathifa, Haaken, and Skarm stood at the base of a rocky hill. Night had fallen, cloaking the land in shadow.

"We've arrived." The lich pointed a dead-white finger at a cave opening halfway up the sloping hillside.

"Doesn't look like much," Haaken said, sounding almost disappointed. "I have to say that so far Trebaz Sinara has failed to live up to its reputation."

"Don't be a fool," Skarm said. "Our journey here was uneventful only because our mistress used her magic to shield us from the island's dangers."

Haaken shrugged.

Normally, Nathifa would've punished the sea raider for his insolence, but she'd envisioned this moment for many long decades, and now that she finally stood here, she was too excited to care about Haaken and his doubts. She glanced up at the sky and judged that it had been night long enough.

"You can come out now," the lich said.

A feminine hand emerged from the rippling black substance that served as Nathifa's robe, and Makala stepped forth from the undead sorceress, detaching herself from the living darkness with some effort.

Once she was free, the vampire shuddered as if caught in the icy winds of an arctic blast. "That was . . . less than pleasant."

"Perhaps, but traveling within me protected you from the rays of the sun. Enough talk: we have work to do, so let's be about it."

Makala smiled. "Well, if you're in a hurry . . ." The vampire's form blurred, shrank, and reformed into the shape of a black bat. Wings flapping furiously, Makala circled around Nathifa's head once before breaking off and soaring up to the cave entrance.

"No!" After all these years, the sorceress wasn't about to permit a lowly servant to enter the cave ahead of her. She pointed at Makala and an ebon bolt of necromantic energy lanced forth from her fingertip, streaked through the air, and struck the vampire precisely on the spot where her bat wings emerged from her shoulder blades. Makala veered wildly for a moment, then dipped toward the hillside and slammed into its rocky surface with a satisfyingly meaty thud. She lay there, only halfway to the cave, stunned and unmoving as her body slowly returned to human form.

"Stupid bitch," Nathifa muttered, and headed up the hill's slope, gliding with eerie liquidity. Haaken and Skarm followed, both having witnessed Makala being chastened by their mistress, and wisely not commenting on it.

The hillside's slope was gradual enough that their ascent proved no difficulty, especially as the three of them possessed unnatural strength and agility to draw upon. Makala had staggered to her feet by the time Nathifa reached her, and the vampire glared at the lich, murderous hate blazing in her crimson-flame eyes. For an instant, Nathifa felt certain Makala was finally going to attack her, but the vampire instead stepped back, bowed, and made a sweeping gesture toward the cave.

"After you," she said, her tone giving an entirely different meaning to the words.

Nathifa smiled. "As it should be," she said, and glided past Makala toward the cave entrance. It had taken a great effort for Makala to restrain herself, and Nathifa knew the next time the woman became angry she wouldn't hold back. The lich was looking forward to it. If Vol's intention in sending the vampire to serve Nathifa was to force the sorceress to prove her ultimate worth, then she welcomed the chance to do so and would not fail. If, on the other hand, Vol wished for Makala to supplant Nathifa for some reason, then she would just have to accept it—but only after doing everything in her fell power to destroy the whore first.

A ledge jutted out from the cave entrance, and they reached it without difficulty. Nathifa paused for a moment, reaching out with her mind, probing the tunnel within to check for any threats. She sensed none, but nevertheless she turned to Skarm and said, "You shall lead the way in your natural form."

Skarm's orange-skinned goblin face paled. "I, Mistress?"

Nathifa frowned. It was unlike the barghest to question her commands. It seemed Makala and Haaken's attitudes had begun to rub off on Skarm. "Your barghest senses are sharp and will alert us to any danger." The lich gave her servant a cold smile. "And, should something happen to you, it will be no great loss."

Skarm nodded, looking miserable, shifted into his lupine-goblinoid form, and padded into the cave. The lich followed, not bothering to give Makala or Haaken any orders. They knew they were expected to come along as well.

They proceeded through the darkness, none of them needing any light to see. The tunnel was wide and the ceiling high and they were able to make their way without difficulty. Naturally enough, Nathifa thought, as this had once been the lair of a green dragon. The tunnel would need to be large enough to allow the beast to enter and exit. The tunnel angled downward and curved to the right, and Nathifa—who'd inhabited her own cavern for a hundred years—sensed they were descending beneath ground level now. Skarm's ears were pricked up the whole way, and he moved with a tentativeness that made Nathifa want to kick him in the rump to hurry him along, but she reminded herself to be patient. Now that she was this close to her goal, she didn't want to make a mistake in her haste to reach the dragon's resting place.

A soft green glow became visible as they approached a bend in the tunnel. They rounded the bend and found themselves standing at the entrance to a large cavern. The source of the green light became instantly apparent: a luminescent substance—moss or mold, Nathifa guessed—covered the cavern's stalactites and stalagmites. The illumination was dim, but it provided more than enough light for the monstrous quartet's night vision, and the cavern seemed nearly as bright as day to them. So much so, that Makala narrowed her eyes to a squint and let out a soft hiss of displeasure. Nathifa ignored the vampire, her attention focused entirely on the skeleton lying in the middle of the cavern's floor: a dragon's skeleton.

"Is that what we've come all this way for?" Haaken asked. "To gaze upon a collection of old bones?"

"Hardly," Nathifa said. "What you see before you are the remains of the green dragon Paganus. Those bones rest in the same spot where the great beast lay for close to three thousand years, guarding the Amahau." The dragonwand lay nestled within Nathifa's interior, swaddled in the same darkness in which the lich had carried Makala during the daylight hours. She thought she felt the Amahau grow warmer inside her as she spoke its name, as if the mystic object was stirring in excitement, joyful to return home after forty years away.

"Until Erdis Cai and Tresslar came along and stole it," Makala said.

"Indeed," Nathifa said. But that was all part of Vol's grand design, she thought. Espial had whispered the story to her many times over the years, and the lich knew it so well, it was almost as if she'd lived it herself.

The Amahau originally belonged to Vol, but a device of such mystic power as the Gatherer was coveted by many. One of those was Paganus. He wanted the Amahau for himself, and he believed he was strong enough to take it. Paganus came up with a cunning plan to steal the Gatherer and, while the dragon succeeded in obtaining the artifact, he did not escape unscathed. Vol discovered Paganus and the two fought a great battle. In the end Paganus—though mortally wounded—managed to flee the palace of ice and bone. He did not possess the strength to heal himself, but he cast a spell so that the Amahau would feed on his innate magical energy and, in return, preserve his body as it was, wounds and all, so that it was as if time did not pass for the dragon. He would not heal, but neither would his wounds cause his death. In excruciating agony, and barely able to fly, Paganus returned to his lair here on Trebaz Sinara. He remained in this cavern for two millennia, hiding from Vol while he attempted to find a way to use the Amahau to heal his injuries.

Vol continued to search for the Gatherer throughout the centuries, and eventually after much effort, she located Paganus's lair. She then set in motion a series of events designed to reclaim what was rightfully hers . . . beginning with Erdis Cai obtaining a map to Trebaz Sinara. Unable to resist adventure of any sort, Cai came to this island and followed the map's route to this cavern. Here he took the Amahau from Paganus and, once the dragon was separated from the Gatherer's protective magic, time began to affect his wounds once more, and the dragon died from injuries sustained two millennia earlier. It was Vol's intention that Erdis Cai travel to her palace in the Fingerbone Mountains and deliver the Amahau unto her and, after some time and various subtle manipulations on Vol's part, the explorer and his crew at last began to sail northward. But something unforeseen occurred. Tresslar, the ship's young artificer, had his doubts about the *Sea Star*'s latest journey, and the coward deserted his captain, stole a longboat, and fled southward.

When Cai and his crew arrived at Vol's palace without the Amahau, Vol—never one to waste a tool if it might one day prove useful—transformed Cai and his first mate Onkar into vampires, and the rest of the crew into ghouls. She gifted the newly reborn vampires with obsidian sarcophagi so that they could withstand the effects of sea travel, and then charged them with finding Tresslar and the Amahau. While that search went on, Vol also tasked Cai with resurrecting an undead army of goblinoid warriors in Grimwall, the ancient subterranean city on Orgalos that Cai used as his base of operations.

Nathifa had been a servant of Vol in mortal life. The woman pledged her soul to Vol in exchange for knowledge of dark magic, and she became even more powerful when she used that knowledge to transform herself into a lich. Thanks to Vol, she was able to gain revenge on her hated brother Kolbyr by cursing his line with the Fury, and as payment, Vol commanded Nathifa to take up residence in a cave outside Perhata and wait until such time as the Dark Queen might have a need for the lich.

Over the decades, Nathifa become aware that despite the Fury, the city bearing her brother's name was prospering, and she decided that her vengeance would never truly be complete until everything he had built—the city included—was destroyed. When Vol became aware of Nathifa's desire, she told the lich that she had decided on a use for the Amahau—a purpose that Nathifa would help to fulfill, thereby gaining her ultimate vengeance in the process. The lich of course eagerly agreed, and settled down to wait until Vol's machinations brought the Amahau into her possession. And now, after all this time and effort, Nathifa stood here at last.

"But now that you have the dragonwand, why return here?" Haaken asked.

The lich's dry dead lips stretched into a hungry smile. "Because the Amahau wasn't the only magical artifact in Paganus's possession, merely the only one he kept on his person."

"So the dragon had a hoard," Makala said. "How original." Her gaze swept the cavern. "I don't see any sign of it in here, though."

"That's because Paganus wasn't foolish enough to keep his treasures out in plain sight," Nathifa said.

"So where are they?" Skarm asked.

"I have no idea," Nathifa admitted. "But I know someone who does. Let's go wake him and ask."

Without waiting for the others, the undead sorceress glided across the cavern floor toward Paganus's skeleton.

◉ ◉ ◉ ◉ ◉ ◉ ◉

Ghaji's elemental axe burst into flame, illuminating their attackers just in time for Diran to duck beneath a set of long, wickedly curved black claws. The creature was a long-limbed, ebon-skinned, rubber-fleshed thing the size of a halfling with large almond-shaped eyes, tiny mouth, and three scimitar-like claws on each hand. As the monster's arm—like its claws—passed overhead, Diran slashed out with both his steel and silver daggers. The dark flesh parted beneath the blades' edges, but it did not sizzle or smoke at the silver's touch. As Diran spun and straightened to meet the next attack, he returned the silver dagger to its sheath within the inner lining of his cloak and drew another steel blade. He only had so many silver daggers, and since the holy metal had no additional effect on this creature, Diran preferred not to waste them.

More shadow creatures attacked from all directions, running at the companions from the ground and leaping at them from tree branches. The creatures came at them in silence, making no noise at all as they advanced, and if Diran hadn't wounded one himself, he might've thought they weren't solid beings at all, but instead ethereal forest shadows that had somehow come to deadly life.

Ghaji's axe slammed into the shoulder of one of the creatures and it released a high-pitched shriek like the piercing cry of a jungle bird as the elemental weapon carved it in two. So the shadowclaws *could* make noise when they wished!

The beast Diran had wounded whirled about for another try, but a backhanded slash at the creature's throat by the priest thwarted the attempt before it had even begun. Black blood gushed from the thing's neck, and it staggered backward, collapsed to the forest floor, and died. Diran didn't pause to take a closer look at the creature, which he'd already begun to think of as a shadowclaw. Though he was unfamiliar with the species, he knew everything that was important: the beasts were trying to kill them and the things died at the kiss of cold steel. Nothing else mattered right now.

It was difficult to estimate how many shadowclaws were attacking. Ghaji's fire axe only provided so much light, and the creatures' black skins blended in perfectly with the darkness that suffused the dark forest. A dozen shadowclaws? Two dozen? More? It was impossible to say.

Leontis was rapidly nocking and loosing arrows, and with every twang of his bowstring, another shadowclaw fell.

"We need more light!" Leontis shouted.

"Happy to oblige!" Yvka called back. She'd taken three small wooden juggling balls from her pouch, and she tossed them into the air. The three balls froze at the apex of their flight and began emitting a dazzling shower of white sparks.

For a radius of fifty feet, the forest became bright as day. The shadowclaws caught in the glare of the sudden light hissed, squeezed shut their overlarge almond eyes, and tried to block out the painful illumination by raising their huge talons. The light didn't keep the shadowclaws from attacking, but it made them hesitant, and that was something.

"Many thanks!" Leontis said, his voice little more than a throaty growl. He continued loosing arrows, but now each shaft plunged into a shadowclaw's eye, penetrating straight into the brain and slaying the creature. With alarm, Diran watched as his friend began to transform. Leontis's eyes glowed a feral yellow, his teeth became sharper and more pronounced, and his hands and face were now almost entirely covered with fur. Nose and mouth merged and stretched into a lupine snout, and his ears became pointed and shifted upward toward the top of his head. His fingernails lengthened into claws, and the priest could no longer get an effective grip on his bowstring. With a snarl, Leontis threw the weapon to the ground, shrugged off his quiver and backpack, and leaped at the nearest shadowclaw, his own claws outstretched and eager to rend flesh.

Diran took a quick glance around to see if anyone else had witnessed Leontis's change of shape, but the other companions had been too busy battling the shadowclaws to notice. Good, Diran thought. The last thing the others needed as they fought for their lives was to be distracted by the realization that they had a werewolf in their midst.

Tresslar knelt on the ground near Solus. The psiforged stood immobile, the psionic crystals that covered his body pulsing with multicolored light. Solus grabbed hold of the shadowclaws in his vicinity with his telekinetic powers and flung them into the air to slam into tree trunks or, just as often, each other. It was as if the creatures were being tossed about by a gale that could neither be seen nor felt.

Tresslar's revealer lay on the ground, and the artificer was furiously working on it with a pair of tools that looked something like lockpicks formed from shimmering light. Diran had no idea what Tresslar was doing, but he had no doubt it was important, so the priest sprinted over to the artificer's side to stand guard over him. Tresslar didn't look up from his work as Diran began slicing at shadowclaws as they attacked, but he said, "Thanks, Diran. If you can just buy me a few more moments . . ."

"That may be about all I *can* do," Diran muttered.

A pair of shadowclaws dropped toward them from the trees, and the priest hurled both of his daggers at the same time, aiming for an eye of each creature. The blades struck, the shadowclaw's eyes popped like rotten fruit, and the monsters fell to the ground, dead.

Leontis had been on to something: the creatures' large eyes made excellent targets.

As Diran grabbed a fresh pair of steel daggers from within his cloak—poison-coated blades this time, for the sheer number of shadowclaws meant they needed every advantage they could get—the priest spared a second to look toward the last place he'd seen Leontis. His fellow priest, now more wolf than man, stood in the midst of a group of shadowclaws, slashing at them with his own claws, tearing at ebon flesh with his teeth, ignoring the deep wounds the creatures' large talons made as they struck again and again, for their claws were not made of silver and therefore did him no lasting damage. His injuries healed almost as swiftly as the shadowclaws could make them. Diran had fought numerous beings that could change their shape, but he'd never seen a true lycanthrope in action before, and the sight was a most impressive one indeed. The speed and savagery were beyond anything he had ever witnessed before, and add to that the swiftness with which lycanthropes healed, and Diran understood why the Purified had once fought so hard to extinguish their kind from the face of Eberron, and why they continued to guard against a lycanthropic resurgence to this day.

Leontis's curse was proving to be a benefit to them now, but what would the werewolf do when there were no more shadowclaws to fight? Would he be so intoxicated with battle-lust that he'd turn on them? If so, then Diran would be forced to do as his friend had originally requested and free him from his curse by plunging a silver dagger into his heart. If that time came, then Diran vowed he would strike swiftly and without hesitation. He owed Leontis that much, at least.

A single shadowclaw rushed at Tresslar, claw-hands held high and ready to strike. Diran stepped between the artificer and his ebon-skinned attacker and hurled a poisoned-coated dagger at the creature's throat. The creature managed to bring down its right claw in time to deflect Diran's dagger and knock it onto the ground. But in the short amount of time it took the shadowclaw to perform this action, Diran had already thrown his second dagger and the blade sank into the base of the creature's throat up to the hilt. The shadowclaw gagged as the poison went swiftly about its work, coughed a spray of black blood, and collapsed onto the forest floor where it laid still, its life fluid soaking into the soil.

Diran quickly moved forward to retrieve his blades. He picked up the dagger that the shadowclaw had knocked to the ground, and then yanked the second blade from the dead creature's throat. He didn't bother wiping the dagger clean, for he wished to keep as much poison on the blade as possible. He shot Tresslar a quick look. "I thought you said you made it through the forest without incident during your last journey!"

"That was forty years ago," the artificer said. He tapped the revealer's metal ring in a rhythmic pattern with his light-picks, moving the tools back and forth rapidly across its surface. "And it was daylight when we crossed the forest—both coming and going. These things don't look like the sort of beasts that enjoy light, do they? Not with those eyes and that coloring. At least, that's what I'm counting on." Tresslar stopped working on the revealer and held it up for inspection. Diran couldn't see anything different about, but Tresslar must have, for he nodded and said, "That should do it." The artificer then rose to his feet, groaning as his knee joints popped. "I really *am* getting too old for this sort of foolishness. Let's go."

Diran slashed another shadowclaw's throat with a pair of cross-handed strikes that nearly decapitated the ebon beast. "Go where?" he asked as the poisoned creature stiffened and fell to join his dead brethren littering the ground.

"I need to reach Ghaji," Tresslar said. "See what you can do to get me there in as close to one piece as you can manage."

Diran nodded grimly. "Yvka!" he called out. "Watch our backs!"

The elf-woman had been flicking tiny seeds at shadowclaws, each one exploding and creating a fist-sized hole in the creatures as it detonated. Yvka ran over to Diran and Tresslar and the three companions started heading toward Ghaji. Yvka continued flicking her deadly seeds, and Diran's hands became blurs as he slashed one shadowclaw after another with his poison-slick daggers. The poison was one of the deadliest that Diran knew—he'd learned how to make it from Aldarik Cathmore—and though little of the substance adhered to the knife metal by now, it remained potent enough to continue inflicting fatal wounds on their attackers.

The companions' situation was bad enough as it was, but to make matters worse, the light-spark orbs that Yvka and thrown into the air were beginning to sink toward, their magic nearly spent, their illumination dimming as they descended. Without the light to deter them, the shadowclaws were becoming bolder, attacking more swiftly and savagely, their numbers increasing. If the companions didn't do something and do it fast, they were dead.

"Everyone gather near Ghaji!" Tresslar shouted.

Solus began making his way toward the half-orc, his psionic crystals still glowing, shadowclaws still flying this way and that as the power of the psiforged's mind tossed them about like ebon dolls. Asenka, Hinto, and Thokk also headed for Ghaji, the halfling tugging on Onu's sleeve to urge the sea captain to accompany them, Onu looking as if he were so enthralled by the battle taking place around him that he was reluctant to move lest he miss something good.

Ghaji wielded his elemental axe in great flaming arcs, slaying shadowclaws with each swing. Dark bodies in various stages of scorched mutilation lay around him in great heaps, and the air stank of burnt flesh and boiling blood. As the companions drew near Ghaji, killing shadowclaws and relieving some of the pressure from the half-orc, Ghaji paused in his efforts to draw the back of his hand cross his sweat-slick brow.

"This is too much like work," he said.

Diran didn't know how many shadowclaws they had killed, but they seemed to have made no dent in their numbers. The creatures kept coming from all directions, vast waves of living darkness with but a single desire: to tear those who had invaded their forest into bloody ribbons.

"Everyone keep close together and crouch down low," Tresslar told them. "Except you, Ghaji. Start swinging your axe in a circle and keep swinging it. We need to create a ring of fire."

"What about Leontis?" Asenka asked. "He's still fighting somewhere out there!"

Diran didn't think the others had witnessed Leontis's transformation, but there was no time to explain now. The area was crawling with too many shadowclaws, and the werewolf was no longer visible. For all Diran knew, Leontis had been torn limb from limb by now, and as powerful as lycanthrope healing abilities might be, Diran doubted they'd save his friend if he were in too many pieces.

"There's nothing we can do for him right now," Diran said. "Proceed, Ghaji."

Ghaji nodded, took a deep breath, and then spun, axe held in a two-handed grip, flames trailing behind the blade. The nearest shadowclaws drew back several feet, leery of the mystical fire generated by Ghaji's weapon, but they did not withdraw far. They sensed their prey's plight and knew it would be only a matter of moments until they would finally get to feed. The shadowclaws edged forward, growing braver by the second. A few more inches . . . a few more . . .

Tresslar raised the revealer until the metal ring touched the flame trailing from Ghaji's elemental axe.

"Everyone face downward, close your eyes, and hold your breath!" the artificer shouted.

The last thing Diran saw was the shadowclaws lunging at them, and then the priest shut his eyes as Tresslar commanded. A split-second later, the world exploded into heat and light, and even through eyelids squeezed closed, Diran saw a bright flash of yellow-white illumination. He felt the skin on the back of his neck burn, and smelled his hair begin to smoke. A loud whooshing sound filled the air, followed by the high-pitched screams of shadowclaws in agony. The heat, light, and noise seemed to go on forever, but eventually Diran realized the only sound he heard was a ringing in his ears, and the only light he saw came from afterimages floating in the blackness behind his eyes.

"It's safe now. You can open your eyes." Tresslar's voice quavered with weariness, but the artificer sounded otherwise unharmed.

Diran opened his eyes onto a nightmarish scene. The forest had been decimated for dozens of yards in all directions. Smoldering stumps were all that remained of the trees, the ground was charred coal-black, and the shadowclaws had been reduced to blackened husks. Flames burned here and there, enough to provide sufficient illumination to see by, especially when their orange glow was added to that of the moons, for there was no longer any tree cover in the area to block the light of the celestial orbs from shining down upon the forest floor. Black snow drifted down from the sky . . . no, not snow, Diran realized. Ash.

Beyond the radius of the fireblast, no shadowclaws could be seen. Perhaps all the beasts had been within range when Tresslar had unleashed the magic that had resulted in this destruction. Or perhaps the surviving shadowclaws had been blinded by the explosion and had fled in terror. Whichever the case, it appeared the companions were safe, for the moment, at least.

One by one the companions stood, helping each other up as necessary. Ghaji held his elemental axe limply at his side, the weapon's flame extinguished, the metal cold.

"Is anyone injured?" Diran asked.

"I don't believe so," Tresslar said. "A few burns, some singed hair, that's all. I was careful to direct the majority of the flame's heat away from us."

"What did you do?" Ghaji asked. He lifted his axe and held it out for Tresslar's inspection. "It feels heavier somehow, more awkward, and the surface has grown dull."

"I'm sorry, my friend," Tresslar said, "but I could think of no other way to stop those clawed monstrosities. I adapted my revealer so that it would function as an enhancer, a device that can temporarily boost another mystic device's power. I used it to enhance your axe's flame so that it would burn hotter and spread outward rapidly. I hoped the resulting flame-blast would destroy the ebon creatures." Tresslar took a moment to survey the carnage he'd wrought. "Looks like it worked."

"Why apologize, Tresslar?" Hinto asked. "You saved us!"

"But at a cost, my little friend," Tresslar said. "Enhancers function by forcing a mystic object to expend all of its energy in a single burst. By employing the enhancer on Ghaji's axe, I forced the elemental within to devote its entire strength into one fiery explosion. Unfortunately, the elemental was drained of the magic that sustained it and was destroyed. I'm afraid your axe is just an ordinary weapon now, Ghaji. I'm sorry."

The half-orc looked at his axe for a moment then shrugged. "I got along without an elemental weapon most of my life. I'll get by now."

"I might be able to restore it some day," Tresslar said. "I can't make any promises, but if I can manage to—"

Asenka broke in, her voice close to a sob. "I can't believe you're standing there talking so calmly about a stupid axe! Have you forgotten that Leontis was outside the circle?"

"We haven't forgotten," Diran said. "Leontis is quite resourceful and not without his own defenses. It's quite possible he managed to get beyond the range of the fire." Diran wasn't lying, precisely. Leontis *did* have the defenses of his lycanthropic metabolism, and there *was* a good chance that—assuming the shadowclaws hadn't destroyed him—he'd either chased the beasts further into the forest or, when the fireblast happened, he'd reacted in animalistic fear and fled. Either way, Leontis would still be alive, though it was possible the werewolf he'd become would find itself at home in the forests of Trebaz Sinara and never return. That might well be for the best, Diran mused. Leontis could live out his life in seclusion, unable to hurt anyone or spread his curse.

"Excuse me," Onu said softly.

Asenka ignored the man and continued. "We have to at least search for his body!"

"How?" Yvka said. "I don't wish to upset you any further, but there are hundreds of dead creatures surrounding us, and their corpses all resemble large lumps of charcoal. Leontis, if he was caught in the blast, will look no different. How will be able to tell his body apart from all the others?"

"Excuse me," Onu repeated, a trifle louder this time.

Again, the sea captain was ignored. Solus spoke next.

"I might be able to detect some faint traces of human intelligence yet lingering in Leontis's mind," the psiforged said. "Assuming at least some portion of his brain remains relatively intact. I'll begin—"

Onu shouted this time, an edge of hysteria in his voice. "Excuse me!"

The companions turned toward the sea captain—or at least, toward a being who wore the captain's garish red longcoat. This being had pale gray skin and thin fair hair. Its arms and legs were somewhat longer than natural for a humanoid, and its white eyes were disturbingly blank. It possessed only the merest hint of facial features—a nub of a nose, a suggestion of lips, and small bumps where ears should be.

Ghaji was the first to give voice to what they were all thinking.

"You're a *changeling?*"

Onu nodded. "But that's not important right now." His voice was soft and nearly devoid of emotion, completely unlike that of the Captain Onu they had come to know. He pointed with a slender gray finger.

The companions turned to look where the changeling indicated and saw the still smoldering body of a shadowclaw a few yards away. In its oversized talons, the creature held the charred body of a small human-like being.

Onu's voice trembled with grief. "He . . . the creature grabbed him just before . . . when the fireblast . . ." The changeling trailed off, unable to say anything more.

Diran understood what had happened. In the moment right before Tresslar had activated the enhancer, a lone shadowclaw had managed to get close enough to sink its talons into Thokk and drag the dwarf off. When the fireblast occurred, Thokk had been burnt to a crisp, along with everything else in range of the enhanced flames.

No one said anything for several moments as the enormity of what had happened began to sink in. Finally, Onu spoke once more.

"I guess this means I really *am* the captain now."

CHAPTER

SIXTEEN

Makala felt no physical aftereffects of Nathifa's energy blast, but she seethed with fury. As the lich led them across the cavern floor toward the skeletal remains of the dragon Paganus, it took all of the vampire's self-control to keep from attempting to tear the sorceress's head off.

Bide your time, whispered a voice inside her. *You'll get your chance.*

Makala hoped so, and she hoped it would be soon.

Nathifa walked up to the dragon's skull and stopped. In the forty years since Paganus died, evidently nothing had disturbed his bones, for his skeleton was not only intact, all the bones remained in their proper places. During her mortal life as an assassin, Makala had had occasion to visit Morgrave University in Sharn. There she'd seen skeletons of ancient creatures displayed on metal frameworks, arranged in what the curators no doubt hoped were lifelike poses. Paganus's skeleton reminded her of those displays. She could even imagine the placard that would accompany it: PAGANUS: ANCIENT GREEN DRAGON, COLLECTOR OF MAGICAL ARTIFACTS, SEEN HERE AT REST IN HIS CAVERN LAIR.

Makala had never seen a live dragon, and the small part of her that was still human marveled at the site of Paganus's bones. But her wonder was forgotten as she saw that the floor around the skeleton was stained a dull reddish-brown. Makala inhaled the rich scent of dragon blood, the odor faint but still tantalizing even after all these decades. She could smell the power in that blood, and she wondered what it would feel like to have a dragon's strength flowing through her veins.

"I want the three of you to stay back while I attempt to rouse the dragon's spirit," Nathifa said. "Such spells require a great deal of power and concentration, and there are . . . dangers. A dragon's spirit is powerful, even in death, so do not interfere or draw attention to yourselves in any way."

Makala hated the way the lich spoke to them as if they were dull-witted children, but she resisted making a snide comment. She wanted to hear what the dragon's spirit had to say—assuming Nathifa succeeded in summoning it.

The lich began simply, lowering her head and whispering arcane words in a language unfamiliar to Makala—words formed of harsh consonants and guttural vowels, words that resonated with blasphemy, as if the sound of them alone was an affront to creation. Nathifa began gesturing with her hands, bone-white fingers contorting into intricate shapes and patterns. Her whispering rose in volume to become a chant, and tendrils of darkness slowly extruded from the hem of her shadowy robe. The tendrils lengthened as they snaked their way across the cavern floor, slithered up the sides of Paganus's skull, and slid into the opening where the dragon's ears had once been. For a long moment nothing happened, and then the tips of the tendrils emerged from the eye sockets and burst upward in sudden growth. The tendrils merged into a single black shape that stretched nearly all the way to the cavern's ceiling. The shadowy substance rippled and pulsated, as if it was trying to assume some manner of form. And then Nathifa raised her arms and gave a last shout that echoed throughout the cavern and resonated within the deepest recesses of her servants' black souls.

The mass of shadow took on the shape of a large dragon with glowing green eyes and wisps of vapor coiling forth from the nostrils. The acrid stench of poisonous gas filled the air, and Makala thought it fortunate that none of them was human, otherwise the dragon's toxic breath might well kill them.

Who summons me?

The dragon's voice wasn't heard so much as felt, as if his spirit was speaking directly to theirs.

Nathifa lowered her arms and spoke with a confident, commanding tone. "I did. I am the sorceress Nathifa, servant of her most great and terrible majesty Vol."

The dragon's gaze fixed on Nathifa, and his eyes glowed a brighter green, as if he were examining her closely. After a moment, Paganus chuckled.

You're nothing but a lich, one of the bitch-goddess's undead puppets. I am insulted that your mistress would send such a lowly creature to speak with me.

Nathifa's voice with tight with barely restrained anger as she replied. "Do not put on airs with me, dragon! You are no mighty lord of your kind. You are nothing but a common thief! You stole the Amahau from my Dark Lady, and though it took almost three thousand years, you paid for your transgression with your life!"

I was happy to give up my life after enduring three millennia of pain. Death was no punishment for me, but rather a release from the prison of perpetual agony in which I was trapped. But enough talk. You have summoned me for a purpose, and the sooner I fulfill it, the sooner I can return to blessed Oblivion. So tell me what you want, lich. But be warned. If you have come for the Amahau you are too late. It was taken by those who granted me my deliverance.

"I have no need to ask for what I already possess." Nathifa reached a hand into her own darkness and withdrew the dragonwand. She held it forth for Paganus to inspect.

The dragon's shadowy form quivered and for an instant seemed as if it might lose definition, but then it solidified once more.

The Amahau . . . even as a shade I can still sense its power.

The dragon lowered his head toward Nathifa, and Makala wondered if it was possible for a spirit to wrest a physical object from its holder. But Nathifa held her ground.

"If you know the Gatherer's power, then you know that it can absorb any mystical energy. Including a spirit. If you attempt to do anything save answer the questions I put to you, the Amahau shall become your new prison."

Paganus hesitated. *My present form is due at least in part to a contribution of your own power. If you absorb me into the Amahau, you will sacrifice that portion of your own strength.*

"Perhaps," Nathifa allowed. "But I am willing to make such a sacrifice for the glory of my dread mistress."

Paganus considered for a moment before withdrawing his head to its original position. *Ask what you will, lich.*

From where she stood, Makala couldn't see Nathifa's face, but she could well imagine the sorceress's triumphant smile.

"The Amahau wasn't the first artifact of power that you stole, merely the last. Where are the others?"

The dragon's glowing green eyes narrowed. *It has been three thousand years since last I gazed upon my treasures, for I was too wounded to move from the spot where my bones now lie. Who knows what fate might have befallen my pretties in all that time?*

"Do not dissemble with me, Paganus! You might have been weakened and in pain, but I refuse to believe that you have no idea what happened to your hoard. Despite how badly you were wounded when you escaped Vol's palace, you managed to fly all the way from the Fingerbone Mountains to Trebaz Sinara. Such a long journey would've been an ordeal given your injuries, yet you forced yourself to continue on until you reached home. Why? Surely it was more than a longing for the comforts of your lair"—she gestured to take in the cavern around them—"meager as they are. You must have had another reason for making the difficult journey, and I submit that it was because you wished to be near your precious treasures. Perhaps you even hoped that one of them, its magic added to that of the Amahau, might heal you."

Paganus regarded Nathifa for some time before finally sighing in defeat.

It is as you say. Over the long centuries, when I could find the strength to move and the will to endure the resulting agony, I made my way to the chamber where my hoard is hidden and attempted to heal myself using one of my pretties. Obviously, I was unsuccessful.

"Then your hoard must be nearby, or else you never would have been able to reach it in your wounded condition."

Paganus said nothing.

"It's not in this cavern, but perhaps it's located in another close by, one easily reachable from here by a creature barely able to move."

Again, the dragon remained silent.

"Tell me, Paganus. Tell me where your hoard is, and I'll release your spirit. Refuse, and I will consign you to the Amahau until such time as I can find a use for your energy."

For three millennia I lay here in agony, protecting my treasures despite my wounds. Even now that I have no more use for my pretties, cannot touch them no matter how much I might wish to, I find it nearly impossible to give them up. Still, I suppose I have little choice.

And so Paganus told them.

When the dragon finished, Nathifa replaced the dragonwand inside herself. "I should absorb your spirit anyway. Three millennia of pain do not begin to redress the wrong you did my mistress. But I'm feeling in a generous mood, so . . . begone, spirit."

Nathifa made a casual wave of her hand and, as if a strong breeze blew through the cavern, the shadowy form of Paganus's spirit dispersed and was soon gone, leaving behind only the harsh smell of poison gas.

The ebon tendrils that had helped give the dragon's spirit shape withdrew, pulling out of the skull's eye sockets, slithering back through the ear holes, and sliding across the cavern floor to rejoin the lich's robe of living darkness.

Despite herself, Makala was impressed by the sorceress's accomplishment, though she would submit to eternal damnation before ever letting on.

"So now we go treasure-hunting?" Makala said.

"Not quite yet." Nathifa turned around to face Makala. "I sense that your former lover and his companions have joined us on the island and are drawing close even as we speak."

"So?" Haaken said, grinning with a mouthful of shark's teeth.

"Let them come. I have a score to settle with that priest and his half-blood friend."

"We have important tasks before us and little time in which to accomplish them," Nathifa said. "We cannot afford to waste what time we have in purposeless battle." More softly, she added, "*I* cannot."

"So what are we going to do?" Skarm asked.

"*You* are going to do nothing," Nathifa snapped. "But I do have a request of Makala."

The vampire raised a skeptical eyebrow. "Yes?"

"I want you tear off one of my arms. Right or left, it doesn't matter. Your choice."

Makala looked at the lich for several seconds before her lips drew back from her fangs in a half smile, half snarl. Now *this* was a command she was happy to obey!

She grabbed hold of Nathifa's right arm with both hands, nails sinking through the darkness of the sorceress's robe and penetrating into the bloodless flesh beneath. Then, using all her strength, Makala yanked.

❂ ❂ ❂ ❂ ❂ ❂ ❂

Though they couldn't spare the time, the companions nevertheless decided to bury Thokk as best they could in the charred mixture of soot and soil. Onu remained in his natural form, as if too weary and filled with sorrow to change shape. The changeling said nothing while Solus telekinetically removed earth from the site they'd chosen for the grave. Tresslar and Hinto prepared the body as best they could, but the heat of the fire had melted the dwarf's mace to his hand, and the only way they could have separated it was to break the hand off at the wrist. So the mace remained in Thokk's grip, which seemed only fitting. When the psiforged was finished excavating the grave, he offered to use his mind powers to move Thokk's blackened corpse into the hole, but Diran thought the Solus should conserve his psionic energy. Besides, the dwarf deserved to be laid to rest in a more respectful manner. So Diran, Asenka, Yvka, and Hinto lowered Thokk into his grave while the rest kept watch.

As the others stepped back from the grave, Solus stepped forward, removed his travel cloak, and gently placed it over the dwarf. Diran knew Solus had no need of the travel cloak to protect him against the elements, so giving it up was no great sacrifice, but it was a nice gesture all the same. Diran was about to perform the rite of the Burial of the Faithful when Onu at last spoke.

"You are a priest, Diran. Is there nothing you can do to restore Thokk to life?"

Diran sighed heavily. He feared Onu might ask this question. "I understand that you are grieving, Onu, and your request comes out of the deep sorrow you feel at Thokk's loss. Please try to understand: the Purified believe that the souls of the faithful join with the Silver Flame after death. This union is a joyful one in which the deceased is reborn into an afterlife of peace and bliss, and the Flame itself is strengthened by the addition of the new soul. To return a spirit to the material world not only weakens the Flame, it brings the deceased back into an existence of further pain and suffering. For these reasons, priests of the Purified have a sacred duty not to raise the dead, regardless of the circumstances. I am sorry."

Diran waited to see if Onu would argue that Thokk wasn't one of the Purified, and therefore the Church's ban on resurrection shouldn't apply to him. It was an argument Diran had heard too many times before. But Onu only nodded, and the matter was closed.

Diran then gestured to Solus, and the psiforged used his mental powers to return the earth he'd taken from Thokk's grave. Diran then conducted the rite of the Burial of the Faithful. He spoke a series of prayers over the grave, asking the Silver Flame to forgive whatever spiritual impurities might have remained in Thokk's soul at the time of his death and to accept the dwarf as part of the divine Flame. Strictly speaking, the rite was intended to be used only for the burial of Purified, but Diran followed the thinking of Tusya on this matter.

It's not for us to judge who is worthy of joining the Flame. We may call ourselves Purified, but no mortal creature can ever be as pure as the Flame itself. To pretend otherwise is a dangerous arrogance that taints the spirit as surely as any wicked deed.

When Diran completed the prayers, he sprinkled a bit of silver dust onto the grave, and the rite was finished. Thokk was at rest.

Ghaji came over to Diran then. "There's no sign of danger yet, but we need to get moving," the half-orc said in a low voice.

Diran looked at Onu. The changeling stood at Thokk's gravesite, hands clasped in front of him, head lowered.

"Let's give Onu another moment," the priest said. "Why don't you go tell the others to get ready?"

Ghaji glanced at Onu, frowning, and Diran knew what his friend was thinking: Thokk hadn't wanted to accompany them onto the island, but he'd come along because Onu had insisted on going. If the changeling hadn't been so adamant, Thokk would still be alive.

Ghaji moved off to see to the others, and Diran walked over to stand by Onu's side. "We have to go," the priest said gently.

"Thokk was the real captain of the *Turnabout*, though I imagine you've already guessed that by now. He was working to repay a great debt of some sort. He never did tell me the details regarding it, but every bit of profit he made went toward that cause. That's why he risked working as a smuggler: he needed to make as much gold as he could in as short a time as possible. But as hardworking as Thokk was, he hated dealing with people and negotiating prices with customers, and eventually he realized he was losing business because of it. He decided he needed someone who was good with people, someone charming and flamboyant . . ."

"Someone who was everything he wasn't," Diran said.

Onu nodded. "And so he hired me, and 'Captain' Onu was born. I'd always loved traveling, being exposed to fascinating new people and places, and my bargain with Thokk granted me those things. And if I do say so, after taking me on, Thokk's profits increased quite significantly. He could be a prickly one to work with, and I must admit that my over-enthusiasm for my role didn't always help us get along, but he was a good man. A good friend. I'll miss him terribly."

Diran laid a comforting hand on the changeling's shoulder. Onu and Thokk's partnership had been an odd one, and Diran wasn't certain he entirely understood it, but he could tell that Onu's grief was genuine.

The changeling's features blurred, shifted, reformed, and his human guise was once more back in place.

"Let us continue with our quest, my good priest! What better way to honor our fallen comrade's memory than by seeing this adventure through to the finish, eh?" Onu clapped Diran on the shoulder and strode off confidently to join the others.

Diran stared after him, puzzled. He'd known changelings before. One of Emon Gorsedd's most trusted assassins was a changeling named Rux. But though Diran understood that in many ways changelings' identities were as fluid and malleable as their outer forms, he'd never seen such a drastic shift in personality as the one he'd just witnessed in Onu. "Captain" Onu had always struck Diran as a trifle erratic, and now he wondered if the changeling might be mentally imbalanced in some way. The man would bear close watching, Diran decided, regardless of which shape he chose to wear.

Diran started off to join the rest of the companions, who'd already shouldered their packs and were ready to move out again, but Asenka broke away from them and approached the priest, meeting him halfway.

"I can't believe that after taking the time to bury Thokk you aren't going to at least attempt to do the same for Leontis. He was a fellow priest—not to mention your friend!"

Diran knew none of the others had seen Leontis change into a werewolf during the battle with the shadowclaws, and he saw no point to reveal his friend's secret now. If Leontis was dead, then let his shame die with him.

"We have no proof that Leontis was killed," Diran said. "But even if he was and even if we could locate his body, he would not wish us to further endanger ourselves by burying him. He came along to help us stop Nathifa, and we would be dishonoring his sacrifice if we failed in that mission." Asenka started to protest, but Diran placed his fingers on her lips to silence her. "When I prayed over Thokk's grave, I prayed for Leontis's soul as well . . . just in case."

For a moment it looked as if Asenka would continue to argue, but in the end she nodded her acceptance of Diran's words. He put an arm around her then and said, "Let's go join the others."

But as the two started toward their friends, they heard a shuffling sound coming from behind. They turned to see Leontis walking unsteadily toward them. The priest was naked, his skin bright pink like a newborn baby's, and he was completely bereft of body hair.

"I appreciate the prayers, Diran, but as you can see they were, unfortunately, a bit premature."

❀ ❀ ❀ ❀ ❀ ❀ ❀

"Why didn't you tell us he was a werewolf?" Ghaji demanded. The half-orc's teeth were clenched, and his voice was pitched dangerously low.

"I don't blame you for being angry with me, but please try to understand. Leontis asked that I keep his condition a secret. It was a request I was bound to keep, both as a priest and a friend."

The companions continued onward. Diran had joined Ghaji at the head of the line, and the others had fallen back a few yards, sensing the two needed a bit of privacy so they could talk. They'd scrounged together some clothing for Leontis, and now the priest wore a pair of Tresslar's extra undergarments and Ghaji's travel cloak. The clothing was poor protection against the night's chill, but Leontis didn't seem to notice. The other companions kept their distance from the priest as they traveled, eyeing him with suspicion and, in the case of Tresslar and Yvka, outright hostility. Though Leontis was in human form, his curse was revealed by how swiftly he was healing. His hair and eyebrows were already starting to grow back, though it would likely be some time before his beard filled in again. His longbow and arrows had been destroyed in the fire, and he no longer carried any weapons, but that hardly seemed to matter since Leontis was a weapon in and of himself.

Diran marveled at the healing powers of Leontis's curse. The fire must have charred his body to a crisp, and yet he was now whole and seemingly none the worse for wear. Even the healing magic granted by the Silver Flame would have been hard-pressed to restore someone who'd suffered such severe burns, especially in such a short time. Diran wondered if Leontis healed so quickly because the werewolf who had infected him had carried an especially powerful strain of lycanthropy or if the healing magic Leontis had learned as a priest of the Silver Flame had somehow combined with his lycanthropic abilities to help restore him to full health so swiftly. The latter possibility raised some intriguing—and disturbing—notions. Could evil and good co-exist within the same individual in some sort of balance? More, could those opposing forces somehow complement each other, becoming stronger than either could be on its own?

"You put us all at risk by not telling us the truth," Ghaji growledd, not mollified in the least by Diran's words. "What if Leontis had changed one night during the voyage on the *Turnabout*? How many men and women might he have slain—or worse, infected with his curse—before we could've stopped him? You should have at least told Solus. He could've kept an eye on Leontis and let us know when he was about to change."

Diran wanted to explain his reasoning to Ghaji, but he realized that his old friend was correct. Diran hadn't really considered all the ramifications of allowing Leontis to come with them. He had told himself that he'd invited Leontis along because of the visions of the future revealed to him by the Fury-demon, and that was true enough as it went. But the real reason—the deepest reason—was far simpler, and it had blinded Diran to the threat presented by Leontis's curse.

"He's my friend, Ghaji. Leontis and I were once as close as you and I are. I . . . wanted to give him the opportunity to come to terms with his condition, to give him a second chance. Tusya gave me a second chance when he drove the dark spirit from my soul and taught me the ways of the Silver Flame. Could I do no less for Leontis?"

"Or Makala?" Ghaji said with a grudging smile. "Or me, for that matter, when you found me working as a disillusioned, cynical brothel guard?"

Diran smiled. "I hate to break it to you, but you're still quite cynical, though I hope somewhat less disillusioned."

The two friends looked at each for a moment, and then Ghaji sighed.

"What's done is done. Let's speak no more of it. But I think we should ask Solus to monitor Leontis's thoughts—as a precaution."

"And a wise one at that. I'm sure Leontis will understand. I'll inform him while you speak with Solus."

The two friends broke rank to do so, and as Diran surmised, Leontis had no objection to the psiforged's mental scrutiny.

"I do have one question," the priest said. "My memories of the battle with the shadowclaws are fragmentary at best, but Thokk's death . . ."

"Was at the hands of the dark beasts, not yours," Diran said.

"Thank the Flame," Leontis whispered.

The companions continued on their way, but Diran noticed how everyone glanced uneasily at Leontis from time to time, as if expecting him to grow fangs and sprout fur any moment. Diran supposed he didn't really blame them.

Once again the party relied on those members with night vision to guide their way. They left behind the burned area of the forest caused by Tresslar's blast, and the going was slow once again. The companions made their way through the thick tree growth and kept close watch for any signs of danger. Tresslar no longer bothered trying to detect the dragonwand. He explained that the process by which he'd converted the revealer into an enhancer couldn't be reversed, at least not with the tools and materials at his disposal. He was, however, attempting to think of a way to repair Ghaji's elemental axe.

Tresslar worked through the problem by whispering to himself, speaking more for his benefit than any of theirs. "If the fire elemental is merely injured, it might be possible to restore it to full strength. But if it's dead, then there's nothing else that can be done but bind a new elemental to the axe. Provided I can find the time and energy to summon one, that is. Perhaps I could make use of the enhancer to . . ."

The companions blocked out Tresslar's monologue as they marched and soon, almost without realizing it, they found themselves leaving the forest. The night sky spread about above them, stars and moons bright and sharp as new-cut crystal. The ground was devoid of vegetation, barren and rocky, and in the nearby distance black hills rose up, forbidding shadows that blocked the horizon.

"These are the hills where Paganus' cave is located," Tresslar said. "I'm sure of it!"

They all were, for their path had been implanted in each of their minds by Solus. They had reached the dragon's lair at last.

CHAPTER

SEVENTEEN

The companions climbed the sloping hillside and entered the tunnel leading to Paganus's lair. The tunnel was wide enough for the group to walk in rows of three: Ghaji, Diran, and Tresslar in front; Yvka, Onu, and Asenka in the middle; Hinto, Solus, and Leontis in the rear. From Tresslar's memory of the place—a memory Ghaji now shared—the half-orc knew they had almost reached the cavern where Erdis Cai, Tresslar, and a handful of sailors from the *Sea Star* had once battled the dragon. The glowing mold clinging to the walls here was a dead giveaway. All they had to do was go around the bend just ahead.

The cavern was huge, lit by luminescent substance covering both the stalactites and stalagmites. The dim greenish glow given off by the mold revealed no sign of life. However, that didn't mean the cavern was free of danger.

Ghaji detected the stink of poison gas before any of the others, and the half-orc quickly called the party to a halt.

"I thought you told us the dragon died forty years ago," he said to Tresslar. "From the smell, I'd say he's still very much alive and breathing."

The artificer looked at Ghaji with concern. "Are your eyes burning? Are you having trouble breathing?"

"I can't say it's the most pleasant smell I've ever encountered, but it's tolerable enough."

Tresslar's relief was clear in his voice. "Good. Let us know if you begin experiencing any discomfort. The fumes emitted by a green dragon are highly toxic, and breathing them is a quick way to an agonizing death."

Onu's eyes widened. "Do you really think the dragon might still be alive?" He peered into the cavern's gloom, as if he were hoping to see a green dragon come charging at them any instant.

Ghaji grimaced in irritation. Of the two personae the changeling had revealed to them so far, he much preferred Onu's natural one. It was the quieter of the pair—not to mention the less obnoxious one.

"I don't see how," Tresslar said. "Paganus was clearly dead when we departed his lair. I suppose it's possible he was restored to life somehow, but someone or something else would've had to do perform the deed, especially as the dragon no longer had possession of the Amahau."

"Before the shadowclaws attacked, Tresslar's revealer indicated his dragonwand lay somewhere ahead of us," Yvka said. "That could mean Nathifa reached the lair before we did."

"Traces of the lich's foul presence linger here," Diran said. He looked to Leontis for confirmation, and his fellow priest nodded. "I am certain Nathifa was in the cavern, but as yet I cannot tell if she remains nearby."

"But if she *was* here—" Yvka began.

"The lich might have resurrected Paganus," Ghaji finished. He turned to Diran. "Is it possible?"

"Liches are powerful sorcerers, so Nathifa undoubtedly has a great deal of mystical knowledge to draw upon," Diran said. "But to resurrect a being forty years after its death would require magic of an extremely high order. I'm not certain she's capable of that."

"She *does* have Tresslar's wand," Hinto pointed out.

"The Amahau could easily provide the lich with enough mystic energy to fuel such a spell," Tresslar said.

"Before we go further into the cavern, Solus should scout ahead using his psionic abilities," Diran said.

The psiforged nodded and stepped for the forefront of the group.

The crystals covering the construct's surface began to pulse with a soft inner light as he mentally surveyed the cavern.

Several moments passed, and then Solus said, "I detect *something*, but I'm uncertain what it is. It's not precisely intelligent in and of itself, but it does possess a rudimentary—"

That's as far as the psiforged got before an ebon serpent dropped from the ceiling and wrapped itself around the construct's neck. It bit down on the top of Solus's head, its curved black fangs penetrating as easily as if the psiforged were made of butter instead of stone and starsilver. The serpent's eyes were a burning crimson, and they flared bright at the creature clamped its jaws tight onto Solus's skull. The psiforged stiffened, and his eyes changed from a glowing green to a baleful vermillion, just like the serpent's fiery orbs.

Diran drew a silver dagger from his inner cloak and lunged forward to strike at the serpent coiled around his companion's neck. At the same instant, Ghaji swung his axe at the giant black snake, not worrying about what might happen if he accidentally struck the psiforged a glancing blow. Solus might lose a chunk of rock from his shoulder, but he wouldn't suffer an injury the same way a being made of flesh and blood would.

But before either the priest or the half-orc could hit the serpent with their weapons, the psionic crystals on Solus's body began to emit crimson light, and the two companions found themselves thrown backward, as if both had been struck by a pair of invisible fists.

Yvka caught Ghaji beneath the arms, her elvish strength belying her petite frame, and Leontis caught Diran.

"Whatever that serpent is, it's taken control of Solus's psionic powers!" Tresslar said. "We must put as much distance between us and the psiforged as we can before—"

"Something like *that* happens," Hinto said, pointing behind them.

The others turned to see a dragon coming toward them. No, not a dragon, but rather the skeleton of a dragon, moving with an eerie liquid grace.

"Diran!" Leontis shouted. "I cannot turn it!"

Ghaji assumed Leontis had lost his silver arrowhead during the fireblast in the forest when his clothing had burned. Perhaps the intense heat had even melted the token.

"I don't think that thing's a normal animated skeleton," Asenka said. "If there *is* such a thing. Look at it. There are spaces between the bones. They're not connected."

It was true. The conglomeration of bones that approached them was configured in the shape of a dragon, but the separate pieces hung floating in the air, moving in concert as if they were a single unified creature.

"It's Solus's doing," Tresslar said. "Or rather, the serpent's. The creature is using Solus's telekinetic power to manipulate Paganus's skeleton!"

Now that Ghaji looked more closely, he could see what Asenka and the artificer were talking about. The skeletal dragon glided toward them with sinuous reptilian grace, but there were clearly gaps between the separate bones. And though they did move in unison, the motion wasn't perfect. Some gaps would widen for a second or two before closing up again. Ghaji was put in mind of the way a marionette sometimes wobbled and drifted even when under the control of a skilled puppeteer.

Hinto moved toward his friend. "Solus, whatever that serpent is, you have to fight it! You can't—"

The halfling reached out for the psiforged's hands, and just as with Diran and Ghaji before him, the little man was flung backwards by an unseen force. Ghaji caught Hinto before the halfling could fly too far, and the pirate's breath whooshed out of his lungs as he collided with the half-orc's sturdy arm.

Ghaji set Hinto down, and the halfling nodded to indicate that he was unhurt as he struggled to catch his breath.

The skeleton of Paganus stopped less than a dozen feet before the companions and reared back on its hind legs, front feet clawing the air, wing bones spreading out behind it, head lifted high, jaws stretching open in a soundless roar. And then the dragon exploded in a shower of bone—the segments of Paganus's skeleton flew through the air, the pieces moving independently of each other, swooping, darting, and dipping as they streaked toward the companions.

Ghaji stepped forward and swung his axe, knocking a femur aside. The bone cracked but didn't break, and it veered away, deflected but not destroyed. Asenka stepped to the half-orc's side, gripping her long sword tight in both hands. Several detached ribs shot at her like curved white arrows, and she cut them into pieces with a single stroke of her blade before they could reach her. But though the ribs shattered, the fragments did not fall, and they continued swirling around Asenka's head, like a cloud of ossified gnats. The majority of Paganus's skeletal structure circled through the cavern air above them, with only one or two bones breaking away from the mass at a time to swoop downward to strike. Ghaji and Asenka were hard-pressed to stop the flying bone segments, but they managed.

A thought struck Ghaji as he batted aside a section of Paganus's spine. If all the pieces of the skeleton attacked at once, there would be no way that the companions could stop them all. They'd be killed within moments. But the segments only attacked a couple at a time, which meant either Solus was resisting the dark magic which had usurped his telekinetic abilities and he was retarding the skeleton's assault, or he wasn't trying to slay them at all, but rather keep them occupied. Perhaps both.

Ghaji swung his axe and broke a rear claw into several pieces. Asenka, using one hand to swat at the bone gnats while holding onto her long sword with the other, struck at a spear-like curve of wing bone. The impact of her blade drove the wing bone into a nearby stalagmite, and the segment broke into a half-dozen uneven fragments.

"The lich is responsible!" Leontis said, his voice close to a growl. *Too* close for Ghaji's comfort. The half-orc couldn't afford to take his gaze off the murderous flying bones to look at the priest, but he could hear the man's words clearly enough. "Can't you feel the stench of her evil wafting off the serpent, Diran?"

"Indeed."

Ghaji didn't have to imagine Diran reaching into his vest pocket with his free hand to remove his silver arrowhead, for he'd seen the priest perform the maneuver hundreds of times before. Ghaji continued batting aside flying bone shards and waited to hear the tell-tale hiss of a supernatural creature recoiling before the holy symbol of Diran's faith. But he heard nothing except Diran's strained breathing.

"I can't move my hand toward my pocket!" the priest said, clearly frustrated. "The serpent is keeping me from reaching my mystic symbol!"

The dragon's skull flew toward Asenka, jaws spread wide as if to devour her. The swordswoman leaped aside and swung her long sword at the juncture where the jaw attached to the skull. The blow knocked the skull to the ground, and the lower jaw shattered. Ghaji dashed forward and split the rest of the skull in half with his axe.

Asenka paused to shout to Diran. "At least you know the arrowhead will work on the serpent, else the damned thing wouldn't care whether you removed it from your pocket or not!"

"I think I might be able to help!" Tresslar called out. "If nothing else, I can buy you a little more time to figure out how to free your arrowhead!"

The artificer was just barely in Ghaji's line of sight, and the half-orc was able to see what the artificer removed from his backpack, and knelt with it on the cavern floor before him. He opened in, reached inside, and pulled out what looked like a large soap bubble. Tresslar stood, cupped the translucent globe in both of his hands and whispered a rapid series of words that Ghaji couldn't quite catch. He opened his hands and the bubble soared up into the air toward where the pieces of Paganus's skeleton spun about like a whirlwind of death. As the bubble rose, a second separated from it and flew upward alongside the original. Then those two bubbles doubled, then those four doubled, and then those eight doubled . . .

Within seconds dozens upon dozens of bubbles filled the air, with more appearing every instant. Each bubble oriented on a specific bone segment and then streaked toward it, growing, expanding, or lengthening to match the size and shape of the bone it headed for. As the bubbles touched the bones, they absorbed the pieces, covering them entirely. The segments of dragon skeleton continued to float in the air, but though they tried to break free of their spherical prisons, the bubbles did not burst.

Tresslar smiled in satisfaction. "Thank you, Illyia," he said softly, then more loudly added, "The water-globes won't last long, so whatever you're going to do, you'd better do it fast!"

Momentarily freed from the task of fending off Paganus's bones, Ghaji turned to Diran. "We can't get close enough to Solus to stop him physically. Can either you or Leontis affect him with a priestly spell?"

Diran shook his head. "There is nothing either of us can do to mystically counter Solus's power."

"We'd need another psionicist," Leontis said, "or a full-fledged wizard."

Tresslar snorted. "I'll pretend I didn't hear that last comment. Solus needs to be able to see the bones in order to levitate them. Even his somewhat weak vision is enough, as long as he can maintain eye contact."

Solus had suffered a serious head injury when he became free of the Kalashtar Galharath's control. Tresslar had done his best to repair the psiforged, but Solus's vision had been weakened somehow during the process. When necessary, Hinto acted as Solus's eyes, and while the psiforged didn't seem to truly need the halfling's assistance, it was obvious to the companions that the construct appreciated his small friend's kindness.

"What are you suggesting?" Ghaji asked. "That we blind him? We can't get close enough, and if Diran threw a pair of daggers at him, Solus would just deflect them telekinetically."

Yvka stepped over to join them. She looked uncomfortable as she began to speak, as if what she were about to say went against her better instincts. Ghaji knew his lover was about to reveal something she preferred to keep private.

"Maybe I can help." The elf-woman rolled her left sleeve up to the elbow then stretched out her arm toward the psiforged. Ghaji gaped to see a shimmering dark blue design on the fair skin of the elf-woman's inner arm. It was a dragonmark, one the half-orc had never seen before, and considering just how much he'd seen of Yvka—not to mention how often he'd seen it—he would've known if she'd possessed such a mark. This was something new.

Yvka's brow furrowed in concentration, and a circle of shadow the size of a large plate appeared before Solus's eyes. The ebon circle darted forward and sealed itself over the psiforged's green orbs, covering them as if with a flap of night-black flesh and cutting off their verdant glowing light.

The instant Solus's eyes were sealed by Yvka's shadows, the dark serpent withdrew its fangs from the construct's head and hissed at the companions. It reared back, eyes returned to their previous crimson color, its coils unwinding from around the psiforged's neck as the foul thing prepared to leave its useless host for another.

But before the serpent could launch itself from Solus's shoulders, Diran managed to withdraw his silver arrowhead from his pocket, and the priest thrust it toward the dark reptile. The arrowhead flared with bright blue-white illumination, and the serpent shrieked its agony in a human voice—a woman's voice. The creature's scream died away, and it went limp as it slipped from Solus's shoulders and fell to the cavern floor. Its sinuous form straightened and shrank somewhat, its head becoming white and separating into five fingers. When its transformation was finished, the serpent had become an arm clad in a sleeve of black cloth, withered hand covered in dead-white flesh.

Diran stepped forward, continuing to focus the silver light of his arrowhead on the arm. He still held a silver dagger in his other hand, and he knelt down and plunged the blade through the back of the bloodless hand. The fingers spasmed once, and then both hand and arm collapsed into dust from which coils of sulfurous wisps like tiny smoke-serpents rose into the air.

Diran stood. The silver arrowhead no longer gleamed with light, and the priest tucked the holy symbol back into its vest pocket. He continued to hold onto his dagger, and Ghaji didn't blame him. There was an excellent chance Diran would have need of a blade again, and soon.

Yvka gestured at Solus, and the patch of darkness covering his eyes dissipated.

The psiforged nodded to the elf-woman. "You have my thanks, Yvka. I struggled to resist the serpent's control, but there was only so much I could do. The creature was very powerful."

Tresslar turned to Yvka as the elf-woman rolled down her sleeve to once again conceal her dragonmark. The artificer was about to speak when the water-spheres dissolved with a series of soft pops, and Paganus's bones fell clattering to the stone floor. Now that Solus was free of the serpent's control, the bones lay where they landed, unmoving.

"I believe that was the Mark of Shadow, was it not?" Tresslar asked.

Yvka nodded. "It manifested in Kolbyr, during the Fury."

"It's not unknown for dragonmarks to appear later in one's life." The artificer looked thoughtful. "I wonder if exposure to high levels of the Fury had something to do with its emergence."

Ghaji looked at Yvka, but the elf-woman wouldn't meet his gaze. The sudden appearance of a dragonmark was a major event in her life, but in the two days since they'd departed Kolbyr, she hadn't mentioned it to Ghaji. And now he knew why she'd insisted they make love in the dark the last several times: she hadn't wanted him to see her dragonmark. Ghaji had always felt an emotional distance between Yvka and himself, and he'd struggled not to let it bother him. But her reluctance to share this latest development with him only made Ghaji feel farther away from her than ever.

Hinto and Onu stood looking down at the black residue that was all that remained of Nathifa's arm.

"Was that really a *lich's* arm?" Onu said. "Most remarkable!"

Hinto frowned at the changeling. "You're enjoying this far too much, you know."

Onu grinned. "My dear lad, one can *never* enjoy life too much!"

Hinto looked back down at the ebon dust. "Seems to me this business has little to do with life."

Ghaji attempted to push aside his feelings about Yvka for the time being, but he vowed that the two of them would have a long talk when the opportunity presented itself. "Why would the lich sacrifice her arm just to slow us down?"

"She gave up more than just an arm," Diran said. "She invested it with a significant portion of her own mystic power so that it could break through Solus's psychic defenses and control him. Now that the arm is destroyed, that power is lost to her forever."

"She's getting desperate," Leontis said in a low, almost guttural voice. "I can smell it in the air."

Ghaji feared the priest wasn't speaking metaphorically. In the time since he'd emerged hairless from the fireblast, Leontis's hair had grown in to the point where it reached past his ears, and he had the beginnings of a mustache and beard once again. More disturbing, his body was dotted with small patches of thick body hair that resembled animal fur. Ghaji had been keeping a close eye on Leontis, and the half-orc was determined to strike the man down if he began to transform into a werewolf once again—and from the way Yvka, Tresslar, and Asenka continued glancing at Leontis, they felt the same way.

"But what's so important about this cavern that it's worth that kind of sacrifice?" Asenka asked. "Nathifa evidently didn't want Paganus's skeleton, and there's nothing else of interest here."

"Nothing obvious," Yvka said.

Ghaji was about to interject a comment of his own, but he was cut off by an ear-piercing—and familiar—scream from the far end of the cavern.

Ghaji looked at Diran, Diran looked at Ghaji, and at the same time they said, "The barghest."

❖ ❖ ❖ ❖ ❖ ❖ ❖

Things weren't turning out as Nathifa had planned. She'd sacrificed her arm to gain enough time to locate Paganus's hoard of magic items and drain their energy into the Amahau. Once she'd accomplished that, she'd no longer have to be concerned about Diran Bastiaan and his retinue of hangers-on. With the mystical power that would be at her disposal, she'd be able to destroy them all easily, and the Amahau would still have more than enough magic left over for Nathifa to fulfill Vol's design for the Principalities.

She'd located the dragon's hoard easily enough. It lay at the rear of the cavern, accessible through a short tunnel concealed by an illusion spell that the lich had been able to remove with ease, even diminished in personal power as she was after the loss of her arm. The hoard chamber contained an impressive collection of stolen magical items: amulets, wands, crystalline figurines, gems of all types and sizes, pendants, bracelets, rings, gauntlets, leather-bound books, yellowed scrolls . . . But the chamber contained more than Paganus's hoard. The dragon's treasures lay piled around sepulchers carved out of black stone, a dozen or more, all with their lids removed, shoved aside, or knocked onto the floor. Strands of white gossamer covered the walls, stretched between the sepulchers, and lay across the magic items as if they had collected there naturally over the course of three thousand years while Paganus lay suffering in the outer cavern from wounds that would never heal. But Nathifa knew the white strands were no natural occurrence.

The lich stood at the chamber's entrance, a rough-hewn doorway that, from the crudity of its construction, had most likely been made by Paganus when the dragon had broken through the wall in order to use the ancient crypt to store his treasures. Makala and Haaken stood in front of the sorceress, and Skarm stood in front of them. There was no sign of life in the chamber, but Nathifa could sense it just the same. Life that was, paradoxically enough, suffused with negative energy.

"What is that stuff?" Skarm asked. "Cobwebs?"

"It's webbing, yes," Makala said. "But not the kind formed from dust."

"The vampire is correct," Nathifa said. "In order to safely drain the mystic energy from this many magical artifacts, I will need several moments of undisturbed concentration. It appears that in the decades since Paganus's death, a new resident has taken possession of the dragon's hoard chamber. You three will enter the chamber, flush out the creature, and slay it for me."

Makala turned to Nathifa. "You're a sorceress. Why not use magic to destroy whatever thing has made this place its lair?"

Nathifa wasn't about to admit to Makala that she'd been weakened by the sacrifice of her arm. Nor did she wish to reveal that she wanted to conserve her power for the task of wielding the

Amahau. Using the device to absorb a vast amount of energy in a short period of time would require precise control. One mistake, and the Amahau would release its captured energy in a conflagration of mystic power that would destroy everything in its vicinity—including Nathifa and her servants.

Nathifa spoke in a low, dangerous voice. "Because I am your mistress, and I command you."

Makala had already had the pleasure of tearing the lich's arm off, and Nathifa thought the vampire—no longer be able to restrain herself—would finally attack. But though Makala's undead eyes flared bright crimson, the vampire made no move toward Nathifa. Instead, she gave the lich a cold, hard smile, and nodded.

"As you desire, my lady."

Makala turned and walked past Skarm into the hoard chamber.

Haakan grinned. "Looks like this is going to be fun!" The sea raider's flesh turned gray, his muscles swelled, a dorsal fin protruded from his spine, and black claws erupted from the tips of his broadening fingers and toes. His face lengthened, teeth grew sharper and more pronounced, hair and ears disappeared, eyes became shiny black orbs, and gill slits opened on the sides of his neck.

The wereshark lumbered into the chamber after Makala.

Of Nathifa's three servants, only Skarm still remained standing at the chamber's threshold.

The barghest turned to his mistress, an expression of mingled fear and apology on his goblin features. "Nathifa, what sort of creature—"

The lich didn't wait for Skarm to finish his sentence. With her remaining hand, she snatched hold of the barghest's cloak, lifted him off his feet, and hurled him into the chamber. Skarm yelped as he flew overtop the heads of Makala and Haaken, arms and legs windmilling as if he might somehow slow his flight. In anticipation of a painful landing, the barghest began to transform into his natural shape of a lupine-goblinoid hybrid. But before he could complete his metamorphosis, a strand of white silk shot down from the chamber's ceiling and struck the barghest in the back. The strand adhered instantly and went taut. Skarm's flight was arrested, and he hung in the air for a split second before the strand withdrew, pulling the barghest along with it.

Nathifa, Makala, and Haaken looked upward to see Skarm being reeled in by a mottled gray spider the size of a horse. The spindly creature clung to the chamber's ceiling and as the barghest—still in mid-change—came within reach, she snatched hold of him with her mouth parts and swiftly plunged her fangs into Skarm's chest. Skarm resumed his goblin shape, almost as if the spider's venom had forced the transformation, and then the huge creature flexed her abdomen and rammed a sharp barb into his stomach.

A scream of sheer agony tore loose from Skarm's throat, and in that instant Nathifa knew the barghest was lost.

She was about to order Makala and Haaken to slay Skarm— though the barghest was next to useless, he had served her for many years and therefore had earned a swift death. But before the words could leave her mouth, a pair of web-wrapped corpses that had been lying hidden in sepulchers sat up. Beneath their gossamer covering, the mummies' skin rippled, as if numerous small creatures squirmed within. The mummies began climbing out of their hiding places, and Nathifa decided that Skarm hadn't been *that* good a servant after all. It would take the spider several moments to finish implanting a fresh batch of eggs inside the barghest's body and wrapping it in silk to turn him into a new web mummy. The mummies needed to be destroyed now, before they had the chance to release the broodswarms that writhed within them.

"Forget Skarm! Stop the others!" Nathifa ordered.

The web mummies had finished lurching out of their sepulchers and now shambled toward the vampire and the wereshark.

"Skarm who?" Makala said with a laugh, and she and Haaken ran toward the web-covered corpses.

"But whatever you do, don't—"

Haaken rammed a gray-fleshed fist the size of a ham through the chest of a web mummy, while Makala took hold of the other's head and ripped it off the creature's shoulders with a single, savage twist.

"—break open their bodies," Nathifa finished with a sigh.

As Haaken withdrew his hand, a swarm of fist-sized bright-red spiders surged forth from the gaping hole he'd created in their host's body. A second broodswarm began to emerge with equal swiftness from inside the neck of the web mummy Makala had decapitated.

"*Now* you tell us!" Makala said.

CHAPTER

EIGHTEEN

As the broodswarm spiders launched themselves at Makala and Haaken, their mother dropped Skarm. The barghest—partially covered in webbing and writhing in pain—hit the floor of the crypt with a sharp crack of snapping bone. The tomb spider released her grip on the ceiling, flipped over as she descended, landed on her legs, and scuttled toward Makala and Haaken.

Tomb spiders reproduced by implanting their eggs in humanoid corpses, which in turn reanimated as undead creatures called web mummies. Once the eggs inside them hatched, the mummies served as both incubator and food source for the spider's young. As they grew within their undead host, the spiderlings began to devour those weaker than themselves until eventually only the strongest individual survived to emerge from the mummy as an adult. But if the immature spiders were released prematurely, they formed a broodswarm, attacking any living humanoids in the vicinity. In turn, the parent spider would seek to replace a ruined web mummy, for the immature spiderlings would never live to reach adulthood once released from their host.

Nathifa knew the tomb spider wasn't trying to save her children, for she could not do so. She was instead seeking hosts in which to implant more eggs. The lich didn't know whether Makala or Haaken could serve as effective hosts, since one was undead and the other a lycanthrope, and she didn't care. All that mattered was that they provided a distraction to occupy the tomb spider so the sorceress could work. Nathifa could have easily used her magic to slay the tomb spider. A simple fire spell would have sufficed, given the flammable webbing that filled the crypt chamber. But she refused to spare even the smallest fraction of her power to aid her servants. She needed every scrap of her magic to accomplish the task before her, especially now that she would be forced to drain the magic from Paganus's hoard as fast as she could. Maintaining control of the energy transference into the Amahau would take a greater effort than she had originally planned, but there was no hope for it. Bastiaan and his followers would be here soon: she could sense it. Swiftness was paramount now.

Besides, Nathifa thought, if the tomb spider managed to destroy Makala, the creature would be doing her a favor.

Makala and Haaken were fighting to shake off the crimson spiderlings they had released, when the two web mummies—even though one was headless—lurched forward and grabbed hold of them. The tomb spider raced toward them, intending to inject the intruders with her venom. Nathifa didn't bother to watch anymore. Whatever the outcome of her servants' battle with the giant spider, she would claim the power of Paganus's hoard in the name of Vol.

Before she could begin, she needed to do one last thing. She reached up, pressed her fingers against her left eye, and gouged it from the socket. The lich felt no pain, but even if the action had caused her excruciating agony, she would have gladly endured it for her Queen. She spoke a series of blasphemous words and tossed her eye into the air. The detached orb swelled to the size of a melon and hovered above its owner's head, facing the crypt's entrance. In case her servants failed to defeat the tomb spider, Nathifa wanted to make certain that someone was guarding her back, and there was no one she trusted more than herself.

She plunged her remaining hand inside her chest and withdrew the dragonwand from her inner darkness. She held the mystical artifact out before her, the golden dragonhead with crystalline teeth and ruby eyes that was the Amahau affixed on the end. She concentrated on activating the Gatherer, and the dragonhead's ruby eyes glimmered as the device began to do what it was designed for: absorb magic power. The undead sorceress shifted her perceptions until she could see multicolored lines of mystic force curl upward from the hundreds of objects Paganus had stolen over the centuries. The energy-tendrils began snaking toward the Amahau, and despite her vow to maintain strict control as the absorption proceeded, Nathifa couldn't help laughing.

● ● ● ◉ ● ● ●

The companions followed the direction of the barghest's scream and discovered a tunnel at the far end of the dragon's cavern. They hurried down it and soon came to a crudely excavated opening leading to a chamber of some sort, and they paused at the entrance.

Diran took the situation in at a glance: ancient crypt filled with webbing, tomb spider, broodswarm younglings, a pair of web mummies (one without a head), a wereshark—where had *it* come from?—Makala (his heart lurched at the sight of her), the barghest lying on the floor half-covered in webbing, and the lich Nathifa, holding Tresslar's dragonwand out before her, a huge crimson eye floating over the sorceress's head as she worked some manner of foul spell. Makala and the wereshark were held in the grip of the web mummies, broodswarm spiders crawling all over them, the younglings' mother rushing in to join her children's attack.

Diran had no idea what the floating eye hovering over Nathifa could do, and he really didn't want to find out. He hurled a dagger at the levitating orb, hoping to spear the eyeball the same way he'd practiced throwing knives at pieces of fruit when he was a boy. But as the dagger flew toward the crimson eye, a beam of necromantic energy lanced forth from the pupil, deflecting the blade. The dagger's new trajectory sent it hurtling toward the tomb spider, and the blade pierced the giant arachnid's abdomen.

The spider screeched and whirled about, as if to shoot an accusing glare at whoever had dealt it such an insulting wound. The monster's inhuman black eyes fixed on the companions and then, though the creature gave no obvious command, a dozen more web-covered figures sat up inside the black-stone sepulchers, their skin writhing from the motion of all the spiderlings growing inside them.

"Solus, Tresslar, Leontis, and I will handle Nathifa," Diran said. "Ghaji, you take the others and deal with the web mummies. But be careful: the spiderlings inside them are just as venomous as their parent."

"Got it. Good luck, Diran." Ghaji turned to the others. "You heard him. Let's go!" The half-orc warrior dashed forward, axe raised and ready for battle, Yvka, Asenka, Hinto, and Onu following close on his heels.

Diran had momentarily forgotten about the changeling. Onu's combat skills were rudimentary at best, and Diran feared for the man's life. But there was nothing the priest could do to help him now. He would have to trust that Ghaji and the others would do what they could to protect Onu.

"The lich is using the Amahau to drain the energy from the magic artifacts in this crypt!" Tresslar said. "Once she has that much power at her command, we won't be able to stop her!"

"And what of that floating eye?" Leontis asked.

"A guardian of some sort," Tresslar said.

The lich is getting desperate, Diran thought, else she wouldn't be sacrificing pieces of her body like this.

"We'll never get close to the lich unless we do something about that eye," Leontis said. His voice was pitched low, the words more growled than spoken. Diran knew his friend was losing his battle against the beast that shared his soul.

Ghaji and the others were battling the web mummies, but since the warriors were restraining themselves to avoid releasing any more broodswarms, they were at a decided disadvantage. The tomb spider had turned her attention back to Makala and the wereshark, and the two monsters ignored the crimson spiderlings crawling over their bodies as they fought the giant arachnid. Nathifa remained motionless as she continued to draw magic power into the dragonwand. If Tresslar was right about what Nathifa was doing, and Diran had no reason to doubt the artificer, then the sorceress was growing more powerful by the moment. They had to stop the lich. Now.

The priest turned to Solus. "I have an idea. I just hope you have the energy to help me make it a reality."

⚇ ⚇ ⚇ ⚇ ⚇ ⚇ ⚇

Ghaji had fought undead of all sorts during his travels with Diran, but he'd never faced tomb mummies before. The things were slow-moving and clumsy like most zombies, and they attacked without any sort of strategy or concentrated group effort. Their strength wasn't out of the ordinary. In fact, they seemed somewhat weaker than most undead. But these mummies possessed two very important differences: the webbing that covered them was incredibly sticky, and their body cavities were filled with deadly crimson spiderlings. So the trick was to fight the damned things while simultaneously avoiding touching them or causing a wound that would release the spiderlings they hosted.

Far easier said than done.

If Ghaji's elemental axe had still functioned, its flames would have made short work of the mummies, as well as the spiderlings they hosted, but the axe was just a weapon of steel now, and there was no point in wishing otherwise. Various objects were scattered across the floor of the ancient crypt, making it awkward to maneuver, but the clutter also hindered the web mummies, so overall it proved an advantage for the faster, more agile living warriors. Dust covered the crypt floor, and Ghaji ordered Hinto and Onu to scoop up handfuls and throw them onto the oncoming mummies. Ghaji hoped that the dust would adhere to the mummies' webbing and nullify its stickiness, making it possible to touch the creatures without becoming bound to them.

Ghaji knelt and rubbed his axe head in the dust for the same reason, and Asenka followed suit for her long sword. Yvka sorted through the magical items in her pouch for weapons that would deter the mummies without damaging them to the point where the spiderlings they hosted were set free. Ghaji didn't know whether Yvka could employ the magic of her dragonmark so soon after wielding it against the dark serpent that had taken control of Solus, but even if she could, he had no idea what use it would be against the web mummies. Though the same luminescent mold grew here on the walls of the crypt just as it did in the outer cavern, the light was so dim that Ghaji doubted Yvka's shadow magic would make any difference to the mummies.

So Hinto and Onu threw dust, Ghaji and Asenka struck the attacking web mummies using the flats of their dust-coated blades, and Yvka tossed a variety of mystic weapons designed by the artificers of the Shadow Network—walnuts that exploded with concussive force, thistles that flew through the air and traced lines that created magical barriers. Thus Ghaji and the others managed to hold back the tide of undead without releasing any more spiderlings.

But the dust covering their weapons soon rubbed off, and Asenka's long sword became stuck fast to a web mummy's chest. As the mummy reached out to grab hold of Asenka, Ghaji started forward, intending to keep the monster from getting its undead claws on her. But before he could do more than take a step in her direction, a hand fell on his shoulder, and a hollow voice said, "Allow me."

Ghaji was startled to see a web mummy walk past him—when had the thing gotten through their defenses?—and stagger toward Asenka. The creature walked with one hand held palm up, and Ghaji saw that the thing carried a handful of crypt-dust. The mummy stepped up to the one reaching for Asenka and rubbed the dust it carried onto the blade of her sword. Asenka looked at the mummy assisting her in disbelief, but she was no fool. She yanked her sword free and quickly stepped back out of reach of either mummy. Their undead benefactor then rubbed its hands together, making sure both were coated with dust, and then shoved the other mummy as hard as it could. The second mummy stumbled backward, bumped into the edge of a sepulcher, and fell into it, web-wrapped legs sticking up and waving uselessly in the air.

The helper-mummy turned back to face them, a familiar grin

on its desiccated, sunken-eyed face, and that's when Ghaji noticed that beneath web-strands covering the mummy lay a bright red sea captain's coat.

"I'm glad that worked," Onu said. "I wasn't sure I could fool the beastly things!"

Ghaji grinned back in relief. After that, the battle went more easily, for Onu—still wearing the shape of a web mummy—was able to walk right up to the real creatures and rub dust on them without interference. Thus Ghaji and the others continued holding the web mummies at bay, the half-orc hoping that Diran was having equal success dealing with Nathifa.

●　●　●　◉　●　●　●

In the confusion, no one—including Asenka—noticed that when she tore her sword free from the web mummy, a tiny red spider no larger than an infant's fist clung to the blade. This youngling had been hiding close to the surface of its host's dead, dry flesh, doing its best to avoid being devoured by its ravenous sisters. When Asenka yanked her sword away, a small scrap of skin came with it, a scrap the youngling was clinging to. The spider, following its instincts to attack anything that threatened its host, scuttled down the length of the sword toward the hilt and onto the back of Asenka's hand. The warrior woman felt the feather-light touch of the spiderling's legs on her flesh, But before she could shake off the tiny creature, it sank its fangs into the back of her hand and released venom into her system.

The bite was painful, but Asenka had endured worse in her time, and her only reaction was to draw in a hissing breath of air that no one else heard. She gave her hand a violent shake, dislodged the spiderling onto the floor, and crushed it beneath her boot before it could crawl away. She then examined the back of her hand. The bite was already swelling and beginning to purple, and she could feel it throb in concert with her pulse. She didn't experience any immediate effects of the venom, though. No lightheadedness, no nausea. She decided that not only had the spiderling been too small to deliver much venom but that she'd managed to dislodge it before it could inject what little it could. Besides, she had more important things to worry about than a tiny spider bite right now. She had to help the others keep the web mummies busy and buy Diran enough time to stop Nathifa.

And so Asenka returned her attention to battle, the spider's bite all but forgotten.

● ● ● ◉ ● ● ●

Makala and Haaken stood wrapped in webbing strong as steel, held captive by a pair of web mummies while crimson spiderlings crawled across their bodies, stinging whatever flesh remained exposed. The younglings' mother crouched in front of them, the tomb spider's fangs glistening with fluid as she prepared to inject them with her venom. The only reason the giant spider hadn't done so by now, Makala assumed, was because the arrival of Diran and his companions had distracted her. But now that the rest of the tomb spider's web mummies were attacking the intruders, evidently the mother was ready to return to the business at hand: namely preparing new hosts in which she could implant eggs.

The spiderlings' stings hurt, but Makala's undead physiology seemed unaffected by their venom. She wasn't certain what effect a full dose from an adult tomb spider might do, though. Haaken roared and struggled against his silken bonds as the spiderlings savaged his body, but Makala thought the wereshark reacted more out of rage and frustration than pain. While Haaken was a lycanthrope, he was still a living creature, and might well react more strongly to an injection of adult tomb spider venom.

Makala didn't care what happened to Haaken, nor did she care whether or not Nathifa succeeded in absorbing the magic of Paganus's hoard. Right now all she cared about was not becoming a repository for a clutch of tomb spider eggs.

As the tomb spider moved forward to bite Makala, the vampire transformed into mist. The arachnid's fangs passed through her insubstantial form harmlessly. The web mummy that had been holding onto her staggered backward as if in confusion, and the webbing that had encircled her, with nothing solid left to hold it up, fell to the crypt floor. The tomb spider scuttled backward and crouched low, wary. Its prey had vanished and its tiny spider mind was attempting to grasp what had happened and whether or not this strange development constituted a new threat.

Makala willed her mist-form to float upward and over the tomb spider, and then she transformed back into her humanoid shape. Makala dropped onto the tomb spider's back and, marshalling all her vampire's strength, she rammed her hands through the creature's body. There was a loud crunching sound as Makala penetrated the spider's outer shell, and then her hands were covered with thick warm fluid. Makala grasped hold of the slippery soft organs inside and pulled.

The tomb spider reared back in agony, front legs waving wildly in the air. Makala was thrown backward off the spider, the guts she held onto trailing out of the creature's back like streamers of bloody meat. She released the organs, transformed into a bat in midair, and swooped up toward the crypt's ceiling. Using a combination of both her bat and vampire senses, Makala was able to form a clear mental image of the battle occurring below.

She "saw" the tomb spider start to come back down on its forelegs. As it did, Haaken pulled free from the web mummy that held him and threw himself beneath one of the spider's legs. The claw on the leg's tip tore through the webbing wrapped about the wereshark's chest, in the process slicing a long wound down Haaken's chest and abdomen. But that didn't matter. Haaken would heal swiftly—and far more importantly, he was free.

Makala was impressed. She hadn't thought Haaken that intelligent.

Haaken let out an elated battle-roar and grabbed hold of the tomb spider's two front forelegs. The giant arachnid brought her mouth parts down in an attempt to sink her fangs into Haaken's broad shark-like head. But before she could strike, Haaken ripped the forelegs legs out of her body, and the tomb spider squealed in pain. She scuttled backward, gore spilling from the gaping wounds were her legs had been attached to her body, but Haaken had scented the blood of his prey, and the wereshark wasn't about to let the tomb spider escape. He leaped forward, claws outstretched, tooth-filled maw open wide, and as he landed atop the spider, he clamped his jaws down upon the spider's eyes and bit down with all his might. The tomb spider's shell cracked open like that of a steamed crab beneath the pressure of the wereshark's jaws and gore sprayed over Haaken. The tomb spider whipped about from side to side in a desperate attempt to dislodge her attacker, but Haaken held on tight with his clawed hands, biting, tearing, and rending.

Finally, the spider's body slumped to the floor of the crypt and its remaining legs curled inward, twitching feebly as the creature surrendered to death. Haaken, his shark's snout smeared with blood and viscera, continued ravaging the tomb spider's corpse, gulping down great mouthfuls of the thing's innards with mindless efficiency.

❀ ❀ ❀ ❀ ❀ ❀ ❀

Leontis stood by, only half-listening while Diran explained his plan to the psiforged and the artificer. The priest watched with increasing frustration as the battle took place around him and, far worse, without him. He was *Sir* Leontis of the Order of Templars, and it wasn't in his nature to stand idly by while others risked their lives in the struggle against evil. He understood why Diran had asked him to stay back, though. If Nathifa was a powerful enough lich, it was possible that both priests would be needed to stop her, but Leontis knew another reason—perhaps the most important one—was that Diran didn't want to risk having Leontis lose control of his lupine side again so soon after what had happened in the forest when they'd fought the shadowclaws. The werewolf had helped the others against those monsters then, but what guarantee was there that the beast wouldn't turn on Leontis's companions this time? None at all.

Leontis recognized the logic in Diran's strategy and even agreed with it, but it still chafed. Diran had played upon their friendship to convince Leontis to come along on this quest, all for the sake of some dubious visions revealed by a demon desperate to make a deal to prevent being cast out of its young host body. Leontis had allowed himself to be convinced, telling himself that perhaps he could do one last bit of good before leaving this mortal plane and joining with the Silver Flame. But he'd contributed little to the group's efforts so far. He'd stopped a Fury-crazed Ghaji from slaying Diran, and he'd killed the flying creature that had been about to attack them as their longboat had approached the island, and that was all. The werewolf had done far more, killing numerous shadowclaws before being caught in the fireblast. It seemed that for all his vaunted training and priestly abilities, Leontis was of less use than the wild animal that shared his soul.

Why should he keep fighting the wolf inside him, then? Perhaps there was a reason he had been infected with the curse of lycanthropy. Perhaps it *wasn't* a curse, at least not in his case. Perhaps it was, instead, a weapon that he was meant to wield in his order's battle against evil. Evil against evil, fire against fire . . .

He shook his head. That was the werewolf talking, not the man. The beast would do anything to be free again, even attempt to persuade Leontis to believe that evil could be used as a tool for good when wielded by one of the Purified. But that was the sort of thinking that led to abuses of power. The ends did *not* justify the means, no matter what. The teachings of the priesthood were absolutely clear on this, and so Leontis vowed to continue fighting to keep the werewolf caged inside him.

But then he heard an animalistic roar, and the sound sent a strange fire surging up his spine and into his brain. Leontis trained his gaze upon a creature that appeared to be half-human and half-shark. In the confusion, Leontis hadn't taken much notice of the creature, but he knew instinctively that it was a fellow lycanthrope. The wereshark attacked the tomb spider, leaping upon the arachnid and biting huge hunks out of her.

Leontis felt the fire in his mind build into a raging inferno at the sight of the wereshark glutting itself on the spider's internal organs, and when the wolf came to the fore, there was nothing he could do to stop the beast from taking possession of his body. And as he felt his persona giving way to the werewolf's savagery, he was horrified to realize that not only did he like it, he welcomed it.

SEA OF DEATH

❀ ❀ ❀ ❀ ❀ ❀ ❀

Diran saw Leontis shift into his hybrid wolf form and bounded toward the wereshark. The sea-based lycanthrope had slain the tomb spider—something Diran supposed they all should be grateful for—and was engaged in devouring the mutilated remains. Diran had been born and raised in the Principalities, and thus knew that sharks would eat virtually anything, but he had a difficult time believing anyone with even a shred of humanity in them would eat a tomb spider, let alone do so with such enthusiastic delight. In addition, tomb spiders were creatures suffused with negative energy, and Diran couldn't see how even a lycanthrope could ingest the horrid thing's meat without being affected somehow by that energy.

Diran shouted Leontis's name, in a vain attempt to call him back, but it was too late. The man was gone and only the werewolf remained. Leontis snarled as he threw himself upon the wereshark, and the lycanthropes began trying to kill each other, two predators that instinctively sensed and loathed a competitor.

Diran wished he could go to his friend's aid, but there was nothing he could do for Leontis right now. He spared a second to wonder where Makala was—he'd seen her transform into mist and attack the tomb spider, but he hadn't witnessed the outcome of her action. Either the spider had wounded her somehow or, more likely, Makala was still close by, either in mist or bat form. He'd vowed to free his former lover from the curse of undeath and undo the mistake he'd made by not slaying her the moment she awoke as a vampire. Hopefully, he'd get the chance to redeem himself soon . . . after Nathifa was stopped. The lich had to be dealt with before she could absorb even more of the magic in Paganus's hoard.

Diran turned to Tresslar and Solus. "Ready?"

The psiforged and the artificer nodded. Both held daggers given them by the priest, one in each hand. Diran held the same number.

"Throw!" Diran commanded, and the three companions tossed the daggers straight up into the air, without even attempting to aim them anywhere in particular. When the daggers reached the apex of their less-than-graceful flight, Solus grabbed hold of the blades telekinetically and sent them streaking toward the oversized eyeball hovering above Nathifa's head.

The guardian eye released a blast of necromantic energy at the six oncoming daggers, but the blades fanned out, and the ebon beam managed to deflect only one. The remaining five encircled the eye and began rotating rapidly around the living orb, moving with such blinding speed that Diran had a difficult time keeping track of the knives. The eye, moving just as swiftly as the blades, oriented on one after the other, blasting them out of the air with dark beams of mystic force. One blade, two . . . three . . . four . . .

At Solus's mental command, the last dagger curved away in the opposite direction from where the three companions stood. The eye tracked the blade, turning away from them as it prepared to deal with this final threat. As soon as the guardian eye faced the other direction and couldn't see them, Diran slipped another dagger out of its cloak sheath, aimed, and hurled the blade at the back of eye. As the eye blasted the last of the rotating blades, the new dagger plunged into it from behind, and the guardian orb exploded in a spray of blood and viscous fluid.

Nathifa cried out in pain and frustration, but she didn't allow her concentration to slacken. The lich continued absorbing magic into the Amahau, but now she had no guardian to protect her. Solus released control of the levitating daggers and the blades fell to the floor. There was no point in the psiforged driving them into the lich. The only way she could be killed was if the phylactery containing her lifeforce was discovered and destroyed. But if Diran could get close enough, he could use the power of the Silver Flame to repel her, giving Tresslar a chance to regain possession of his dragonwand.

The priest drew a silver dagger from his cloak and removed his arrowhead symbol from his vest pocket. He then turned to Solus and Tresslar.

"Be careful," he warned his companions. "Even diminished as Nathifa is by the loss of her arm and eye, she is still most powerful—all the more so because she possesses the dragonwand."

"I shall remember," Solus said.

"You take care of the lich," Tresslar said, a determined look on his face. "You let me worry about the Amahau."

Diran nodded, and together the three started toward the lich.

⊛ ⊛ ⊛ ⊛ ⊛ ⊛ ⊛

Nathifa was no stranger to mystic power, but she'd never experienced anything like the Amahau before. The sheer amount of magical energy that it could hold was astonishing. It had already drained a good portion of Paganus's hoard, and Nathifa could sense that it wasn't near to being full. How much magic could the dragonhead contain? With its power hers to command, she would be like unto a god herself. She could keep the artifact for herself, continue traveling throughout the Principalities and absorbing magic wherever she went. And when she finally had enough, she could travel to the Fingerbone Mountains and challenge Vol. With the power of the Amahau, she could defeat the Lich Queen, cast her down, and take her place on the throne of bones.

But Nathifa knew it was a foolish dream. She'd made a bargain with Prince Moren to get the supplies to repair the *Zephyr*, and the bill would come due soon—long before she could ever hope to acquire enough power to challenge Vol. Nathifa wondered if perhaps this wasn't how her Queen had planned it all along. Vol might well have sent the Ragestorm, and Prince Moren *had* answered her summons rather quickly. Perhaps he'd been waiting close by at Vol's command.

No matter, Nathifa decided. The die was cast, and events would play themselves out as they would. Let Vol's reign continue. As long as Nathifa finally had her vengeance on Kolbyr, she would be satisfied.

Though the bulk of her concentration was focused on controlling the Amahau, she was able to spare a fraction of her awareness to monitor the progress of the battle around her. Skarm writhed on the crypt floor, his barghest physiology doing its best to fight off the web spider's venom. Nathifa knew he was fighting a losing battle, though. The venom was simply too strong. Nathifa was pleased that

Haaken had killed the web spider, but she was surprised to see the wereshark now fought with another lycanthrope. The lich had been aware that a werewolf numbered among Bastiaan's companions, and she couldn't conceive of a priest—especially one devoted to the Silver Flame—associating with such a monster. There was obviously more to that story than met the eye.

Nathifa saw no sign of Makala, and she wondered if the vampire had betrayed her and fled. Most likely not, Nathifa decided. Makala had many annoying qualities, but cowardice wasn't among them. Makala was probably lurking about somewhere, alert for an opportunity to turn the tide of battle in her favor.

She was pleased that the web mummies and her dark-eye were proving effective at keeping Bastiaan and his friends busy. If the priest and his companions could be held off for a few more moments, she'd be able to—

Pain blossomed in the empty socket where Nathifa's left eye had been, and the lich cried out, more in anger than in hurt. She didn't know how, since she was only subconsciously connected to the dark-eye, but she knew Bastiaan had somehow managed to destroy it. This knowledge was confirmed a split-second later when warm viscous fluid pattered down onto her head and shoulders.

Not now! I'm so *close* . . .

But Nathifa knew her time was up. Weakened as she was by the sacrifices of her arm and eye, she couldn't hope to stand against Bastiaan, especially not without the aid of her servants. Whatever power she had managed to drain into the Amahau would have to serve.

The lich had no need to check if Bastiaan was attacking. She knew he was as surely as she'd ever known anything in her long, foul life. She commanded the Amahau to cease absorbing magic from the items in Paganus's hoard, and she pushed the dragonwand back into the inky-black substance of her shroud. Her body burst apart into dozens of shadowy scraps that resembled ebon leaves, and they swirled about the crypt as if in the grip of turbulent winds. One scrap passed near the ceiling, close to the ear of a black bat, and Nathifa whispered, "Time to leave." Another scrap blew by Haaken's head, and it whispered the same thing to the wereshark. The shadow-leaves then tumbled end over end toward the rough-hewn entrance Paganus had created when he first discovered the crypt millennia ago. She was aware of Bastiaan holding forth his arrowhead symbol, the silver light blazing painfully as she passed. But her form was too diffuse and moving too swiftly for the burning illumination to do more than cause her momentary discomfort. And then Nathifa was through the entrance, a black cloud of shadow-leaves tumbling down the tunnel toward the dragon's cavern lair, her voice a chorus of delighted laughter as she made her escape.

⊛ ⊛ ⊛ ⊛ ⊛ ⊛ ⊛

Asenka watched as the web mummies broke off their attack and began a slow, shuffling retreat to the far side of the crypt. The undead things seemed almost afraid of them now, and she couldn't figure out why, until she turned and saw that the tomb spider had been killed—and in an extremely messy fashion. Without their parent to command the web mummies, the egg-hosts had a new purpose: to preserve the lives of the spiderlings growing inside them. They would no longer risk damaging themselves, for to do so would endanger the lives of the children they carried. A distorted reflection of parental instinct, she supposed, but one that proved an advantage for her and the others.

Her hand throbbed from where the spiderling had bitten her. But though sweat dripped down the sides of her face, and she felt light-headed and sick to her stomach, she forced herself not to worry. Even if she had taken a large enough dose of venom to prove deadly, all she had to do was hold out long enough for the battle to end, and then Diran could heal her. She was Commander of the Sea Scorpions, the elite warriors of Baron Perhata. She could deal with a little bit of poison in her veins. After all, the ale in Perhata was so awful, it practically qualified as poison in its own right, and she'd quaffed enough of the bitter stuff over the years to build up immunity to any toxic substance, right?

She was horrified to see Leontis—in werewolf form—battling the wereshark, and the scene was so nightmarish that for a moment she feared the spider venom was making her hallucinate. But then she saw Nathifa break apart into a flurry of shadows, and she decided it had to be real. Even in delirium, she wouldn't have been able to dream up something that bizarre. As the shadows flew out of the crypt, a bat descended from the ceiling and headed for Leontis and the wereshark. The bat changed as it landed, and Makala reached out and grabbed hold of Leontis by the scruff of his neck and saw that the werewolf was bleeding from dozens of cuts made by the wereshark's claws The werewolf spun around, intending to sink his claws into whoever had the temerity to interrupt his battle with a fellow lycanthrope. But before Leontis could land a blow on Makala, Haaken took advantage of his foe's distraction to snatch the werewolf from the vampire's grasp. Before Leontis could react, Haaken hurled him away, and the werewolf soared through the air—

—straight toward Asenka.

She tried to avoid being struck by the werewolf, but he was moving too fast. Leontis slammed into Asenka, and she saw bright white flash behind her eyes, followed by darkness.

CHAPTER

NINETEEN

Ghaji ran toward Asenka, hoping to shove her out of the way before Leontis could hit her, but he was too late. The werewolf struck her and they both went down hard.

Leontis was momentarily stunned by the impact, but Ghaji doubted he'd stay that way for long. Though the half-orc's axe wasn't made of silver and no longer produced flame, it was still razor-sharp, so Ghaji rushed forward. As Leontis struggled to rise—broken bones already setting themselves and beginning to knit—the half-orc swung his axe and cleaved the werewolf's skull in two. Blood and bits of gray matter sprayed the air as Leontis let out a sharp whine and slumped to the ground. Ghaji knew that as devastating as the blow appeared, it would do no more than slow Leontis. A creature that could heal as swiftly as he had from the fireblast in the forest would have little trouble recovering from even a serious head wound, but at least they wouldn't have to deal with the werewolf while he healed.

Ghaji wanted to go to Asenka's side and tend to the injured woman, but he was too experienced a warrior to lose his focus in the midst of battle. He forced himself to ignore his wounded comrade as he swept his gaze around the crypt, searching for the next threat. The web mummies had retreated, the tomb spider was dead, the crimson spiderlings that had been released earlier had scattered, the barghest was half-wrapped in webbing, and Nathifa was nowhere to be seen. The lich had evidently escaped, and Makala and the wereshark were running for the crypt entrance, obviously intending to follow their mistress's lead. Diran, Tresslar, and Solus were moving toward Makala and Haaken, but the two monsters ran with inhuman speed, and it was obvious the priest and the others wouldn't reach them in time. Diran held a silver dagger, and he hurled it at the wereshark, but Makala—no doubt anticipating Diran's move—knocked the blade out of the air before it could strike the lycanthrope. Solus's psionic crystals glowed as the construct marshaled his mental abilities, but as the wereshark ran he grabbed an object from Paganus's hoard, a golden shield, off the ground and flung it at the psiforged with all his might. The shield whirled through the air and struck Solus a ringing blow in the face. The psiforged staggered backward, his concentration broken.

Tresslar rummaged in his backpack for a mystic device he might be able to use to prevent Makala and the wereshark from fleeing, but he was too late. The two passed through the opening in the crypt wall and disappeared into the tunnel beyond.

"We must not let them escape!" Diran shouted as he ran toward the tunnel.

Ghaji called out to his friend. The half-orc was unable to keep a note of concern out of his voice, and that, more likely than anything else, is what caused Diran to stop and spin around. When the priest saw Asenka lying on the floor near Ghaji, her body bent and broken, he forgot about the lich and ran over to kneel at the woman's side. Diran saw Leontis then, lying on the floor close by, his lupine skull rent in two by Ghaji's axe. The priest seemed to hesitate a moment, as if unsure who needed his help more. But then he turned away from Leontis and focused the entirety of his attention on Asenka.

Ghaji knew that Diran's order forbade raising the dead, and as much as his friend might love Asenka, if she died, the priest would not bring her back.

"Is she . . . ?" Ghaji couldn't finish his sentence.

Diran placed two fingers against the vein in Asenka's neck. "Her heart still beats, but weakly."

Ghaji let out a breath he hadn't realized he'd been holding. As long as there was a spark of life remaining in Asenka, then there was hope.

The others gathered around as Diran clasped Asenka's hand, closed his eyes, and called upon the power of the Silver Flame to work its healing magic through him. Ghaji had seen Diran heal people who looked as if they'd been chewed up by a tarrasque and spit out, but he couldn't help thinking how awful Asenka looked. Her skin was almost white, and blood ran from her mouth, nostrils, and ears. Her head lolled at an odd angle, indicating her neck was broken, and both her arms and her right leg had snapped when Leontis had collided with her. The leg was especially bad, with a jagged end of bone protruding from the flesh. And though Ghaji was no healer, he'd seen enough battlefield injuries in his time to know that there was a strong likelihood that Asenka had suffered internal damage as well. Ghaji had never known his friend to fail in an attempt to heal, but the half-orc feared that even the power of the Silver Flame might not be enough this time.

A moment passed without any sign that Diran's efforts were having any effect. And then Asenka's eyes flew open wide and she drew in a gasping breath of air. Diran opened his own eyes and gazed down upon her face with tender concern.

"Asenka?" he said gently. "Can you hear me?"

Blood bubbled past her lips as she struggled to speak. "Diran? I . . . I . . ."

And then a gout of dark blood sprayed from Asenka's mouth as she screamed. Her body stiffened as if her skeleton were trying to tear free from the flesh that trapped it, and then she fell still. Her eyes remained open, but they were glassy and empty, and Ghaji knew she was dead.

Diran, still holding Asenka's hand, gazed down upon his lover's slack features and staring eyes without comprehension at first. And then he turned her hand over to reveal a purple-black welt the size of a bird's egg.

Tears flowed down Diran's face, and when he spoke his tone was detached and devoid of emotion.

"The tomb spider and its progeny are creatures of negative energy. Once injected into a victim, their venom causes healing magic to have the opposite effect. Instead of repairing injury and restoring health it . . ." He took in a shuddering breath before going on. "Asenka must have been bitten by a spiderling, and though the amount of venom injected into her body was slight, the rest of her injures were so severe that when my healing magic interacted with the venom . . ." He trailed off, but there was no need to complete the thought. It was clear enough. Asenka had been on the edge of death, and Diran's attempt to heal her had, thanks to the poison of the tomb spider, killed her.

Asenka was gone.

Ghaji wanted to say something, anything, to comfort his friend, but no words came to him. All he could do was step forward and lay a hand on the priest's shoulder. Diran didn't seem to notice. He just continued staring at Asenka's face.

No one spoke for several moments, and then a scuttling sound broke the silence. The companions turned to see that Skarm was using a single clawed hand to pull himself toward the crypt entrance. But the wounded barghest was too weak to do more than scratch his nails against the stone floor.

Diran's tears stopped as if a switch had been thrown somewhere inside him. He gently lay Asenka's hand down and rose to his feet. He walked over and briefly knelt by Leontis' side, then after a quick examination, he stood once more.

"Leontis should make a full recovery," Diran said, his voice more toneless than that of a warforged. "Even now his curse is working to repair his wounds."

Ghaji had to repress a shudder upon seeing the cold, dispassionate look in his friend's ice-blue eyes.

"The barghest knows where Nathifa and the others are bound next," Diran said. "I'll go talk to him and find out. Alone."

The priest turned and started walking toward the web-covered creature. He paused at the spot where Nathifa had been standing to gather up the daggers that had fallen when Solus stopped levitating them. Most of the blades he slipped back into their cloak sheaths.

But a couple—the sharpest ones—he held onto with tight, white-knuckled fists.

Diran reached the barghest, crouched down next to him, and began speaking softly. So softly that even Ghaji's excellent hearing couldn't make out what the priest said.

Ghaji turned toward the others. "Now that the web mummies are no longer aggressive, it should be simple enough for us to destroy them. All we need to do is make a few torches and set them on fire, keeping watch for any escaping spiderlings as their hosts burn."

"I have little psionic energy remaining to me, but I believe I have enough left to start a fire," Solus said. "Unfortunately, it takes more energy to maintain control of such an ability than it does to merely wield it. If I attempt to create a flame right now, I might very well create a conflagration that will fill the entire crypt."

"Don't worry about it," Tresslar said, glancing sideways at Diran and the barghest. "We can manage by making torches the old-fashioned way."

"You can help by guarding Asenka's"—Ghaji had been about to say *body*—"guarding Asenka. If any spiderlings get past us, you can levitate them away from her."

The psiforged inclined his head somberly. "It will be my honor to take care of our friend."

Ghaji was about to tell the others to begin looking for material to make torches when the barghest's first scream tore through the air. It was far from the creature's last.

CHAPTER

TWENTY

The first rays of dawn were just beginning to tint the eastern sky when they laid Asenka to rest. The companions stood before a funeral pyre fashioned from rocks and tree limbs, watching as flames tinted with silverburn wreathed the woman's body. Though they had burned out the infestation of spider spawn in the ancient underground crypt, Diran had insisted on cremating Asenka, just in case any more of the giant arachnids might be laired elsewhere in the vicinity. The followers of the Silver Flame usually buried their dead, but Ghaji knew Diran couldn't bear the thought of Asenka becoming a web mummy, and the half-orc didn't blame him.

As Diran prayed for the Silver Flame to accept Asenka's soul, Ghaji kept close watch for any sign of threat. They'd already lost two members of their party on this expedition, and he was determined that no one else would die, not as long as the merest scrap of strength remained to him.

Ghaji doubted Nathifa, Makala, or Haaken would return. For one thing, daylight was swiftly approaching, which meant Makala would need to seek shelter from the sun. For another, Skarm had told Diran everything about Nathifa's plans, and the companions now knew all that had transpired since the lich had stolen Tresslar's dragonwand at the psi-forge facility within Mount Luster. According to the barghest, his mistress and her servants were on their way to Regalport right now. Skarm had been vague on what Nathifa hoped to accomplish once she arrived at the port city. It seemed the undead sorceress had only shared so much information with her underlings. But Ghaji knew that whatever the lich had planned, it didn't bode well for the citizens of Regalport.

Ghaji glanced at Diran. The priest stood with his head bowed, speaking prayers in hushed, reverent tones. Leontis, in human form once more, stood next to his old friend, intoning the same prayers along with him. After Ghaji had split the werewolf's skull with his axe, the beast had remained unconscious for some time as it healed, and by the time its wounds had finally vanished, the wolf had become a man again.

Ghaji was worried about Diran. He had traveled with the priest for some time now, and they had seen each other at their best and their worst. Ghaji understood that his friend had lived the first half of his life as a killer for hire, and he'd witnessed the assassin within Diran come to the fore on a number of occasions. But the half-orc had never seen Diran do anything as cold-blooded as the methodical way he'd "questioned" Skarm. Diran had taken his time, patiently waited for the barghest's screams to die away so that he could ask the next question. And if he didn't like the answer he got—or if Skarm was too hesitant in answering—Diran used one of his blades and the screaming would start anew. When Diran had been satisfied the barghest had told them all it could, Diran had told the creature that he was going to heal it. What the priest didn't tell Skarm was that since he had a strong dose of tomb spider venom inside him, the healing magic would have the opposite effect. At least the barghest had died quickly.

Ghaji had no sympathy for Skarm, and he certainly wasn't sorry the creature was dead. But he worried about the effect of Asenka's death on Diran. The priest had worked long and hard to put his former life behind him, to become something new, something *better*, and he'd inspired Ghaji to do the same. To one degree or another, in ways great or small, Diran had inspired the others as well. Now Ghaji feared Diran would turn his sorrow, anger, and guilt over Asenka's death inward, until the emotions fused into self-hatred.

Ghaji was afraid his friend would return to killing for the sake of killing, slaying out of a need for revenge rather than to protect others. And if that happened, the good man Diran Bastiaan had fought to become might well be lost forever.

They'd built Asenka's pyre on the other side of the hill near the entrance to Paganus's cavern. They'd found another tunnel leading out of the crypt and had followed it to the surface. The outer entrance was just large enough for a humanoid to slip through—or a tomb spider, if she drew her legs in close to her body. They'd discovered a small semi-permanent camp at the base of the hill: lean-tos and simple shacks, most of which had fallen into disrepair. The camp was deserted, and from the few meager possessions they'd found inside the crude shelters, they guessed that this had been the temporary home for an expedition that had fallen on bad luck, perhaps even been shipwrecked and stranded upon the island. The adventurers had experienced even worse luck when they'd chosen to make camp near a tomb spider's lair. Ghaji felt confident those hapless adventurers had been taken by the giant arachnid, impregnated with her eggs, and transformed into the web mummies the companions had encountered in the crypt. Poor devils.

They kept silent vigil while Asenka's body was reduced to bones, and when the fire died out, they buried her remains on the site of the pyre. Solus used the last dregs of his psionic energy to levitate a rock from the hillside and onto the grave to serve as a marker. The psiforged apologized for not having enough energy to chisel words into the stone, but Diran told him it didn't matter. Asenka's soul had joined with the Flame, and she was beyond the need for words now.

And then Diran turned and walked away from Asenka's grave, and one by one the companions followed. Of them all, only Diran never glanced back. Not once.

●　●　●　◉　●　●　●

It was noon by the time the companions reached the *Turnabout*. They all took turns rowing since Solus could no longer use his psionic abilities to power the craft. And it was another hour after that before the elemental galleon set sail for the island of Greentarn, where Regalport was located. The trip would take a day and a half, though Hinto, who volunteered to serve as first mate in Thokk's absence, promised that he'd do everything he could to motivate the crew to squeeze as much speed as possible out of the ship. Onu, wearing his guise as a human sea captain, accompanied the halfling, speaking good-naturedly with the *Turnabout*'s sailors and offering them words of encouragement. Hinto wasn't as harsh as taskmaster as Thokk had been, but Ghaji thought the crew responded better to the halfling for he seemed more like one of them than the dwarf ever had. Ghaji had no idea what would happen to the ship with Thokk's death. The dwarf had been the vessel's owner and true captain, but none of the crew knew that. As far as they were concerned, the ship belonged to Onu. Ghaji supposed she did now, at least until any of Thokk's heirs could be notified. The changeling might be a good actor, but he was a lousy seaman, and the half-orc didn't see how Onu could make a go of commanding the *Turnabout* on his own. But that would be something for the changeling to worry about in the future. Right now, all Onu and Hinto had to do was keep the crew working hard until the ship reached the island of Regalport.

All during the first day back at sea, Diran stood at the ship's prow, face expressionless, blue eyes fixed on the horizon, speaking only when spoken to, and even then only responding in one or two word phrases. Ghaji tried to get his friend to open up several times, but without any success. The half-orc asked Solus if he could speak to Diran, hoping the psiforged might be able to somehow employ his mental powers to reach the priest. But Solus demurred, saying that Diran's desire for solitude was obvious, even to one bereft of psionic abilities. Ghaji didn't bother asking Yvka to speak with Diran. The elf-woman had been avoiding Ghaji ever since their return to the ship, as if she sensed he was upset about keeping her dragonmark secret from him and wished to avoid discussing the subject as long as possible. Tresslar was no good, either. The artificer was holed up in his cabin, working. Tresslar had recovered several magical artifacts from Paganus's hoard that Nathifa hadn't had time to drain the power from, and the artificer was attempting to adapt their mystic energy in order to repair Ghaji's elemental axe.

That left only one person for Ghaji to turn to: Leontis.

Reluctantly, Ghaji went to the priest's cabin and knocked on the door. A moment later, Leontis answered.

"What is it, Ghaji?"

Leontis's hair and beard had grown back, and despite all the injuries he'd suffered, the man looked healthy and strong. He had on a new set of clothes, a simple white tunic, leather belt, brown trousers, and black boots he'd borrowed from Onu. It turned out the changeling had a wide variety of clothing—for both men and women—in numerous sizes to accommodate whatever masquerade he might be called upon to perform, and these clothes were the closest to a perfect fit for the priest.

"I wanted to say I'm sorry for what I did back on Trebaz Sinara . . . you know, when I split your head open."

Leontis smiled faintly. "No need to apologize. I have no memory of it." The priest's smile fell away. "My only regret is that your weapon wasn't forged from silver."

Leontis's words took Ghaji by surprise. "You *want* to die?"

"Of course. Wouldn't you if you were in my place? That's why I sought out Diran: to ask him to kill me."

"Diran talked you out of it."

A ghost of Leontis's smile returned. "He always *was* persuasive. And he believes that I have some role to play in the events to come."

"You sound doubtful."

"The visions of the future Diran saw were given to him by a demon desperate to remain on our plane and thus cannot be trusted. But even if the visions are true, I cannot see how any good can come from the evil that taints my soul."

Ghaji was beginning to see Leontis in a new light, and he felt his resentment and suspicion of the priest beginning to fade. "I once asked Diran how he could still use his assassin's skills in the service of good. Can you guess what he told me?"

Leontis nodded. "That while Good and Evil are real forces in the world, it isn't always easy for us to know which is truly which. It's the sort of thing our teacher Tusya would've said."

"I think it would be wise of you to try to remember that," Ghaji said. "I also think our mutual friend could use a reminder himself right now. I have a feeling it might mean more coming from you."

Leontis hesitated. "I don't know . . ."

"Maybe this is part of the reason you were destined to come along on this voyage," Ghaji pointed out. "But forget destiny and visions. Diran's hurting, and regardless of whatever else you may be, you are still a priest of the Silver Flame. Our friend needs healing."

Leontis looked at Ghaji for several moments before finally nodding his acceptance of the half-orc's words.

❋ ❋ ❋ ❋ ❋ ❋ ❋ ❋

Diran's face and hands had long ago gone numb from the constant buffeting of frigid sea winds, but he scarcely noticed. He'd taken no food or water since Asenka's burial, but as a priest he was used to privation, and so he ignored the empty ache in his stomach, the weakness in his limbs, and the pounding in his head. He concentrated on the waves ahead of them, mentally ticking off the miles as the *Turnabout* raced toward Regalport, going over the visions the Fury-demon had revealed to him and attempting to divine some insight into Nathifa's ultimate plan.

"Punishing yourself isn't going to help make Asenka's loss hurt any less."

Diran didn't turn to look at Leontis as his fellow priest joined him at the prow.

"Ghaji has already tried to speak with me several times since we departed Trebaz Sinara," Diran said. "I'm surprised he hasn't told you that I'm poor company right now."

"Who do you think suggested I take a turn at you?"

The two priests stood for a time, listening to the waves breaking against the ship's hull and the wind whistling past their ears. Eventually, Leontis spoke again.

"Though I did not spend my youth near the sea, I must confess that I find its sights and sounds soothing. The water seems almost to be calling me, whispering something that I can't quite make out . . ." Leontis shook his head. "But you're a Lhazaarite born and bred. The sea probably holds little mystery and even less attraction for you."

Diran gazed out upon the slate-gray surface of the water, knowing that this time of year the Lhazaar was cold as liquid ice. "You might be surprised . . ."

Leontis changed the subject. "Ghaji is a good man, and the two of you make an effective team. He's worried about you, and truth to tell, so am I."

"There's nothing to worry about. I'm preparing for the battle that lies ahead of us . . . weighing various strategies, calculating odds . . ."

Leontis laughed. "I hope you were a better liar back when you were an assassin."

Despite himself, Diran smiled. "I guess I've fallen out of practice."

"It's not your fault that Asenka died, Diran. If I wanted to, I suppose I could blame myself. After all, if the werewolf hadn't gone after Haaken, the wereshark wouldn't have thrown him across the crypt, and he wouldn't have collided with Asenka—"

"That's ridiculous!" Diran snapped. "You had no control over your lupine half, and you certainly had no control over what Haaken did or didn't do."

"And you had no control over whether Asenka was bitten by a spiderling."

"I should've checked. If I'd known . . ."

"She would've died anyway. Her injuries were too severe. Without the benefit of healing magic, it was only a matter of time. Though you didn't mean to end her life, by doing so swiftly, you saved her from suffering any further."

Diran's tone hardened. "That's cold comfort, Leontis."

"Do you remember what Tusya used to say about that? 'Sometimes cold comfort is the only kind we get in this life.' "

"I remember. I found it a rather facile saying at the time, and I find it even more so now."

"As an assassin, your training centered entirely on control," Leontis said. "Control of your emotions, your body, your weaponry, your victim, and the circumstances under which you would confront him . . . Control is also vital to the Purified. We attempt to purge ourselves of negative emotions and desires, and strive to adhere to a strict code of moral behavior. Control is even more important for priests. It allows us to open ourselves to the power of the Silver Flame so that we might become effective conduits for its holy energy. But we mustn't forget what Tusya taught us."

Diran didn't want to say the words. He wanted to hold onto the icy fury that had encased his heart. But he found himself speaking them nevertheless. Words he'd first heard years ago around a campfire near the bank of the Thrane River. "Fire consumes wood for its fuel, and in so doing, the wood is transformed. It becomes one with the fire, fulfilling its true purpose. To serve the Flame well, we must willingly give ourselves over to its heat and light."

"I've been thinking about this a great deal lately—for obvious reasons." Leontis gave Diran a rueful smile. "Evil attempts to control the fates of others for its own selfish ends. That's what you did when you were an assassin. You killed because Emon Gorsedd accepted money for your services and sent you forth to slay whoever his client chose. Good, on the other hand, seeks to preserve the rights of individuals to choose their own fates. It tries to teach by example, rather than force others to order their lives as it wishes. That's who you are now, Diran. You are Purified, a servant of the Flame, and a force for Good in a world that sorely needs people like you. Don't let your grief turn you back into a heartless killer. You have a choice in this matter. Some of us do not."

Leontis put his hand on Diran's shoulder and squeezed once before turning and walking away.

Diran remained standing at the prow for some time after Leontis's departure, thinking over all that his fellow priest had said. He had a good idea what Asenka might say if she were present, could almost imagine hearing her speak the words.

We had little time together, Diran Bastiaan, but what we had was good. Don't spoil it by turning my memory into a millstone around your neck. There are people—good people—depending on you. Don't you dare let them down because you're too wrapped up in sorrow and self-pity. You're a

Lhazaarite, and you know our way: Live hard, love hard, die well. As far as I'm concerned, I did all three. Mourn me if you must, but you're still alive and you have work to do. So get to it!

Despite his grief, Diran smiled. He then turned away from the sea and the wind and headed off toward the passengers' quarters.

❁ ❁ ❁ ❁ ❁ ❁ ❁

Diran knocked on the door to Tresslar's cabin.

"Go away! I'm busy!"

"It's me," Diran said.

Tresslar opened the door. The artificer gave the priest an appraising frown. "Did you finally realize you aren't to blame for what happened?"

"I could ask you the same, holed up in your cabin, working feverishly on your magic items . . ." Diran smiled to take any sting out of his words. "You aren't to blame, either. None of us are."

Tresslar's frown eased, and he looked haggard, far older than his sixty-odd years. "If I hadn't lost the Amahau, none of this would've happened."

"My former teacher used to say that *if* is like a double-edged blade: it cuts two ways. It can spark imagination and creativity or cause regret and sorrow. It all depends on how you wield it."

Tresslar smiled. "Wise words." The artificer let out a long sigh. "Very well. Let us look to the future, eh? I'm still working on restoring Ghaji's elemental axe. I think I've found a way to infuse a fire elemental within the metal, but I still need some time."

"That's good, but I've come to speak with you about a different magical artifact. One that I believe you removed from Thokk before we buried him."

Tresslar looked suddenly uncomfortable. "You speak of the Oathbinder. To an artificer, burying a mystic object with the dead is a terrible waste. We would rather our greatest enemies take the devices we create than have them never used again. It's a way for a small piece of ourselves to live on after our deaths." He lowered his gaze. "I didn't say anything about taking the Oathbinder because I didn't want anyone to think I was robbing the dead. None of you are artificers . . . I was afraid you wouldn't understand."

"I do understand," Diran said, "and I'm glad you had the foresight to salvage Thokk's medallion. I think I know how we might put it to use."

● ● ● ◉ ● ● ●

Ghaji found Yvka in their cabin. She sat cross-legged on their sleeping pallet, her left sleeve rolled up to expose her dragonmark. She gazed down upon the swirling design, the fingers of her right hand poised above it, as if she wanted to touch the mark but was afraid to.

She looked up as Ghaji closed the hatch and crossed over to the pallet. The cabin was small, but compared to the cramped quarters on the *Zephyr*, it was nearly palatial. Ghaji sat next to Yvka. He wanted to give her a kiss and put his arm around her, but he didn't. They had things to discuss, and one kiss would lead to another, which in turn would lead to something else, and before long all thought of talk would be forgotten. Better to maintain a certain distance for now. But before Ghaji could say anything, Yvka spoke.

"This changes everything, you know."

Ghaji understood that she was talking about her dragonmark, but that was all he understood. "No, I *don't* know. Tell me."

Yvka looked at Ghaji for a long time, her face unreadable, but her eyes revealed the inner struggle she was going through. Finally, she told him everything—about going to the Culinarian to meet with Zivon, how the Fury struck while she was there, and how her dragonmark had manifested during her fight with the half-elf.

"Zivon not only wanted me to regain possession of the *Zephyr*— for though I've used the vessel for decades, she belongs to the Shadow Network—he also wanted me to deliver Tresslar's dragonwand to them . . . as well as Solus."

Ghaji wished he was shocked by Yvka's words, but he wasn't. The Shadow Network had a reputation for absolute pragmatism in all things, but most especially when it came to the acquisition of the organization's twin loves: power and profit.

"And what did you tell him?" Ghaji asked.

"I tried to put him off by pretending that I wanted to negotiate a better reward for myself. But then the Fury overwhelmed Zivon and our discussion ended when he tried to kill me. After Diran exorcised the Fury-demon, Zivon regained his senses. He was so pleased by the appearance of my dragonmark that he said no more about Solus or the dragonwand."

"But that doesn't mean he's forgotten about them, does it?"

Yvka shook her head. "The Network never forgets anything. If they want Solus and the wand, they will stop at nothing to get them. Whether I deliver them or not. They'll simply send someone else, and if that person fails, they'll keep sending new people until someone finally succeeds. But a dragonmark, even a Lesser one, raises my status in the Network. I may be able to bargain with the Hierarchs so that they'll . . . *overlook* their interest in Solus and the dragonwand."

Ghaji didn't like where this was headed. "Bargain with what?"

"My services. I've worked hard for more years than you've been alive to earn the freedom to roam the Principalities as I wish. And the Network has allowed me to retain my liberty as long as I furthered its interests. But dragonmarks are a valuable commodity, and the Hierarchs prefer to keep a tight rein on those individuals who possess them. I've given the Network both Grimwall and Mount Luster. Now I will give them myself—but *only* if they'll leave Solus and the dragonwand alone."

"It sounds like indentured servitude! I admire that you want to protect Solus and Tresslar—assuming the artificer ever gets his wand back for anyone to take it away from him again—but do you really believe the Network will live up to its end of the bargain?"

"It may be difficult for someone not part of the Network to believe, but once the Hierarchs make a bargain, they keep it. Especially within the organization. We have a saying: 'True loyalty is the only item that cannot be bought.' That's why it's so highly prized in the Network."

Ghaji understood now why Yvka had been so reluctant to talk with him the last few days, and why she'd seemed to be hiding something more important than usual. On one level he was relieved to know the truth, and he was pleased that she'd finally told him something of her life working for the Shadow Network. But he also feared the implications of what she intended to do.

"So just how tight a rein will these Hierarchs wish to keep on you? And what will this mean for us?"

"It will mean the end of my freedom, at least, the kind I enjoy now. As for you and me . . ." She looked away, tears forming in the corner of her soulful eyes. "The Hierarchs are unhappy enough that I have friends outside the Network as it is. Once I start working for them as a dragonmarked operative . . . I just don't know."

There were so many things Ghaji wanted to say to Yvka. In the end, too many. Instead he took her in his arms and held her tight. Holding eventually led to kissing, and kissing in turn led to other things, and for a time the two lovers forgot their troubles as they lost themselves in each other.

And the *Turnabout* sailed on, slicing through the waves like a finely honed sword as the elemental galleon ran full out for Regalport.

CHAPTER

TWENTY-ONE

Moonlight painted the water lapping at Regalport's central dock a gleaming silver. Nathifa thought of Diran Bastiaan and his companions—who surely were on their way to Greentarn even now—and she hoped the reflected moonlight wasn't an omen of ill fortune. The sorceress told herself to forget such foolish thoughts and have faith in the machinations of her Queen. Even if Bastiaan and the others managed to arrive this night, there was nothing they could do to stop her. Failure was impossible.

Still, the water's silver glimmer seemed to say otherwise.

Nathifa stood on the dock next to where the *Zephyr* was berthed. With Skarm left behind on Trebaz Sinara and most likely dead, Haaken had taken over piloting the elemental sloop. Since the spells that allowed one to activate and control the vessel's wind elemental were built into the pilot's chair, no special skill with magic was necessary. In his previous life as commander of the Coldhearts, Haaken had captained a ship called the *Maelstrom*, and he proved quite adept at piloting the *Zephyr*, so much so that Nathifa had no regrets over abandoning Skarm. In fact, it was something of a relief to be rid of the bumbling fool.

They'd approached Regalport at dusk, but the bay had been cluttered with fishing boats, pleasure craft, and trading vessels, and night had fallen by the time they'd maneuvered through the maze of ships and managed to reach the central dock. No berths were available, so Haaken jumped over the side, took shark form, located a small sail boat and bit through the mooring line. He gave the vessel a shove, and the boat drifted away from the dock, making room for the *Zephyr*.

Once the sloop had taken the sail boat's place, Makala stepped onto the dock and tied the *Zephyr*'s lines to rusted iron cleats. Just as she finished, there came the sound of boots pounding on wood as two men ran down the dock toward them, swords drawn.

"Here now! What do you think you're doing?" one of the men shouted.

Guards, Nathifa thought. What a nuisance.

"Slay them," she told Makala.

Grinning, the vampire stepped forward to meet the guards' advance. She backhanded one man, sending him into the water for Haaken to deal with. She grabbed hold of the other by his throat, slammed him down onto the dock, and fell upon him like a starving animal. Moments later, both guards were dead, their bodies tossed into the sea.

Nathifa had kept watch for other guards while her servants dispatched the men, but she'd sensed none. Nevertheless, she ordered Makala and Haaken to perform a quick search of the docks and slay any other guards they might find. A short while later, the vampire and the wereshark returned to the *Zephyr*, the blood covering their mouths and hands telling Nathifa that the docks were now clear for them to go to work.

Haaken and Makala brought up the statue of Nerthatch from the *Zephyr*'s hold. Centuries ago, the evil priest had attempted to raise the bodies of those who'd lost their lives in the unforgiving waters of the Gulf of Ingjald to create an undead army. This night, Nathifa would use the priest's petrified form to raise something entirely different—and far more deadly—from the frigid depths of the Lhazaar.

Makala had hold of the top half of Nerthatch's stone body, and she carried it with ease. Haaken gripped the lower half, but as he was in human form, he was having a harder time of bearing his share of the statue's weight. Protruding from the statue's chest was the hilt of a silver dagger. Both Makala and Haaken were most careful to avoid touching it. It took several minutes for the two of them to get the statue onto the dock and positioned facing seaward, as Nathifa wished.

Once the statue was in place, Haaken said, "You still haven't told us what we're going to do tonight. But whatever it is, wouldn't it make more sense to do it out in the bay aboard the *Zephyr?* That way we'd be certain no one could interfere before we were finished."

"Mere servants such as yourselves could never appreciate the full majesty of Vol's grand design," Nathifa said. "Suffice it to say that the mystic rite we are going to conduct needs to be performed on a passageway between land and sea."

Haaken continued to look her with a blank expression on his face.

"A passageway such as this dock," Nathifa added.

Haaken grinned as his face lit up with comprehension.

Nathifa sighed. If the imbecile wasn't so useful when in were-shark form, she might've slain him on the spot for his stupidity. But no, as satisfying as it would be, she couldn't harm the idiot. Haaken Sprull had a very important role to play in what was about to occur.

"I've never been to Regalport," Makala said. "It's impressive." The vampire had turned away from Nathifa and Haaken and now stood gazing shoreward.

Nathifa had been too caught up in the excitement of knowing that everything she had sacrificed so much for was finally on the verge of being fulfilled to pay much attention as they'd approached Regalport. But now she turned and for the first time took a good look at the city that was known as the Jewel of the Principalities.

Nathifa and her brothers had traveled here once, over a century ago. Regalport had been a major city even then, one that both Kolbyr and Perhata had attempted in their own small, inadequate ways to emulate when they'd founded the cities that bore their names. But Regalport had grown a great deal since Nathifa's breathing days. Music and laughter drifted out from numerous dockside taverns, and everbright lanterns dotted the city like a field of stars that had fallen from the heavens. There were so many buildings that the cityscape resembled a mountain range silhouetted against the night sky, and Nathifa was surprised to find herself feeling a twinge of homesickness for her lair in the Hoarfrost Mountains. She'd thought herself beyond such emotions.

Regalport was full to bursting with life, and Nathifa could sense its energy, almost see it shining in the darkness like a miniature sun, warm and glowing and above all, *alive*. For an instant she questioned what she had come here to do. What purpose would destroying this life serve? How would it grant her desire for vengeance against her brother Kolbyr, dead now for a hundred years? How long had it taken for Regalport to become the great city it was now? How many men and women had worked to make it so? For the first time in her long life, Nathifa realized how easy destruction was and how arduous the process of creation, how fragile the result. Destruction was the act of a moment. Simple, mindless, pointless. But creation was complex, thoughtful, and shaped toward an ultimate goal: to make meaning. Destruction was, in the most profound sense, meaningless.

"Don't tell me that after everything we've been through you're losing your nerve."

Makala's words startled Nathifa out of her thoughts, and the lich glared at the vampire with her sole remaining eye. "Stand guard while I prepare the ritual. Once I have begun, I must not be interrupted. Kill anyone who approaches." Without waiting for Makala to respond, Nathifa turned to Haaken Sprull. "Stand behind the statue of Nerthatch and place your hands upon the shoulders. Once you've done that, transform into your hybrid form. I shall begin my spell shortly afterward."

The sea raider looked skeptically at the sorceress. "That's all? I just have to . . . stand there?"

Nathifa allowed herself a slight smile. "Your role is a bit more complicated than that, but you are essentially correct. Now do it."

Haaken gave Makala a look that said he was beginning to doubt their mistress's sanity, but he did at Nathifa commanded. He stepped behind the statue of the priest, placed his hands about the stone shoulders, and shifted to his transitional form of half man, half shark.

Nathifa then reached inside her dark substance and brought forth the dragonwand. She had carried the Amahau inside her during the entire journey from Trebaz Sinara, the artifact full to bursting with the mystic power she had drained from Paganus's hoard. Having that much magical force contained inside her had been uncomfortable, and she felt relieved that the dragonwand was no longer housed within her darkness. The Amahau fairly hummed, so full of power was it, but Nathifa knew that the dragonwand could've held even more energy. If only she'd had more time in the crypt. But she hadn't, so however much power she'd managed to take would have to serve. She only hoped it would prove sufficient.

The lich leveled the dragonwand at Haaken and concentrated on releasing the Amahau's stored energy. A bolt of crackling energy surged forth from the mouth of the dragonhead at the tip of the wand, lanced through the air, and struck the wereshark just below the point where his dorsal fin emerged from his back. Haaken bellowed in pain, muscles spasming as mystic power filled his being. He thrashed back and forth like a captive beast trying to escape a trap, but he was unable to remove his clawed hands from the statue's shoulders. His flesh was bound to the stone now, and he would not be able to let go until the enchantment was ended. Nathifa continued releasing magical energy into Haaken's body as she at last began chanting a spell that she'd learned a century ago.

The sorceress sensed the dark power contained within the statue of Nerthatch begin to respond to the magical force flowing into it through Haaken's body. Then, though Nathifa couldn't see it from where she stood, she knew the statue's stone mouth opened to emit a soundless cry, one that not even she could not hear. But the summons wasn't intended for her.

Several moments passed in this manner before they heard the sound of roiling water, as if something large were surging toward the dock at incredible speed. A few seconds later a pair of gray-skinned hands, fingers tipped by black claws, reached up over the dock's edge, took hold, and a man-shark pulled itself out of the water. It was followed by a second, and then a third. The weresharks regarded the bizarre scene before them for a moment and then, as if obeying orders only they could hear, the three aquatic lycanthropes stalked past and lumbered down the dock toward shore.

Toward Regalport.

* * * ◉ * * *

Jahnu followed the flow of people out of the tavern, his wife at his side, her hand resting in the crook of arm.

"Did you enjoy the bard, my love?" Dirella asked.

Once outside, the tavern-goers began to head in different directions, strolling slowly in pairs or groups of three and four, enjoying the night air. It was somewhat chilly for a walk, Jahnu thought, but the buildings, two and three-stories, made an effective windbreak here. Plus he and his wife were hardy Lhazaarites who knew to dress for the weather in heavy clothing and fur cloaks.

Jahnu turned left and Dirella allowed herself to be led. She was a very independent person. Her family owned several dockside warehouses, and though it pleased her to defer to her husband at times, there was never any doubt between them as to who was the more dominant in their marriage.

He shrugged in answer to his wife's question. "There's no denying the skill with which the man played, but his voice often seemed harsh to me, like he was . . . I don't know. Singing between the notes somehow."

"That's because you're *human*, dear. Elvish music is composed for people with *elvish* hearing."

Dirella spoke with a patronizing voice, as if she were pointing out something that should be blindingly obvious. She used that voice a great deal more than Jahnu appreciated. He worked to keep his tone neutral as he replied. He didn't want to spoil the evening by getting into a fight.

"But if I'm not elvish, then how can I . . ." He trailed off. Coming toward them, washed in the eerie green illumination of everbright street lanterns, was a creature out of nightmare. Roughly humanoid, though larger and more muscular. Naked, with slick, tough-looking hide, and clawed hands and feet. Most disturbing was its shark-like head with its maw full of triangular teeth.

Jahnu stopped and stared at the strange apparition walking down the street toward them. Dirella, still holding onto her husband's arm, stopped as well.

"Do you see that?" Jahnu asked in a hushed voice. He knew what he *thought* he was seeing—a monster stepped straight out of childhood bedtime stories—but such a thing couldn't possibly be here. Not on the streets of Regalport! High Price Ryger made sure his city was one of the safest in the Principalities. The city watch was well trained and well paid, and the Prince's Sea Dragons diligently patrolled the waters beyond Regalport.

"It looks like a, a walking shark," Dirella said, a note of wonder in her voice. "Do you think it's a joke of some kind? A drunken sailor playing a prank in costume?"

Jahnu let out a relieved sigh. Yes, of course! It had to be something like that!

The "wereshark" stopped as it drew near. Its dead-black eyes narrowed, and Jahnu caught a whiff of saltwater mixed with the scent of rotting meat wafting forth from the thing's tooth-filled maw. Suddenly, he wasn't so sure that this was a joke.

The wereshark lunged and sank its teeth into Jahnu's shoulder. The man screamed as his blood geysered into the air, splattering his wife who was also screaming now and desperately attempting to pull free of her husband—his arm had folded back reflexively when the creature bit into his flesh, trapping her hand in the crook of his elbow. The wereshark didn't look at Dirella as it gnawed at Jahnu's bloody shoulder, serrated teeth sawing gobs of meat off the bone. But the woman's scream rose to a high-pitched shriek and, as if to silence her, the wereshark lashed upward with a clawed hand and disemboweled her. It worked most effectively. Dirella became instantly quiet as her intestines spilled down the front of her expensive gown and onto the ground.

The wereshark ripped a hunk of meat from Jahnu's shoulder, and the man fell sideways onto his dying wife. Dirella, unable to support her own weight any longer, let alone that of her husband, slumped to the cobblestones below, and Jahnu landed in a bloody heap on top of her. Through blurred vision swiftly going black, Jahnu saw the wereshark swallow his flesh and then, grinning in a way a true shark never could, the beast crouched down as it came toward them to continue its grisly feast.

The sight Jahnu saw as life left him was a hazy image of other weresharks filling the street, and the last sound he heard were the screams of other victims as the monsters ran forward to join in the slaughter.

❀ ❀ ❀ ❀ ❀ ❀ ❀

More weresharks arrived, and more after that, and they all walked past Nathifa, Haaken, and Makala and continued on into the city. Dozens of them.

Nathifa paused in her chanting, unable to stop herself from laughing in delight. It had begun! Nothing could stop Vol's conquest of the Principalities now! Nothing!

The lich resumed chanting and the weresharks kept coming.

And that's when Nathifa saw the prow of an elemental galleon coming fast toward the dock.

CHAPTER

TWENTY-TWO

"She's already started!" Diran said.

The priest stood at the stern of the *Turnabout*, peering through the lens of a hand-held telescope, long black hair trailing behind him in the wind. The sky was clear, and the moons provided sufficient light for him to make out Nathifa standing on Regalport's central dock. He recognized the statue of the priest Nerthatch that Ghaji and he had been forced to deal with on Demothi Island. Haaken Sprull, in the shape of a half-man, half-shark, stood behind the statue, clawed hands gripping its shoulders, blunt snout pointed skyward as he bellowed in pain. Behind Haaken stood Nathifa, holding the dragonwand and blasting the wereshark with a stream of mystic energy released from the Amahau. Makala stood close by, watching the procedure with a malicious grin, clearly amused by Haaken's pain.

A steady parade of weresharks climbed out of the bay one by one, pulled themselves onto the dock, and lumbered past the lich and her servants as they headed into Regalport proper.

Diran handed the spyglass to Ghaji so the half-orc could see for himself. The other companions gathered around, and though they didn't have telescopes of their own, the elemental galleon was only a quarter of a mile away from the docks and closing fast. They could see well enough to give them a good idea of what was happening.

272

Ghaji lowered the spyglass. "This is Vol's grand scheme? To send a bunch of ugly fish-faces into Regalport for a late dinner? It's an awful thing, but I don't see how that will help her conquer the Principalities."

"You forget that a lycanthrope's bite is infectious," Leontis said. "Though I have no doubt the weresharks will kill tonight and take great pleasure in doing so, my guess is their primary purpose is to infect as many of Regalport's citizens as they can with their curse."

"At Grimwall, Erdis Cai sought to create an army of undead soldiers for Vol," Tresslar said. "It seems that Vol has decided to create an army of sea-based lycanthropes instead."

"Any army of weresharks . . . under the Lich Queen's control," Diran said. The vision the Fury-demon had shown him was coming to pass, and its implications were staggering. "They could move throughout the Principalities without the need for vessels, traveling undetected beneath the waves."

"They could infiltrate any city or settlement in human form," Onu added, "attacking whenever they wished."

"They'd keep on attacking until they'd either killed or infected everyone," Yvka said. "And then the whole lot would move on to the next settlement."

"They'd board ships at sea too" Hinto put in. "Killing or transforming the crews."

"Their numbers would grow swiftly," Solus said. "So much so that the Principalities would fall before they could muster a sufficient defense."

Even if the barons and princes had advanced warning of the wereshark threat, what sort of defense could there be? Diran wondered. This was precisely the hellish scenario the Purified had envisioned that had caused them to embark on the Purge. The Purified had succeeded in preventing the scourge of lycanthropy from destroying all of Khorvaire. But what the servants of the Silver Flame hadn't considered—hadn't the resources to even *attempt* to consider—was dealing with those lycanthropes who lived in the world's rivers, lakes, seas, and oceans. Those beasts were too well hidden, too well protected in their watery lairs, to make hunting them practical. So, out of necessity more than anything else, the Purified had adopted a you-don't-bother-us and we-won't-bother-you attitude toward aquatic lycanthropes that had worked well enough for years.

Until tonight.

"We have to stop her," Diran said.

"Who?" Ghaji asked. "Nathifa or Vol?"

"Both," the priest said grimly. He turned to Onu. "Have your crew head for the dock where the lich is casting her spell."

"At once!" the changeling said. "I assume you'd like them to get a longboat ready as well?"

Diran shook his head. "You misunderstand. I don't want the *Turnabout* to get *near* the dock. I want to *ram* it."

Onu looked alarmed for a moment, but then a slow grin spread across his face. "Sounds like fun. Come, Hinto! I'll need your help to convince the crew we haven't lost our minds!" The changeling hurried off with the halfling in tow.

"I'm not so certain we *haven't* lost our minds," Tresslar said.

"I understand that you want to slay the lich," Ghaji said, "And why. But to damage the *Turnabout* like that . . ."

"I'm not acting out of a desire for vengeance, my friend," Diran said. "We must stop Nathifa. We can worry about dealing with the lich and her servants—not to mention the weresharks already in the city—once we've interrupted her spellcasting."

Yvka eyed the rapidly decreasing distance between the elemental galleon and Regalport's main dock. "The water may not be deep enough so close to the dock. What if we run aground?"

"The ship will be traveling swiftly under the power of the wind elementals," Diran said. "Hopefully their combined force will prove enough to push us past any reefs."

"Or reduce the *Turnabout* to kindling," Tresslar muttered.

Diran turned to Solus. "Can you use your telekinetic abilities to cushion the impact?"

The psiforged considered for a moment. "The forces generated by any collision will be formidable. I have been able to strengthen my crystals somewhat using the excess psionic energy generated by the ship's crew, but I am not up to my full strength. I shall do what I can, but I cannot guarantee the outcome."

Diran nodded. The construct's answer was only what he expected. "I know you shall do your best, my friend. That's all anyone can ask."

"And more than many offer," Ghaji added.

The *Turnabout* surged forward, the sudden increase in speed almost knocking the companions off their feet. A moment later Onu and Hinto returned.

"We convinced the pilots to continue running the elementals full out," the changeling said. "They'll deactivate them just before we hit the dock. We've ordered all hands to prepare for impact and, uh . . ." Onu paused, and then looked to Hinto, like an actor who'd forgotten his lines.

"Make ready for combat," the halfling provided.

Onu nodded. "Yes, yes. Just so. After all, we can't have our crew stand idly by while those beastly were-creatures run rampant through the streets of Regalport, can we?" Onu looked at Leontis, an expression of sudden embarrassment on his face. "Sorry, my friend. I meant no offense."

Leontis waved the changeling's apology away.

Diran looked toward shore. Regalport loomed large now, and the priest knew it would be only a matter of moments before the ship reached the central dock.

"I suggest we split into two teams," Ghaji said. "Yvka and I go into the city to warn the watch—assuming they aren't already aware of what's happening—or perhaps alert the Sea Dragons."

"I have a better idea," Yvka said. "House Thuranni has an enclave near the docks. If we can reach it, I can inform the Hierarchs about the attack. They will be able to reach Prince Ryger and the Sea Dragons faster than we could."

Ghaji nodded. "Sounds good. Diran?"

Diran couldn't argue with the logic of Yvka and Ghaji's plan, though he couldn't help worrying that they would be going on what was essentially a suicide mission. "The streets of Regalport will be deadly tonight, my friends. Go swiftly and go with caution."

Ghaji grinned. "Caution? Who do you think you're talking to?"

Diran couldn't help grinning back.

"Besides, who needs caution when Tresslar managed to repair my elemental axe?" The half-orc warrior drew his weapon and held it up to emphasize his point.

"No more talk," Leontis said. "Brace yourselves!"

The companions turned and saw the galleon was only seconds away from colliding with the dock.

"Do you know a prayer for situations like this?" Ghaji asked Diran.

"Hold tight, grit your teeth, and close your eyes!" the priest shouted. Diran took his own advice and then the world became a riot of splintering wood, splashing water, and grinding rock.

He opened his eyes, half expecting to find himself looking into the luminescent glory of the Silver Flame. Instead he saw Regalport's central dock—a good two dozen yards from where the *Turnabout* had run aground. Yvka had been right; the water was too shallow here for a craft as large as their galleon.

The *Turnabout* listed to the right, and the ship now had a huge gaping hole in her prow. The middle of the vessel's three masts had broken and fallen forward, her sails becoming entangled with those of the first mast. An almost deafening quiet filled the air, and Diran realized he could no longer hear the roaring of the rushing winds created by the ship's elementals. The pilots had deactivated them just before the *Turnabout* had crashed, just as Onu had said they would.

The companions were shaken but unharmed. Evidently Solus had succeeded in shielding them from the worst of the impact. Diran looked to the dock, hoping that the wave created by the galleon's approach had inundated Nathifa and the others, knocking them into the water and halting the sorceress's spellcasting. But though the lich, Haaken, and the statue of Nerthatch were sopping wet, they remained where they'd been, and the sorceress continued her chanting uninterrupted. Diran saw no sign of Makala.

"Good to see you again, lover!"

Diran looked up and saw a large black bat coming toward him, its eyes burning with crimson fire, its face half human. The creature's form blurred and shifted, and Makala was now falling toward Diran, clawed hands outstretched, fangs bared in a cruel, mocking grin. Diran had seen that grin before, not on Makala's face but on Aldarik

Cathmore's. The priest knew the grin came not from the woman he had once loved above all else, but rather from the dark spirit she had unwittingly inherited when she'd attempted to drain the master assassin's blood within Mount Luster.

Diran didn't hesitate. He pulled out his silver arrowhead and brandished it at Makala. Silver light poured forth from the holy object, and Makala hissed in pain, throwing her hands over her face to shield her eyes. An instant before she would have collided with Diran, her body collapsed into mist, and the ethereal tendrils streaked upward and away from the *Turnabout*'s deck.

The arrowhead's light dimmed and Diran lowered it to his side. He did not return the holy symbol to its pocket, though. He would soon have further use of it. Instead, he turned to Ghaji and Yvka.

"Get to the House Thuranni enclave as fast as you can!"

Ghaji nodded. "May fortune favor you, my friend." The half-orc wrapped his free hand around Yvka's waist and turned to Solus. "You heard the man. Can you give us a lift?"

Solus glanced toward shore. "I believe I can get both of you to the far end of the dock. I do not know how comfortable a landing you'll experience, however."

"Don't worry," Ghaji said. "I'm used to uncomfortable landings. Just do it."

Solus's psionic crystals glowed bright, and Ghaji and Yvka shot upward into the air as if they'd been launched from a catapult. Yvka whooped in delight as they soared over Nathifa, Haaken, and the procession of weresharks lumbering down the dock toward the city. Diran imagined the curses that were likely pouring past Ghaji's lips right now, and he couldn't help smiling. Diran wanted to watch to see if the two made it safely to the other end of the dock, but he knew they couldn't afford to waste even the few seconds it would take. He turned to Solus.

"Can you levitate the rest of us over to Nathifa and Haaken?"

But before the psiforged could reply, a gray-skinned, black-clawed hand dripping with seawater clasped the ship's railing. Another followed, and a wereshark pulled itself up. At first Diran thought it was Haaken, but this beast possessed a flat, horizontal head. Diran was looking at a hammerhead shark that seem half-formed into a man's face.

The remaining companions backed away as the monster heaved itself over the rail and onto the deck. But before either they or it could attack, two more weresharks climbed over the railing—one a lean creature with bluish hide and a narrow snout, the other a large creature easily twice the size of the others, with a gray back, white belly, and sickle-shaped fin. Diran understood at once what was happening. Nathifa was sending some of the weresharks she'd summoned to prevent the priest and his companions from stopping her.

Diran drew a silver dagger with his free hand and prepared to battle the lycanthropes, but he hesitated when he heard an animalistic snarl erupt from Leontis. He turned to look at his fellow priest and saw that, just as in the crypt on Trebaz Sinara, being in the presence of other were-creatures had triggered Leontis's own transformation. Fur burst out in great tufts to cover Leontis's skin, and his face elongated into a wolfish snout. But then something different happened. His head and face broadened, and a series of slits opened up on the side of his fur-covered neck. His mouth grew larger, his teeth even more pronounced, and the cloth on the back of his tunic ripped as a triangular fin jutted forth.

Diran couldn't believe what he was seeing, had never read about such a thing happening, hadn't believed it was even possible. But there was no denying the evidence of his eyes. During Leontis's battle with Haaken on Trebaz Sinara, the priest must have been bitten by the wereshark, and the infection contained in Haaken's body had been passed onto Leontis. The twin infections now raging within the priest had merged somehow, making him into a creature that was half werewolf, half wereshark.

Leontis let out a cry that was part howl, part roar, and raced toward the weresharks. The three lycanthropes didn't react at first, seeming almost as startled by Leontis's strange new form as Diran was. But then the weresharks roared and ran forward to meet the wolfshark's attack.

Diran, Tresslar, Hinto, and Onu moved well away from where the four lycanthropes fought. Diran then tossed his silver dagger to

Hinto, drew another, and handed it to Onu. "Use these if Leontis can't keep the weresharks busy. If more of the creatures swarm onto the ship than you can handle, make sure you and the crew take shelter below. Hopefully, once Tresslar, Solus, and I attack Nathifa, the weresharks will lose interest in the *Turnabout* and you'll be safe."

Hinto frowned. "Do you have any more silver daggers, Diran?"

The priest held up his holy symbol and smiled. "I have this." He glanced toward the central dock and the statue of Nerthatch—or more accurately, at the hilt of the dagger protruding from the statue's stone chest. "And I know where there's another I can get hold of." Before the halfling could question him further, Diran turned to Solus. "Do you still have enough power to levitate the three of us onto the dock near Nathifa?"

"There is much ambient psionic energy to draw on in a city this large," the psiforged said. "Now that we are this close to Regalport, my crystals are growing strong once more."

"I'll take that as a yes," Diran said. "Let's go."

Diran stood on Solus's right, Tresslar on the psiforged's left. They each put a hand on one of the construct's shoulders, and Solus's psionic crystals glowed with power. The three companions rose into the air and soared toward the central dock.

❖ ❖ ❖ ❖ ❖ ❖ ❖

Ghaji was considerably less enthused than Yvka to be flying through the air, though *flying* wasn't exactly the right word for the sensation they experienced. It felt more like they were in the grip of a giant invisible hand that was carrying them swiftly from the now lopsided deck of the *Turnabout* to the far end of the central dock.

As they descended to the wooden planks of the central dock, Ghaji did a quick estimate of the number of weresharks in their landing zone. Four. All of them big, overly muscled, and exceptionally ugly. But if Yvka and he could deal with them, or at least make it past them, they stood a good chance of reaching House Thuranni. He didn't know how long Nathifa had been summoning weresharks, but unless the streets were chock-full of the damned things, they could fight their way through. And if the streets *were* thick with the monsters, it wouldn't matter if they reached House Thuranni or not. Regalport—and likely the entire Principalities—would be lost.

Suddenly Ghaji and Yvka were falling. He removed his arm from Yvka's waist. Yvka would be far safer landing on her own that she would if held by him. He pulled his elemental axe from its belt sheath, willed it to burst into flame and fixed his gaze on the wereshark closest to where he was going to land, one with copper-colored hide. Ghaji wished he was going to hit Copper-Skin directly in order for his landing to do the maximum amount of damage, but he was going to come down two feet to the creature's left. Still well within striking distance of his axe, though, and that was all that mattered.

Ghaji bellowed a war cry at the last instant to get Copper-Skin to turn its face. The creature whirled and looked up, giving Ghaji a clear view of two curved sharkskin-covered mounds protruding from the wereshark's chest. Definitely a her, Ghaji thought, and swung his flame-wreathed axe blade at Copper-Skin's snout, directly between her nostrils. Blood sprayed, Copper-Skin shrieked, and the shock of impact jarred up Ghaji's arm, ran through his shoulder, and rattled his teeth. The half-orc held tight to his axe as he hit the dock, and as the blade was still embedded in Copper-Skin's snout, she was pulled down with him. The wereshark continued shrieking in pain and clawed at her snout, which was fast becoming a blazing inferno of its own.

Ghaji rose to a crouching position, ignoring the protests of various joints and muscles that weren't happy at how they'd just been treated. He was pleased at the effect of his axe on Copper-Skin. Lycanthropes couldn't be killed by fire, as Leontis proved in the forest of the shadowclaws on Trebaz Sinara, but they could still be injured by it, enough so that it took them a while to heal. He'd hoped that since weresharks were aquatic monsters, they'd suffer even more from being set aflame, and it appeared his hope had been born out. Ghaji smiled in grim satisfaction as he yanked the axe free from Copper-Skin's flaming face and stood, spinning around as he did so, ready to meet the next attack that was sure to be coming his way.

Another wereshark lunged at him, this one with hide colored

bluish-black on the back and pinkish on the underbelly. Ghaji hit this beast with an upward swing that laid open his abdomen, causing wet loops of intestine to spill out onto the dock. Ghaji brought his axe down in a return strike and set fire to Pink-Belly's exposed innards. Pink-Belly staggered backward, his screams of agony added to those of Copper-Skin, and he threw himself off the dock and into the water. The flames generated from Ghaji's elemental axe were mystical in origin, and though water would extinguish them, it would take a few moments for it to do.

Ghaji turned to see how Yvka was faring. He hadn't seen her land, but she stood nearby in a fighting stance, and he knew she'd completed their descent without injury, just as he'd expected. She faced two weresharks—both possessing sharply pointed snouts and mouthfuls of long, sharp projecting teeth. Both of the creatures were hissing in pain and rubbing their eyes. Their heads were covered with fine yellowish powder, and though Ghaji didn't know precisely what substance Yvka had used to bedevil the monsters, he was grateful for the distraction. It was going to make his job much easier.

Ghaji dashed forward, swung his axe several times, and stinging eyes suddenly became the least of the weresharks' problems. Like Copper-Skin, these two fell to the dock, slashed, mutilated, and on fire. The flames from all three weresharks lying on the dock spread rapidly, merging to create a solid wall of fire. Good. Hopefully, the flame barrier would at least slow the procession of weresharks into the city. Ghaji ran forward and grabbed Yvka's hand.

"Come on!" he shouted, but the elf planted her feet and refused to budge.

"Wait! I want to try something." Yvka rolled back her left sleeve to expose her dragonmark. She closed her eyes and as she concentrated, the mark grew black and seemed to spread down her fingers and up along her arm. The darkness moved swiftly over her body, and within seconds she was completely enveloped in shadow.

She spread arms black as night. "Well? What do you think?"

Ghaji was impressed. Even with his night vision, he had a difficult time seeing her.

"I wasn't sure it was going to work, or else I might've asked Solus to transport me here alone," she said. "Then again, I couldn't have taken care of four weresharks by myself." He couldn't see her smile, but he heard it in the tone of her voice. "Cloaked in shadow like this, I'll be able to sneak past any weresharks without difficulty. I can make it to House Thuranni on my own, and you can go back to help the others."

"I'm not sure this is a good idea," Ghaji said. "You have no experience with this new shadow magic of yours. What if it fails and you can be seen again?"

"Then I'd better get moving, eh?" She came forward, moving with such silent elven grace that she really did seem to be nothing more than a shadow. But when she put her ebon arms around Ghaji's waist, they felt real enough. "I'll be all right. Trust me . . . please."

And that's what it came down to, didn't it? Did he trust her? Could he? He thought of Kirai. He'd gotten to know her well during their time together on the Talenta Plains. In many ways he had known so much more about her—her past, her likes and dislikes. Where Yvka was secretive and reluctant to share information about herself and her work, Kirai had been an open book. But he knew how Kirai had made him feel about himself, and it couldn't compare to the way Yvka made him feel.

Ghaji wanted to hug Yvka, but he was afraid of disrupting the shadow-spell that concealed her. Instead, he smiled and said, "Good luck to you, my love."

"And to you." She leaned forward, rose on her tip-toes and gave Ghaji a quick kiss on the lips. And then she pulled away, turned, and melded with the darkness.

Ghaji said a quick silent prayer for Yvka's safety—not that he'd ever admit it to anyone—before turning seaward once more, only to find himself facing the rising wall of flame that he'd created.

He sighed. Wielding an elemental weapon had its drawbacks sometimes.

He took a deep breath, held it, and ran toward the flames.

CHAPTER

TWENTY-THREE

Diran, Tresslar, and Solus came to rest on the dock directly in front of the statue of Nerthatch. It appeared to Diran that Nathifa and Haaken had become integral parts of the enchantment the lich was casting, and neither would be able to move without disrupting the spell. At least, he hoped that would prove to be the case. All the trio needed was a few moments in which to act.

Coils of mist drifted in from the sea and wrapped themselves around Diran's body, and the priest knew he was under attack by Makala.

"Tresslar, Solus, forget about me! Go and—" Diran's words were cut off, and he found himself unable to breathe. He understood what was happening. Makala had filled his lungs with her vaporous substance, preventing him from breathing. Could she transform while within him, take on human form, and tear him apart from the inside out? He was unfamiliar with any vampire lore that spoke of such a capability, but if it was possible, he certainly didn't want to learn about it firsthand. He opened his mouth and pressed his silver arrowhead against his lips. White light shone forth from the holy symbol, pouring into his body, filling him with its warmth.

Diran sensed more than heard a scream from somewhere inside

him, and then tendrils of mist raced out of his mouth and nose. His lungs began to work again, and he drew in a gasping breath as Makala's form solidified in front of him. The vampire hunched over on the dock, flesh smoking from dozens of burns.

Diran knew it would take Makala a moment to recover, and he took the opportunity to glance over to see how Tresslar and Hinto were doing. The psiforged had stepped in front of the statue of Nerthatch and now placed his three-fingered hands on the sides of the stone head. As soon as contact was made, the psionic crystals covering Solus's body began to flicker erratically, and he threw back his head and screamed. Diran wasn't certain what the psiforged was trying to accomplish. How could one create a psionic link with the petrified body of a long-dead priest? But whatever Solus was attempting, it was clearly causing him great agony.

Tresslar had reached into his backpack and removed a glove made of wire mesh. He slipped it over his right hand, stepped toward Nathifa, and grabbed hold of the dragonwand. Sparks of necromantic energy flew off the mystic artifact, and the shaft of dark power lancing forth from the mouth of the golden dragonhead began to shrink, as if it were a stream of black water that was slowly being cut off at its source. Nathifa turned to Tresslar and glared at him with her sole remaining eye. She couldn't use magic against the artificer, for her power was bound up in maintaining control of the Amahau, and she couldn't strike Tresslar as she only had one arm and couldn't spare it at the moment. But the lich had other ways of attacking. Ebon tendrils of shadow emerged from the black substance that served as her cloak and shot toward Tresslar fast as striking snakes. The tendrils coiled tight around his arm, and the artificer cried out in pain. Diran had fought enough liches in his time to know what was happening: Nathifa was draining Tresslar's lifeforce. The artificer was in good health, but he wasn't a young man and wouldn't be able to withstand Nathifa's assault for long.

Diran started to go to Tresslar's aid, but before he could do more than take a single step, Makala leaped upon him with the speed and grace of a jungle cat. She knocked him down to the dock, rolled him onto his back, straddled him, and with inhuman strength pressed his shoulders against the wooden planks, pinning him in place.

Makala grinned. "Tell you what, lover. How about I let you live long enough to watch your friends die?"

"How about I tell you a secret first?"

Makala frowned. "What?"

"During the voyage from Trebaz Sinara I sharpened the edges of my arrowhead." Diran still held his holy symbol in his right hand, and he had just enough range of movement left to raise the silver object and ram its razor-sharp tip into the vampire's leg.

Makala screamed and rolled off Diran. The priest maintained his grip on the arrowhead, and it tore free of the vampire's leg in a gout of foul-smelling black fluid. Makala tried to scuttle away, but before she could escape, Diran jumped on top of her and pressed the holy symbol to her forehead. Makala's scream rose in volume and pitch until it no longer had anything even remotely in common with a sound produced by a human throat. Then in a loud, commanding voice, Diran spoke three words.

"Begone, foul spirit!"

❂ ❂ ❂ ❂ ❂ ❂ ❂

Hinto was both impressed and terrified at the savagery with which Leontis fought. Though he faced three weresharks, the priest was more than holding his own. The new transformation Leontis had undergone seemed to have made him stronger, as if he now possessed the combined strength of both a werewolf *and* a wereshark. Leontis bled from dozens of wounds, but they were little more than scratches. The three weresharks weren't so lucky, however. They were covered with deep slash marks thanks to Leontis' powerful claws. Hinto was beginning to think that the priest would be able to handle the weresharks on his own when the largest of the creatures managed to clamp its jaws down on Leontis's left arm. The wolfshark howled in pain and clawed furiously at the white shark's snout with his free hand, cutting long bloody furrows in the creature's flesh. But no matter how fiercely Leontis fought, the white shark refused to let go.

Hinto was about to race forward and attack with the silver

dagger Diran had given him when he saw that Onu had shucked off his crimson captain's jacket. The changeling then tore off the white shirt he was wearing and dropped it to the deck. He gave Hinto a wink and then started toward Leontis and the wereshark, his body shifting and reforming with each step until Onu resembled a smaller version of the wereshark. The changeling walked straight up to the wereshark, silver dagger held down at his side. The wereshark didn't let go of Leontis's arm as Onu approached, but his gaze shifted to take in the newcomer. When the wereshark saw that the creature that approached was apparently of the same species, its mouth widened into a grin, and it looked away.

That's when Onu plunged the dagger blade into one of the wereshark's dead-black eyes.

The wereshark roared, let go of Leontis's arm and staggered backward, blood gushing from his eye socket. He reached up in an attempt to pull out the dagger, but silver was as poison to lycanthropes, and the wereshark was already too weak to do more than claw feebly at the dagger's hilt. The creature fell and hit the deck with a loud thump that shook the planks beneath Hinto's feet. The wereshark was dead.

Snarling, Leontis took a step back and cradled his wounded arm. The other two weresharks—the hammerhead and the blue—hesitated, unsure what had just happened and what, if anything they should do about it. Hinto saw his chance. He dashed toward the hammerhead, the bigger and more deadly of the two, and rammed his dagger into the monster's chest. The monster screamed once, stiffened, and then fell to the deck.

The blue shark looked back and forth between Onu, Hinto, and Leontis. The lycanthropic priest stepped toward the surviving wereshark, growling low in his throat. The blue might have looked like a mindless animal, but he was anything but. He knew bad odds when he saw them. He turned, ran toward the railing, leaped over, and plunged into the water below.

Hinto didn't know whether lycanthropes would heal if the silver weapons that slew them were removed, so he left the dagger buried in the wereshark's chest and walked over to Onu. The changeling was in the process of transforming back into his human guise of Captain Onu, and the metamorphosis was complete by the time Hinto reached him.

"Not bad, eh, lad?" Onu said, grinning. "But then the beastly things should've known better than to go up against a couple of hardy old salts like us!" The changeling clapped Hinto on the back hard enough to nearly knock the halfling off his feet. Hinto was about to congratulate Onu on the success of his ploy when he realized that Leontis was growling at them.

The wolfshark's arm had almost healed. While the flesh was still ragged in places, the wounds no longer dripped blood. Leontis's eyes—large fish-like orbs that shone lupine yellow—were fixed on them with murderous fury. Hinto feared that there was nothing of the priest left inside that monstrous body, and the evil thing he'd become would, lacking any other prey, now attack them.

Hinto glanced sideways at the dead body of the wereshark, gauging his chances of reaching the corpse and pulling the silver dagger out of its chest before Leontis could leap forward. He decided they weren't good.

Hinto stepped in front of Onu. Perhaps the changeling had become the true captain of the *Turnabout* by an accident of fate, but he *was* the captain, and it was Hinto's duty as acting first mate to protect him.

Onu attempted to push the halfling out of the way. "Lad, I appreciate the gesture, but there's no need."

Before the changeling could say anything more, Leontis stopped growling. His prominent brow furrowed, and a look of confusion came into his eyes. Then he spoke, his voice a gravely rumbling that was difficult to make out, but not impossible.

"Hinto . . . Onu . . . ?"

Hinto grinned. "That's right, Leontis! It's us!"

The wolfshark's arm was completely healed now, and he rose to his feet. Hinto almost stepped forward to help Leontis up, but he restrained himself. Just because the priest recognized them didn't mean he was no longer dangerous.

Now that the weresharks had been deal with, they should go

help Diran and the others. But before Hinto could broach the subject, he felt a chill breeze against the back of his neck. The cold seeped into his skin, penetrated his bones, and seemed to permeate his very soul. Coils of greenish mist slithered across the deck of the galleon, moving as if they were somehow alive, vaporous serpents probing, exploring, seeking something, though Hinto couldn't have said what. The halfling turned toward the ship's railing and there, out in the bay, he spied a dark vessel that every sailor who plied the waters of the Lhazaar Sea feared and prayed never to set eyes upon.

The *Ship of Bones.*

CHAPTER

TWENTY-FOUR

Nathifa felt the artificer's lifeforce draining into her body, and she welcomed it. Not only because it weakened one of her enemies, but because it helped restore a small portion of the power she'd lost on Trebaz Sinara by sacrificing her arm and her eye.

The old man was clever; she had to give him that. His mastery of mystic arts couldn't begin to approach hers, but he'd created a device that allowed him not only to take hold of the dragonwand while it was in use without being damaged, but also to dampen the Amahau's energy output. If he were allowed to continue, he might well be able to stop the Summoning and regain possession of the dragonwand. But he would be dead long before that came to pass.

A cold breeze wafted in from the sea, bringing with it tendrils of greenish mist, and Nathifa's feelings of triumph gave way to fear and despair. She looked out across the bay, knowing what she would see upon its waters. The *Ship of Bones*. Prince Moren had come to collect the debt she owned him.

The lich cast her thoughts out toward the dark vessel.

Not yet! I'm not ready!

She wasn't surprised when she received no answer.

❂ ❂ ❂ ❂ ❂ ❂ ❂

Ghaji—singed and smarting from the burns he'd taken from leaping through the wall of fire—ran to the end of the dock, elemental axe held tight, flames trailing behind him. There were only three weresharks between the half-orc and his destination, but that was three too many as far as Ghaji was concerned. He whirled the axe over his head, bared his teeth ,and roared as he came, trying to make himself into what he hoped was a fearsome apparition. He had no illusions that he'd frighten the weresharks off, but he hoped that his ferocity and the flames generated by his axe might give them enough pause so that he could get the first strike in as he attacked.

But the weresharks didn't appear intimidated in the slightest, and they matched Ghaji's display of ferocity with their own, showing their teeth, raising their claws, and bellowing a challenge. But then they stopped and as one turned to look toward the bay. A green mist that seemed almost to glow with a sickly illumination covered the surface of the water, and there was a sudden drop in air temperature. A moment later the trio of weresharks leaped off the dock, transforming into full shark form before they plunged into the water.

Ghaji kept running, but out of the corner of his eye he saw the sharks swim away, their dorsal fins cutting through the layer of green mist that hung over the water. He had no idea what the mist was or why it should frighten the weresharks so much, but he was too grateful to question it.

As the half-orc approached the end of the dock, he saw that his friends had already engaged Nathifa and her servants in battle. Solus gripped the head of the statue of Nerthatch, Diran was struggling with Makala, and Tresslar was trying to wrest the dragonwand from the lich who, in turn, had wrapped tendrils of darkness around the artificer's arm. Ghaji had faced enough liches alongside Diran to know that Nathifa was draining Tresslar's lifeforce. He knew what he had to do.

He raced toward Nathifa and Tresslar, raised his flaming axe, and brought it down upon the ebon tendrils protruding from the lich's body. The blade sliced through the shadowy substance of the sorceress's cloak, making the lich hiss in pain. The black coils around Tresslar's arm relaxed and fell to the dock, and the artificer gasped with relief. But he did not release his grip on the dragonwand. Ghaji knew they had only seconds before Nathifa unfurled more tendrils and renewed her attack, so the half-orc did the only logical thing: he swung his axe at the sorceress's wrist.

The flaming blade cut through Nathifa's undead flesh as if it were dry kindling, and Tresslar yanked the dragonwand away from her, the lich's hand still holding tight to the other end. The shaft of necromantic energy emanating from the mouth of the Amahau winked out the instant Nathifa's hand was severed from her body, and the lich shrieked in rage. Tresslar shoved the end of the dragonwand into the flames of Ghaji's axe, and the hand was instantly charred black. The fingers released their grip, and the blackened hand fell to the dock. Nathifa lurched forward, as if intending to retrieve her hand, but Tresslar kicked it out of her reach. The lich's hand flew into the water with a small splash and sank from sight.

Nathifa, her bleached-white features twisted into a mask of sheer hatred, lunged at Tresslar, but Ghaji stepped in front of her and barred her way with his flaming axe. The lich shrank back with an angry hiss, and Tresslar pointed the dragonwand at the statue of Nerthatch. Streams of black energy began to flow from the statue's stone surface and drift into the mouth of the golden dragonhead, almost as if the mystical device was devouring them. Ghaji understood what was happening: Tresslar was draining the magical power from the statue of Nerthatch.

"No!" Nathifa cried out.

Ghaji grinned. "Oh, yes."

❋ ❋ ❋ ❋ ❋ ❋ ❋

Makala's body writhed as the burning light of the Silver Flame poured from the holy symbol pressed to her forehead. The Flame blazed through her being. She tried to dislodge Diran, but her strength had deserted her. She felt weak as a newborn kitten, and she feared the power of the Flame was going to consume her. She squeezed her eyes shut, and deep inside the inner recesses of her mind, Makala saw herself standing on Regalport's dock, but she wasn't standing alone. Before her stood an old man in a fur cloak with roiling pools of shadow where his eyes should be.

"Resist!" the old man shouted, blood-flecked spittle flying from his fanged mouth. "The priest is trying to drive me out! Fight him, damn you!"

Here within the core of her soul, Makala was still human, and she knew the dark spirit that she'd inherited from Aldarik Cathmore was desperate to maintain its hold on her.

You present yourself as a benefactor that provides both strength and cold-blooded ruthlessness, Makala said. *But you're nothing. Just a parasite afraid to be separated from its host. You heard what Diran said: begone!*

The dark spirit threw back its head and roared its fury to the night sky. A small dot of silver light began to grow on the spirit's wrinkled forehead. It quickly assumed the shape of a glowing blue-white arrowhead, and then the light spread rapidly across the spirit, blazing brighter and brighter, until Makala could see nothing but its light . . . a light that no longer hurt to gaze upon.

She opened her eyes and found herself looking up at Diran's concerned face. The priest knelt beside her. He'd removed the arrowhead from her flesh, holding it clasped in his fist to hide it from her sight. Her forehead felt as if a white-hot branding iron had been pressed to it, but the pain was already beginning to recede.

She smiled at the man who had once been her lover. "You did it, Diran. The dark spirit's gone. Am I . . ." She reached up and touched the sharp point of her right incisor. She was still a vampire.

"I'm sorry," Diran said.

Makala sat up. "Don't be. Thanks to you, my soul is free of Cathmore's taint. That's enough of a miracle for one night, wouldn't you say?"

Diran smiled, but before either of them could speak again, they heard Nathifa cry out in a voice like thunder. "I'll see you all dead!"

The shadowy substance of the lich's cloak rose up to cover her head, and her ebon form began to grow, its shape rearranging as it expanded. Slender sections separated from the central core, forming a dozen writhing tentacles. Makala realized what Nathifa was doing: she was using up the remainder of her magic for one last attack. Perhaps she would snatch them up in her tentacles and squeeze the life out of them, or perhaps she would simply drain their lifeforces. It didn't matter. Whatever the sorceress intended, Makala wasn't going to stand by and allow it to happen. Diran had saved her soul, and now she was going to save his life, regardless of the cost to herself.

She gave the priest a quick kiss.

"Don't say I never did anything for you."

Before Diran could react, Makala transformed into a bat and flew directly into the tentacled monster Nathifa had become, disappearing into its shadowy substance.

⊚ ⊚ ⊚ ⊚ ⊚ ⊚ ⊚

Solus's mind was lost in a raging storm of psionic chaos—a riotous cacophony of blinding images and deafening sounds. Thanks to the memories of his kalashtar creators that he had absorbed long ago, he understood what was happening. When Solus had first descended to the dock, he had sensed that Nathifa was summoning and controlling the weresharks through a psionic link with Haaken, who in turn was linked to the stone body of the priest Nerthatch. Solus, drawing on his creators' knowledge, knew that if he could disrupt that psionic chain Nathifa had established, he could stop her enchantment. But what he hadn't paused to consider—and what was the cause of his current predicament—was that while there was at times a certain overlap in the disciplines of psionics and magic, their power came from very different energy sources. The power Nathifa used to fuel her spell was corrupted by the foulness of her undead form, and the substance of Nerthatch's stone body was suffused with the evil energies of the dark power that had cursed him. Thus, when Solus had attempted to establish his mind-link to Nathifa using the statue and Haaken as conduits, he'd opened himself up to the dark energies surging through all three. Now he could not break the link, and evil filled his mind, threatening to plunge him into madness, and though he was fighting as hard as he could, he feared it was a losing battle.

He thought of Diran and Ghaji, of Tresslar and Yvka, but most of all, he thought of Hinto. He and the halfling had formed a special bond, right from the beginning, and while Solus felt sorrow at the thought of failing his friends, he regretted letting Hinto down most of all. The psiforged hoped his friends would find a way to defeat Nathifa and stop the weresharks attacking Regalport without him.

But just as Solus was about to surrender to the whirlpool of insanity that threatened to pull him under, he felt the pressure in his mind ease. The storm of madness that swirled around him lessened, and though it did not abate entirely, it diminished to the point where Solus was no longer in danger of being lost to its fury. He didn't know precisely how it happened, but he sensed that Nathifa's link to Haaken, and therefore to the statue of Nerthatch, had been broken. He was about to sever his own link to the statue since he could no longer use it to strike against the lich, but now that his mind was free to focus more clearly, he sensed that all the weresharks Nathifa had summoned remained linked to the statue.

And that meant they were all linked to him.

If Solus had possessed the physiognomy for it, he would have smiled. To the weresharks still at sea, he sent a single command: *Stay away!* But he had something a bit more special in mind for those lycanthropes rampaging through the streets of Regalport.

Solus concentrated on sending a very specific image into their minds.

❧ ❧ ❧ ❧ ❧ ❧ ❧

It had been a glorious night of slaughter so far for the weresharks, and the fun showed no signs of abating. True, there had been some minor resistance. The city watch was putting up a fight (though not much of one), and the Sea Dragons had given a much better account of themselves—and continued to do so in isolated spots throughout Regalport. Operatives from House Thuranni were striking silently and swiftly from the shadows, though not doing much permanent damage, and of course there were various swordfighters, artificers, wizards, and more who had taken to the streets in order to protect their city. But what of it? The defenders' efforts only added to the weresharks' amusement, and every person the lycanthropes wounded but did not slay became infected with their curse, adding to their numbers, if not this night, then on the morrow. There was nothing anyone could do to stop the weresharks' rampage. There were simply too many of them, and they had struck swiftly and without warning. Regalport had already fallen. Its citizens just hadn't realized it yet.

But then something strange happened. The cobblestone streets shimmered and became coated with smooth metal. The buildings changed as well, stone and wood now overlaid with bluish-white until everything in Regalport gleamed with reflected moonlight. Throughout the city, the weresharks reacted in horror as they realized they were entirely surrounded by silver. Their feet burned from the silver cobblestones they stood upon, and the moonlight reflecting off the silver buildings seared their eyes. The weresharks panicked and ran blindly, following their instincts back toward the sea, and those few who were not slain by Regalport's defenders—none of whom saw the illusion that so terrified the weresharks—actually made it.

❀ ❀ ❀ ❀ ❀ ❀ ❀

Solus's perceptions shifted back to the material plane in time to see Tresslar, once again in possession of his dragonwand, lower the magical device. The psiforged's fingers were still pressed to the head of Nerthatch's stone body, but he could no longer sense any evil power within the statue. He guessed that Tresslar had used the Amahau to absorb the statue's energy, but he felt confident that he had gotten his twin messages to the weresharks through the statue's link before Nerthatch's body was completely drained of magic. Solus lowered his hands from the statue's head and turned to see what further assistance he might render his friends. That's when he saw Haaken remove his hands from the statue's shoulders, and he realized that he hadn't dealt with *all* the weresharks in Regalport this night. He had failed to follow the link back through the statue to Haaken's mind.

Haaken didn't recover right away, however. He swayed on his

feet as he struggled to shake off the effects of serving as a conduit for Nathifa's magic. Solus had witnessed the recuperative powers of lycanthropes enough times to know that it wouldn't take long for Haaken to recover, and the psiforged didn't intend to give him the chance. Solus concentrated on using his telekinetic power to grab hold of the wereshark and fling him far out into the bay, but nothing happened. Solus looked down at his chest and saw that his psionic crystals had gone dark. He'd expended his entire storehouse of psionic energy to resist the mental maelstrom he'd been caught in and then to deal with the weresharks. It would be quite some time before his crystals were able to restore themselves, and in the meantime, he was helpless.

No, he thought as he looked down at his hands. Not entirely.

The psiforged curled his stone fingers into a fist, stepped forward, and punched Haaken on the snout as hard as he could. Unfortunately, Solus hadn't been built for strength, and all he managed to accomplish with his blow was to clear Haaken's mind. The wereshark glared at Solus and lashed out with a vicious backhand strike, and suddenly the psiforged was the one who found himself flying off the dock and plunging into the bay.

❖ ❖ ❖ ❖ ❖ ❖ ❖

Ghaji saw Haaken knock Solus into the water. The half-orc didn't know if the psiforged could swim, but since the construct didn't need to breathe, Ghaji decided the point was moot. He took a quick look around and tried to decide on his next move.

The weird greenish mist now covered the entire bay, and tendrils were just starting to curl up over the edges of the dock. Ghaji didn't know what the stuff was, but he knew it wasn't good. Tresslar still held the dragonwand, but something had happened to it. The Amahau and the wand it was attached to had both turned pure black. Ghaji was no artificer, but he doubted the wand was going to be of much use in the immediate future. Strangest of all, Nathifa had transformed into a mass of shadow tentacles approximately ten feet tall. Nathifa—or whatever she was now—had folded over on herself, as if she were a giant fist squeezing something tight within her grip. Ghaji had no idea what it could be, until he remembered seeing a small dark object streak into Nathifa's shadowy form right after he had cut the dragonwand free. Ghaji glanced in Diran's direction and saw his friend rising to his feet, silver arrowhead held in his right hand. There was no sign of Makala.

That's when Ghaji realized what Nathifa was squeezing within her shadowy grasp.

Diran dashed to the half-orc's side. "Makala's inside Nathifa! We have to do something before the lich destroys her!"

Ghaji wasn't sure what Diran was talking about, but it never occurred to him to question his friend.

"Let's do it," the half-orc said.

Together the two friends started toward the tentacled beast, Ghaji gripping his flaming axe tight, Diran raising his silver arrowhead, preparing to wield the holy object against the evil sorceress.

That's when Haaken grabbed them both by the neck and slammed their heads together.

Bright light flashed behind Ghaji's eyes, the world spun, and his vision went gray. When his eyes cleared, he found himself looking up at Haaken, and he realized that he was lying on his back. The wereshark must have dropped him and Diran to the dock after knocking them together. Ghaji tried to rise, but his head felt as if it had been shattered into a million pieces, and he was too dizzy to move. He turned to look at Diran, and though his friend was consciousness, he looked to be in just as bad a shape as Ghaji. Blood ran from both Diran's ears and nostrils. Not a good sign. Ghaji turned the other direction and saw his elemental axe lying on the dock several feet out of reach. Once out of his hand, its flames had extinguished. He supposed it didn't matter that he'd dropped the axe. He was too weak to lift it right now anyway.

Haaken looked down at them, grinning with a maw full of shark teeth. "You don't know how good it feels to finally have a chance to pay the two of you back for wrecking my ship and stranding me on Demothi Island. I suppose I should thank you, though. If it wasn't for you, I'd never have become the magnificent creature I am today. I *did* manage to extract a bit of revenge on Trebaz Sinara, though." The wereshark focused his gaze on Diran. "It was no accident that I threw your werewolf friend at Asenka. She was a pain in my rump back when I was human, and I was glad to end her life. Her bones made such lovely snapping sounds when the wolf hit her, didn't they?"

Haaken laughed then, the sound hideous coming from his inhuman throat.

Ghaji saw Diran struggle to rise, an expression of mingled sorrow and fury on his face, but the priest was too injured to get up and slumped back down onto the dock.

"I was just going to kill the two of you," Haaken continued, "but now that I think of it, that would be too easy. Instead, I'm to give you each a little love nip. Just enough to draw blood—and pass along my gift to you. I think you'll eventually come to enjoy being weresharks. I know *I* love it."

Haaken started forward, mouth open wide—

"Get away from them!"

Haaken paused and turned to look at Tresslar. The artificer held forth the blackened dragonwand, the Amahau pointed directly at the wereshark.

"Take another step and I destroy you!"

"Don't bluff, old man," Haaken growled. "If that thing still worked, you'd have used it already." The wereshark looked back down at Ghaji and Diran. "You two aren't going anywhere soon. I'll wet my appetite for you by slaying the old man first."

Haaken turned back to Tresslar and began to advance on the artificer. Tresslar held his ground, but Ghaji could see that the dragonwand was shaking in the artificer's hand. Tresslar *had* been bluffing, and now that Haaken had called his bluff, it appeared that the artificer had run out of tricks.

"I don't suppose you're going to give me a chance to say any last words?" Tresslar said, backing up slowly.

"Why should I?" Haaken snarled.

"Pity," Tresslar said. "Because if you did, I'd say, 'Look out.'"

Haaken scowled and spun just in time to see a strange creature— part wolf and part shark—leaping at him.

SEA OF DEATH

❀ ❀ ❀ ◉ ❀ ❀ ❀

Diran watched as Leontis—at least, he assumed the hybrid monster was his old friend—tore into Haaken with a savage fury that was both wonderful and terrible to behold. Leontis knocked Haaken onto the dock and clawed at his chest with his hands, ripped at his belly with his feet, and ravaged his neck and face with his teeth. Haaken screamed as his blood fountained into the air and his viscera spilled onto the dock. Diran knew that Haaken was no longer a threat to them, so he turned his attention to Nathifa.

The priest didn't know what was happening inside the lich, but from the way her shadowy form was shaking, he assumed that Makala was doing something to attack the sorceress from within. Nathifa couldn't drain Makala's lifeforce, since she was a vampire and thus undead, but Makala couldn't hope to do any lasting damage to the lich, since the only way to slay her kind was to locate and destroy the phylactery in which she'd stored her essence. The best Makala could hope for was a stalemate, but even weakened as Nathifa surely was from the effort of casting her summoning spell, she was still a powerful sorceress, and Diran knew it was only a matter of time until Nathifa bested Makala. Diran hadn't driven the dark spirit from Makala's body only to abandon her now. He had to do something, and he had to do it fast.

He struggled to rise up on his left elbow, ignoring the throbbing in his skull, and the resulting wave of nausea that twisted his gut. He knew he had a severe head injury, but he couldn't afford to waste the time it would take to heal himself. He could tend to his wounds later—after Nathifa was defeated once and for all.

Diran retained his grip on the silver arrowhead. He held it lightly between the thumb and forefinger of his free hand and, though it wasn't a dagger, he'd sharpened its edges, and Nathifa's transformation into a giant tentacled monster had made her a satisfyingly large target.

Diran whispered a quick prayer and hurled the holy symbol toward Nathifa. The silver arrowhead spun through the air, struck the lich's ebon substance, and passed into her darkness.

Perhaps it hadn't been the most skillful throw he'd ever made, Diran thought, but he'd take it.

❋ ❋ ❋ ❋ ❋ ❋ ❋

Nathifa felt Makala, in humanoid form now, clawing at her from the inside. The lich wished she had never transported the vampire within her body on Trebaz Sinara, for surely that had given the woman the notion to attack this way. Normally, Makala's efforts to harm her would have been laughable, but Nathifa's power had been greatly diminished by the events of the last several days, and it was taking her longer to muster the strength to deal with the vampire than she would've liked—especially considering the fact that Prince Moren had arrived to claim his due. If she were to have any hope of slaying Bastiaan and the others, she had to deal with Makala swiftly.

She felt a small sharp-edged object slice into her. Not only was the damnable thing fashioned from silver, it also bore a holy blessing, imparted by Bastiaan, no doubt. The object burned like white fire inside of Nathifa, causing so much agony that she could no longer hold onto Makala. She ejected the vampire from her dark substance and flung Makala onto the dock. The woman landed near the priest and his half-orc companion, but Nathifa had no more attention to give the vampire. She had to expel the silver object from her body before—

She sensed tendrils of green mist curl onto the dock, stretch toward the ebon tentacles that supported her, and gently, almost lovingly brush against her dark substance.

Her time was up.

❋ ❋ ❋ ❋ ❋ ❋ ❋

In his quarters aboard the *Ship of Bones*, Prince Moren sat in a chair fashioned from the unfulfilled dreams of dead sailors. Resting before him atop a table made from memories of regret and betrayal was the obsidian skull named Espial. Nathifa had bartered the skull in order to obtain the material she needed to repair her damaged vessel, and Moren had agreed not to leave Espial alone for a short time to give the lich an opportunity to achieve her vengeance. Moren had kept his word. He hadn't laid a finger on the skull, though that hadn't stopped him from examining it in other ways. It was a most intriguing object. The lich used it to communicate with Vol—or rather the Lich Queen used it to pass along her orders to Nathifa. But Espial served a dual purpose: it was also the lich's phylactery.

Prince Moren reached out and lifted Espial off the table. The skull was about to serve a third purpose. Nathifa's lifeforce was contained inside, and Moren—like the rest of his cursed crew—fed on the life essence of others. And the Prince was hungry.

Moren raised the skull to his mouth and, as if Espial were nothing more than a piece of rotten fruit, he pressed his decayed teeth onto its obsidian surface and bit down hard.

He chewed, swallowed, and grinned as black juice dribbled over his dry, leathery lips and onto the exposed bone of his chin. Delicious.

He took another bite.

❧ ❧ ❧ ❧ ❧ ❧ ❧

Nathifa screamed.
But not for very long.

❧ ❧ ❧ ❧ ❧ ❧ ❧

Diran watched as the lich's form broke apart into scraps of shadow that swirled about like black leaves before dissipating like smoke. He didn't know how—his arrowhead certainly hadn't done the deed—but he knew that Nathifa had been destroyed. Tresslar rushed to Diran's side and helped him to a sitting position. The priest looked out over the bay. The greenish mist that had covered the water was receding, and Diran could sense the presence of an evil much greater than Nathifa withdrawing. He was too hurt to worry about it now. Whatever the mist was, and whatever role it had played in the events here tonight would have to remain a mystery for the time being. Diran had more important tasks to tend to. He placed his hand over his heart, closed his eyes, and willed the healing power of the Silver Flame to work its divine magic through him. He then repeated the procedure for Ghaji, and when both men were whole and healthy once more, Tresslar helped them both to stand.

Makala stood on the dock, gazing out to the sea. Diran didn't know what she was looking at, and he wasn't sure he wanted to. He turned to Leontis, fearing they would still have a battle on their hands if the lycanthropic priest remained in the grip of a killing frenzy. But Leontis stood apart from Haaken's ravaged body. He was covered with blood, but he was human once again, his fury spent. Without speaking, Diran, Ghaji, and Tresslar walked over to examine Haaken. Makala joined them a moment later.

Haaken had also returned to human form, but he was a grisly sight. His chest and abdomen had been ripped open, ribs broken, internal organs shredded or torn out and cast aside by Leontis in his bestial fury. There was blood everywhere, and Haaken was covered in it, so much so that his skin looked black in the moonlight. But even mutilated as he was, Haaken was not dead.

Haaken coughed, and a froth of blood oozed from between his lips. Then he spoke in a gurgling, wet whisper.

"I can . . . already feel myself . . . healing." He coughed again and swallowed. "Hurts. But . . . I can take it. I'm . . . going to kill every last one of you . . . bastards."

Ghaji had retrieved his axe, and with a thought he caused its flame to ignite. "Big talk from a man who's been gutted like a fish. Since Leontis has already gone to the trouble to fillet you, maybe I should go ahead and cook you." Ghaji started forward, but Diran placed a gentle hand on his friend's shoulder to stop him.

"Fire won't kill him, Ghaji. You know that."

"Maybe not normally," the half-orc growled. "But wounded as he is, flame just might kill him. Let's try it and see." He glared at Haaken. "If nothing else, it'll make me feel better."

Diran shook his head. "There's only one way to be sure." The priest walked over to the statue of Nerthatch and gripped the hilt of the silver dagger protruding from the chest. He pulled, and though the dagger was wedged tight, Diran managed to work it free. He then walked over to Haaken and stood by the lycanthrope's side. Haaken's heart was visible, and though it had several large gashes in it, the organ continued to beat, and Diran could see that the gashes were already beginning to heal over.

"Are you going to . . . stab me?" Haaken asked. His voice had grown stronger and steadier in the few moments since he'd last spoken. "Coward!" Haaken spat a gob of bloody sputum at Diran, but it fell far short of hitting the priest.

"Go ahead, Diran," Ghaji said. "If he heals, he'll just go on killing. Worse, he'll spread his infection to others. He doesn't deserve to live. He's just another damned monster."

Diran looked at Haaken, then he looked at Leontis, and finally at Makala. He remembered what Leontis had told him during the voyage from Trebaz Sinara.

You are Purified, a servant of the Flame, and a force for Good in a world that sorely needs people like you. Don't let your grief turn you back into a heartless killer.

"Let the city watch or the Sea Dragons decide what to do with him," Diran said. "I've had enough of death for a while." He turned his back on Haaken and started to walk away, but Makala took hold of his wrist and stopped him.

Diran turned to her, a questioning look on his face. She reached out and gently took the dagger from his hand. As soon as her flesh came in contact with the silver hilt, her hand began to sizzle and smoke, but she gritted her teeth and held onto the blade. She stepped over to Haaken's side, knelt down, and plunged the blade into his heart. Haaken's eyes went wide and he let out a last gasp as he died.

Makala stood and turned back to Diran.

"I never did like the son of a whore."

CHAPTER

TWENTY-FIVE

Ten days later, in the hour just before dawn, the companions once more stood upon Regalport's central dock. A longboat was moored on the dock's northern side, and the *Turnabout*, whole and hardy once more, floated out in the middle of the bay. Onu, wearing his human shape and clad in his signature crimson jacket, stood gazing at the northern horizon.

"Looks like we're going to have good sailing weather today," the changeling said. He glanced at Hinto for confirmation, and the halfling nodded.

Diran smiled. "It seems as if you're well on your way to becoming a true seaman, Onu."

Onu reached down and patted Hinto on the back. "My recent gains in nautical knowledge are due entirely to the tutelage of my new first mate."

"Do you really think you'll be able to pay off Thokk's debt?" Ghaji asked. "From what you've told us, he spoke little about it to you. Do you even know where to start?"

Onu shrugged. "As to whether or not I'll succeed, only the gods of fortune may say. But I must try." The changeling smiled. "It's my own debt to Thokk, you see. We'll return to Kolbyr and begin there. Thokk did a great deal of business in that city, and perhaps there are some there who knew him better than I. At any rate, it seems a logical place to start." The changeling looked at Tresslar and smiled. "Besides, I have a passenger to conduct there."

The artificer looked suddenly uncomfortable. "Even with the aid of the best artificers in Regalport, I haven't made much progress cleansing the Amahau of the taint it incurred when I used it to drain the mystic energy from the statue of Nerthatch. But I believe there's a chance that the magic of Illyia's water spheres might prove effective where other approaches have failed. Water does have inherent cleansing properties, you know, and if I can adapt her spheres—"

"You want to do a lot more to her spheres than adapt them," Hinto said, grinning.

Tresslar scowled at the halfling, but then he just shrugged and smiled sheepishly.

"I think it's sweet," Yvka said. "But be wary. I've managed to convince the Hierarchs of House Thuranni to . . . table their interest in the Amahau, especially now that it's been tainted. But if you do manage to repair the wand, the Hierarchs might decide to renew their interest in obtaining it."

"I'll be careful, Yvka," Tresslar said. "Thanks for the warning."

The elf-woman turned to Solus. "The Hierarchs are still most interested in obtaining your services, though. While they've abandoned the idea of doing so through force or trickery, they've authorized me to make an offer of employment to you, and the compensation would be most handsome indeed."

"Please thank the Hierarchs for me, Yvka, but I must decline. The uses House Thuranni would put me to would be no different that what Aldarik Cathmore and Galharath would've done with me. Though I was given life some time ago, I have only recently begun to learn what it means to truly live. I believe I can continue to best do that be remaining my own person. I hope you understand."

Yvka smiled. "I do indeed, my friend. I not only understand your decision, I applaud it."

"Besides, Solus is going with us," Hinto said. "I'm going to teach him to be a sailor."

"I find the open sea calming," Solus said. "The thoughts of its denizens are simple and unclouded by negative emotions like deceit and greed."

"You've never run into any pirates," Tresslar muttered.

"I fully understand what Solus means," Leontis said, looking toward the eastern horizon. "The world below the waves is a very different place from the world of land, air, and sun. It has its own rhythms of life, rules of existence, and codes of behavior. In many ways it's a much harsher world than this one, but it's more honest as well."

There was nothing else to do then than to say farewell to those who were bound for the *Turnabout*. Words were exchanged, as well as handshakes and hugs. Then Onu, Hinto, Tresslar, and Solus boarded the longboat. The halfling untied the mooring lines, and the psiforged used his telekinetic powers to back the boat away from the dock.

Onu called out, "Good sailing to us all!" Then Solus propelled the longboat across the bay toward the waiting elemental galleon. It didn't take long for the party to board the vessel, and the ship set sail soon afterward. The remaining companions watched as their friends sailed out of Regalport's bay. The vessel looked like a normal galleon, but that was just its illusion in effect. Once out to sea, Onu would order the air elementals to be activated, and the ship would head off at full speed toward Kolbyr.

"I'm surprised the shipwrights were able to repair the *Turnabout* in such a short time," Ghaji said. "Actually, given the severity of the damage she sustained, it's a wonder they even tried."

"Prince Ryger was most grateful for our efforts to stop the wereshark invasion," Diran said. "I imagine he instructed the shipwrights to make every effort to do the job as quickly as possible."

Yvka smiled. "Or else."

Diran had mixed feelings about the aftermath of the wereshark invasion. Solus had managed to drive off the weresharks that Nathifa had summoned, but the monsters had killed many of Regalport's citizens before fleeing. The lycanthropes had infected many more, and Prince Ryger had ordered those now cursed with the taint of the wereshark to be rounded up and imprisoned. Ryger had wanted to execute them, though the Prince took no joy in the thought, but

Diran had talked him out of it. The goal was to prevent the newly infected lycanthropes from slaying anyone or further spreading their contagion, not to kill them for possessing an affliction over which they had no control. It wasn't a satisfying solution, but it would have to do. Diran remembered once more Tusya's words: *Sometimes cold comfort is the only kind we get in this life.*

So true.

"It is time that I take my leave as well," Leontis said.

Diran turned to his friend, surprised by his fellow priest's pronouncement. "I take it you no longer wish me to kill you?"

Leontis smiled. "Perhaps another day. I've spent much time over the last ten days exploring my new abilities and trying to decide what, if anything, I should do with them. I meant what I said earlier about the sea, Diran. It's . . . different there. Good and Evil still exist, of course, but the expressions they take are unique to their world. Perhaps I have been cursed, but what I choose to do with that curse is up to me. Look at you. You were born with a talent for knife work that borders on genius. You were sold into slavery, raised by a brotherhood of assassins, and implanted with an evil spirit to make certain you remained cruel and heartless. You've since managed to put that dark past behind you and dedicate your life to helping others, but instead of discarding your knowledge of the art of killing, you now use your skills in service of the Silver Flame. You've taught me that it's possible to employ darkness in the fight against Evil. Perhaps I am no longer one of the Purified, but that doesn't mean I still can't fight for the Flame in my own way."

The priest paused and smiled, and his teeth seemed slightly sharper than they had a moment ago.

"Besides, I used to hunt lycanthropes on land, where they are few and far between. But the seas are full of the creatures. The hunting will be good there."

Diran wasn't certain what to make of his friend's words, but before he could think further on the matter, Leontis disrobed, dropped his clothes to the dock, waved once, then turned and dove into the water. The priest entered the sea as a man, but the creature that swam away was an amalgamation of wolf and shark.

Ghaji stepped to Diran's side. "Do you regret letting him go?"

"He seemed to learn a measure of control over his bestial side during his time with us. And as he said, the sea is a very different world from ours. Perhaps he was destined for it all along."

"That still doesn't answer my question," Ghaji said.

Diran smiled. "I never said it did."

"I'm afraid I must go as well," Yvka said.

The two friends turned to the elf-woman.

"Will you be gone long?" Ghaji asked.

"It's difficult to say. The Hierarchs would prefer that I reveal as little about my destination and goals as possible. But they had the *Zephyr* repaired, so she's just as swift as she ever was. I'll return as fast as I can. I promise."

Diran looked at Ghaji, attempting to gauge his partner's reaction. The priest knew Yvka's tendency toward secrecy was something of a sore point with his friend, and now that she possessed a dragonmark, the Hierarchs of House Thuranni were going to send her on missions of greater import than before. Which, in turn, meant she could tell Ghaji even less about where she was going or what she was supposed to do there once she arrived.

But Ghaji smiled and simply said, "I wish you success. Come back to me when you can."

The two lovers embraced and kissed, and Diran knew Ghaji had made his peace with Yvka's lifestyle.

"I won't be going alone, however," Yvka said. "The Hierarchs have assigned me a partner."

Coils of white vapor drifted onto the dock, gathered together, and coalesced into human form.

Makala grinned. "Guess who it is?"

Diran turned to Yvka and Ghaji, and from the amused look on the half-orc's face, it was clear he'd known about this development for some time.

"Leontis isn't the only one who's decided to use his abilities for good. Well . . . assuming you can term House Thuranni's goals as *good*. But at least I'll have a purpose in life—or undeath."

Makala stepped forward and took both of Diran's hands in hers.

"I just want to say that I'm so sorry about Asenka. If I could've stopped Haaken—"

"Don't," Diran interrupted. "You weren't in control of your actions then." He smiled sadly. "Asenka would've understood."

"Well, I am in control now, and I'll do everything in my power to resist the darkest part of my nature."

"I may be able to help with that," Diran said. He reached back into his cloak and pulled an object from within one of its pockets.

Makala let go of his hands and stepped back, as if she feared Diran was going to attack her.

"Don't worry. It's not something that will harm you." Diran held up a lump of misshapen iron on the end of a chain. "This is the magic medallion Thokk used to make certain no one could reveal . . . a certain secret." Even now, Diran could not speak the truth about the elemental galleon, even though Makala already knew it. "Tresslar called it an Oathbinder. He salvaged it from Thokk's body before we buried him."

Makala looked at the Oathbinder warily. "I don't understand."

"I want you to swear on this medallion that you will never take an innocent life," Diran said.

Makala stared at him in disbelief. "I don't see how a simple promise—even one that I'm magically bound to keep—can combat the bloodthirst, Diran. It's . . . too strong."

"That's why I asked Tresslar to make some adjustments. It took him longer than he thought, and he only finished a few hours ago. I asked Tresslar to increase the power of any oath sworn on the object so that the swearer would be unable to break that oath, no matter what the provocation—even if magic of a very high order was used against the swearer. Magic such as that contained in a vampire's curse."

Makala looked upon the Oathbinder with mounting wonder. "You mean if I swear on that thing, I won't be able to harm anyone, even if I want to?"

"You won't be able to take an innocent life," Diran said. "It will be up to you to interpret those words for yourself. But I trust you to interpret them wisely."

"Are you certain it will work?"

"Tresslar thinks it will, though he said such an oath will use up all the remaining magic within the object, rendering it forever useless afterward." Diran held out the object. "Place your hand upon the Oathbinder, Makala. That is, if you want to."

Makala hesitated for a moment before laying her hand atop the iron medallion.

"Speak these words: I shall never take an innocent life, no matter how long I may exist."

Makala repeated the words, her voice quavering slightly. Light glittered across the surface of the medallion, and when it was finished, the iron collapsed into gray dust in Diran's palm, leaving only the chain unaffected. Diran shook the dust off his hand, and it was carried out over the water by the breeze. He then tucked the chain back into his cloak.

"It is done."

"I don't *feel* any different," Makala said doubtfully.

"As with all things, only time will tell," Diran said.

"Time I now have, thanks to you." Makala came forward to embrace him, and though her body was cold, she felt good in Diran's arms. When they parted, Makala glanced toward the eastern horizon. The sky was growing lighter as dawn drew near.

The vampire turned to Yvka. "We should go. If I'm not sealed in my sarcophagus before daylight, our partnership will end up being extremely short-lived."

Yvka laughed, and the two women walked away toward shore. Diran didn't know where the *Zephyr* was moored. Presumably House Thuranni had private docks. Ghaji and he watched Yvka and Makala go until the women were lost to their sight.

"We'll see them again," Ghaji said.

"I hope so."

The friends stood in silence for a time after that, watching as the sun rose in the eastern sky. Gulls drifted on the air currents, and the wharf began to come to life as men and women started their workday.

After a time, Ghaji said, "So, what's next?"

Diran considered. "Breakfast, I think."

"And afterward?"

"Whatever fate brings our way." The priest smiled. "What else?"

Ghaji grinned. "What else, indeed?"

And the two companions walked down the dock, heading back into the city.

RaVeNLoft
the covenant

RaVeNLoft's LoRDS of DaRKNess HaVe aLWaYs WaIteD foR the uNWaRY to fIND them.

From the autocratic vampire who wrote the memoirs found in *I, Strahd*
to the demon lord and his son whose story is told in *Tapestry of Dark
Souls*, some of the finest horror characters created by some of the most
influential authors of horror and dark fantasy have found their way to
RAVENLOFT, to be trapped there forever.

LaUReLL K. HamILtoN
Death of a Darklord

chRIstIe goLDeN
Vampire of the Mists

p.N. eLRoD
I, Strahd: The Memoirs of a Vampire

aNDRIa caRDaReLLe
To Sleep With Evil

eLaINe BeRgStRom
Tapestry of Dark Souls

taNYa HUff
Scholar of Decay

RICHARD LEE BYERS

The author of *Dissolution* and The Year of Rogue Dragons sets his
sights on the realm of Thay in a new trilogy that no
FORGOTTEN REALMS® fan can afford to miss.

THE HAUNTED LAND

BOOK I
UNCLEAN

Many powerful wizards hold Thay in their control, but when one of them
grows weary of being one of many, and goes to war, it will be at the head of
an army of undead.

BOOK II
UNDEAD

The dead walk in Thay, and as the rest of Faerûn looks on in stunned horror, the very
nature of this mysterious, dangerous realm begins to change.

March 2008

BOOK III
UNHOLY

Forces undreamed of even by Szass Tam have brought havoc and death to Thay, but
the lich's true intentions remain a mystery—a mystery that could spell doom for the
entire world.

Early 2009

anthology
REALMS OF THE DEAD

A collection of new short stories by some of the Realms' most popular authors sheds
new light on the horrible nature of the undead of Faerûn. Prepare yourself for the
terror of the *Realms of the Dead*.

Early 2010

RICHARD A. KNAAK

THE OGRE TITANS

The Grand Lord Golgren has been savagely crushing
all opposition to his control of the harsh ogre lands of
Kern and Blöde, first sweeping away rival chieftains, then
rebuilding the capital in his image. For this he has had to
deal with the ogre titans, dark, sorcerous giants who have
contempt for his leadership.

VOLUME ONE
THE BLACK TALON
Among the ogres, where every ritual demands blood and every ally can
become a deadly foe, Golgren seeks whatever advantage he can obtain,
even if it means a possible alliance with the Knights of Solamnia, a
questionable pact with a mysterious wizard, and trusting an elven slave
who might wish him dead.

December 2007

VOLUME TWO
THE FIRE ROSE
With his other enemies beginning to converge on him from all sides,
Golgren, now Grand Khan of all his kind, must battle with the
Ogre Titans for mastery of a mysterious artifact capable of ultimate
transformation and power.

December 2008

VOLUME THREE
THE GARGOYLE KING
Forced from the throne he has so long coveted, Golgren makes a final
stand for control of the ogre lands against the Titans . . . against an
enemy as ancient and powerful as a god.

December 2009